JERRY POURNELLE
S.M. STIRLING

A Novel of Falkenberg's Legion

PRINCE OF SPARTA

BAEN

A Baen Books Original

Baen Publishing Enterprises
P.O. Box 1403
Riverdale, NY 10471

ISBN: 0-671-72158-5

Cover art by Stephen Hickman

First Printing, March 1993

Distributed by Simon & Schuster
1230 Avenue of the Americas
New York, NY 10020

Printed in the United States of America

"A well-hidden secret of the principate had been revealed: it was possible, it seemed, for an emperor to be chosen outside Rome."

— Tacitus, *HISTORIES*, I, 4:

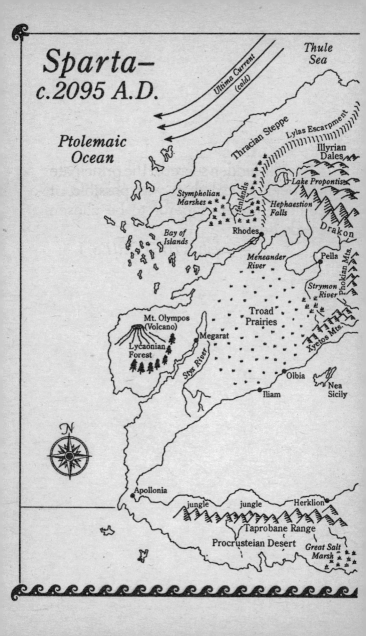

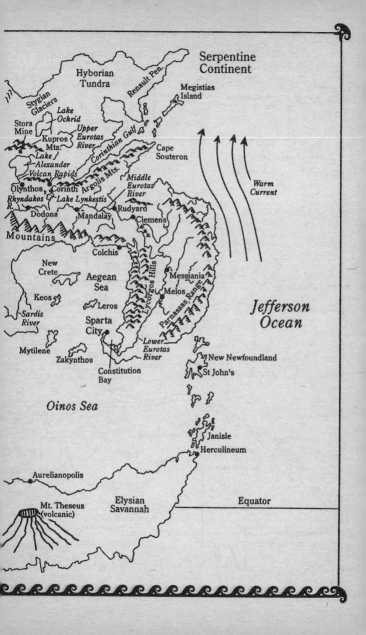

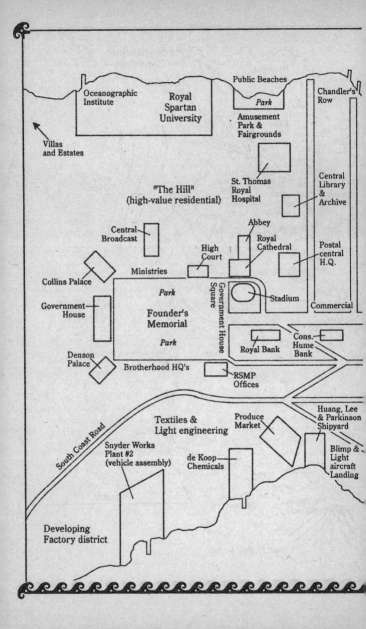

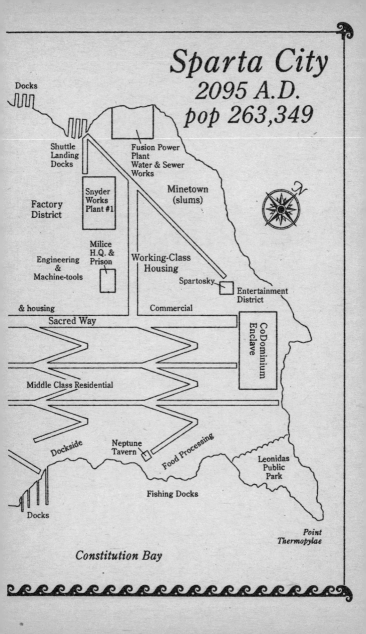

Sparta City
2095 A.D.
pop 263,349

Docks

Shuttle Landing Docks

Fusion Power Plant Water & Sewer Works

Minetown (slums)

Factory District

Snyder Works Plant #1

Milice H.Q. & Prison

Engineering & Machine-tools

Working-Class Housing

Spartosky

Entertainment District

& housing

Sacred Way

Commercial

CoDominium Enclave

Middle Class Residential

Dockside

Neptune Tavern

Food Processing

Leonidas Public Park

Fishing Docks

Docks

Point Thermopylae

Constitution Bay

✧ CHAPTER ONE

The soldier stands alone. In the time when he must either succeed or encounter failure that will follow him beyond his grave, he has only a little time and only two considerations — his mission, and what strength he has within himself by which he may accomplish it. Whether he commands a million other men or only the weapon in his own hand, the soldier in the moment of decision is of all men most alone. Whatever of harmony he has achieved in his adjustment to the world as he knows it is the source of his strength. If he has adjusted himself only to chaos, it is in this time that he will dissolve and lose himself in its nothingness.

— Joseph Maxwell Cameron, *The Anatomy of Military Merit*

✧   ✧   ✧

The most important fact of the first half of the Twentieth Century is that the United States and England both speak English. The most important fact of the second half will be that the dominant race in both the United States and the Soviet Union is white.

— *Herman Kahn, 1960*

✧   ✧   ✧

Crofton's Encyclopedia of Contemporary History and Social Issues (3rd Edition):

CoDominium: The first attempts by the United States to forge a CoDominium alliance were defeated by the failure of an attempted Communist Party coup and the consequent deposition of Gorbachev. The Soviet Union splintered along national and ethnic lines; but when the economic situations of both the former Soviet Union and the United States continued to deteriorate, many in both nations looked back on the Cold War with nostalgia. When a new series of military and political coups resurrected the USSR, the United States was quick to join its former enemy in an alliance that established the supremacy of the two dominant nations over the rest of the world. The alliance was one of convenience rather than genuine friendship. . . .

The Exodus 2015—2050: In the first generation after the perfection of the Alderson Drive in 2010 more than forty planetary colonies were founded, not counting closed-environment mining settlements and refueling stops in systems without Terresteroid planets. While the CoDominium did not encourage governments (other than the US or Soviet Union) to establish direct settlements, corporations or settlement associations clandestinely backed by governments were common. Private colonization ventures were typically either commercial (e.g. *Hadley*, q.v.) or religious-ethnic in nature; see *Arrarat* (q.v.), *Dayan* (q.v.), *Friedland*, (q.v.), *Meiji*, (q.v.), others, spp. During this phase, several million emigrants left the solar system, almost all voluntary — although both the CoDominium Powers offered increasingly strong "encouragement" to politically inconvenient individuals and groups. Thus there are now planets whose population is purely Mormon (*Deseret*), American Black Separatist (*New Azania*), Russian nationalist (*St. Ekaterina*), Finnish (*Sisu*), and even Eskimo/Innuit (*Nuliajuk*).

The second phase of interstellar colonization began with the extension of the Bureau of Relocation's mandate to include involuntary transport of colonists (in addition to the already existing flow of convicts, many merely petty criminals). During this period (2040 to date) voluntary emigration has remained roughly stable, but involuntary has increased to levels exceeding fifteen million persons per year; at the same time, more than seventy new planetary colonies have been founded, many specifically by the Colonial Bureau as relocation settlements. Given the sometimes extremely marginal habitability of the planets concerned (see *Haven, Frystaat*) and the endemic shortage of capital in the outsystem colonies, casualties among the transportees are often heavy, with life expectancies averaging as little as three years in some cases.

❖   ❖   ❖

Whump.

A globe of violet fire bloomed for an instant against the southern horizon, down in the lowlands, actinic brightness through the gathering dark and the light cold rain. Firefly streams of tracer began to stitch across the ground in long shallow arcs, and the reddish sparks of exploding munitions.

The mercenary sergeant smiled in satisfaction at the picture his facescreen showed. He turned in his foxhole, away from the action to the south and toward the valley below the ridge where his men lay concealed. The twelve-man SAS section was dug in on the low crest, invisible in their spider-holes under chameleon tarps. Only the thread-thin tip of the fiber-optic periscope showed above the sergeant's camouflage.

It was dark, Cytheria was just a sliver on the horizon, but that was no problem with nightsight. The enemy column was spread out down the wooded vale beneath them, winding through the tall grass and eucalyptus trees; the slope was in reddish-brown native scrub and shamboo. Men and mules halted at the sound of the explosion, then scattered to shouted orders.

"*Now*," Sergeant Taras Miscowsky said into the throat-mike. *Not what the bastards expected*, he thought with a hard grin in the private darkness of the hole.

A heavy droning whistle came through the low clouds overhead. Then: *crump . . . crump . . . crump*. Points of red fire flashed over the valley, proximity-fused 160mm mortar rounds bursting at ten meters up. Circles of vegetation bent away, crushed by blast and flayed by the steel-wire shrapnel. Men and animals screamed or writhed or lay still under the iron flail; the faint bitter scent of explosive joined the smells of wet earth and grass. Another salvo came in, and another, the air whistling continuously. The observers called fire on the clumps of guerrillas forming around officers and noncoms, throwing men into panic flight and chopping into dog-meat any attempt to rally.

"That's doing it to them, Captain," Miscowsky said as he threw back the tarpaulin. Then more formally, "Sir, they're taking heavy casualties. I estimate thirty percent casualties on a full company. Better than half the mules are down, too. They're moving, one six five degrees true."

"Roger that. Tracking. We'll get the blocking group in fast."

"Sir. We'll lose most of them if we don't act fast."

"Right. Thank you, Sergeant."

Some of the enemy troops were moving straight west up the slope toward his position; the hill was gentle, and there was good cover. Mortar shells landed closer, probing for them as they moved up toward the ridge. The SAS unit was well dug-in, but they were infiltration scouts, not a line unit, and there were only a dozen of them. Miscowsky flashed a ranging laser at the center of the enemy group.

"Fire mission. Personnel, not armored. Five-fifty-six meters, bearing one hundred seventeen degrees."

"On the way," his commander's voice sounded in the helmet mike. Seconds later Corporal Washington spoke:

"Getting troop movement noise to our rear, Sarge. Multiples, light vehicles and infantry."

"Roger. Cap'n, the Royals are coming in from my west."

"Roger that, Miscowsky; the other side of the trap's moving in from the southeast around now."

Miscowsky turned his head in that direction and switched his facemask to IR sensors. There was a hell of a firefight going on down there a couple of klicks away, at the works the guerrillas had been planning to attack. Small arms, mortars . . . and the lance-shaped blossom of a Cataphract light tank's 76mm cannon. Several of those, coming toward him fast; he could see the faint waver of heat from their engines. Relayed sound-sensor data gave him the push from behind the SAS position. Boots thudding on turf, and a quiet whine from fuel-cell electrics. Then a louder *shoop-wonk* as their mortars opened up, lighter 81mm's and 120mm mediums.

He tapped at the side of his helmet to switch to the Royalist unit's push.

"Miscowsky, Falkenberg's Legion," he said.

A dark machine shape came bounding up the low reverse slope behind him. A cycle, boxy body slung between two wheels that were balls of Charbonneau alloy monomolecular thread. It braked to a stop and a figure in bulky Nemourlon combat armor jumped down.

"Captain Lewis, 2nd Royals," the man said.

Others in the same camouflage uniforms and armor were swarming up the ridge; teams set up machine-guns as the riflemen fanned out and opened fire. Behind them light four-wheel vehicles like skeletal jeeps hauled ammunition and heavy weapons, recoilless rifles and rocket-launchers.

Miscowsky straightened and threw a formal salute. "Sir. Falkenberg's Legion presents one enemy column, badly used," he said.

The Royal officer returned the gesture, grinning as he scanned the action below. His night-sight goggles were flipped up, and he was using a blocky pair of sensor-glasses; less efficient than the multitasking facemasks of the Legion, but Sparta was not a rich planet.

"Some of them are putting their hands up already," he said. A signals tech came up behind him and put a handset into his outstretched palm. *"First platoon,"* he continued into it. *"Deploy in skirmish order and advance. I want prisoners, but don't take unnecessary casualties. If in doubt, shoot."* Men fanned out and began to filter into the scrub downslope.

"Well done, Sergeant," he went on, nodding to Miscowsky.

           ✦   ✦   ✦

"Next insertion, sir?" Miscowsky said hopefully.

The Royal Spartan Army helicopter was still turning over its turbines behind the SAS squad.

"That's the last of them." Legion Captain Jamey Mace, Scout Commander, twitched his thumb toward the column of enemy prisoners as they shambled past under guard down to the river docks.

The Tyndos flowed north from here into the Eurotas, the great river of the Serpentine Continent. McKenzie's Landing was a riverside town, like most on this world; not much of one, which was also typical. There was an openpit rare-earth mine cut back into a smooth green hill, a geothermal plant and a kilometer of railway down to the loading docks. That and housing for a few hundred people, ranging from tufa-block Georgian houses for the mine-owner down to plastic-stabilized rammed earth for the miners' barracks. A fuel station by the docks, stacked logs for steamers and peanut oil tanks for diesels. A bar, a seedy-looking hotel, a Brotherhood meeting hall, two churches — established and non-conformist — and a tiny Hindi temple, a three-man Mounted Police station-cum-post-office. . . .

Not many of the Spartan People's Liberation Army — Helot — guerrillas had gotten to anywhere useful. Rosie's Bar and Grill was burning, and one of the steamers down at the pier was sinking at its moorings. The rebel plan had probably been to overrun the settlement just long enough to wreck the mine — it brought the Royal government off-planet hard currency — kill the Citizens resident, harangue the convict-transportee section of the labor force. . . .

"Let me go after them, Cap'n."

"Can't do that." Mace shook his head. "Back to training duty, Sergeant. We're going to need every Royal up to the mark—"

"Yes, sir, but —"

"If I thought there was one chance in ten thousand she was still alive I'd *order* you to go look for her."

"You wouldn't have to order me or anyone else. Captain, dammit, I know she's dead. But I want—"

"A head?"

"Balls would do."

"You'll have your chance," Mace said. It was easy to see what Mace was thinking. Taras Hamilton Miscowsky came from a culture that took blood feuds seriously. "Right now we've got a war to win, Sergeant."

"Sir." Miscowsky was silent; obedience, not agreement. Two months ago the war had stopped being a job to him; when Lieutenant Lefkowitz died. Lieutenant Deborah Lefkowitz, wife of Jerry Lefkowitz, who had been Miscowsky's first officer in the Legion. Miscowsky would not have lived past his first battle if Lefkowitz had not put his men ahead of his personal survival. Deborah Lefkowitz had been an electronics tech, not a combat soldier; sheer bad luck had put her observation plane over enemy Skyhawk missiles, in the Dales campaign. Miscowsky hadn't been able to rescue her, nobody had, after her plane augured in still spitting out data. Data that had probably saved the Legion's detachment here on Sparta, but nobody had saved Deborah. They found her torn clothing and some blood, but nothing else, despite the efforts of the Legion's best trackers.

That's the official story, Miscowsky thought. *But Mendota was there, and he's not talking, and I think he found something more. Maybe the skipper has some reason to keep things to himself, but God damn —*

Jerry Lefkowitz was far away, eight months inter-stellar transit, though only half that for the fastest messages, on New Washington with Colonel Falken-berg and the bulk of the Legion. Sparta had originally been intended as a quiet training assignment for the 5th Battalion and a haven for the noncombatants. He wouldn't even have the news about his wife yet. Mis-cowsky scowled. At least he wouldn't have to break the news. The chaplain-rabbi would do that. *But I have to write him. And when I do I want an enclosure.*

A man in the uniform of a Brotherhood militia cap-tain came up. "Captain McKenzie, sir," he said to Mace. "Did I hear something about pursuit?" He was a middle-aged man, stocky and sandy-haired. There was a wolfish eagerness in his tone.

"The 18th Brotherhood's authorized to send fight-ing patrols into bandit country," Mace said, nodding northwestward. There lay the Himalayan-sized Drakon range and the vast forest-and-prairie expanse of hill country known as the Illyrian Dales.

"Not your SAS?" McKenzie said. He looked admir-ingly at the mercenary troopers squatting stolidly in the rain and leaning on their weapons. "We'd have been royally screwed if you hadn't spotted those ter-rorist scum massing up in the ravine country. We've only got an under strength company of the Brother-hood here; if they'd hit us without warning . . . "

Captain Mace pulled a pack of cigarettes out of a shoulder-pocket in his armor, offered one to the Spartan. They lit, sheltering their matches from the steady drizzle.

"That's just it," he said. "Look, the enemy *never* attack if they think we know they're coming; they just call it off and split up and concentrate somewhere we're not. And we can't give you long warning . . . "

They both nodded. Legion communications were secure — mostly — but the Brotherhood comm lines were leaky, and there didn't seem to be much that anyone could do.

Most of the three-million population of Sparta was spread out along the nearly ten thousand kilometers of the Eurotas. Most traffic moved at the pace of the riverboat, with the faster alternative being a blimp. There was very little high-tech transport; Sparta saved its money for building its industries, and imported little in the way of personal luxuries. Even military helicopters were still rare, just now starting to come off the lines in quantity. Away from the little towns and scattered ranches of the Valley were mountain, swamp, forest. Easy to hide in, now that the satellites were down. The Helots crept through it like rats in long grass, massing secretly, striking without warning and scattering before the Royalist forces could respond.

"It's like stomping on bloody cockroaches," the Spartan said in frustration. "Can't *find* the buggers. When you do, there are always more of them."

"Mm-hmm," Mace said. "And the Legion doesn't have enough SAS to make much of a difference. We've got to train your own Regulars, your SAS" — which in the Royal forces stood for Spartan Air Service — "to give you a broad-based capacity."

McKenzie nodded unwillingly. "We'll pursue anyway," he said. More softly: "My boy Phyrros was in the Dales. He got the Star of Leonidas . . . posthumously."

"Be cautious," Mace said.

"Sir." Miscowsky leaned forward. "Sir, I've been thinkin'." His provincial accent roughened a little, the Anglic harshened with the tones of Haven, his home planet. "Either the enemy's going downhill, or these were recruits. Prob'ly sent in for a little on-the-job training."

"Yes?" Mace looked at the prisoners thoughtfully.

A lot of them *did* look a little raw, without the stripped-down appearance you got after six months or so in Sparta's heavy gravity. *Transportees.* Convicts and political prisoners from Earth; most of the Helots were, like a majority of Sparta's population. *And they did break up a bit easily.* Not much unit cohesion, as if they were just out of the enemy equivalent of basic training. The Spartan People's Liberation Army probably hadn't expected much resistance here.

"Well," Miscowsky went on, "if this was a training exercise, they had a command group somewhere close watching. Might be worth going after, Cap'n. Maybe even that bastard nephew of Bronson's, the one we got the voiceprint on in the Dales."

That would *be worth it,* the mercenary officer thought. *With Geoffrey Niles in our hands, we'd have more of a lever.* Grand Senator Bronson was illegally backing the rebellion . . . not that anyone on Earth seemed to give a damn anymore about little things like the CoDominium's Laws of War, or treaties, or anything else.

"No." He shook his head. "Niles may be dead . . . or still wandering around the Dales looking for the Helot survivors. We've got orders; mount up, Sergeant."

❖   ❖   ❖

Crack. A branch broke underneath a boot.

Geoffrey Niles started awake and then crouched lower under the overhang of blue rock. It was screened by tall canes of witch hazel and thick crystalline snow, only feet from the little brook that purled down the shallow valley under a skin of ice.

He forced his breathing to calm, clenching his jaw as it tried to chatter with cold and the effects of malnutrition. The skin on his fingers was cracked where it gripped the rifle; his body felt like an arthritic seventy instead of the twenty-eight Terran years it actually bore. Few would have recognized the sleekly handsome blond Englishman of a scant half-year before in the scarecrow figure that crouched in this cave. The heavy gravity of Sparta dragged at him, as sleep dragged at his eyelids. The air smelled of wet limestone and muddy earth; beyond the stream the first buds were showing on the rock maples, and strands of green among the yellow stalks of grass.

Another crack, and a voice swearing softly. Men dropped past him to stand on the edge of the stream, and another walked up it leading a flop-eared hound. Men in uniform . . .

Royalists, he thought. Camouflage uniforms, Nemourlon armor and helmets, but the shoulder-flashes showed Brotherhood militia. Not Royal Army regulars, and thank *God* not the mercenary SAS-scouts of Falkenberg's Legion. The relief was irrational, he knew; there were a dozen of them, and he had only five rounds left in the clip. The militia were countrymen used to tracking, and well-trained; they would check this overhang eventually. He had escaped from the last battle in the Dales by drifting downstream on a river that eventually fed into the Eurotas. It had carried him far into Royalist-held territory, and it had been a long slow journey back into the wilderness.

I can't even blame Grand-Uncle for sending me here, he thought bitterly. He had *asked* to go to Sparta, to serve in the revolution Grand Senator Bronson was clandestinely backing. *I wanted adventure. God!*

❖   ❖   ❖

"Lost him, Sarge," the man with the dogs said disgustedly. "He went into the creek downstream where it's clear, but I'm damned if I can find where he came out."

The militia noncom grunted. "Everyone, spread out; he may be lying low around here. And keep alert — we've come a long ways west, he isn't the only Helli around here. Sparks, get me —"

Pffft.

The soldier doubled over and fell backwards into the water with a red spot blossoming on his chest. The others went to ground in trained unison, scrambling back up the overhang to return fire. The sharp crackling of their New Aberdeen rifles echoed back overhead, answered by others out in the woods; the silenced sniper weapon fired again, and a light machine-gun opened up on the Royalist patrol. A body slid back downslope to lie twitching at the edge of the water next to the bobbing corpse. Branches and scrub fell after it, cut by the hail of bullets; a man was screaming, an endless high keening sound.

Niles flogged his mind into thought. He had been running far and fast ahead of this pursuit; it was unlikely there was another Royalist patrol near enough to intervene. From the sound of the firing the guerrillas outnumbered the government soldiers handily, and according to Spartan People's Liberation Army — Helot — tactics they should . . .

God. If there still are *any Helots* — The attempted ambush in the Dales had fallen apart so fast the Royalists might have mopped up everything but scattered bands.

Fwhump. A rifle-grenade blasting off the muzzle of a rifle some distance away. It landed on the lip of the rise over his head and detonated in a spray of notched steel wire. Then more rifle fire came from the other side of the creek bed, into the backs of the Royalist soldiers, and more grenades. The noise rose to a crescendo and then died away with startling suddenness. Niles waited while the Helots made their cautious approach, waited until their leader whistled an *all clear*. Then he called out:

"I'm coming out! Senior Group Leader Geoffrey

Niles, SPLA!" Spartan People's Liberation Army, the formal name of the Helots.

"Out careful," a hard voice replied.

He pushed through the witch hazel, leaving his rifle behind. The tough springy stems parted reluctantly, powdering him with snow. He stood with his hands raised. Half a platoon of Helot guerrillas surrounded him, most busy about their chores. A few leveled rifles at him.

"Police it up good, don't leave nothin' for the Cits," the Helot sergeant was saying. Men moved briskly, stripping the Royalist militiamen of weapons, armor, kit and clothing.

One Brotherhood fighter was still alive, despite the row of bullet-holes across the small of his back. The guerrilla noncom stepped up behind him as he crawled and fired with the muzzle of his rifle an inch from the back of the other man's head. The helmet rolled away in a spray of blood. Then he turned back to Niles.

"Who did you say —" he began, then stopped. His eyes widened as he recognized the scarecrow figure in the rags the winter woods had left of his uniform.

The sergeant was a short man, as were most of the guerrillas, a head shorter than the Englishman's 185 centimeters; virtually all of the guerrillas were transportees from Earth's Welfare Islands, chronically malnourished as children. American, from his accent, and Eurasian by the odd combination of slanted eyes that were a bright bottle green color.

"Jesus and Maria, it *is* Senior Group Leader Niles," he said, saluting and then holding out a hand. "Sergeant Andy Cheung, sir — hell, we thought you were dead meat for sure!"

"So did I for a while, Sergeant, so did I," he said. Relief shook him, and bitter regret. *I wanted out*, he thought. Out of the Helots certainly, after the horrors of the campaign last year; poison gas and slaughtered prisoners, capital crimes under the Laws of War. But the Royalists would hang him; the only chance he had of getting off this world alive was with the guerrillas. Off this world and back to a place where the Bronson power and wealth could buy immunity from anything.

"We gotta get out of here real quick," Sergeant Cheung was saying. "Lost half a platoon to them SAS buggers around here just last week; they're seven klicks of bad news." The noncom grinned at him. "Field Prime will sure be glad to see you again, sir."

Skilly, he thought, with a complex shiver. *Oh*, God.

❖   ❖   ❖

"Are you telling me, gentlemen, that there is *nothing* we can do to rid our world of these murderous vermin?"

Crown Prince Lysander Collins paced back and forth before the broad windows that looked out over Government House Square; the Council Chamber where the Cabinet met was on the second floor of the Palace. It was a rainy spring day, and the breeze carried in odors of wet vegetation from the gardens, together with a damp salty smell from the Aegean. He was a tall young man in his mid-twenties, with short-cropped brown hair and regular features. Until recently it had been a rather boyish face.

Peter Owensford, Major in Falkenberg's Legion, Major General in the Spartan Royal Army, looked up from his readout and files to the prince. *Not so young as he was*.

A good deal had happened to Crown Prince Lysander Collins over the past eighteen Terran months. Sent to the CoDominium prison-planet of Tanith as unofficial ambassador to Falkenberg's Mercenary Legion; he had "seen the elephant" there, as a volunteer junior officer, and incidentally earned the respect of many of the Legion officers. Owensford suspected Lysander Collins would have been more than happy to maintain his pseudonym of "Mr. Cornet Prince" and remain in the Legion's ranks. That was impossible, of course, despite Lysander's bravura performance, highjacking the rebel shuttle and the smuggled drugs . . . as impossible as his brief and doomed affair with Ursula Gordon, sometime hotel girl on Tanith. Sparta was too important to civilization, and to the plans of Grand Admiral Sergei Lermontov, for Lysander Collins to have åny role but the straight one laid out for him by hereditary duty. *If there's to be any civilization left once the CoDominium collapses.*

Lad's grown up a lot, Owensford thought. Lysander had returned to Sparta to find a full-fledged rebellion in progress. *Did all right, too. Decent as battalion commander. Even better as field commander in chief. I've fought for worse ones.* Now even that was denied him; with his father's judgment impaired by the enemy's viral sabotage he was *de facto* ruler of the Collins half of the Dual Monarchy's executive. *He's seen the elephant with a vengeance.*

"No, sir," Owensford said aloud. "There is a great deal that we can and must do."

The Crown Prince was in uniform at this meeting; as a Lieutenant General, he could be addressed as a military superior rather than sovereign, a useful fiction. "But I am saying for the record that under present conditions it will be very difficult to achieve *swift* and *decisive* victory over the enemy."

He looked over at Hal Slater, the other mercenary present. Commandant of the Royal War College, making him a Major General in the Royal Army. Possibly a more permanent one. Owensford would revert to his mercenary rank of Major whenever the Fifth Battalion of Falkenberg's Legion left Sparta . . . *if* they left; quite probably this would be permanent base for at least part of the mercenary outfit. *And I'm running a whole army here. Challenging.* Long-term if he wanted to stay here and become a Spartan Citizen. *Tempting. Sparta's a good place, and I'm tired of running from planet to planet.* Owensford looked again at Prince Lysander. *He's grown up. I could accept him as sovereign. I think Hal already has.*

Hal Slater wouldn't be filling any active commands. He had gone to the regeneration tanks once too many times, too many bones were titanium-titanium matrix, and his wounds would keep him behind a desk for the rest of his life. Running the War College was a good final berth. One he would do well; Hal Slater had taught Owensford and many another young officer, back in his days with the Legion. His son George was a Legion Captain, and a Brigadier in the Royal forces.

And Hal Slater is Falkenberg's oldest friend. If anyone knows what Falkenberg's game is, Slater will.

Lysander halted at the window and looked out over the square. "I had hoped to get more out of the Illyrian Dales campaign," he said bitterly. "We certainly paid enough for it."

Owensford nodded. The battles against the Helots in the northwestern hills had been bloody. Bloodily victorious, in the conventional sense . . . and a good deal of that was due to Crown Prince Lysander's refusal to accept a truce offered by the enemy when the battle was won. That had cost the Royal Army, but they had harried the enemy units into rout with a relentless pursuit. Lysander, he knew, was still haunted by the casualties. They'd lost some of those wounded in the enemy's poison-gas attacks, because many couldn't be flown out while the battle continued.

"We paid, but never doubt it was worth it," Owensford said. He looked to Slater and got a nod of agreement. "I doubt if one in five of the enemy escaped on the southern front. High cost in their trained leaders."

"Not enough to break them," Lysander said.

"No, sir. But we stopped them. Sir, they were in a fair way to taking and holding a good part of the Dales. That would have given them a sanctuary area. More than that. It would have given them a territory, making this an actual planetary war instead of an insurgency. They could have called on the CoDominium to intervene. Depending on CD politics that might even have worked. Instead, we got most of their leaders, maybe half of their lower ranking Meijian technoninjas, a lot of their equipment. Some of their units evaporated. Lots of deserters. One unit surrendered just about to a man."

"Good recruits?" Hal Slater asked.

Owensford nodded.

Prince Lysander frowned. "You're accepting *Helots* as military volunteers?"

Owensford grinned slightly. "Not for you, sir. For the Legion. We'll get them part trained and ship them off as reinforcements for Colonel Falkenberg on New Washington. The point is, sir, don't doubt that you made the right choice. We not only robbed them of their victory, we came close to breaking them."

Slater said, carefully, "It should have been enough to break them."

"But it didn't."

"No, sir," Peter Owensford said. "They've got too much off-planet support."

"Not just off-planet."

"No, sir." A sore point: Sparta hadn't yet suspended constitutional civil rights, and the Helots had allies in the Senate and elsewhere.

"Look at it this way. You forced them back to classical Phase One guerrilla operations," Hal Slater said.

"Vigorous Phase One operations," Owensford said.

"Well, yes," Slater said. "It hurts, but Phase One can't win if you keep your nerve."

Lysander slammed the heel of his hand against the stonework. That was the antiseptic Aristotelian language of a military professional; "Phase One" meant ambush and sabotage, burnt-out ranches and civilians killed by land-mines, every sort of terrorist atrocity.

He looked at Slater. "This is what you meant at the first Royal Strategy Lecture, isn't it?" He quoted: " 'Insurgency against a modern state requires powerful allies operating from sanctuary. Unfortunately, given supply of war material from a sanctuary, insurgency can be continued practically forever.' "

"Yes, sir," Hal Slater said. "Under the present circumstances, patience is as important a weapon as explosives." He shrugged. "It's also all we have just now."

Lysander nodded curtly. Both the professionals were older than he — Owensford in his thirties, Slater over fifty — and between them they had a generation's experience. He would use that accumulated wisdom.

"I agree. I don't have to like it," he said. "What else can we do?" He held up a hand. "Not tactics, that's obvious — what can we do to bring the war to an end?"

Slater smiled thinly; it was not every man Lysander's age who could keep the need to have strategy driving tactics firmly before his mind.

"There are essentially three ways to defeat an enemy," Slater began formally. Teaching had been a large part of his military career, even before he became head of the Spartan War College. "Physically smashing them is one — killing so many that the remainder give up in despair. We can only do that with the Helots if they are obliging enough to gather in one place where we can get at them.

They *nearly* made that mistake last year in the Dales, but I doubt they will again. Their leaders are evil men —"

And women, Owensford thought; he remembered the mocking contralto voice of the Helot field commander in the Dales, with its soft Caribbean accent. By the look on his face, so did Lysander. Neither of them had forgotten the helpless prisoners slaughtered on her order.

"— evil to the point where 'vile' is an appropriate term, but they are not stupid. Inexperienced in real warfare, but they are cunning, they have experienced mercenary advisors, and they learn quickly."

Slater sipped water and continued. "As is often the case in war, we cannot force battle on the enemy if they are not willing to meet us; the ratio of force to space is too low. There is nothing they must stand and die to defend; they have no towns, farms or families as the Royal forces do, and no base of supply." Slater paused. "None within our reach, anyway."

Sparta had three million people, a tenth of them in the capital; the Serpentine Continent had eighteen million square miles of territory. Even the heartlands along the Eurotas River were thinly peopled.

"Particularly with the limits on surveillance, we are unlikely to catch large numbers of them at any one time." Skysweeper missiles had knocked down every attempt to loft more spy satellites; observation aircraft were impossible, of course, and even drones were high-cost and short-lived if the enemy had countermeasures. In addition, the Helots' Meijian hirelings were simply better at electronic intelligence and counter-intelligence than anything the Dual Monarchy of Sparta could afford, and they were running rampant through every computer on the planet with the exception — he devoutly hoped — of the Legion's. At that, his own electronics specialists were spending a counterproductive amount of time checking for viruses and taps, and vetting Royal Army machines. The Royalist forces were back to what scouts and spies could discover, and whatever the Legion computers could massage out of the data.

"Of course there's an unpleasant implication to our lack of surveillance," Slater said. "Low orbit satellites they can knock down fairly easily, but geosynchronous? They had to have cooperation from the CD Navy for that."

"Are you sure?" Lysander demanded.

"Near enough," Slater said. "The CD may not have knocked our geosynch out, but they had to look the other way when it happened. And you'll note they haven't offered to replace it."

"No. When we ask for cooperation, they never say 'no,' but nothing happens. Delays, red tape, forms not properly filled out . . . Do you think they're actively against us?"

Slater shrugged. "Or tilted neutral at best."

"What can we do about that?"

"I presume you've filed a formal protest."

Lysander nodded. "And you?"

"We've done what we can," Peter Owensford said. "I've sent off urgent signals to Falkenberg and Admiral Lermontov. With any luck Lermontov can use this to order active CD intervention on our side."

"How did you send the message?" Lysander asked.

"With your permission I would rather not say," Owensford said.

Lysander nodded quickly. "That's probably best. Do you think we can get CD Navy support? When?"

Hal Slater shook his head. "It won't be soon. CD politics is thick soup." His voice went back to lecture mode. "The second method of defeating an opponent is to strike at their rear — at the sources of their supplies and support. Unfortunately, we cannot for the same reason we can't locate them. As long as they have even tacit CD support, their rear area is off-planet."

"Bronson," Lysander said; he made the word an obscenity.

"Exactly. Grand Senator Bronson. Somehow Bronson's people are still landing supplies. His shipping lines regularly transit Sparta's system, and the supplies get here. It's like the geosynchronous satellites. We have no proof, but it's hard to imagine any other explanation."

The Treaty of Independence had left spatial traffic control in the hands of the CoDominium forces, and the Grand Senator was a power in the CoDominium. So were Sparta's friends — Grand Admiral Sergei Lermontov and Grand Senator Grant, the Blaine family . . . and the result was deadlock. No new thing. It was a generation since the CoDominium as a whole had been able to *do* anything of note. The Soviet Union was dissolving again — but so was the United States. Between them they ruled the world, but neither nation remembered why they had wanted to.

"Bronson," Slater went on, "is also behind most of our economic problems."

Sparta's main exports were minerals and intermediate-technology products for planets even less industrialized than she. Markets had been drying up, contracts been revoked, suppliers defaulting, loans being called due. The planetary debt was mushrooming, and Standard and Poor's had just reduced the Dual Monarchy's credit rating once more. The financial community was more and more jittery over the situation on Earth, in any case. Capital was flowing out to the secure worlds, places like Friedland and Dayan, and sitting there.

"What does Bronson want?" Lysander demanded.

Hal Slater shook his head. "We don't know."

"He seems to have an active hatred for Falkenberg."

"Yes, sir," Slater said. "But that's a very old story."

"Falkenberg ruined his Tanith operation," Lysander said.

"Yes, sir. With your help." Slater shrugged. "Bronson never forgets an enemy. You'll have noticed that he hasn't even tried to negotiate with you. But given the resources he's putting into this operation, there has to be more at stake than personal animosity. Unless —"

"Unless?"

"Unless he's feeling old and useless and has nothing left but his hatreds," Slater said.

"Whatever his motives, this has to stop." Lysander stared out at the Spartan landscape. "Even if we called out every Brotherhood militiaman," he said slowly, "we wouldn't have enough to finish this quickly. Would we?"

"No, sir," Owensford replied flatly. "They'd disperse, go to earth and wait for new supplies. We can't keep any militia unit in the field for more than a month or so. Helot attacks are planned long in advance; if we detect them concentrating and mass to defend or counterattack, they simply call off their assault and pick another target somewhere else. They never attack without a locally superior ratio of forces, and we don't have enough mechanical transport to respond quickly in such cases."

There were a million Citizens; the first-line militia of their Brotherhoods could field a quarter of a million troops. Unfortunately, when they did the entire planet had to shut down; the Citizens were over a third of the total labor force, and a much higher percentage of the skilled and managerial classes.

"We're keeping fifteen battalions under arms at any one time as regional reaction-forces, and we're building up the standing forces of the Royal Army to twenty-five thousand troops," Owensford said. He ran a hand over his short-cropped brown hair. "Whatever else the Dales campaign did, it certainly gave us plenty of combat-tested men." Action was the best way to identify potential small-unit leaders. "And the cream of the newcomers as recruits, too. Everyone wants to fight for a winner. We'll keep grinding at the enemy."

Hal Slater grimaced slightly. "Now you see why professionals hate guerrilla wars, sir," he said. "It's pure attrition, unless we can kill or capture their top leaders."

Lysander smiled sourly. "I've known mercenaries who liked that kind of thing. A long war and no resolution— no, of course I don't suspect that of Falkenberg."

Slater didn't say anything.

"All right," Lysander said. "Attrition with Grand Senator Bronson sending the Helots weapons and money, and the CoDominium Bureau of Relocation sending convicts and involuntary transportees for them to recruit from. It takes twenty years to produce a Citizen, gentlemen, and only eight months to ship a transportee from Earth to Sparta. And yes, I know, you can recruit among those as well as the enemy. But damn it, no offense intended, Sparta needs Citizens, not more mercenaries."

He moved his shoulders, the unconscious gesture of a man settling a burden he means to carry. "We can also proceed on the political front," he went on. "Breaking up the enemy's clandestine networks. And nailing Croser."

For a moment all three men shared a wolfish grin. Senator Dion Croser, head of the Non-Citizen's Liberation Front . . . and almost certainly leader of the whole insurrection. Almost all the insurgents were transportees and non-Citizens; Croser was the son of one of the Founders, and there was as yet no smoking-gun proof of his involvement with the insurrection.

"He won't be the last," Lysander went on softly. Even the mercenaries were slightly daunted by the look in his grey eyes. "We can't attack a man who's a power in the CoDominium — we can't even *defy* the CoDominium — yet. But Croser we *will* get; and eventually, beyond him, those responsible for backing him. As God is my witness, I'm going to see that nobody is ever in a position to do this to Sparta again. Or," he went on, "to anyone else, if I can help it."

"Meanwhile," he continued more briskly, "we should prepare for the War Cabinet meeting."

❖   ❖   ❖

The rain had been hitting harder as the Helot patrol moved northwest. The horses hung their heads slightly, wearily placing one hoof down at a time. For Geoffrey Niles the trip was rest and recuperation, after starving and freezing for the better part of two months. By the end of the second week he was strong enough to curse the cold drops that flicked into his face as they rode and trickled down inside his camouflaged rain-poncho, to realize how much he detested the constant smells of wet human and horse. The forest thickened as they moved closer to the foothills of the Drakons, spreading up from the low swales and valleys to conquer the slopes of the hills, leaving only patches in the tallgrass prairie that was so common elsewhere in the Illyrian Dales. Occasionally they passed other patrols — once they nearly tripped an ambush — and more often saw foraging parties, out cropping the vast herds of game and feral cattle.

"Not many enemy in this far?" he asked the Helot NCO.

"No, sir," the man replied; he kept his rifle across his saddlebow, and his eyes were always moving.

"Leastways, not big bunches of 'em. Sometimes they send in fightin' patrols, battalion or better, but we scatter an' harass and they go away. Hard to supply this far in, too. They got no satellite recce now, can't put aircraft anywhere near us. Keep tryin' t'locate our bases, though. Lots of infiltrators. Ambush and counter-ambush work — helps with training the new chums, anyway."

Niles nodded. They were riding up a long slope; the rain had a little sleet in it now, they must be at least a thousand meters above sea level. Well into the foot-hills, and Sparta's 1.21 G gave it a steep atmosphere and temperature gradient. The slopes on either side were heavily wooded with Douglas fir and Redwoods, oaks and beech; the genetic engineers and seeders had done their work well here. Branches met over-head, and the hooves clattered through gravel and broken rock. They turned a corner; it took a moment's concentration for Niles to pick out the bunkers that flanked the pathway. They were set deep in the lime, with narrow firing slits hiding the muzzles of 15mm gatlings. His shoulders crawled slightly with the knowledge that Peltast heavy sniper-rifles had prob-ably been trained on them for the better part of an hour.

"Sir," an officer said, as he swung down from the saddle. "We've got transport for you. Field Prime is anxious to debrief you herself."

Niles raised a brow at the sight of the jeep; it was a local model, six balloon-wheels of Charbonneau thread, but the Helots had had little mechanical transport before. *We're coming up in the world*, he thought.

The new base-headquarters was a contrast to the old, as well. It was a rocky bowl several kilometers in extent, a collapsed dome undercut by water seep-age. That was common in the Dales, with multiple megatonnes of water coming down off the Drakon slopes every year and hundreds of thousands of square kilometers of old marine limestones to run through. The edges of the ring were jagged fangs thrusting at the sky; his eyes widened at the sight of detection and broadcast antennae up there, and launching frames for Skyhawk and Talon antiaircraft missiles. Cave-mouths ringed the bowl, busy activity about most, but the rolling surface itself was occupied as well.

Not afraid of aerial surveillance any more, he thought. Neat rows of squared-log cabins, and troops drilling in the open. More troops than he expected, many more, but what was really startling was the equipment. Plenty of local make, everything from rifles and machine-guns up to the big 160mm mortars that were the local substitute for artillery; Dion Croser had been siphoning off a share of local production and caching it in cave-dumps here in the Dales for a full decade before the open war began. But there was off-planet material as well, in startling quantity, items he remembered from Sandhurst lectures. A dozen stubby 155mm rocket-howitzers, Friedlander-made, with swarms of Helot troopers around them doing familiarization. Six Suslov medium tanks, slab-and-angle composite armor jobs with low-profile turrets and 135mm cannon in hydraulic pods. *Those* were Co-Dominium issue, made on Earth.

And bloody expensive, he thought.

The jeep pulled up at one of the cave entrances. A man was waiting for him. Niles recognized the figure; 190 cm tall and broad enough to be squat. Skin the color of old mahogany, a head bald as an egg, and a great beak of a nose in the round face. Over his shoulders were the twin machetes that had given him his nickname, and dangling from one hand was a light machine-gun looking no bigger than a toy rifle in the

great paw. The only change he could see was a certain
gauntness to the face.

"Two-knife," he said, nodding to the Helot commander's right-hand man.

"Niles," the other answered, equally polite and
noncommittal. The big Mayan had not minded when
Skilly took the Englishman as her consort; that was the
Donna's privilege. Niles was privately certain that he
would also have no hesitation in quietly killing an
unworthy choice. . . .

The caves were larger than the old Base One that
had fallen to the Royalists last winter, but the setup
within was similar, down to the constant chill and smell
of wet rock. Glowsticks stapled to the walls,
color-coded marker strips, occasional wooden walls
and partitions, rough-shaping with pneumatic
hammers. There seemed to be a lot more modern
electronics, though. He passed several large
classroom-chambers with squads of Helots in
accelerated-learning cubicles, bowl-helmets over their
heads for total-sensory input. Then they went past
alert-looking guards into a still larger chamber, where
officers grouped around a computer-driven map table.
One looked up at him.

"Hiyo, Jeffi," she said quietly when he was close
enough to salute.

Geoffrey Niles' throat felt blocked. He had *thought*
he remembered her, but Skida Thibodeau in the flesh
was something different from a memory. Very tall,
near two meters, much of it leg. Muscled like a pan-
ther and moving like one, a chocolate-brown face
framed in loose-curled hair that glinted blue-black.
High cheekbones and full lips, nose slightly curved,
eyes tilted and colored hazel, glinting with green
flecks. His nostrils flared involuntarily at her scent,
soap and mint and a hint of the natural musk. And the

remembered thrill of not-quite-fear at meeting her eyes, intelligent and probing and completely feral.

"Skilly is glad to see you back," she said.

"Glad to be back, Field Prime," he said. Realized with a slight shock of guilt that it was true. *God, what a woman.*

She smiled lazily, and sweat broke out on his forehead; then she dropped her gaze to the map table. "We having de post-mortem," she continued. "Little training attack go wrong, a bit."

He cleared his throat, looked around at the other officers. Many he recognized: von Reuter, the ex-CD major; Sutchukil, the Thai aristocrat and political deportee, a man with a constant grin and the coldest eyes Niles had ever seen. Kishi Takadi, the Meijian technoninja liaison. Another man he almost did *not* recognize. Chandos Wichasta, Grand Senator Bronson's trouble-shooter. That was a shock; the last time he had seen the little Indian was back on Earth, during the humiliating interview with great-uncle Adrian at the Bronson estate in Michigan. The Spartan mission had been a last chance to redeem himself. . . . *Which means Grand-Uncle has managed to get two-way communication going.* There were big glacial lakes in the Drakon foothills where high-powered assault shuttles could land and take off.

"Brigade Leader Niles," Wichasta said discreetly. Another surprise; Niles had been Senior Group Leader —roughly a Major—in the SPLA in the last campaign.

Skilly smiled and shrugged. "You was right about Skilly's plan last time, Jeffi," she said. "Too complicated; or maybe we have de intelligence leak here. Or both; Skilly think both. Howsoever, de wise mon learn from mistake."

"Ah . . . " *Come on, you bloody fool, don't sound like a complete nitwit* " . . . things seem to be well in hand."

Skilly nodded. "Numbers back up some," she said judiciously. "Lots more fancy off-planet stuff coming in —" she nodded to Wichasta "— and money, *lots* of money. The Royals, they doan' know how much we have hid, too. We bleeding them pretty good now, gettin' ready we give them the real grief."

"Hmmm. Won't the CoDo naval station on the Aegis platform —" He broke off at the ring of wolfish grins around the map table.

She laid her light-pencil down. "Field Prime think that enough analysis," she said. "Von Reuter, you breaks up that group and uses the personnel at you discretion." She looked at Niles, and the pulse hammered in his temples. "Brigade Leader Niles need a debriefing."

◆ CHAPTER TWO

Crofton's Essays and Lectures in Military History (2nd Edition)

Professor John Christian Falkenberg II:
Delivered at West Point, June 17, 2073

The soldier and the spy have always been uneasy bed- fellows doomed to unwilling cohabitation. First and foremost among the military virtues is loyalty, above all to one's salt. Correspondingly, the most despised military sin — beyond even cowardice — is betrayal of the oath of service. There are, of course, sound and obvious functional reasons for this ethic; the primary emotional cement of armies is and must be, trust. Without it, no military force can operate for a moment. The spy proper — the clandestine operative — is above all one who wears a mask, who dons a uniform and takes an oath under false pretenses, who abuses trust to pass vital information to the enemies of those whom he infiltrates. Accordingly, none of the protections of the Laws of War apply to the spy. Indeed, historically some military forces have hesitated to use information from such "tainted" sources.

Yet there is no substitute for HUMINT — direct intelligence of the inner councils of an opponent. Even where the full panoply of technical intelligence-gathering is available, HUMINT is priceless; it gives direct access to the *intentions* of the enemy, always the most difficult aspect of military intelligence-gathering. Just as important, the knowledge that one's own ranks have been infiltrated is a powerful tool, sowing suspicion and dissolving the bonds of mutual loyalty that sustain the operational capacity of a military unit.

◆   ◆   ◆

Both principal intelligence officers of Falkenberg's Legion sat at the table. Captain Jesus Alana was a short man, dark and slim with a well-trimmed mustache on his upper lip. His wife Catherine was two fingers taller and flamboyantly red-haired, and also a Captain. As the joke ran, virtually everybody in the Legion was; the chain of command depended on your job, not your pay-scale. Apart from them the office in Fort Plataia was empty. The spring rain was falling, mild here only a few kilometers outside Sparta City; it carried a smell of wet adobe clay through the slit of open window. Over that came a sound of boots splashing down on wet gravel and a voice counting *heep . . . heep*. Cadence for another group of recruits; they were pushing them through as fast as possible. Three Legion battalions now, spawned by the 5th, and the Royal army had doubled and redoubled.

"Not very hopeful," Jesus Alana said.

The files lay in front of him, in hard copy. Only two names . . .

"Not very hopeful, that one, eh, *mi corazon*?"

"Thick as a brick," Catherine replied. "He could take the biofeedback, but he's hopeless for anything requiring an imagination. With luck, he'll make a passable rifleman."

"That leaves the young woman."

"From the file, much more hopeful. Finished basic training, and non-com school. Very reasonable to make her an officer. Higher IQ. Also, lots of determination, with that background."

"I know. Yet —"

"Yet you're a romantic, Jesus. She got out of a Welfare Island."

"Yes," he sighed, and touched a control on the table. "Recruit Talkins, please."

Margreta Talkins was a young woman. The russet eyes were harder than her twenty years would justify. Medium height, olive skin and dark-mahogany hair cropped to a short cap of curls, with a wary edge to her expression. Looking a little weary; neither the Royal army nor the Legion accepted women for combatant positions, but their basic training didn't reflect that. *We may not want them to fight, but it happens often enough*, Jesus thought. *Firm body, looks good on her. She will have no difficulty seducing her targets.* Talkins returned Jesus's hard look, then her eyes darted to the equipment on the table, a set of flat screens and a few crackle-finished milspec electronics modules.

"Sir. Ma'am." Her Anglic was North American, almost-but-not-quite Taxpayer class, the voice of someone who carefully copied the upper-class accents on the Tri-V.

"Please sit, recruit Talkins," Catherine said. "Now, I'm going to ask you a series of questions. The answers aren't important in themselves — just say what comes into your head.

"First, how do you feel about the Helots?"

When the interrogation finished an hour later, Talkins' hair was plastered to her forehead, although her face was still calm.

"Perfect," Catherine said. "Not only can she do it, she'll volunteer to do it."

"Volunteer for what, ma'am?" Talkins said.

Jesus Alana leaned forward. "Clandestine operations. Very secret, very dangerous."

"Will this hurt the Helots?"

"If it works, it'll be very damaging to the enemy. We need your agreement, first."

Silence stretched; then she nodded with a bitten-off: "Yes, sir."

"Why?" Captain Jesus Alana said to the young woman in recruit coveralls. "The machinery —" he indicated the book-sized display unit, open on the table "— tells us you mean it. But that doesn't tell us why you are willing to take the risk."

There was a trace of anger in her voice; Alana frowned slightly at that, then recognized it. She was volunteering, and she had the slightly bitter self-accusatory air of a veteran cursing himself as he volunteered for something he knew was stupid. The young woman spoke at last.

"My brother," she said flatly.

"Killed in action," Catherine Alana said. "Revenge?" she went on, keeping half an eye on the Voice Stress Analysis readouts. There was plenty of data to be authorized in more detail later.

"I told George not to enlist," she said. "Look, sir . . . ma'am. We both came from Columbia Welfare Island, you know?"

Jesus nodded. He did know; he'd heard that something like half the population of the US lived in places like that now. Of course the intentions had been good. Make the cities safe, get the festering legions of the underclass out of the downtown ghettoes, put them where they can be educated, learn to be somebody, leave the underclass. And, incidentally, put them in controlled areas. Let them riot, they couldn't get at the wealthy.

Now the Citizens — some bureaucrat seventy-five years ago had a sickly sense of humor to name them that — sat and rotted, and the Taxpayers paid for it, and paid more for the police who guarded them from the Citizens. Borloi from the convict-worked plantations of Tanith kept the Welfare inhabitants pacified, that and cheap booze and the Tri-V. But some escaped. It was possible, barely.

"Yet you managed an education," Catherine said. "How? Or perhaps better, why?"

"Sister Mary Margaret cared. After a while, I did too."

Catherine smiled reassurance. "Not unlike me, then."

"You're from Welfare? Ma'am?"

"The Legion cares no more where you came from than Sparta does," Jesus said. "Nor do either of us usually care why you joined, but in this case we must know more." He touched the personnel forms on the table. "Edison Technical School in Pittsburgh. No record of drug use. Minor crimes — I assume you were intelligent enough to avoid being caught at anything major. You and your brother did well on Earth. With your education you should have been welcomed into the — normal society."

"As trained seals," Margreta said. "Our sosh worker was proud of us. Offered us a shot at civil service."

"Which is the dream of half those in the Islands," Catherine said. "So why are you on Sparta? It says you were voluntary emigrants."

"Didn't seem like a lot of future on Earth. What's the use of reading books if you don't think? Clear to us, United States wasn't like what the history books said. We wanted —" She stopped. "Damn if I know, ma'am. I guess it seemed like a good idea at the time."

"Your intentions here?"

"Start a business. Own our own life. Make Citizen. That was why George enlisted — I told him it was better I do it, less dangerous. George and I always looked out for each other. There was nobody else but the two of us, but I couldn't in the Army. He thought the stats looked good, but *somebody* has to be unlucky."

The Alanas nodded. Private George Talkins had been in the field one week, as a communications tech, when the truck he was riding in went over a land mine.

"Anyway," Margreta said, "George and I . . . George made it sort of personal. I was always for the Royalist side — I like the way this place is run — but George, that makes it personal."

Talkins looked up, and the Alanas both felt a slight cold chill at the intensity. "Sir, what is it exactly you want me to do?"

"Infiltrate," Jesus Alana said. "Both sides have been trying that, of course. And we've combed out a lot of people from the Royalist organization with this." He reached out a finger and tapped the Voice Stress Analyzer.

"The problem is, the enemy evidently have something like this too. They also have better computer equipment and more and better technicians than we do; the Meijians are expensive but they have the best there is, a slight edge even on Fleet Intelligence standards. They've been running rampant through the local computer nets, and only the fact Legion equipment is ROM-programmed has saved ours from penetration — we hope. *Per Dios*, every time we compare hard copy with government or Royal Army computer files, we find discrepancies! Any operation we *really* want to keep secret is to be word-of-mouth only."

Talkins blinked. "How can I help you beat their screening, if they have that, sir?" she said, nodding to the equipment.

"Well," Catherine said, "it *is* possible to beat voice-stress detection. Not without elaborate hypnoconditioning and biofeedback training, and even then only a very small minority can hope to get through more than a superficial scan. Then, only a small minority of *that* minority is qualified for the job in other respects."

Talkins closed her eyes in thought for nearly half a minute. "And I fit? Must be. And the Legion is handling this because of security. Does this count for Citizenship?"

"Assuredly," Jesus Alana said.

"It's dangerous, Margreta," Catherine said. "If you want to walk out of here, no one but us will ever know we talked."

"How long?"

"A year. Perhaps two. No more than that. But understand, it will not be easy. For one thing, the Helots are certain to require your participation in an atrocity. To prove your loyalty to their cause."

"You mean like —"

"Like shooting prisoners," Catherine said. "Perhaps not so clean as shooting."

"Jesus. Like back in William Penn Island." She was quiet for a moment. "I can really make a difference?"

"Yes."

"And Citizenship when it's over."

"Yes."

"Okay. I'll do it. What happens next?"

"You'll be sworn in to the Legion — that's plausible, we need people with your sort of educational background, and we've started recruiting locally for a lot of positions. You have been through the Royal non-com school. Assuming you can get past our OCS, you will become a Cornet, a very junior officer in training."

"That counts for Citizenship?"

"In your case, certainly. Whatever your Legion rank on discharge, you will have been a commissioned officer in the Royal Army."

Margreta nodded thoughtfully.

"It will all appear to be entirely natural. We train you, then send you on temporary duty to the University. It is certain that the Helots will try to recruit you once you are there."

"You've tried this before."

"Yes."

"What happened to — my predecessors?"

Catherine grinned. "Not what you think. She married an exchange student, and went to Friedland with him."

"You let her go without finishing her hitch?"

"Special circumstances," Catherine Alana said.

"I don't see that happening to me. Not that I wouldn't do it if the right guy asked. Or was that last one really special?"

Jesus shrugged. "We will cross that bridge when the chickens are hatched. For now, you will be transferred to the Legion and sent to officer candidate school. Understand, you must do well there, your instructors will have no hint that you have any special status. When you are commissioned, Catherine or I will speak with you again. No one else will know of your assignment, not now and not later."

"No records?"

"When next we meet we will tell you how to prove your status in the event that both Catherine and I are unavailable. Otherwise, no, no records. Now, we meet again in six weeks' time."

❖   ❖   ❖

Good tradecraft, Cornet Margreta Talkins thought, as the waiter brought her lunch, with a sideways glance for her blue and gold Legion walking-out uniform. *Nobody's going to suspect* this *as a Helot dropshop*.

She very much doubted the owners knew that the underground arranged rendezvous here. Half the patrons in the courtyard tavern were in Royal Army uniform, mostly recruits out on their first post-basic furlough, sitting with their buddies or girlfriends or both; there was a sign outside offering them a discount. Many of the rest were machinists or fitters from the Works, in grease-stained overalls. Von Alderheim was running three shifts now, with the war effort.

The Cock and Grill was on Burke Avenue just off the Sacred Way, not far from the CoDo enclave at the northern end of Sparta City's main avenue. West of here and stretching to the edge of the Minetown slums was working-class housing, two or three-story buildings divided into modest apartments; within easy walking or bicycle distance of the docks, the big von Alderheim plant to the south, and the tangle of small factories that had grown up around it. Many of the buildings had shops or service industry trades on the ground floors, like this one. A brick-paved courtyard facing the sidewalk across a low wall, set with wrought-iron tables and wooden chairs under umbrellas; even on an early spring day like this, Sparta City's climate was comfortable enough, so long as the rains held off. The traffic in the sidestreet beyond was light, an occasional van or horse-drawn dray, bicycles and electrocars.

"Here you are, Miss," the waiter said. "One garden salad —" a heaping bowl of greens and vegetables, colorful and neatly arranged "— one mixed grill —" a wooden platter of spiced steak strips, pork loin and lumps of rockcrawler claw with mushrooms and fried onions "— and a wine seltzer."

She reached into her belt-pouch for the tenth Crown piece; about what a dockworker made in an hour, fairly steep by local standards.

"No charge for Falkenberg's Legion, Miss," the waiter said. He looked about seventeen, with a pleasant freckled face and was probably the son of the owners. "Compliments of the proprietors."

"Thank you," she said sincerely; he reminded her of George, a little. More naive, but then, on Sparta a kid could find time for childhood. And the Legion was popular in this district. She remembered the cline-graphs from briefings at Fort Plataia; about a quarter Citizen around here, and most of the rest established family people, ones who hoped to see their children make Citizen, or were saving to homestead in the outback. The Non-Citizen's Liberation Front didn't route demonstrations through here, since the inhabitants tended to turn out with baseball bats and shotguns to stand in menacing silence.

She took a bite of one of the steak strips; beef still tasted a little odd to her. Few enough on Earth ate much meat these days. *Taxpayer food*, she thought. A far cry from the endless starches, synthetic protocarb and bacteria-vat protein they issued in the Welfare Islands.

Still no sign of the contact when she had finished. *Waiting. Soldiers and spies, they both spend a lot of their time waiting.* Students evidently did, when they could afford to actually attend a University and not cram the study in where sleep ought to go. At the University of Sparta she had met Mary Williams; conversation had led to talks about her background on Earth, the squalid poverty of the Welfare Islands. That made a bitter radicalism plausible — plausible to the children of privileged who seemed to make up the Non-Citizen's Liberation Front at the student level.

Idiots, she thought contemptuously. *Wealthy enough to despise money.* She — *and George, God damn them to hell* — had worked their butts off to get *into* the middle classes, not overthrow them. Casual meetings had led to the legal NCLF organization, and then to the clandestine.

Mary had hinted that this would be a *real* contact, someone she couldn't reach herself except through a series of blind drops and cutouts. No listening bug woven into her uniform, that was far too risky against opposition of the quality the Alanas suspected. There *was* a team observing her, a reaction-squad and snipers with heavy Peltast rifles, so she was probably quite safe.

And she had the biofeedback training that made it possible to baffle detectors. Had that, and her native wit.

Datamonger, soldier and spy — and all before my twenty-first birthday. What's next, the circus?

Swallowing the last of the food turned out to be a little difficult. She concentrated, breathed deeply, used the trick Catherine Alana had taught her of thinking of a pool of still water, it was quicker and less de-energizing than the techniques she had used to overcome fear back home. *No-Nose Charlie was nerve-wracking enough.* They had never been part of the Organization back on Earth, but they had been contractors. Too many licenses for legit operation, too much paperwork and graft and pull. Everything outside the Welfare Islands was sewn up tight by the guilds and the unions and the big government-favored corporations. *Who else was there to work for,* she thought. All No-Nose cared about was whether you could make computer systems sit up and beg. She and George could do *that*, any day of the week.

After a moment her pulse slowed and the muscles in the back of her neck relaxed. Margreta sighed, ordered coffee and pulled some lecture notes out of the attaché case she was carrying. They were on software design, the University was trying to resurrect that, along with a number of other sciences. The problem was that the CoDo Intelligence people had made more effort to corrupt those files than any others, even to falsifying the early history of its development; BuInt's attempts to suppress all dangerous science — which turned out to mean all science, period — had been all too successful. Reinvention had to go back almost to the beginning to do anything more than assemble the standard premade blocks in new positions. Xanadu and Meiji were rumored to have made a good deal of progress, but if they had nobody was talking.

A shadow fell across the paper. "Yes?" Margreta said, looking up and around. It was the waiter; the place had grown a little more crowded, extra tables set out for more soldiers and the afternoon shift from the factories. "I'm sorry, I was expecting someone; I'll leave if you need the table."

"No problem, Miss," the waiter said. He smiled shyly. "Besides, I may need to keep on your good side." At her raised eyebrows. "Just accepted as an ephebe of the Brotherhood last week, Miss, and reporting to Fort Plataia for training with the 7th Royal Infantry Monday next. Anyway, your friend called. Says they'll be by any time now."

"Thank you. And good luck in the army; I hope you haven't been listening to too many romantic stories. It's hard work." Even by her standards; still, it would be very useful to have a scientific understanding of combat. The Talkins' twins had learned a good deal on the streets, and there was teaching available there if you could pay, but the Legion was a different category altogether.

"You're welcome, Miss, and my brother's in the 1st, he fought in the Dales — you'd think they crawl up cliffs pulling themselves along by their lips, to hear *him* talk."

Margreta smiled and shook her head as the young man bustled away, catching a tray of beer steins at the serving window and weaving between the tables to a boisterous party in high-collared gray tunics and stubble-shave haircuts. Imagining himself one of them, she supposed, as she clipped the attaché case closed. *Babies,* she thought. *All overgrown babies.* Trying to prove how tough they were.

She started slightly when the dark man in the conservative brown tunic and tights stopped at her table.

"Do not be alarmed," he said, moving forward with fluid smoothness. He took her hand in a grip like a pneumatic clamp, as impersonal as a machine too.

"We have now," he went on, seating himself and laying an attaché case on the table, "eliminated the obvious; police tailing efforts, implanted electronics, and the rest. Passive observation is possible, of course."

❖   ❖   ❖

The man was about 175 centimeters, brown-skinned, Latino from the cast of his features. Unusually fit, not massive but broad-shouldered and moving lightly as a racehorse. Not a native Anglic speaker, she judged; an ear for the nuances of language was another thing common to her new profession in Intelligence and her old life on the fringes of the illegal. The mystery man had no trace of a regional or planetary accent. That was rare. Definitely not a Spartan, their dialect was so archaic that it was almost English; it retained the final "g," differentiated between "c" and "k," and had fewer of the Spanish and Oriental loanwords that made up so much of the modern language. This man's Anglic had a pellucid clarity like a very good AI language program or someone high up in the CoDominium information services.

"I should think the information I've delivered over the past weeks would be proof of my *bona fides*, sir," she said; a combination of respectfulness and firmness was best here.

A slight chuckle. "Yes, but as we both know, Miss Talkins, it is often worth the sacrifice of real data to plant a double agent who can feed disinformation into an opponent's information-bloodstream. Granted that the files you have contributed are mostly useful, and all have been corroborated independently, this possibility remains."

Margreta allowed herself to lick her lips; they tasted of salt. "Paranoia is also a threat in this business, sir," she said.

A quaver? No, too much. He's got to think I'm valuable, and an agent with weak nerves is a walking invitation to disaster. "Properly safeguarded, an agent in place in the Legion's intelligence section would be a priceless asset."

"Quite. But an exceedingly risky occupation for an agent with a comfortable position elsewhere," he said dryly.

"I'm scarcely comfortable where I am, sir," she said coldly. "My origins . . . I have abundant reason to sympathize with the Movement."

A skeptical silence. *All right, girl, time to* really *act.*

"All right. Sir." A calculating viciousness in her tone now. "I've seen enough to know the Helots stand a good chance of winning. If I get in on the ground floor, I can really get somewhere — all the best jobs in the Legion go to Falkenberg's cronies, and you can't get ahead unless you hold a line command and women can't. I don't want to spend thirty years being a glorified commissioned clerk, or marry some po-faced whiskey-swilling mercenary and breed a litter of officerlets. I want to *be* something, *myself.*

"And," she added, panting slightly, "I want the satisfaction of seeing those bungling incompetents who got my brother killed stood up against a wall and *shot*. All my life — all my and George's life — we've had to wade through wet cement to get a living, while morons without a tenth our brains sat fat and happy up on top, rigging the game against us. We couldn't break in back home because we didn't have parents in the business — bad as bloody India. And here, these so-called generals couldn't figure out anything better for a man with George's brains to do than carry a field computer over a minefield."

Amazing what buried resentments you can find, she thought with a slight tremor of distaste, turning her head aside and controlling her breathing. *Be what you want to seem, as Socrates said.*

The unseen man laughed. "Better. Altruists are unreliable, while resentment and spite are the unfailing twin engines of conspiratorial politics." A long silence, while he looked into the briefcase. "Sincerity, or so my equipment assures me. Well.

"However, another problem arises. You have made yourself an object of suspicion to your superiors by associating with members of the NCLF which is popularly —" a shade of irony "— suspected of having links with the Helot Movement and the Spartan People's Liberation Army. 'No politics in the Legion' will scarcely stretch to cover that."

"I never joined," Margreta said. "Just hung around with them and didn't win many arguments." *God, don't let the deal be queered by its own camouflage!* Gradual disaffection was much more credible than a Saul on the road to Damascus conversion; those were rarer than hen's teeth had been before genetic engineering.

"I've staged some quarrels with the NCLF people at the University" — *which was no problem, what a group of geeks, Mary apart; she's quite nice in a spoiled-brat way* — "and made friends with Royalists. They've welcomed me back like a strayed lamb."

"Perhaps. Although I have a healthy respect for the Captains Alana. The Legion is a small organization and tightly-knit, its officer corps very difficult to infiltrate; particularly as they also have access to voice-stress equipment."

Another pause. *Who* were *these people?* she

thought. Not Spartans, not part of the NCLF's underground apparat. Off-planet hired specialists — she almost snorted at the irony. *Mercenaries*. Meijians, from the captured equipment — although possibly other Orientals, say from Xanadu or even Earth, trying to make everyone *think* they were Meijians. Clandestine ops were like that.

"You are correct, though," the man continued. "Such an asset is too precious to risk. Continue to use the present dropoffs; a call to this number —" he slid a slip of paper across the table "— will give you an emergency contact. Please remember that emergency is the operative word. Please also remember that you are now committed; refuse to carry out orders, and we will simply let your Legion superiors know what you have been doing." The Legion's punishment for treason was hanging.

"We won't use this location again?"

"No, its utility is at an end. Good-bye, Cornet Talkins. Leave the location quickly, please."

He nodded and rose to go, brushing past her. She waited a safe ten minutes, then rose and packed the satchel, remembering to leave a decent tip, and flagged a taxi.

"Definitely Meijians," she said, sliding into the back seat. "They've got voice-stress equipment, too."

"Good to have confirmation," Captain Jesus Alana said from the front seat. "It would be splendid," he went on wistfully, "to pull in that son of ten fathers and sweat out what he knows. Not with a Meijian, though."

Margreta nodded; the technoninjas used a suicide-conditioning process, they could stop their hearts by willing it. And would, if captured.

"Feeding them disinformation will be even better," he said. "And now . . . debriefing."

❖   ❖   ❖

Julio McTieran grinned to himself as he saw the young woman hail a taxi-van and drive away.

God, talk about cute, he thought. *Walks like a palm swaying in a south breeze. On her, red hair looks good.* It was very *dark* red, of course. His younger sister had an orange thatch, and in his private opinion she was homely enough to stop a clock. *So that's one of the terrible slave-driving mercenaries Mike's always moaning about.* He'd have to tell his brother about *that* one when he came back from Mandalay on leave.

"Julio, you good-for-nothing, stop dreaming and help me with this!"

"Yes, mother," he said resignedly, throwing the towel over his shoulder and taking the trays.

A big order for the new bunch of soldiers and their dates; five roast chicken, six burrito platters, seven orders of home-fries, ice-cream to follow, three sarsaparillas, a carafe of the tavern red, two half-liter steins of Pale Brewmaster. This bunch weren't recruits; they had the Dales campaign ribbon, and one ferret-faced trooper with monitor's stripes had the Military Medal. Yellowed teeth showed as he sprawled back in his chair, stein in one hand and the other arm around the waist of a girl.

Transportee, Julio thought. He lifted one tray on each hand, corded forearms taking the strain easily; Julio believed in being prepared, and he had been working out more than the Brotherhood training required. Running up and down Thermopylae Point with hand-weights fifteen times every morning, then back home through the streets before the traffic started. *If a transportee can get the Military Medal, I certainly can.*

His mother was laughing and talking with the soldiers; some were from the neighborhood, some from the Valley, a few even from the Minetown slums, but they were all enjoying her banter. Julio felt invisible as he held the trays for her to serve, watching the way the soldiers' girls clung to their arms, smiling and looking pretty and fresh in their thin print frocks. *Only one more week*, he thought doggedly. *One more week till I report.*

He was turning with the empty trays when he noticed the bicycle stopping outside. Nothing unusual about it, a two-seater commuter model, thousands like it. The two men on it were dressed in ordinary clothes, except that they were wearing white Carnival masks weeks and weeks before the season. The young man recognized the shape one drew from beneath his cloak easily enough; the Walther 10mm machine-pistol was part of the training program for his Brotherhood. It was the fact that it had no place *here*, that it was so *strange*, that was what kept him standing and staring blankly while the man raised it, finger tightening on the trigger.

One of the soldiers had better reflexes. The snaggle-toothed monitor kicked the table over for a barricade and drew his sidearm in the same motion, firing without even getting out of the chair. The terrorist gunman lurched backward off the bicycle, and most of the burst went high, cracking into the rooftiles. Diners were shouting, trying to get to their feet, but they were blocked by the table and their chairs and the screaming, milling patrons, bottles and food and wine and blood. The soldier fired again, not quite quick enough to stop the second man on the bicycle as he jerked the pin from a grenade and lobbed it into the Cock and Grill's courtyard. Julio's eyes followed its arc.

Five second fuse, he thought with detachment. The men on the bicycle were both down now; the soldier who had shot them was prudently behind the heavy oak of the table, and his hand reached up to jerk down the girl who had been sitting beside him. Few of the other patrons had that training, most had not even seen the weapon land.

Three seconds. The oblong grenade clattered to the brick not far from him, spinning on its side like a top. *Fragmentation model*, he realized; that was part of ephebe training too. Lined with coils of notched steel wire, kill-radius of fifteen meters.

It detonated less than a second after he dove onto it and flattened himself to the ground.

◇ CHAPTER THREE

Crofton's Encyclopedia of the Inhabited Planets (2nd Edition):

Terraforming: techniques whereby an extrasolar planet is rendered more habitable for humans and/or other Terran life. Prior to the discovery of the *Alderson Drive* (q.v.), terraforming referred primarily to hypothetical projects to render planets such as Mars and Venus inhabitable. While technically practical, the discovery of worlds with oxygen-nitrogen atmospheres and carbon-based life cycles has made such endeavors non-cost-effective. Habitable planets have proven to be relatively common, and the basic similarities in their biologies — e.g. the prevalence of close analogs to DNA — has given considerable support to the "panspermia" hypothesis that the basic building-blocks of life are introduced from space, where complex hydrocarbons and amino acids are formed spontaneously. Differences in detail, for example the "handedness" of sugars or, less seriously, the presence or absence of various vitamins, pose severe problems to human colonization. A random introduction of Earth bacteria, plant life and simple animals is an excellent trial indicator of the suitability of a roughly Earthlike world for human settlement.

As a general rule, the less advanced the ecology, the easier the introduction of Terran forms will be. On *Tanith* (q.v.), which contrary to surface appearances is in a post-Miocene, post-mammalian stage of evolutionary progress, only intensive protection by man allows any Terran plant or animal life to survive at all. The native species are simply more efficient. Most oxygen-atmosphere planets are less formidable, and selective introduction of higher animals is possible once the native ecosystems are disorganized by human activities. Most favorable of all are worlds like *Meiji* (q.v.), *Xanadu* (q.v.), or *Churchill* (q.v.), where the native ecologies are notably simpler than the Terran; here the introduced forms, with some simple genetic engineering to compensate for factors such as differences in length of year, often replace the local life-forms spontaneously.

An extreme example is *Sparta*, (q.v.), where the relative youth of the planet and the great rapidity of continental formation and subsidence meant that the local ecology had barely begun to colonize the landmasses at all. Faced with an entire planet of virgin ecological niches, the introduced plants and animals exploded across whole continents, completely replacing the meager native species (analogs of mosses, lichens and ferns, with some amphibious insects) almost overnight. In turn, the introduced species have engaged in complex and fluctuating interactions as plant-herbivore-predator associations are worked out to fit the patterns of a world never *quite* like Earth. A stable ecology may take millennia to form. . . .

❖   ❖   ❖

"Excellent," Dion Croser said, lighting his pipe. *Thank god the geneticists got the gunk out of tobacco*, he thought absently. *Greatest aid to concentration ever invented.* "Excellent work." He was a tall man, 180 centimeters, rangily athletic; his face was mostly Anglo-aquiline, and the eyes were blue. Their slant and the high cheekbones were a legacy from a California-nisei mother, but Croser was Sparta-born, the second generation after the Founding. "Particularly getting someone inside the Legion's Intelligence service.

"Not a high-ranking source; and our contacts through the Royalist secret service indicate the double agent may be under suspicion already. We are developing plans to replace this agent, and to extract maximum asset-value in the meantime."

The man sitting across from him in his study did not look much like Kenjiro Murasaki, head of Special Tasks Inc., of New Osaka; more like an American of *mestizo* background, if anything. But then, he had seen Murasaki in his own *persona* only once — if that. *A knight of ghosts and shadows indeed*, Croser thought. Mercenary technoninja, an ironic ally for the Non-Citizen's Liberation Front. Politics made strange bedfellows, and Bronson's money even stranger ones.

"Still, we've gained valuable information already," he said aloud.

Kenjiro made an expansive gesture; even his body-language had changed with the disguise. "Largely a confirmation of material from other sources, Capital Prime," he said. "We are still working on cracking the control codes for the computers of the Legion itself; even that will be of limited utility, since they are ROM-programmed. Best to proceed very cautiously, very cautiously indeed. Our probes have positively identified CoDominium Intelligence security and counter viral systems, Fleet HQ level. Excellent work, if unsubtle; BuInt has been keeping many of the people they 'disappeared' over the past century working in their own research institutes."

"Certainly," Croser said. "Well, Earth Prime was right, they are working hand-in-glove with Lermontov. Damn the CD anyway."

Once the Democratic Republic's established, I have to get a priority effort going on computers. We can't depend on foreigners. He glanced up, into the mask of North American affability that Murasaki was wearing. *And I'm uneasy at the extent I depend on this one* already, he mused. Meijians had a reputation for fanatic loyalty to their employers. *But Bronson — Earth Prime — is the employer here, and what does the Senator really want?*

Murasaki inclined his head. "Even so, Earth Prime is not without influence on the CoDominium. More may come of that. As for now, Capital Prime, I would recommend certain selective assassinations."

Croser frowned. "I thought you'd started on the regional governments?"

"Yes. I was referring to key personnel in the upper structures of the enemy."

"Not the kings, I hope?" That would be a little too much, at this point. For that matter, he intended to exile rather than execute them, after he won.

"No." Murasaki spread his hands. "David I is a very competent administrator and economist, but is emotionally incapable of adjusting to harsh conflict. We would not wish him replaced. As for Alexander —" a thin smile "— he is still too popular and trusted, among many non-Citizens as well. Removal would be counterproductive. His judgment is still uncertain" — the news of the viral psychopoisoning of the King had come out some time ago — "and Prince Lysander is alarmingly capable, and has a wide following among the young. A heroic soldier-king is not our need at this point. No, I was referring to technical personnel; the Royalist government's mobilization is proving alarmingly effective."

"Agreed," Croser sighed, rubbing thumb and forefinger on the bridge of his nose. *I wonder if the fear aroused by Alexander's poisoning was worth the anger?* "Try to be a little less sloppy than you were with the Armstrongs, won't you?"

He had felt a little sick, when the pictures came in. Oh, Senator Steven Armstrong was a bull-headed reactionary of the worst sort — typical new-money greed and pushiness — but Alicia had been charming. It was a pity about the children, as well. Wife, children and hard-won ship all destroyed in an afternoon; it was no wonder the man had gone crazy.

Murasaki's bow was slightly out of the character he was playing. "Still, Capital Prime, Armstrong's Secret Citizen's Army has been of immense value to us," he pointed out.

"Feh," Croser said, using a pipe cleaner to tamp down the tobacco. "Mad dogs, the lot of them, even if they are throwing more and more of the non-Citizens our way."

Two more bombings this week, one of a group of transportees just off the shuttle and heading for the CoDo enclave, the other of a meeting of the new Migrant Farmworker's Union, the first all-non-Citizen labor organization. Armstrong's group was mad with fear and hate, but their actions might as well have been dictated from Movement headquarters.

"We'll have to dispose of them all, first thing after we take over," he said. *Actually, there are an uncomfortable number of people to be disposed of. I should take some time to think about this; granted you can't make an omelet without breaking eggs, no point in beheading the chicken.* He could not govern Sparta without *some* of the old ruling class. "Still, they help our recruiting considerably. Beautiful symmetry." He grinned. " *'See, the Royalists have their extremists too, and they can't control them any more than the NCLF can the Helots.'* By the way," he added, reminded. "Field Prime says that she needs more of your people if they're going to get things rolling again after the Dales campaign."

The Meijian bowed again. "We sacrificed a number of assets," he said judiciously. "But an early breaking of the myth of Citizen invincibility is some compensation. Granted that the Royalists held the field, we demonstrated that our troops could fight the Royal Army."

"Well, the dice rolled that way. Could have been much better, could have been *much* worse." Sitting by the receiver during those crucial hours had aged him a year. Unbelievable exultation, when it looked like the mercenaries and the Royal forces had walked into a trap, then the savage disappointment of seeing it close on his own people instead. The combat experience of Falkenberg's people had been enough to offset Murasaki's penetration of the Royalist intelligence computers.

"My next political move," he went on, "is a direct assault on the legitimacy of the Royalist government. Best to get it done before they proscribe the NCLF and me, personally; that's coming, although we'll fight to delay it. Here's how the open and clandestine wings can help —"

❖　❖　❖

"Don't you have to be at the meeting, Lynn?" Melissa von Alderheim said.

"No, they've put it off until tomorrow," Prince Lysander replied to his fiancee; loudly, as the noise from the factory floor was fairly heavy, even up here in the control booth. "They've brought in some political analyst from Earth that Falkenberg's people think will get to the bottom of our problems; he'll be addressing the War Cabinet."

This was the new von Alderheim works, barely a decade old and on a greenfield site on the southeastern fringe of the city, with its own dock on Constitution Bay. From this station they could see out over the huge machine-littered concrete bay of Assembly Hall Three. The vehicles were moving down the length of it on wheeled pallets guided by the central Works computer, stopping at each team station while groups of overalled machinists swarmed around it. Overhead trolleys lowered sheets and components, welding torches flashed, pneumatic tools shrilled. The air was full of a low electric humm, the smell of ozone and oil and hot metal.

All like something out of a historical documentary on the First Industrial Revolution, Lysander thought wryly. *Something to be proud of, nonetheless.* Most worlds had a thin scattering of modern equipment over a mass of hand-tools. He extended an arm around Melissa's waist as she came to stand beside him; she was wearing overalls too, but the contents were very pleasant.

"Lynn!" she said, in mock protest, as his hand wandered slightly. "Not here!"

"We've got to stop meeting like this, then," he said, straight-faced. "People will begin to suspect, if we keep traveling to the same factories." They had been friends from childhood, their eventual marriage an understood thing. Lately it had been something he looked forward to more and more. *Melissa's not just smart and pretty, she's a real friend, and someone who wants the same things I do.*

"Forgotten your hotel girl?"

"Yes."

"I don't believe you."

"Melissa—"

"It's all right. It's nice that you say it. And we have our duties." Suddenly she was all business. "I have a surprise for you."

"Pleasant, I hope."

"The war isn't going well."

"Depends on what you mean by well. We're not losing." He waved expressively at the factory. "But we're putting effort into the war that ought to go into building civilization."

"Have you thought of negotiation with — with Croser?"

"Sure," Lysander said. "All he wants is for us to dismantle everything that brought us here. Build a welfare state and all that implies. No thanks. But the worst of it is, I think we're just a sideshow," Lysander said.

"Sideshow?"

"Something like that. The real war is political, and it's being fought in the Grand Senate. If the CoDominium would help us — hell, just stop helping the God damned enemy! — we'd end this damned war and get on with our lives. Including our wedding."

"It's bad, then."

He grimaced. "Bad and getting worse," he said. "The enemy can move faster through the Dales than we can down in the lowlands, and they're starting to stick their heads out again. Nothing decisive, but they're killing ranchers — We've got to move faster and hit harder, or there won't be a ranch standing within a day's ride of the hills come summer."

"Well then, come see the present I've made for you," she said, leading him down another staircase into Bay Six, past a bank of humming fabrication machines. "We made, I helped."

He spared the machines a glance. Smooth man-high shapes, with nothing on the exterior but a console, screen and the ingress and egress ports. Put your metal in one end, program, and any possible shape came out the other, formed by everything from powder-deposition to an ultrasonic beam, untouched by human hands. Earth-made by Hyundai, bought forth or fifth-hand, and still representing an investment so huge that the Finance Ministry had had to handle it. Here they were the tiny heart of the great plant; making machines to make machine tools that human operators could use to do the actual production work. *Some day* . . . Some day Sparta would have real factories, robot-run.

They went through a big sheet-metal door with two armed company guards. Inside white-coated technicians were working around an armored vehicle, with parts of several more nearby. "Here it is!" Melissa said. "Behold: the *Cataphract*." She stood to one side and clapped; there were good-natured cheers from the technicians doing the final testing.

"Your Highness, Miss von Alderheim." A bow from the chief engineer.

"Sorry to interrupt, Mr. Azziz," Lysander said

absently. Suddenly even the woman at his side receded from consciousness for a moment as he looked at the sleek gray-green bulk of the machine before him. "I didn't think you could actually come up with a tank worth building," he said.

"More of a light armored gun system, sir," the engineer demurred; his swarthy face split with the smile of a professional who sees a difficult problem solved. "We're just not up to cermet composites, and no realistic thickness of steel is much use. Miss here did it, on that CAD-CAM machine over at the University."

Melissa made a dismissive gesture. "Just playing with the program," she said, blushing. "Thank Andre Charbonneau."

"Charbonneau?" Lysander said.

He knew the name, a French materials engineer arrested for illegal research and sentenced to transportation by BuInt thirty years ago. The Frenchman had been lucky enough to be sent to Sparta, and had been a fixture of the von Alderheim industrial empire for two decades. The single-crystal iron-chrome alloy he had developed was one of Sparta's few really cutting edge products and a staple export.

The new vehicle was a box about six and a half meters long and three and a quarter wide, no more than two and a half tall, sharply sloped in the front and sides. Suspension was on broad treads with seven road wheels and drive sprockets at the front; the wedge-fronted turret mounted towards the rear of the hull carried a long cannon and coaxial machine-gun.

"The armor's a sandwich," Azziz said, slapping it affectionately. "Twenty mm of steel, then a layer of interwoven Nemourlon and iron-chrome thread in insulac, then another 20mm of steel. With this on top." He held up a square of some hard glossy material, on a sheet-metal backing. "High-stability explosive. Fire a shaped-charge warhead at it, and it explodes and disrupts the plasma jet. Old Dayan idea."

"From Earth, really," Melissa said, smiling indulgently at the enthusiasm of the men. "But I dug it out of a big load of datadump we bought as part of a job-lot from them with those used shuttles."

Azziz nodded and dropped the plate of explosive casually to the deck of the Cataphract.

"Whole thing is bulkier than cermet, and gives about 75% of the protection for the same weight," he said. "It'll stop most light antitank weapons if they hit on the frontal slope. Thirty tons total weight; the track's woven Charbonneau thread again, with inset tungsten cleats, the suspension's hydrogas units taken from our heavy mining truck, and the engine likewise — seven hundred horse-power turbocharged diesel, top speed of 80 kph and a range of 700 klicks. Three versions, this one with the rapid-fire 76mm gun, one with a 125mm rocket howitzer, beam-guidance, and an infantry fighting-vehicle.

"Nothing but basic four-way stabilization on the weapons and a laser range finder, I'm afraid," he continued, with gathering excitement. "But if we could get modern electronics and sensor kits to upgrade them, I swear there'd be a big export market. Not quite as effective as the stuff North American Motors or Daimlerwerk Friedland AG put out, but a lot cheaper — a fifth the cost, and hell of a damn sight easier to maintain on a nonindustrial planet."

"Toys for the boys," Melissa said. At their surprised glances: "It's just machinery to me, Lynn. I don't get that, ah, sensual satisfaction from it. We've done up a set of duplicate jigs, by the way, for the plant in Olynthos, and we're starting series production immediately. We can —"

Whunnnnng. The explosion seemed to go on forever,

vibrating from the pressed-metal internal partitions and off the high ceiling of the plant.

"Where was that, where *was* that?" Lysander barked, hand clearing the sidearm he was wearing with his undress grays. Nobody was down, nothing burning. But close. The communicator on his belt squawked:

"*On the way, Prince!*" Harv, with the headquarters reaction squad. *Thank God I let him talk me into bringing them,* Lysander thought.

The technicians had taken cover; an alarm klaxon was blaring. Melissa had vanished. A moment's panic, before he saw her head emerge from the Cataphract's turret. *Smart girl.* Probably the safest place in miles. The prince cocked his head; his ears were still ringing, but he knew where those screams were coming from. Azziz was at his side, one hand clutching a piece of steel bar stock.

"Stay back, man," Lysander snapped.

"Stay back, hell," the engineer said, although he did drop behind a little. "I didn't sell everything I owned on Earth and move here to lose it all to convict scum."

They dodged through the door to the next bay. "My God!" Azziz exclaimed in horror.

Lysander did not think the emotion was for the two workers lying on the ground; Harv's reaction squad was there, spreading out to search and giving first aid to the wounded. The object of the engineer's attention was the first of the four Hyundai fabricators. The exterior telltales had gone dead, and one side of the boron-fiber outer sheathing was bulged and blackened.

"Ruined!" he screamed, slapping his hands to his head. "Two million CD credits and a year's shipping time, and it's *ruined*."

His piece of bar stock clattered to the floor as he rushed over to the machine. Harv rose from beside one of the wounded technicians and went over to a robot trolley stacked with sections of 75mm steel-alloy square beams, bent to examine them and lifted the end of one, then another.

"Think I've found it, sir," he said, saluting. "Quick work, Sergeant," he replied. Harv Middleton, body guard and Phraetrie-brother, would never qualify for a commission, but then he wouldn't want one. All he wanted was to stay close to his Prince.

"Sabotage, Prince. The operator there, he said he and his buddy came round and fed the square steel billets there into the machine every half-hour or so, and saw that the bin of parts moved off."

Lysander walked over and looked at one of the neighboring fabricators. There was a feed-arm that gripped the raw stock, with an automatically adjusting chuck to hold it while the interior mechanisms got a firm grip.

"They had a fresh trolley here. They put the first one in, turned away to check on the finished parts, and just when they walked around behind it blew. Must be something in the steel, sir."

"Probably," the Prince agreed grimly. His sidearm was still in his hand; he slapped it back into the holster with a sense of angry futility. "Cordon it off, until the Milice get here. Don't disturb the site, the forensic experts will want it that way." *Probably was the bars*, he thought. *Which either came from the smelter right here, or down from Olynthos on a barge. The barge, I'd bet; thousands of klicks of opportunity to substitute.*

"Sorry to spoil your furlough, Sergeant," he continued.

Harv smiled broadly and tapped the butt of the rifle slung over his shoulder. "We were figuring on doing a night-patrol exercise around your hunting lodge," he said. "To see that you and Miss weren't disturbed, sort of."

"That won't be necessary; we won't be using the cottage," Lysander said flatly. "Neither of us will be leaving the Palace."

The NCO's face fell slightly. Lysander forced a smile and clapped him on the shoulder; Harv could be a bit of a trial sometimes, but he was a good man and a Brother.

"Visit your own girlfriend, Sergeant," he said.

"Which one?" Harv said, returning the smile. Then he looked to his men: "Excuse me, sir?"

The officer nodded, turned and walked back through the doors, brushing aside the crowd of frightened technicians and their questions. Melissa was sitting on the side of the Cataphract, waiting.

"Bad?" she said.

"Two men injured," Lysander replied. "One of the Hyundai's is wrecked."

She winced. "That *is* bad." He explained, and she shook her head ruefully.

"Don't tell me we're going to have to inspect every shipment of raw stock!"

"I'm afraid so," he said. Softly: "I'm afraid it's too risky for us to visit the Theramenes. Personally, the Palace will do me quite well, and to hell with appearances." He held out his hand.

✧ CHAPTER FOUR

Confusion is often apparent in discussions where the terms *guerrilla*, *partisan*, *insurgent*, *terrorist*, and *mercenary* are used. *Guerrilla*, *partisan*, and *insurgent* are interchangeable. These three words refer to one whose aim is to overthrow a government by armed force, largely through use of indigenous resources. International conventions provide for the treatment of guerrillas, insurgents, and partisans. They must bear arms openly, wear an identifying symbol that is recognized at a distance, and conform to the laws of war. Compliance with these simple rules places the insurgent, guerrilla, or partisan in the category of a legally recognized combatant, one who is due prisoner-of-war status if captured.

Terrorists enjoy no legal protections. They normally conceal weapons, mingle with the civilian populations for personal protection, and may take hostages to achieve their aims. Defying international conventions, they are usually treated as common criminals. Terrorist methods often involve armed and illegal coercive propaganda. The most typical terrorist goal is to achieve widespread recognition for a cause through outrageous actions that compel international attention.

One term, *mercenary*, is apt to be much in evidence during the 21st Century, and it may be used as inappropriately then as it is now. Commercial contractors currently maintain some weapons systems, perform housekeeping duties at military and naval installations, and conduct military training. They have even drafted military plans. The use of commercial firms in military affairs is growing, and their staffs are often composed of ex-military and -naval personnel. But are these companies and their employees properly labeled as mercenaries?

The word *mercenary* is more often used in perjorative descriptions. The term usually has more to say about the writer or commentator's political orientation than it does about the person described. A true mercenary's sole motivation is financial reward, the acid test being whether he would switch sides for more money. In other words, the mercenary does not discriminate between political causes or nations to which he offers his services. His work simply goes to the highest bidder. As a practical matter, most people who are described as mercenaries are actually adventurers who discriminate between the political causes they support . . .

—Rod Paschall
LIC 2010: Special Operations and
Unconventional Warfare in the Next Century
(Institute of Land Warfare, Association of the US Army, 1990)

❖ ❖ ❖

Letter found in War Office general delivery box, Sparta City:

Dear Major-General Owensford:

Hiyo, Petie! This Skilly dropping you a line to thank you for the seminar in operational art you give us Helots back in the Illyrian Dales. That will teach Skilly not to make she plans so fancy! Skilly, now she understand more of what Clausewitz write about friction and other thing as well.

Expensive lesson, Petie, but as old Socrates say, knowledge be a treasure nobody can take away.

We Helots love the knowledge, so we want to learn everything you can teach. We be coming back for more. Again . . . and again . . . and again. As many times as it take until we get it *right* and pass Final Victory exams. Protracted Struggle, hey?

Give Skilly's regards to Baby Prince. He getting so hard-nose, pretty soon maybe he go into her line of work? But he right not to care nothing about those prisoners and wounded.

You and you gunboys was lucky, but you earned it.

Skida Thibodeau
Field Prime, Spartan People's Liberation Army

PS: Maybe you be lucky again. Maybe twice. But we only need be lucky *once*.

❖ ❖ ❖

"The important thing," Peter Owensford said, "the great thing, is not to lose our nerve."

There were murmurs of approval around the Council table. "Are you going to give that letter to the press?" someone asked.

"I don't know. Would it be more likely to stiffen resolve, or frighten people?"

"Both, I think." Alan Hruska, Milice chief for Sparta City, looked thoughtful. "Me, I'm for telling the Citizens everything we can."

"Right," Owensford said. "It's our major advantage. Citizens are our partners, not our slaves. Besides, she could send a copy to the press herself. All right, I'll hand it to Harold Preston at the *Tribune*. We owe him — that was a good job he did on the Cock and Grill bombing."

Hruska nodded. "I'd say so."

"How's the boy?" someone asked.

Hruska shrugged. "No change. He'll be months in the regenn tanks, but they figure they can rebuild him. I want him on the force when he gets out—"

"And we could use him in the Army," Owensford said. *Pancake on a bomb and get a choice of careers.* "Whatever happens with him, he's got a medal coming. I take it his medical's paid—"

"Sure, his phratrie took care of everything."

"That's good — ah." Owensford stood to greet a newcomer. "Dr. Whitlock. Gentlemen, Dr. Caldwell Whitlock, political consultant."

There was a flurry of greetings. Horace Plummer, secretary to the War Cabinet, stood. "I will inform their majesties that we are ready to begin."

Roland Dawson, Principal Secretary of State, indicated a place at the table next to Owensford, and Whitlock went to it. He bowed slightly. "Madame Attorney General. Gentlemen. My pleasure to be here." He spoke with a thick Alabama accent.

"I wish that were true." Attorney General Elayne Rusher looked more like a society lady in her thirties than a grandmother of fifty-five, or would if there hadn't been so many worry lines at the corners of her eyes. "But it's nice of you to say so."

"Ma'am." Whitlock took his seat. He was a tall lean man in his early fifties, looking younger from careful exercise and expensive regeneration treatments; even under Sparta's heavy gravity he was loosely relaxed. A blond mustache and trimmed goatee set off long carefully-arranged yellow locks, and he was dressed with foppish care, in multihued tunic, tooled boots, black-satin tights, broad sash and an emerald stickpin in his cravat, the height of Earth fashion.

"How long will you be here?" Peter Owensford asked.

"I won't be leavin'. Closed out my affairs on Earth before I came."

"Good God."

"Not easy," Whitlock said. "My family settled Montgomery, you know. And we've had the Jackson-ville plantation ever since the Yazoo Purchase."

"It's that bad on Earth, then?"

Whitlock looked up to see that everyone was listen-ing, and nodded. "I'll have a few words about that in the meetin'. But yes, things are happening on Earth. With John Grant dead, I wouldn't be surprised to see Unity out of office next election. If things last until then, which—"

The door at the far end of the chamber opened. "Gentlemen, ladies — their Majesties."

Everyone stood as the kings, Alexander and David, entered with Lysander.

The King looks better, Owensford thought with relief. Lysander had told him that Melissa and the Prince's mother Queen Adriana had been working on him in relays to take a vacation at the summer palace on the island of Leros. Two weeks among the orange trees and olive groves had worked wonders in speeding the cure; Alexander's skin was tanned and firmer, his eyes had lost most of the desperate hunted look, and he moved less like a man carrying a double-weighted pack. By contrast, his co-monarch David looked as if he were still in mourning. He'd been Crown Prince Regnant for years until his near-invalid father quietly died. *At least the Helots had the decency to let us bury the king without incidents.* David's rather low key coronation was marred by three car bombings and an attempted riot. The riot was suppressed with casualties to the rioters; relatives of the police were killed by the car bombs. *Another incident of oppression for the opposition to exploit.*

On the other hand, David Freedman always looks like that when we have to increase taxes. The Freedman kings had been economics professors of a very laissez-faire bent, back when Sparta was the dreamchild of the Constitutionalist Association on Earth. Every regulation or tax was like tearing off a piece of skin, to them. One could sympathize, but that money was buying what his men needed to fight and win.

The royal party took their places at the center of the table. Alexander nodded to Horace Plummer. "Mister Secretary."

"Your Majesties. Your Highness. The first order of business is a report on the current situation. General Owensford."

❖   ❖   ❖

" . . . so by the end of spring, we'll have better than thirty thousand people under arms in the Royal Army, under the Emergency Program," Owensford concluded. "In addition we have a full two regiments of the Spartan Legion. We've got four companies of Helot deserters trained and heading out to New Washington as reinforcements for Colonel Falkenberg."

"Tell us about that," Attorney General Rusher said.

"Not much to tell," Owensford said. "We offered amnesty to any captured enemy enlisted troops who'd join the Legion, and got about two thousand. Half that many made it through training. We turned the others, the ones who wouldn't volunteer, over to the Milice."

"What happens to the washout volunteers?" Roland Dawson asked.

"Turned over to the Milice same as those who told us to go to hell," Peter said. "Provides an incentive to finish training."

"They go to the far end of the island," the Milice chief said. "Separated from the ordinary POW's. Right now both groups have enough work just building their camp and raising their own food, but we hope to have an education program for those that stay out of trouble and want to get back into mainland life." He shrugged. "One more thing to do, and we're in no big hurry to do it, not until the war's over."

"So none of your trained Helot warriors will stay on Sparta," Elayne Rusher asked.

"That's correct, ma'am, we couldn't trust them here. Off-planet —" Owensford shrugged.

"Legion's been making troopers out of that sort forever," Dr. Whitlock observed.

"All true," Owensford agreed. "And finally, we've reinforced the Fifth Battalion, Falkenberg's Legion, almost to full regimental strength, mostly with recruits just off the CD transports. Unavoidably, this means temporary compromises with unit quality, but we're working on that."

"Nothing like combat to sharpen up the troops," Whitlock said dryly.

"Quite true," Owensford said. "Especially NCO's. Of course we've accelerated officer and NCO training. We're combing the CD transports for men with

Marine experience. But the best training is still live fire. Unfortunately we're getting all too much of that." The map wall sprang to life.

"Notice the pattern of incidents." He called up an arrow and traced the line of southern Drakons, south and east from the Rhyndakos toward the coastal town of Colchis. "Attempted infiltrations, here and here. And too many successes, because we have no satellite reconnaissance, and not much aerial."

"Dr. Whitlock," Alexander said. "Do we dare renew the satellites? The local CoDominium commander won't answer. Says the question is insulting. But we haven't infinite resources—"

Whitlock nodded. "I wouldn't, just yet. Admiral Lermontov is aware of the situation, but his efforts to make some changes here were blocked by Vice Admiral Townsend."

"Townsend?"

"A Bronson grandson," Whitlock said.

"That sounds ominous," Hal Slater said.

"Ominous indeed, Colonel Slater. Excuse me. General Slater," Whitlock said. "Control of the Fleet is very much in dispute just now, and unfortunately there are other critical situations demanding Admiral Lermontov's attention and influence."

"Such as New Washington?" David Freedman asked.

"Yes, Majesty," Whitlock said. He looked around the room. "Do you want that report now, with all these people?"

"Yes, I think so," Alexander said. "If we can't trust this group, we're finished."

"All right. But with your permission, Sire, I'll let General Owensford finish telling us how he sees the situation before I begin."

"All right," Alexander said. "I take it that we won't be getting a new satellite."

"Maybe not just yet, Sire."

"I see. General —"

"There's not a great deal more to report," Owensford said. "There have been actions here, up the valley of the Jason and into the Lycourgos Hills. We know they've gotten small forces into the foothills of the Pindaros and Parnassus ranges east of the river. Meanwhile, activity of all sorts is increasing throughout the Middle Valley; their latest trick is to drop mines into the river. We've recovered a few. Big box of plastique with a simple pressure trigger; blows the bottom out of a river boat quite thoroughly."

Lord Henry Yamaga, Minister of Interior and Development, made a sound of disgust. "What's the *point*, beyond sheer sadism?"

Owensford shrugged. "The same *point* as putting small units into the Lower Valley," he said. "We have to divert resources to sweep for mines, and every man we keep in the Lower Valley is another we don't send to the Middle."

"The plan was to keep them bottled up," Yamaga said. "That's not working."

"No, my lord. I haven't enough troops for that. Actually, Alexander the Great and Julius Caesar together couldn't seal that area air-tight, not with a *million* foot-infantry. Controlling guerrilla warfare of this type sops up soldiers the way a sponge does water."

"So what will we do?" *Freiherr* von Alderheim affected a monocle and looked very Prussian, but his voice was friendly. He'd been suspicious of the Legion mercenaries when they first arrived, but lately had become one of their chief supporters.

"We hold on," Owensford said. "And continue to build strength. Majesties, my original assignment here was to train mercenaries you could hire out off-planet for hard currency. That we're doing. As Dr. Whitlock observes, there's nothing like live fire training to cement unit cohesion. In that sense this war has actually helped us get ahead of schedule—"

"At fearsome cost," David Freedman said.

"Yes, Majesty, but the costs of recruiting and training this many soldiers would have been fearsome anyway. When this is over, we'll have trained cohesive units under battle tested leaders. I should think they would command a good price."

"Perhaps," David said. "But I never liked that scheme to begin with." He shrugged. "Of course if we hadn't begun when we did, we wouldn't have had troops ready to fight this — rebellion. We might have lost already. Your pardon, General. Please continue."

"Majesty. Some things go well. The Coast Guard Reserve, our brown-water navy, has got control of a lot of our rivers, and contests the rest with the rebels. They used to get nearly a free ride. Not any more.

"Production of Thoth missiles is up. We don't have as many as I'd like, but the pace accelerates. *Freiherr* von Alderheim's factories are ahead of schedule in helicopter and small aircraft production. We don't have aviation company up to TO&E in every regiment, but at least they all have some kind of aircraft, and brigade levels have more. That gives us considerably more strategic mobility.

"We can't use those for tactical engagements, of course. The rebels have quite enough anti-air to prevent that. On the other hand, having to carry air defense missiles cuts down on their mobility and complicates their logistics, and they don't have air capability.

"The result is that we've cut way back on their ability to resupply from our arms factories. They used to steal us blind, but they can't do that any more. The bad news is they stockpiled a great deal, and they're still receiving off-planet supplies from somewhere. Every time we cut into their quantity, there's new increase in the quality of what they get. Almost as if it's a game."

"Ah," Whitlock said. "And there's where you put your finger on it."

"Sir?"

"In a very real sense, it is a game. Very high stakes game, but a game right enough."

"I expect you're going to explain that," Owensford said.

"Yes. I'll have to lecture."

"Dr. Whitlock, I assure you, you have our full attention," King David Freedman said. "Perhaps you should begin your report now."

"Sire. Well. All along, it must have been obvious to y'all that this rebellion hasn't got a coon's chance without help from off-planet."

"Yes, of course," Alexander said.

"And not just a little help. I don't know what all Bronson has put into this, but it's got to be more than a billion credits."

"That much," David Freedman mused. "Yes, I believe that — but Dr. Whitlock, *why*?"

"That's the question," Whitlock said. "What could he want that's worth that much? There's only one answer that makes sense. Empire."

There was a long silence. "With himself as emperor," Alexander said at last.

"Himself, an heir, a whole group of heirs," Whitlock said. "Yes."

"Why in God's Name would he *want* the job?" Alexander demanded.

" 'Cause he thinks it's got to be done, and he's sure he and his people are the only ones that can do it," Whitlock said. "I know y'all think of Bronson as purely mean and selfish. I can understand Spartans seeing him that way, but I'm surprised you two —" he indicated Peter Owensford and Hal Slater — "bought into that. Colonel Falkenberg always knew better."

"Bronson? A misguided idealist?" David Freedman asked.

Whitlock shrugged. "Call him a patriot if you prefer. He'd think of himself that way."

"And we stand in his way," David said. "Why? Because we — the Collins kings anyway — early on chose to be part of Lermontov's scheme? Is that why our people are being bled to death in a filthy little war we can't win? Because of this ill conceived alliance with Lermontov?"

"David," Alexander said gently. "Please excuse my colleague, Dr. Whitlock. Still, he has a point. Have we merited Senator Bronson's attentions because of our support of his enemies? Could we have avoided all this by remaining neutral?"

"I very much doubt it, Sire. And now I really will have to lecture. If you'll excuse me, I think better on my feet." Whitlock rose and strode to the map wall, where he paced back and forth. "Always did like blackboards," he said absently. "I take it that everyone in this room is cleared for — for everything."

"Yes, of course," Alexander said.

Whitlock was silent as he looked at them one by one.

"You can proceed," Hal Slater said.

"As General Slater says," Lysander said carefully.

Whitlock nodded to Slater, then bowed slightly to Prince Lysander. "Thank you, Highness. All right, let's start from the beginning. The CoDominium's coming apart. When it does, there'll be war on Earth, and it won't stay confined to Earth. Enough of the nationalist elements on Earth have close ties with their colonies that the war will spread beyond the solar system. We have a name for that. Interstellar war. But we don't know much about what that means. Just that it'll be pretty bad, bad enough that it's worth a lot to stop it. We okay so far? Good.

"So. The Grants and the Blaines saw this coming twenty years ago. Earlier, probably, but that's when they hired me to study their options. Problem was, there weren't many options. Too many colonies hate each other. Some areas, the Fleet's all that keeps the peace. Remove the Fleet, war starts like that." He snapped his fingers. "Obvious conclusion is that the Fleet, or a good part of it, has to keep operating if we're to have any chance of holding onto civilization.

"That'll cost money. A lot of money, and a Fleet's no good without bases, recruiting grounds, retirement homes, home ports for families. You going to keep civilization, you got to have a civilized home base. You need forward bases, too, out among the barbarians. Outposts, listening posts, refueling facilities, bases. Some of those can be enclaves, but it's better to have whole planets.

"That takes soldiers. Long time ago, man named Fehrenbach said it, you can fly over a territory, you can bombard it, you can blow it to hell, you can even sterilize it, but you don't own it until you stand a seventeen year old kid with a rifle on top of it. So. Where to get soldiers? Can't hire 'em. Not enough money, but worse, when you hire mercenaries, what have you got?"

Everyone looked at Slater and Owensford, then looked away.

" 'Course there's mercenaries and mercenaries," Whitlock said. "They ain't all alike by a long shot. Take Falkenberg's outfit. It started as the 42nd CoDominium Line Marines. Decorated all to hell, elite outfit even before Falkenberg took it over. No surprise that it stayed together after the CD ordered it disbanded. Lermontov helped find 'em work. Figures. Falkenberg and Lermontov go back a long way. Lot of loyalty in both directions. You can think of Falkenberg's outfit as a kind of Praetorian Guard for Lermontov, except that Lermontov's no would-be emperor.

"But that's one regiment. Need a lot more troops to hold things together. Where to get them?"

"Sparta," King David said. "You and my father —"

"Let's don't get ahead of ourselves, Sire," Whitlock said. "What we've established so far is a need for bases, and troops to guard them with. There's another need, planetary governments interested in civilization. Places without any grudges to work off, no ambitions to drive them. That's Sparta. Not much wonder you were one of the first they tried to sign up."

"There was no commitment. Then," Alexander said. "We were friends with Lermontov and Grant, and we got some trade concessions, favorable interpretations of regulations—"

"All of which ended when the Grants and Blaines lost control," David said.

"Sure, but anyone could foresee that would happen," Whitlock said. "You had to know it, there wouldn't have been no need for this conspiracy if it hadn't been clear things were going to hell and nobody could stop the trip. What were your alternatives? Join up with Bronson?"

Alexander shrugged. "That was never offered to us. If we had —"

"If you had, you'd have ended up with no independence at all," Whitlock said. "Bronson planets have puppet governments, with a Bronson resident calling the shots. Can't see Sparta going along with that."

"Nor I," Baron von Alderheim said. He looked thoughtful. "But is this what will happen if Croser and his people win?"

"Yep."

"Do they know this?" Sir Alfred Nathanson asked. Nathanson was Minister of War, but that was an administrative rather than a command position. Under the Spartan constitution the Kings were the commanders in chief, and could issue orders directly to their generals. For all practical purposes, Crown Prince Lysander was the actual War Minister, with Nathanson handling administration and details.

"I doubt it," Whitlock said. "Y'all know Croser better than me. Would he find the role of puppet very attractive?"

"Attractive, no," Alexander said. "But I really don't know if he would accept it. I knew his father well, but Dion is a bit of an enigma. Would he take the trappings of power without the substance? Probably. He would persuade himself that this was for the best, would serve some higher good."

"And that he'd be able to use his position to take charge some day," Roland Dawson said. "Yes, I think that's how his mind would work. But surely he expects to gain both substance and trappings."

"Well he sure ain't got much chance of it," Whitlock said. "Not given who he's running around with." He clicked the screen controller, and an image formed on the wall screen.

"Field Prime. That's what the Helots call their military commander, just like Croser is Capital Prime, and Bronson is Earth Prime. Interesting set of designations, no? Don't show any one of them subordinate to any other. Anyway here she is."

The woman on the screen was in her early thirties, clearly Eurafrican. 175 centimeters, according to the scale beside the image, with a high-cheeked, snub-featured handsomeness and a mane of loosely-curled hair. Startlingly athletic-looking. An insolent half-smile was on her lips.

"Ms. Skida Thibodeau, aka 'Skilly,' born Belize City, Belize, 2061; mother Mennonite, kidnapped into prostitution, father a pimp. Orphaned at six, primary education in a Catholic charity school. Transported by the Belizian gov'mint — gallows-bait themselves — for 'offenses against public order' in 2083. Better lookin' than your average terrorist, but hoo, lordy, look at that record! Arson, insurance fraud, illegal substances trafficking, assault, intimidation, murder, racketeerin', you name it and she's dabbled in it. When your police people closed in on her accounts and suchlike, they found she'd managed to accumulate better than six million crowns."

"No small sum," Lysander said dryly.

"Right. Got most of the money out, too. Presume it's stashed where she can get at it if she has to vanish fast. She was an, ah, *intimate* friend of your good Citizen Dion Croser fo' six years, but no trace of political ties. No paper trail."

Chief Hruska nodded sourly. "No criminal record, except for the one assault charge that got her in jail. We've known she was a criminal for years, but no evidence. She moved around a lot, but she stayed with Croser every couple of months. They openly went to night spots together."

"And of course Croser is simply shocked to discover she was involved in criminal activities," Attorney General Rusher said.

"The point is, she's not likely to knuckle under to anybody," Whitlock said. "Doesn't fit her personality. So here she is, out there carryin' water for Croser, and if Croser's not smart enough to see what Bronson has in mind for Sparta, this one is. Leavin' us with the question, just what in hell is her game?"

"Do you have an answer?" Alexander asked.

"Only the obvious, she thinks that when the fightin's over, Field Prime'll be runnin' the show and Capital Prime and Earth Prime can dance attendance." He shrugged. "If she can outmaneuver Bronson she's a rare bird for sure."

"Devious, but inexperienced," Hal Slater said. "Inexperienced at this kind of intrigue, that is. She will have been the cleverest around where she came from. Able to outsmart anyone. Look at her battle plan in the Dales campaign. Intricate, fine tuned, clever — and utterly unworkable. I suspect it's the same thing here. She simply has no experience at dealing with really clever people, people served by an equally intelligent general staff. Her experience with Croser probably has done little to disillusion her — and of course Bronson's people aren't going to."

"Until it's too late," Whitlock said. "Yeah, I reckon that's the size of it. She figures when it's over she'll be in charge with Croser to help her, and he reckons the same thing only reversed."

"They really do intend to become the government," David mused. "They *want* to govern."

"No, Sire, they don't want to govern. They want to *rule*," Caldwell Whitlock said. "Not quite the same thing. And as General Owensford's report shows, they've made a fair bit of headway."

Alexander shook his head in wonder. "How could people like that put together an army, an army capable of fighting real troops, right under our noses?"

"Careful plannin'," Whitlock said. "An eye for conditions. And a lot of help from off-planet. Conditions first. I was just remarking to General Owensford here, this isn't the sort of war he's used to. It's revolutionary war, the type they had on Earth a hundred, hundred and fifty years ago. You see, you're the victims of your own success. Oppression and despair don't produce revolution; there's been exactly *one* successful slave revolt in all of recorded history. No, what produces revolutions is *hope* — combined with a certain amount of social disorganization. Defeat in war will do it but BuReloc's given you the equivalent — and frustrated ambitions. The underclasses may furnish the troops, but it's people on the make who lead them.

"Places like Meiji or Churchill, they're too homogenous and stable for this kind of war. They'd have to be outright invaded. Frystaat, say, or Diego are quite effectively oppressive. They'd have shot your Croser years ago. You, I'm afraid, are stuck right in the middle. In most places civilization is a thin crust on a sea of barbarism; Rome had her Goths and Saxons, Earth bred 'em in its own guts. Still, the system's had a certain stability. The masses never get to *see* the rulers, mostly they're left to rot while dangerous ones are shipped out, or recruited fo' the Marines and the Fleet; the productive workin' minority is kept in line by the threat of the — pardon me, usin' Earth terminology — Citizen hordes. An' the tiny oligarchy that runs things is secure. Except from itself, which is where the system's breakin' down there, a lot like old Rome.

"Now," he went on, drawing on his cigar, "out here, you've got problems from the bottom *up*, instead. Y'all understand, you've got an unusual rulin' class here. A full third of the population, and *visible*. Then the CD sends you Earth's barbarians. And what do you do? You give them a chance. You give them no excuses. None. You make it plain, their failures are their own fault, and you rub it in by making the rewards of success visible and believable.

"That worked fine so long as you didn't get over-whelmed. Lots of them made good, you've achieved a remarkable and admirable social mobility. But a lot just don't make good. Too many generations of failure, too long away from even suspecting what citizenship is. They see you as rich slavemasters, and they get told all they got to do is take what's coming to them. Okay, you can handle that if you don't lose your nerve, but nobody ever said it was going to be easy."

"We give them every opportunity to get ahead. Become Citizens, or, more likely, their children will," Lord Yamaga said. "My grandfather was a transportee!"

"Yessir, but don't forget how things change. First generation transportees got here into a working soci-ety, lots of opportunity. No opposition to speak of. Now you get floods of these barbarians. Most raised in cesspits ruled by two-legged rats. Example, Skida Thi-bodeau, of Belize. Only difference there between the street gangs and the gov'mint is firepower. Miz Thi-bodeau grew up in an environment where there's no law nor morals either; she's got enormous ability, and the moral outlook of a hammerhead shark." Another meditative puff.

"Of course, the demographic mix here doesn't help. The surplus of males, that is. Big concentration of young, socially alienated and sexually frustrated males with no prospects of startin' a family is a recipe for trouble. Recruitin' them into an army and sending them offworld was a good idea, only too late. Because of the next factor: who's taking *advantage* of the condi-tions."

"Croser," someone said; they made the word sound like a curse.

"True. Typical in Utopian settlements to get a rebel-lious element in the second generation. Your bad luck to get one who's perversely brilliant, with a childhood grudge against your whole social system. Knows history, knows the weak points of your society — I've read some of his papers from his university days. Also a charismatic leader who can win loyalty, not afraid to delegate, and he knows how to pick able people.

"Been plannin' this for the better part of two decades, I'd say. Accumulatin' funds — does it shock you if I say he controls more money than *Freiherr* von Alderheim here?"

The industrialist *did* look shocked.

"Lot of debts," Whitlock said. "But lots of power, too."

"Where did he get it?" van Alderheim demanded.

"Lots from off-planet," Whitlock said. "Easy to guess the source."

"So Bronson has bought him? Why? What does Bronson want with us?" Alexander demanded.

"Regiments. Same thing Lermontov wanted," Whitlock said. "You set out to build a regiment factory. That was fine by Bronson. He'd figured on Croser doing that anyway, you might as well get a good start. Then two things happened. Ms. Skilly got anxious to start things movin' — don't know why, maybe she's beginning to feel her age — and you brought in Falkenberg's Legion to train these troops. That was enough to get Bronson's attention."

"Because he hates Falkenberg," David said.

"Well, Sire, that's a piece of it, but if you bet on Grand Senator Adrian Bronson gettin' carried off by his emotions, you'll lose every time. Not that he minds indulging his grudges when he can, he's got a hell of a streak of mean, but think on it. If you'd built normal mercenary regiments for use off-planet, who'd they be loyal to?"

"The paymaster, I presume," Lysander said quietly.

"Exactly. But Your Highness was with Falkenberg's Legion on Tanith. Who are they loyal to?"

"Falkenberg. I see," Lysander said. "Suddenly what Bronson saw as an asset — mercenary regiments he could subvert — became a possible threat."

"That's about the size of it," Whitlock said. "Before that, his support for Croser was nominal, the kind of thing he does lots of places for insurance, a way to keep his hand in. Sparta didn't look like having any special ties to Falkenberg and Lermontov. Then all of a sudden, Prince Lysander here goes to Tanith, where Falkenberg and one of the Blaines are in cahoots to mess up Bronson's plans to get more control over the Fleet. Crown Prince Lysander becomes Mr. Cornet Prince, and that right there would be enough to take notice of."

"Why?" David asked.

"Reckon you never met Falkenberg," Whitlock said. "If you had, you wouldn't ask. Anyway, pretty soon he don't have to guess whether Prince Lysander's going to choose the Lermontov side in the upcoming struggles, 'cause Mr. Cornet Prince goes and ruins Bronson's whole operation for him."

"Game. You said game," Lysander said.

"Up to not long ago that's what it was," Whitlock said. "Bronson didn't want Croser to win and consolidate his position, but he didn't want him to lose, neither. So he sends just enough to keep him going. But that all changed last year. Now it's all out."

"And so he sent the technoninjas," Slater said. "And stepped up his off-world support by a lot."

"So what will happen now?" Lysander asked.

"Not to get ahead of ourselves," Whitlock said. "First look at what you're facing. For twenty years Croser's been laying a political framework without much opposition. After all, it didn't occur to anyone that organizin' the non-Citizens was anything but an exercise in futility. Developin' an ideology: I mentioned this was an archaic sort of place? Well, you've got something *really* old-fashioned here. A real, honest-to-god Leninist-Maoist vanguard party that believes in itself. Oh, not strictly Marxist — elements of that — more like National Socialism, really. Then he started buildin' up an army. The brigadier here knows more about the ways that might be done."

Owensford nodded. "We've put together something of a picture from the prisoner interrogations," he said.

"You'd start small, with some committed partisans. Get them military educations, and bring in small parties of people with training — there are plenty of good officers and NCO's on the beach on Earth, and the NCO's would be more valuable than the officers, at first. Not all that many who'd be willing to link up with this gang, but enough. Send others off to enlist in merc units on other worlds, which would get you combat-experienced men. Use all those to train selected local recruits who're committed to your cause. It would start small, but once you got well started expansion could be geometric. We've also determined that they — presumably Croser — started stockpiling weapons and equipment, in the Dales and elsewhere, a full decade ago. Skimming export shipments, mostly. Croser's companies would get export orders, over-order enough to cover the five or ten percent they'd take, then use the profits on the real sale to cover the excess. Complicated, but workable, and you wouldn't have to have many people in the know."

Alexander rolled a pen between his fingers. "But surely Croser — if it is he — couldn't think that such a force could overthrow the government? After all, the Brotherhoods can call out hundreds of thousands of troops in an emergency."

Whitlock waved the tip of the cigar to emphasize

his point. "Not attack and displace — but you're thinkin' in terms of modern warfare, small decisive campaigns, your Majesty. The enemy is usin' an older model. Their target isn't really your armed forces, it's your society as a whole. They give you nothing to attack, while you have to guard *every-thing*. You can't call out the Brotherhoods *en masse* for long; too much shuts down. And many of them are scattered on farms and ranches miles from any-where when they're not under arms. There's a military saying —"

"Frederick the Great," Owensford supplied. "*Who defends everything, defends nothing.* Quite true."

"And a Chinese saying," Whitlock continued, "which sums up the method: death by a thousand cuts." Another puff. "Won't work, not the way Croser had it planned original. The rebels are underestimatin' the solidarity of your Brotherhoods; also how mad they're getting." A bleak smile. "Ruthless people don't understand how mean good folks can get when their codes are violated. But he has outside help now, an' that makes all the difference."

" 'Death of a thousand cuts' applies politically as well as militarily," Whitlock continued. "This referen-dum he's pushing, for example."

David snorted. "A farce. A referendum on universal suffrage, when we don't *have* universal suffrage? Nothing but an opinion poll."

Whitlock chuckled. "Thing is, you people have made a big thing of votes. Back on Earth, not three countries left where votin' means a thing; doesn't in the US, certainly. Here, it's a jealously guarded privilege. Rest of the population figures since Citizens' put so much store in it, vote must be a good thing to have. Since most Citizens won't go within ten yards of Croser's poll, give you odds it'll be done scrupulous honest and still win big. No legal force — but it'll polarize the population even more. Who's going to come right out and admit: *yes, I'm lower than a snake's belly in a wagon rut and don't deserve a say?* There'll be some appeal to those workin' towards Citizen status for themselves or their kids, too.

"It's psychological-political jujitsu. After he wins, he'll claim a popular mandate. Then again, some of the measures you're being forced to adopt will push the fringe of the Citizens towards Croser. Higher taxes, fo' example. Then, limitin' access to firearms. Necessary, but many of yourn have what amounts to a religious taboo against regulation of guns; 'armed men are free men.' Likewise war regulations of all sorts. Those who don't go to Croser will be pushed towards the radicals on the other fringe, that poor fool Armstrong and his Secret Citizen's Army, or the radical Pragmatist Party crowd. Lot of pure self-interest there, too. Frontier planets with labor shortages always have a tendency towards bound labor systems, slavery or indentured. Thin profit margins, an' with full employment, workers tend to be mobile. Real, real temptin' to use extra-economic means to get secure supplies of workers at a price that leaves some margin. Most of your Citizens've shown commendable restraint, but they're getting mad and scared. And every move in that direction frightens the non-Citizens still more."

"Wage slavery. Enserfment," Alexander said. "I know it happens, but it is contrary to every principle on which this government was founded."

"Sure," Whitlock said. "But the enemy of every free man is a real greedy successful one. Biggest enemies of capitalism are successful capitalists. That's why you got to have governments, but just havin' one ain't enough either. There's plenty of people start at the bottom, get rich on freedom and hard work, and then try to take over the government so they don't have to work any more.

"Fact is, when all this is over, I got some advice for you on tinkerin' with your system. Give your individual workers a bit more power and union bosses and owners a bit less. But that's for happier times. Right now, this random terror campaign gets you tightenin' the screws, giving more power to the owners 'cause they're loyal, scaring the little guys. That, and showin' the Royal government can't offer protection even to the Citizens. Goin' after non-Citizen loyalty and Citizen morale."

The ring of faces around the table was set in grim anger; they had known the outlines of it, but the Earthman's dispassionate assessment was a shock.

Owensford turned his uniform cap in his hands.

"It shows in their military approach," he said meditatively. "Puzzled the hell out of me, at first. They didn't seem to be *fighting*, as I understood the term. As Dr. Whitlock said, we've become accustomed to a certain style of warfare. Essentially limited, careful not to damage the prizes we're fighting for, in societies too fragile to stand the strain of mass mobilization. War between *condottieri* captains; maneuver warfare, we're prepared to fight, but only until one side has an unbeatable advantage. Then we make terms. Soldiers are few and expensive and very carefully trained, and the mercenary captains don't expend them easily.

"Our enemies here," he said, "aren't fighting that kind of war. At all. And they're willin' to expend troops, 'cause they got more than you do."

Dr. Whitlock ground out his cigar. "The details are in my report, gentlemen," he concluded. "Sorry I couldn't be more optimistic. You got some real problems. Nothing you couldn't handle by muddlin' along if they didn't have offworld help, but they've got that. Lordy, do they ever."

"And Bronson really wants to be emperor," Elayne Rusher said.

"More likely Chairman," Whitlock said. "But yes."

"Emperor of what?" David Freedman demanded.

"As much as possible, Your Majesty."

"That's impossible," Peter Owensford said.

Whitlock shrugged. "Maybe. Maybe not. Look at it like this. Sparta's neutralized. Far from having an army and the beginnings of a fleet, you won't have control of your own planet. Get the Grand Senate to depose Lermontov before things come apart, while people are still listening to the Senate, and put a Bronson man in as Grand Admiral—"

"Would the Fleet permit that?" Alexander asked.

"They might. Strong tradition in the Fleet, obey orders and stay out of politics. And stay together. As long as Bronson is careful about who he puts in, there'll be a lot of pressure to go along, stay together. The last thing most of those captains want is war with each other."

"Will that happen?" Lysander demanded.

"Probably not. First place, he hasn't got the votes to depose Lermontov, won't so long as Grant hangs on."

"We can presume you have done all you can do on that score," Lysander said. Whitlock nodded. "So. Since there's no more we can do, we concentrate on our own problems. You can prove that it's Bronson who's aiding the rebels?"

"Yes, Highness, and not long ago that would have been enough. Grand Senators aren't supposed to be pursuin' wars of their own. But the fact is, the CoDominium's coming apart fast. It's every senator for himself. Or herself. And Bronson will offer what it takes to get what he wants."

"Because he doesn't intend to honor his debts."

"Maybe, but don't count on it. Good politicians keep promises, and he's been in politics a long time.

Don't matter anyway, what's obvious is that Bronson's got massive resources on and off Earth. The Bronson family's disposable income is certainly greater than the Dual Monarchy's."

"And he's willing to spend billions supporting our enemies," Alexander said.

"Sure. He needs a regiment factory. You have one," Whitlock said. "When the CoDominium collapses, it'll be like the fall of the Roman Empire. Bronson's Earth-side money'll be gone anyway. Right now it's use it or lose it time."

"New Washington," Lysander said. "What about that?"

Whitlock nodded. "That's going well. Falkenberg and his employers have a good half the planet under control, and a handle on the rest as long as the Fleet doesn't interfere. It won't, because Lermontov's seeing to it, but that's using up a lot of the Blaine and Grant clout."

"Leaving none for us, which is why we can't count on the local CD fleet to protect our recon satellites," Lysander said.

"That's the size of it, Your Highness. On the other hand, the New Washington situation won't last forever, and when that's done, you're the top order of business." Whitlock shrugged. "All you have to do is hold on. We got us a political war here, and we going to have to make some political plans. I'll be talkin' with y'all about that another time."

"I just realized," David Freedman said. "If we hadn't become involved with Lermontov, this would have gone on anyway. Croser would have built his strength, with help from Bronson, and we'd never have known it was happening."

Lysander's voice was not much above a whisper. "And no one cares about Sparta. We're just a catspaw in a larger game."

Whitlock nodded gravely. "Wouldn't put it quite that way, Highness. I do see what you're driving at. Both Lermontov and Bronson think they're protecting civilization, civilized values in a world going to hell. Difference is, Falkenberg and Lermontov ain't quite so certain they're the only ones who know what's best for the universe. Hell, they like free people. They're looking for friends and allies, not just subjects."

"I wish I could believe that," David said.

"What choices have we?" Alexander asked. "The whole basis of civilization is collapsing."

"No more law," Owensford said.

They all looked at him.

"The Laws of War and the Mercenary Code — we've been able to enforce them because everybody who mattered believed in them, and those who didn't were militarily contemptible; we could *force* them to abide by the customs. Dr. Whitlock mentioned our internal barbarians; that's where our armies are recruited from, but they've been under the command of civilized men. Now we've got an army — not a mob, but a real army — whose *leaders* are barbarians themselves. For a lifetime, we've managed to make war a limited thing. Putting a wall of glory around it, making it terrible but splendid. Now it's going to be terrible and squalid."

Lysander didn't say anything, but Peter Owensford felt a chill when the Prince looked at him.

✧ CHAPTER FIVE

Crofton's Encyclopedia of the Inhabited Planets (2nd edition):

Treaty of Independence, Spartan: Agreement signed between the Grand Senate of the CoDominium and the *Dual Monarchy of Sparta* (q.v.), 2062. The Constitutionalist Society's original settlement agreement with the Colonial Bureau of the CoDominium had provided for full internal self-government, but the CoDominium retained jurisdiction over a substantial enclave in *Sparta City* (q.v.), the orbital transit station *Aegis* (q.v.), and the refueling facilities around the gas-giant planet *Zeus*. In addition, during the period of self-government a CoDominium Marine regiment remained in garrison on Sparta and its commander also acted as Governor-General, enforcing the residual powers retained by the Colonial Bureau, mostly having to do with the regulation of involuntary colonist and convict populations.

In line with Grand Senator Fedrokov's "New Look" policy of reducing CoDominium involvement in distant systems where practicable, negotiations began with the Dual Monarchy in 2060. Under the terms of the Treaty, the Royal government became fully responsible for internal order and external defense of the Spartan system, and all restrictions on local military and police forces were removed. The transit station and Zeus-orbit refueling stations were also turned over to the Royal government. However, the treaty also stipulated that certain facilities were to be maintained, at Spartan expense, for the use of the CoDominium authorities and the Fleet; these included docking, fueling and repair functions, and orbit to surface shuttles. Also mandated was the continued receipt of involuntary colonists at a level to be set by the Bureau of Relocation, and for this purpose the CoDominium enclave in Sparta City was retained with a reduced garrison. Penalty provisions in the Treaty authorized direct intervention by the Commandant of the enclave should the Royal government fail to fulfill these obligations. . . .

❖   ❖   ❖

"Leader selection and development in Western special operations forces began a departure from military norms after a perception of battlefield failure during the Malayan Emergency in the 1950s. The leadership of the SAS, dissatisfied with the unit's performance against communist terrorist bands, determined that a revision of the induction and initial training of SAS personnel was warranted. The program that was developed not only applied to the enlisted ranks; officers were also included in a demanding and wholly new selection process.

"The SAS selection system eliminated candidates who are physically inferior, cannot exhibit sound independent judgment under stress, and lack determination. The system involves several weeks of arduous, individual land navigation treks. The candidates carry heavy rucksacks. Each man plots his own lonely course day after day and cannot rely on others to make the decisions. During the trial, candidates are not encouraged, but instead given every opportunity to drop out of the course, an action that would eliminate their chances to join the unit. Normally only about 15 to 25 percent of candidates are able to complete the course and be selected for membership in the regiment. The qualities of those who pass the trial include a high IQ, superb physical condition, and demonstrated ability to choose wisely despite conditions of great fatigue and mental stress. Only the determined, self-reliant, and quick-witted are selected to serve in the SAS. . . .

—Rod Paschall
*LIC 2010: Special Operations and
Unconventional Warfare in the Next Century*
(Institute of Land Warfare, Association of the US Army, 1990)

❖   ❖   ❖

. . . at the beginning of the war it was easy, we could walk into Kabul and attack where we wanted. We had our bases 2 to 3 kilometers from the enemy positions, even at 6 to 7 kilometers from the biggest Soviet base of Darlahman . . . In 1982, they had a 3 kilometer security belt, but it wasn't very effective . . . eventually we received 207mm rockets with 8 kilometer range, and targets inside the capital were constantly under fire.

. . . eventually, they spread out around their belts of outposts, trying to control an area around the city wide enough to keep it out of range of our rockets. In spite of the three rings of defensive positions they built, we are still regularly slipping through and our operations are still going on . . . Of course we have to be very professional now. All operations have to be carefully planned. We have to have a lot of protection groups because all positions in their area must be engaged . . . routes must be clearly known. Alternative retreat routes have to be studied. We have to take care of mines, booby-trapped illuminating flares that give away our positions, even dogs.

—Mujahideen commander, Afghanistan, 1985

❖ ❖ ❖

The tiltrotor engine changed pitch. The plane circled the military base before landing.

"Good to see the Battalion again, Prince," Harv Middleton said.

Lysander smiled briefly before turning back to the window. "Regiment, now. Or will be when we leave." Below, the First Royals, Prince Royal's Own, was encamped on and around three small hills set in the endless grasslands. They were supposed to be on light rear area security duty, a kind of working rest and recreation. Soft duty, but Lysander was pleased to see that hadn't stopped them from building a fortified camp, with perimeter wire and plowed minefields, and mutually supporting fields of fire. They were doing good work. He was eager to talk with them. There'd been a lot of personnel changes in the First Royals since Lysander had been Major Collins in command of the Scouts in the Dales campaign, but the Regiment would remember him.

"Good campaign, Prince," Harv said.

Reading my thoughts. Yep, we didn't do bad at all. He laughed softly as he caught himself thinking how much simpler his life had been in those days. *Simpler, maybe, but it sure got frustrating.* It had been a monumental violation of the principle of the unity of command to have the Crown Prince serving as a unit commander, and as soon as he'd proved himself to the men, Owensford had moved him out, back to politics and staff schools and desk work and pretending to

coordinate the entire war. It was important work, but
Lysander was glad of any excuse to get out among the
troops. *When this war's over I'll let David run the
economy. I'll take military affairs. Maybe even lead the
Spartan Legion off-planet.*

The hold of the tiltrotor transport plane was
crowded with a full platoon of the Life Guards. All
Citizens or advanced candidates, they were theoreti-
cally under the command of an aristocratic young
lieutenant, although Sandy Dunforth was unlikely to
contradict Staff Sergeant Harv Middleton in a conflict.
When the plane touched down, Harv would be first
off, and the Guards would take stations all around the
field, as if it were dangerous for the Prince Royal to
visit his own regiment.

*Hell, I'm safer here than walking the streets of
Sparta City,* he thought mordantly. *The Helot assassination campaign has to be stopped. We can only guard
so many of our people. Death of a thousand cuts, but
we don't have to die. As Owensford keeps saying, the
great thing is not to lose your nerve. They can't win by
killing teachers and administrators. Not as long as
we're willing to fight back.*

The sound of the turbines deepened as the plane
came in toward the hilltop and the engine-pods tilted
backward. The pilot was an artist; the big craft
touched down with scarcely a jar, and the guard platoon fanned out as the rear ramp went down with a
sigh of hydraulics. Lysander waited obediently until
Harv signed the all-clear. Harv was Lysander's oldest
friend, a Phraetrie-brother, but also playmate and
companion when they were children. *Not that we're
all that older now.* Middleton knew he wasn't intellec-
tually gifted, and didn't care: Prince Lysander could
do the thinking for both of them, about everything but
Lysander's safety. When it came to protecting his

Prince, Harv's humorlessly intense sense of duty gave him a monomaniacal intelligence.

Lysander blinked at the bright sunshine outside. Sentries and messengers were scurrying all over the field. A group of three officers came out of the Headquarters building to stride briskly toward them. The leader was Major Bennington, a short competent-looking man, Spartan-born, Citizen, an engineer turned soldier. When he saw who had come, he shouted back into the orderly room. Bugle notes sounded, and a company hastily formed as an honor guard.

Bennington saluted. "Highness, they told us to expect visitors, but not who. Apologies —"

"No problem," Lysander said. He returned the salute, then went over to clasp Bennington's hand and clap him across the shoulder. "It's good to see you, Jamie, my Brother," he said formally. He raised his voice, "And all of my Brothers."

"And you, Brother." Bennington was careful to clasp hands with Harv as well. Then he led the way to the waiting troops.

They walked past the leading ranks of the honor guard. Lysander stopped. "Sergeant Ruark. Good job spotting that minefield in the Dales," he said. "Saved my arse."

Ruark grinned, and so did the men around him.

Lysander stopped to talk with several more of the men he recognized, before letting Bennington lead him away.

"It's good to see you, sir," Bennington said. "But you should have told us—"

"Our communications have been leaky, and headquarters thought it better not to say who was coming. Surprising you wasn't the purpose, but no way to avoid it."

"Yes, sir."

"You look tired. So do the troops."

"A bit, sir. It was tough out there. But we've had three weeks to rest up, and it's getting time to go back into the line. But first — With your permission, we'll have 'dining in' at the mess tonight. Not often we have our Battalion Commander with us."

" 'Fraid it will have to be 'dining out,' " Lysander said. "Owensford and some of the staff will get in shortly. Please see they're invited — Who's mess president?"

"Captain Hooker, sir. Preston Hooker. Demartus Phraetrie."

"Ah. Platoon commander in heavy weapons support."

"Company commander now. Yes, sir."

"Lots of new faces," Lysander said. "I don't get here often enough. I know I'm only nominal commander but dammit, I ought to know my officers, all of them in this regiment anyway!" He grinned. "Yes, I said regiment. First Royal Cavalry, Prince Royal's Own. You'll get the official word soon enough, along with a promotion."

"Thank you, sir."

"Not much of a surprise, the way we've been adding to your duties, but I thought I should bring The Word myself." He looked around the compound. "Yep. New faces, now, more coming. I've got my work cut out learning them all. I knew all of Falkenberg's people when we had them showing us how. Things working all right without them?"

"Yes, sir. We miss their technical skills sometimes, but this is a Spartan regiment now."

Lysander nodded, pleased at the pride in Bennington's voice. "Right. Sparta needs — our own people. Now show me around. Only you'll have to indicate where we're headed, else Harv will have kittens."

Bennington led the way to the edge of the raw-earth berm. They looked out over the rolling lands below. The 1st Mechanized Battalion, 1st Royal Spartan Infantry, was encamped on three hilltops near the working parties they were helping to guard. The hill camps were leaguered behind earth berms thrown up by 'dozer blade. The troops were in undress uniforms, weapons stacked, a few doing useful things, but most seemed to be just enjoying the mild weather. They were a hundred kilometers inland and north of the Aegean, but the gentle hand of the sea lay across the rolling volcanic hills. This district was warm enough that there were palms in some of the sheltered swales along the Aegean coast.

"Good land," Lysander said.

"Sir." Bennington grinned. "Like most of Sparta. Hasn't quite made up its mind what to be."

"Grassland, I think," Lysander said. He used his binoculars to scan the terrain around them. A few trees, some scrub brush. An occasional live-oak. "Grass. I bet you get some spectacular fires come summer."

"Yes, sir, that we do."

Long rolling hills faded into haze on the distant horizon of a planet larger than Earth. The pale three-quarter sphere of Cytheria sat on the edge of the world. Something moved out at the edge of what he could see. Antelope, he thought, running free in the knee-high mutant kikuyugrass on the hilltops. Bluegrass in the rocky areas, higher growths on the slopes and flats, feathery pampas grass, sloughgrass and big bluestem taller than a man's head. Everything was vivid green from the cool-season rains, starred and woven with cosmos and crimson meadow rose. The scent was as heady as chilled white wine.

"God, I love this planet."

"Yes, sir. Wish everyone did," Jamie answered

grimly. "The Prince Royals have been taking it on the chin. We needed the rest. Thanks for getting us this assignment."

Lysander nodded. A rest from the brutal late-winter campaign in the northwest, trying to stop raids out of the Dales. A war of ambushes and burnt-out ranches and endless cold and mud and low-level fear, seasoned with continuous frustration and spiked with moments of raw terror. Always wondering if the next step would be onto a mine, if that clump of trees held a sniper. Too many recruits and never enough time to teach, as the Royal Army doubled and redoubled and units were mined for cadre; newcomers making stupid newbie mistakes, rushing in straight lines towards a noise, showing lights, walking against the skyline. Getting drunk alone in an Olynthos cathouse and ending up knifed in an alley, for that matter.

"The problem is, the rest gives people time to think," Jamie said. "Everyone was feeling fairly good after the Dales campaign; we'd whipped their butts. The men were walking tall. Then we landed on a greased slope and spent the whole winter running as fast as we could to stay in one place."

Lysander ran a hand through his short brown hair. "Don't I know it, Jamie," he said. "Look, that's one reason I came out here to talk to you. We've got to start thinking beyond the next year; beyond settling this war, come to that. We both know the Helots wouldn't last six months without outside help. Hell, without the CoDo shoveling their human refuse on our heads, there wouldn't *be* any Helots."

"True enough," Jamie Bennington said, narrowing his eyes slightly. "Meaning?"

"Meaning we're in this mess because we're helpless. Not just against Earth. Whitlock says the CoDominium won't last five years. Without the Fleet —"

"Yes, sir," Bennington said. "That gets discussed in the mess of a night. Friedland's friendly enough now, but —"

"Or Meiji. Look at what's happening to Thurstone and Diego, and that's with the CoDominium still trying to keep order. Without it there'll be no order at all out here any more."

"And so, Lysander my Brother, you are saying that we should not plan on soft garrison life after we kill off the Helots."

"More than that."

"More than that," Bennington mused. "More than that, my Prince. So. You will want more than just the Spartan Legion ready for expeditionary duty. And we are chosen?"

"I've thought of it. What will the men think? Will they follow orders?"

"Depends on who gives the orders," Bennington said. "They'll follow their Prince. Just about anywhere, after the Dales."

They went back toward the orderly room. Inside were the duty sergeant and two corporals. The sergeant jumped to his feet. "Sir. I'll inform the officer of the day that you're here."

Before he could do that, a corporal came in from the next room. "Sergeant, urgent message from —" He stopped when he saw Lysander and Bennington.

"Carry on," Bennington said.

"Sir. Urgent signal, sir. Message through the Rural Emergency Network from the Halleck ranch at Three Hills. Oldest son and three hands missing. Suspicious tracks. The local constabulary requests assistance."

"Right," Bennington said. "Sergeant, alert the ready team —"

"Halleck?" Lysander asked.

"Yes, sir."

"Damn," Lysander said. "Would that be Aaron Halleck's place?"

"Sergeant?" Bennington asked.

The duty sergeant typed at a console. "Says here Roger Halleck, let's see, Roger Halleck, Divine Twins Phraetrie, son of Senator Aaron Halleck, sir."

"That's torn it," Lysander said. "Senator Halleck's grandson missing. Major, I'd count it a favor if you sent the best you have on this one."

"Right." Bennington conferred with his duty master sergeant. "Who've we got?"

"Sir, the ready platoon is Lieutenant Hartunian's scouts. About as good as we have for this sort of thing."

"Get them moving," Bennington said.

"Sir." The sergeant turned to his console.

"What's the situation out there?" Lysander asked.

Bennington activated the map wall. "We're pretty sure there aren't any big gangs operating around here — they'd love to get at the road to Colchis before we finish it, but there's no cover south of the Drakons." He waved toward the mountain chain to the north and west. "Snow up there. Hard to get through without leaving tracks. But there's canyon country over here. Anything could hide in those caves."

"Hartunian's ready to roll, Major," the sergeant said.

Bennington eyed the map. "Lousy roads. Sergeant, tell the chief constable we'll have troops there in about two hours."

"No planes?" Lysander asked.

"Only have three," Bennington said. "All down for maintenance. Try not to let that happen, but sometimes there's no help for it. Sergeant, you'd best have them speed up the work on those ships—"

"Just did, sir. First plane operational in ninety minutes."

"Right."

"I can speed things up," Lysander said. "Sergeant, have Lieutenant Hartunian load his men into my tiltrotor. You sending anything else?"

"Yes, I thought I'd send a troop of light armor," Bennington said. "The exercise won't do them any harm, and Hartunian may need help."

"Whose?"

"'B troop. Captain Reid."

"Thank you. OK, mount them up and get them on the road. Mind if I tag along with Hartunian?"

"Is that wise, Highness?" Bennington asked.

"Given it's the Hallecks, it might be," Lysander said. "We won't get in the way." He went to the orderly room door. "Harv!"

"Prince!"

"Pick a squad of Life Guards and load up. Alert the pilot we're moving out. We're going hunting."

Harv grinned wolfishly. "Yes, *sir!*"

⋄   ⋄   ⋄

Three Hills Ranch was typical of the Colchis Gap district, a fairly small operation. Not in area — the Hallecks had patented better than two thousand hectares — but in scale. Most of the rangeland the armored column passed through might never have known the hand of man. Except that the grass itself, the grazing herds of buffalo and impala, mustang and onanger and pronghorn, even the wild geese migrating north in sky-darkening flocks, were all of them a sign of man's presence; Spartan evolution hadn't produced much native life on land. Closer to the ranch headquarters they saw black-coated Angus cattle and shaggy brown beefalo under the guard of mounted vaqueros, and around the ranch house itself waving strips of contour-ploughed cropland. Not much, because there would be little market here; what cash-money this spread saw would be from herds driven down to the slaughterhouse in Colchis town on the coast, or wool hauled there by bullock wagons.

The Senator's younger son, setting up on his own. And looking to make good as a farmer. There were new fields under cultivation, sprouts showing green against the raw-red soil. Beets and sunflowers and soyabeans, some cotton; powered vehicles on Sparta ran mostly on alcohol or vegetable oil, and the new road would provide a market. The ranch house was single-story and not particularly large, with whitewashed walls of rammed earth, roofed in home-made tile that supported a satellite dish. Half a dozen vaquero cottages nearby, and a bunkhouse; much like the rancher's dwelling except for size. Outbuildings were scattered, sheds, barns, a set of windmill generators and a stock-dam fringed with willows. Modest but carefully cultivated flower beds and lawns and tall trees surrounded the houses to make an oasis in the huge rippling landscape.

Exactly what we're trying to build here. Frontier people. The frontier of humanity, and the bastards won't let us alone. It's not Spartans who are destroying us.

A windsock marked a landing area near the house, an open pasture beyond a row of big gum-trees. Better than thirty people and two light armor vehicles awaited them there, which was quick work in a district as spread-out as this. Most were in militia cammo uniforms and body armor. A couple of the vaqueros were in their normal leathers, probably non-Citizens, but their rifles were as much a part of their working equipment as their clothes, and they looked just as determined as the rest. Off to one side a pack of hounds that looked to be more than slightly mixed with gray wolf lay in disciplined silence.

"Junior Lieutenant Cantor, 22nd Divine Twins Brotherhood Battalion," a man introduced himself, as Lysander swung himself down from the tiltrotor. Nobody jumped distances like that in Sparta's gravity. Except new chums, who wondered why they ripped tendons and sprained ankles. "Brother Halleck," the militia officer went on, introducing the owner. Roger Halleck was a stocky rancher in his forties with gray in his shag-cut brown hair, a finger missing from one hand and a bulldog determination to his square face. *A lot like the Senator, actually,* Lysander thought.

"This is Lieutenant George Hartunian, Prince Royal's Own," Lysander said. "And Lieutenant Sanford Dunforth, Life Guards."

"Highness—" Cantor began.

"And for the moment I'm Colonel Collins, First Royals Regimental Commander," Lysander said. "No point in getting too formal, Citizens. Now what's our situation?"

"My boy Demetrios was up north about six klicks, scoutin' for a new watering dam. Had a handset, reported all well at sundown yesterday. Nothing this morning, so I sent my top hand out. Miguel?"

"Don Roger," the vaquero said, nodding with dignified formality. "My Prince, I took young Saunders with me" — a big-boned blond youth, another of the vaqueros, shuffled his feet in acknowledgment — "to the stream where the camp was. We found a campfire still warm with unburied embers; this Don Halleck's son would never do, he was well taught. Also we found this."

He handed a small object to Lysander. A spent cartridge case, standard 10mm magnum caliber. He brought it to his nose. *Recent.* Sparta City Armory marks on the base, which meant little . . .

"See," the vaquero said. "The firing pin imprint is a very little low and to the right of center? The young

Don Demitrios's gun, *veridad.* Also we find this, a thousand meters north." A ring. Lysander's brows rose.

"It's his," Halleck said. "His grandmother left it to him."

"Twenty horses, maybe more, came during the night from the south," Miguel continued. "Before the rain, because the marks were almost washed out. Only in the mud by the stream we see them, you understand." Lysander nodded. The grasses which had claimed this countryside so quickly after the terraforming package made a deep tough sod. "They paused, then went on with the young Don's horses as well."

Lysander started to speak, then stopped and turned to Lieutenant Hartunian.

George Hartunian straightened. "Not much doubt about what happened," he said. "Lieutenant Cantor, what do we know of enemy activity in the area?"

"Sporadic. Largest group we've seen was a dozen, on horseback. This group may be twice that size, but they shouldn't be any problem, no heavy weapons. Except—"

Except they've got the squire's son as hostage, Lysander thought.

"Anyway," Cantor said, "we had instructions to call on the regulars, and since I don't have any experience with hostage situations—"

"Neither do I," Hartunian said. He hesitated, clearly looking to Lysander for orders he wasn't going to get. "A troop of scouts will be here in an hour," Hartunian said. "Send them after us. I guess it's time for the rest of us to move out." He looked to the dogs. "Is that pack well trained?"

"They can follow a scent," Halleck said. He looked at Hartunian and shrugged, a gesture that clearly said he didn't believe that waiting for the regular troops had been worth the delay. "Colonel, the best thing will be for us to get on the trail, and you look with that tiltrotor. That way we just might find something."

Lysander glanced up at the sky. "Three hours of daylight, maybe a bit more." He projected a map onto the ground. "Dunforth, you'll take the tiltrotor. Cover this area, but stay away from the canyons. I don't have to tell you the whole purpose of this just could be to lure that plane into range of a missile."

"Sir. Shouldn't I stay with you?"

"No. Now get looking, and be careful. Keep Regiment up to date on your location." Lysander looked to the available transportation. Two Cataphracts, and three von Alderheim 6x6 trucks. Little enough. "There'll be a light armor cavalry column coming up before dark. Send it after us. And I'm ordering Regiment to send another cavalry troop."

"Fuel," Hartunian said.

"I'll authorize air resupply," Lysander said. *Expensive. Damned expensive, but Senator Halleck's always been one of the team, and by God we can take care of our own.* "Now load up."

"I'll be going," Halleck said quietly.

"And me." A girl not more than twenty. Freckles, strawberry blond hair and furious blue eyes, in militia gear. "*I* trained those dogs, as much as Demetrios did, Dad. I ride and shoot as well as he does, and he's my *brother*."

Lysander raised his brows at the rancher. Unwillingly, he nodded. "Lydia is the best hunter on the place, next her brother. My family," he added, nodding to two mutinous looking boys of about fourteen, "runs to twins. And no, Isagoras and Alexias, you're not going."

"Load up, then," Lysander said. He waited until the Hallecks were in the trucks. "You go with her," he told Middleton. "Hartunian will take the lead Cataphract. I'll be in the other one until Reid's troop catches up."

Harv started to protest and thought better of it. "Yes, Prince."

.   .   .

"Missile attack. Taking evasive action."

Lysander noted the tiltrotor's location on his map projection. "OK, you've found them," Lysander said. "Now get well back, refuel, and stand by. If they had one missile they'll have more."

"Yes, sir."

"OK, driver, push it," Lysander said. They rolled onward.

.   .   .

"Bloody hell," Lysander cursed quietly. "There goes the chance of using the IV sensors."

The hills to the west were aflame for better than a kilometer to either side; there was a strong easterly wind, enough to move the fire briskly despite the early season. Tall grass will burn even when green, if the fire is set with torches and fanned by moving air. The higher partial pressure of oxygen on Sparta made it even more deadly than prairie fires on earth. . . . Haze and smoke and the pale-yellow disk of the setting sun made it difficult to see the mountain peaks beyond.

"Halt." The burbling roar of the diesels sank to a low murmur, no louder than the roar of the fire approaching them from a kilometer away. He could smell the thick acrid smoke of it, over the hot metal of engines and the overwhelming sweetness of crushed grass.

The tracking force was advancing along a front as wide as the fire itself, Cataphracts in the lead with the trucks a hundred meters behind. He swiveled to look around; nothing, except the clouds of birds fleeing the grassfire, and the twin-track marks the armored vehicles had beaten through the turf. They were tending south of west, up into the higher country on the fringes of the Drakons. Not the nine- and ten-thousand meter peaks of the midrange, but still more than high enough to carry eternal snow and glaciers. The hills here were already several hundred meters higher than the Gap country proper, unclaimed land, with tendrils of brush and forest down the valleys. Perceptibly colder than the Halleck ranch, too.

"Regimental command push," he said.

"Bennington here," the Major replied after a second.

"Collins here. We're getting closer, but they set a grassfire. We'll have to stop and find the scent again on the other side."

"They were laying mines back here," Bennington said grimly. "New wrinkle. Anti-vehicle mines in the track, as a decoy; laser trigger rigged to a directional mine off to the side. Lost two of the sappers."

"Goddam!" Lysander said.

"My sentiments exactly. Not to mention a farm wagon further down the road, another fatal. Get them, sir."

"Will do, Jamie."

The 6x6 jounced up, with the dogs and the Hallecks. The trucks had excellent cross-country mobility, Charbonneau-thread tires gripped like fingers, but the ride was rougher than the broad treads and hydrogas suspension units of the Cataphracts. Miguel, the chief vaquero, swung down, wiping at his soot-streaked face with a bandanna.

"The *hijo de puta* picked the spot for their fire well, my Prince," he said. "No deep valleys, the ground only rolls. More broken country beyond. Someone among them must be himself an *llanero*, a plainsman. Donna Halleck says that the forest begins only ten kilometers beyond, very bad country with many ravines and cliffs; oaks, firs, deodar cedar and rhododendron thicket."

"I've hunted leopard there," she said from the bed

of the truck; her father and Harv were beside her. "Tricky. Pumice soil and rock, pretty steep. Landslide country in the rains."

We'll never get them in there, Lysander thought. His speed advantage would be lost; ambush country, and easier for the bandits to disperse. Roger Halleck was looking grimly furious.

"Backburn?" the vaquero asked, looking at the approaching fire.

"Nix that!" Lydia Halleck said. "Too long — look, we can run it, if a couple of your lobsters go through first right ahead of us. We'll only be in the flame-front for a second or so and nothing flammable will be touching the ground. Hose everything down, and the dogs will be able to take it."

Hell of a risk, he thought. Then: *God damn it, these are my people, I'm not going to let their kinfolk be dragged off by those scum.*

"OK," he said. "Citizen, Miss Halleck, if you'd prefer to ride in one of the Cataphracts?" A family muleishness confronted him.

"The dogs need me to stay with them," the girl said. *Well, not much chance her father won't stay with her,* Lysander thought.

"Sir?" Harv, standing next to the Hallecks. "Sir, if we cover everything with a couple of ground sheets and soak it, we'll be safe enough under."

Lysander blinked in surprise; he had expected another polite-but-firm request that Harv ride in the Cataphract with him. "Carry on, Sergeant." He looked west. An hour of daylight left. "Let's move."

❖   ❖   ❖

Lysander buttoned the hatch down and looked at the wall of smoke ahead of them; it towered into the sky, and the flames were twice the height from the ground to the top of the Cataphract's turret.

"Goose it!" he said.

The armored vehicle gathered speed with a pitch-and-yaw motion like a boat beating through a medium sea. For a moment there was darkness shot with red outside the vision-blocks, and his ears popped as the overpressure NCB system pumped air into the fighting compartment through its filters. Then they were through, on a broad expanse of smoldering black stubble kilometers wide. The truck was through as well, covered in soot and smut but still functioning; as he watched the tarpaulin over the rear deck was thrown back, revealing grinning humans and hysterical dogs pulling against the short-staple leashes tied down to the railings.

The column pulled to a halt on the unburned grass, the familiar *shhhh* against the hulls replacing the popping crunches of the burn. The Hallecks and Miguel moved efficiently to quiet the dogs; the cycle-mounted scouts pulled up from their wide circle west of the fire. As steady in their way as the humans, the dogs soon settled down and began to cast about, tails high and wagging furiously; they had been following the on-again, off-again trail all day, and they were getting into the spirit of it. *Well-trained pack, too*, Lysander thought, studying the ground ahead. *No yelling off after something else once they've been given a scent.*

The land was rising again, the ridges getting sharper. It suddenly occurred to him how different it would have looked in his grandfather's time. Olive green pseudomoss then, and scraggly patches of semibamboo, scarred by the erosion the introduced vegetation resisted so much better. Grass and brush all mixed in, just beginning its long march to conquest. One long human lifetime, an eyeblink in the history of a world. Even the insects and bacteria beneath his feet were of strains that had come here less than a century ago.

"Message, sir," his driver called.

Lysander frowned. "Right." He retrieved the head-set from the Cataphract. "Collins here."

"Suggestion."

Owensford's voice. *And he's not using honorifics because there's only one person out here he would say "sir" to. OK, he thinks someone is listening. Someone with our scrambler codes . . .* "Yes, sir," Lysander said.

"Wait five right where you are."

"Dammit, they'll get away—"

"Strong suggestion."

Lysander started to protest and thought better of it. "Roger."

      .   .   .

The tiltrotor landed on a level spot close by. A dozen men, led by Owensford in combat dress. "Like to talk to you for a minute, sir," Owensford said.

Lysander let himself be led away from the others. "What's all this, General?"

"Highness, do you know what the hell you're doing?" Owensford demanded.

"I'm chasing down those scumbags—"

"No, sir, you're making certain that the Senator's grandson is killed, and probably endangering every-one around you," Owensford said evenly. "You don't think this was a coincidence, do you?"

"Eh?"

"Senator's grandson gets kidnapped. Not killed, kid-napped, just before the Crown Prince visits the regiment assigned to security duty here. The Prince Royal's Own regiment to be exact. May be coinci-dence, sir, but more likely leaks in the Palace."

"To what end?"

"God knows," Owensford said. "But they run to complicated plans. My guess is they hoped you'd be sucked into this operation."

"Am I that easy to predict?"

"Senator's grandson, kidnapped in your regiment's sector, plain trail to follow." Owensford shrugged.

"I see. So now what?"

"They plan a surprise for us, I think," Owensford said. "Just maybe we have one for them." He turned to the group who had come with him in the tiltrotor. "Miscowsky."

"Sir." Sergeant Taras Hamilton Miscowsky was a stocky man, dark, clearly of Eurasian descent.

"Got a reading?" Owensford asked.

"I think so, sir." Miscowsky squatted and used his helmet to project a map onto the ground in front of him. "They'll be here, in canyon country. They'll have split up into smaller groups, but there'll always be an obvious main body—"

"It's been that way so far," Lysander said.

"Yes, sir. Point being to get you to divvy up your force while they lead you by the nose." The stocky sergeant grinned slightly.

"By the nose," Lysander said. "You mean the dogs."

"Yes, sir."

"So what do we do now?"

"Chase 'em," Miscowsky said. "The trail will divide somewhere about here, where you'll be just about at dark. You'll want to follow on after dark. Don't. Instead, make camp, but not on the main trail, off here somewhere, like maybe you're going to follow the wrong branch. Keep a good watch, and I mean good, sir."

"You expect them to attack us? In the dark?" Lysander asked.

"Be more likely if you was to camp in the obvious place," Miscowsky said. "But they might try and hit you anyway. And they'll sure as hell send out scout parties to look you over. What they'll want is to get you chasing them out there in the canyons and woods in the dark. I don't suppose I have to tell you, don't do it?"

"I see. And then?"

Miscowsky shook his head. "Then comes the fun part," he said, but his grim look denied the words.

.   .   .

The dogs barked in glee, then milled in confusion, casting along two diverging trails. Lysander cursed loudly. "Bring us up level, Delman," he said to the driver.

The Cataphract quivered and flowed forward with an oilbath smoothness; there were grinding sounds as the tungsten cleats of the treads met an occasional piece of pumice rock.

"Six horses that way, sir." Sergeant Salcion pointed to the left, southwest over a small hillock. "The rest went straight west."

Lydia Halleck squinted into the vanishing sun. "West over that ridge is the beginning of canyon country," she said.

Miguel had been quartering the ground while the others spoke, occasionally stopping and going to one knee to part the grass gently with his hands; it was over a meter high here, new green shoots mingling with winter's pale gold straw.

"Here," he said, indicating a spot of bare wet reddish earth between two tufts. "This horse is shod by the Three Hills farrier; the others have machine-made shoes." He looked up at Lysander. "Ours are hand-hammered from bar stock," he explained.

"It's nearly dark," Lysander said.

"We're gaining on them!" Lydia said. "Come on!"

"Right," Hartunian said. "Mount up!"

"No, I think we make camp," Lysander said. "Cancel that order." *An hour ago I'd have been right with them. There's so damned much I don't know, and it can get my people killed.* He looked at his map. The trail divided almost precisely where Miscowsky had said it would. Lysander pointed southwest. "We'll camp on that hill. Full perimeter. Get set up while there's still daylight."

"But we can catch them!" Lydia shouted. "No, you can stay if you're scared of the dark, but some of us aren't! Who's with me?"

Peter Owensford had been talking quietly with the girl's father. Halleck said, "Not enough, Lydia. Not enough."

"But —" She stood defiantly. "Miguel—"

The vaquero looked to the rancher.

"You'll stay here, and that's an order," Lysander said. "Owensford!"

"Sir!"

"See that they stay and camp is made."

"Sir."

"Damned cowards," Lydia said. "I never thought I would have to say that about a Prince of Sparta. Coward."

• • •

The hilltop was largely dirt, with some boulders, which they used as part of the fortifications Owensford insisted on. Foxholes, trenches, ramparts; tanks hull down in earth bunkers, truck revetted. The work wasn't finished until well after dark. Finally Owensford was satisfied. "Larraby, you'll take first perimeter patrol."

"Sir."

"Highness, Mr. and Miss Halleck, there'll be hot tea in the command bunker. Care to join me?"

The command post was more trench than bunker. Owensford's orderly handed out mugs of tea and left them.

"This is crazy," Lydia said. "We could have caught up to them—"

"Very likely," Owensford said carefully. "At least they certainly hoped we would."

"They —" Lydia's eyes widened. "Oh." She turned to Lysander. "Highness — I'm sorry, really, I didn't —"

"It's all right," Lysander said.

"Better than all right," Owensford said. "I just hope they were listening."

"Real earful," Halleck said. He put his arm around his daughter. "Somebody had to protest," he said. "Knew you would, and it came more natural if you didn't know."

"I should have guessed." She blushed. For just a moment, embarrassment overcame her frantic concern for her twin. Embarrassment, and something else, fear of a loss greater even than her brother.

"I didn't," Lysander said. "It took General Owensford to show me. And that sergeant, Mis —"

"Miscowsky," Owensford said. "Havenite. Grew up thinking like a bandit." He glanced at his watch. "Another couple of hours, if they're coming."

"Coming. You expect them to attack us here, then?" Lydia asked.

"Ma'am—"

"I'm Lydia, General Owensford," the girl said quietly.

"Lydia. You put it stronger than we would. We don't exactly expect an attack, but if they have the strength we think they do, it's one of their options. We need to be prepared, that's all. My guess is they won't. We built a fortified camp in a place they didn't expect, and one thing we've learned about the Helots, they don't do much on the spur of the moment. They like complicated plans, and they won't have time to make one up. Hartunian will see to the watch. I think what we should do is try to get some sleep."

"That won't be easy," Lydia said.

"For any of us," Lysander said. "Good tea. Now I think I'll take General Owensford's advice."

It was dark outside. Two hours until moonrise. Lysander paused to let his eyes adjust, and heard steps behind him.

"Not much chance for my boy, is there?" Halleck asked.

"I don't know," Lysander said.

"Probably dead already."

"Maybe not," Lysander said. "Miscowsky thinks they'll use him as bait."

"For what? For you," Halleck said. "God damn— Highness — Oh God damn it. Well, we can't let them do that."

•   •   •

"Prince."

Lysander woke from a pleasant dream. Dawn light, hardly bright enough for shadows. "Right, Harv."

"General Owensford's respects, he's in the command bunker with coffee," Harv said.

"Right." Lysander pulled himself out of the bedroll and pulled on his boots. Owensford and Lydia Halleck were seated close together in the command bunker. Lysander wondered if she'd been there all night. He got his coffee and sat across from them.

"Good morning," Owensford said. "There are over a hundred of them. With heavy weapons. Big mortars. Rocket launchers. Maybe more. Well dug in, too."

"Christ."

"I'd have walked right into that," Lydia said. "Worse, I'd have taken you—"

"The point is, it didn't happen," Owensford said. "Anyway, now we know what we're facing, the news gets better."

"Such as?"

"They have three live prisoners. The bad news is

they know how many we are, and they didn't run away," Owensford said.

"How do we know all this?" Lysander asked.

Owensford grinned. "They're not the only ones who can sneak around in the dark."

"Miscowsky."

"Followed their scouts back, of course. This is an eyeball report."

"That *is* good news. All right, what next?"

Owensford looked pointedly at Lydia Halleck. She stood. "Whatever happens, thanks, Highness," she said. "And — thank you, Peter, for explaining things."

"Wish I had more hope for you," Owensford said.

"Yeah." She climbed out of the bunker, leaving Lysander and Owensford alone.

"You asked what's next," Owensford said. "I can make a suggestion."

"Make it."

"Order me to handle the situation, then get the hell out of here."

Lysander frowned. "I can't do that—"

"With all respect, Highness, you should do that. There's a lot at stake here—"

"Damned right—"

"A lot more than Senator Halleck's grandson," Owensford said. "Look, this situation is all fucked up. We're out here in the middle of nowhere. We have one ace in the hole, but otherwise we're outnumbered and out gunned. If we bring up reinforcements they'll kill their hostages and run for it into the badlands. If we go straight in they'll likely cream us. The whole deal is tailor made for a defeat, and the biggest disaster of all will be that the Prince Royal was in charge and fucked it up! Bluntly, Highness, losing that kid will be bad enough, but it'll be a lot worse if it makes you look incompetent. Which, by the way, I'm pretty sure was one object of this exercise in the first place."

"How the hell could they have known I'd be here? For long enough that they brought in all that stuff?" Lysander demanded. "Damn it, I didn't know myself I was coming until last week!"

"Yes, sir, but your favorite regiment was here long enough," Owensford said. "The original objective would have been giving the Prince Royals a bloody nose. For that matter, it was predictable you'd visit when the Battalion was upgraded to Regiment. Then they heard when you were coming, and that made it all the better."

"And I took the bait," Lysander said. "I see. But damn it, Peter, I can't just abandon that boy! His grandfather is one of my father's oldest friends! Even if he wasn't— they're my people! This, this ranch, this is what Sparta is *for!* I can't let them take risks I won't take—"

"You can, and you will," Owensford said. "Remember the enemy's objectives, Highness. They can't defeat us as long as we keep our nerve, but if they can make the people lose confidence in the government, they're halfway to winning. And for all practical purposes right now, *you are the government.* You're already the good luck charm for half the soldiers in the Royal Army. That doesn't mean you can't risk getting killed, but it sure as Hell does mean you've got to be careful not to look like a fool."

"I'll work on that," Lysander said. "Now show me the situation, and tell me what you think we should do."

"That still doesn't work," Owensford said. "I may have it all wrong too." He grinned suddenly. "Hell, neither one of us should be here, come to that. This is a job for a captain." He projected a map on the bunker wall. "An expendable captain."

Lysander didn't answer. After a while Owensford said, "Here's the situation. They're dug in, here, a natural redoubt, with heavy weapons. They won't want us to get close enough to spot for artillery and missile fire, so they'll try to intercept us well short of their main area, probably here. They don't know Miscowsky's group has them under surveillance, which means we can pound them with Thoth missiles."

"We didn't bring any Thoth missiles—"

"I took the liberty of using Legion communications to send for the SAS support unit," Owensford said. "I didn't have them report to anyone in the Royals, but they're out there. Anything Miscowsky can see, we can hit without warning."

"You suspect a traitor in the Royals?"

"I suspect leaks in the Royals," Owensford said. "Not necessarily a traitor, but that's possible. Those Thoths are our main advantage, and we'll want to use them properly."

"So we can kill them any time," Lysander said. "If we don't mind killing the hostages too."

"Something like that."

"What happens if we wait for the rest of the regiment to come up?"

"Don't know," Owensford said. "But they have to worry about that. My guess is if they get worried enough, they kill the hostages and scatter."

"But if they think they have a chance of getting me—"

"They'd take risks for that," Owensford agreed. "But they're not fools. They aren't going to wait until you have a whole battalion of armor here—"

"What if we don't bring the reinforcements here at all," Lysander said. "Suppose I send the regiment around behind them, here. The main body won't be in position until dark, but a scout platoon can be in position a lot earlier than that."

"And then we go in after them?"

"More or less," Lysander said.

"They outnumber us, you know," Owensford said.

"Sure. But it's what you'd do if I weren't here, right?"

Owensford shrugged. "It's what I'd expect from my hypothetical captain who ought to be in charge of this cockamamie deal."

"Then we'll do that."

"An expendable captain."

"So we're not expendable," Lysander said. "We'll be careful. Now let's go."

. . . .

Nearly dusk. Peter Owensford used the command tank's optics to peer into the shadows ahead. *Christ, here I am acting like a captain again.* He grinned slightly. *At least by God I've got someone to fight. Not just chasing ghosts. And someone to fight for . . .*

Just ahead would be the enemy's redoubt. This would be the tricky part. "They see you coming," Miscowsky's voice said in his ear. "They're all spread out, waiting."

"Command push," Peter said. "Halt the column."

The two lead Cataphracts slowed, stopped. The infantry fanned out to both sides. Ahead lay a four hundred meter escarpment topped with a dense stand of trees, the sun already lost behind it. Somewhere along the base of that escarpment, no more than two kilometers away, was the rebel ambush. Minutes ticked by.

"They're getting nervous," Miscowsky said. The signal was faint but clear. "Timing's gonna be tricky."

"The great thing," Peter said aloud, "is not to lose your nerve." His driver grinned slightly, then nodded. Five long minutes . . .

"Here he comes," the driver said. He opened a port in the armor of the tank, and brought in a thin cable which he handed to the communications sergeant who sat in the loader's seat.

After a moment the sergeant handed Peter a headset and microphone. "Secure communications, sir."

"Right. Thank you. Report by sections. Report."

"Section One set and loaded, sir."

"Section Two in place and loaded sir."

"Armor units ready."

That would be Lysander, of course. *If I let that kid kill himself, John Christian will have my hide. Christ, he's all that's holding this goddam planet together, and here we are playing company commander.* "OK. Here's the situation. They don't suspect the SAS team is observing them. They know we're here, and they're stirring around, wondering why we've halted. It's a war of nerves."

"It will be dark soon enough." A female voice. *I might have known Lydia would be talking for her father.*

"We'll give Mobile One a little more time," Peter said.

The wait seemed endless.

"There's a group moving out. Riflemen. One grenade launcher. I count eleven, moving toward your position," Miscowsky said. "Bearing one niner five at four five zero meters relative my position. They're moving out now. Call it vector niner zero."

Somewhere out there, miles away near the horizon, a Legion SAS signal section had sent up a balloon and tethered it in line of sight to Miscowsky. It would be able to receive Miscowsky's narrow beam signals without any possibility of interception. Of course signals the other way to Miscowsky wouldn't be secure at all, but there was nothing they could do about it. Owensford plotted the enemy patrol's position on his helmet display. "Visitors coming," Peter said. "Call it a dozen, moving due east. If they continue on course that will put them right on top of Section One."

"Scout Section Four moving to intercept."

"Roger that."

"Getting dark, General."

"Scout Four here. We see them. They'll have Section One in sight in six minutes."

And here we go. Peter punched in codes. "Thoth Daddy, fire mission, roll four anti-personnel," he said. "I say again, Thoth Daddy, roll four anti-personnel. Relay to SAS One they're on the way." Then without waiting for acknowledgment he changed channels. "Scout Four. Intercept and destroy that patrol, Scout Four."

"Will intercept and destroy. Scout Four out."

"Sections One and Two load concussion. Armor units stand by."

"Acknowledge four birds on the way," Miscowsky said. "They do not appear to have intercepted the alert to me, I say again are not reacting. Thoth Daddy, give me four more, anti-personnel, I say again, four anti-personnel."

"Thoth Daddy here. On the way."

Timers on Peter's console began their countdowns, flickering sets of red numbers.

From ahead and to the left came a sudden stammer of rifles and machine guns, then grenades. Contact. "Execute alpha," Peter said. "I say again, all units, execute plan alpha, I say again, execute plan alpha. Move out!"

The Cataphract engines were loud in the falling dusk. There were more shots and the bright flash of grenades to Peter's left. Then the Cataphracts moved over the ridge.

"Incoming!"

Something burst overhead. Cluster bombs rained around Owensford's position. Any uncovered infantry out there would be in trouble. More bombs fell around them. *They're using their big stuff. Good.*

Peter stared at his console. There was nothing he could do now, it was up to the computers. Green lights flickered. Antennas they'd spent the afternoon putting out a klick to each side backtracked the enemy's artillery shells. Pulses came into the command computers. Analysis. A light flashed. *Locked on.* More lights, as information went at the speed of light from the command unit to the tiltrotor aircraft twenty kilometers away, then to Miscowsky and his missile control unit . . .

"Got it," Miscowsky said. "Four missiles acquired. Guidance set. Locked."

There were flashes from over the ridge. Four missiles, lofted from the aircraft named Thoth Daddy, landed among the enemy's heavy weapons with an accuracy better than one meter.

"Thoth Daddy, give me more," Miscowsky said. "Anti-personnel, stream it."

"On the way."

. . . .

"Rebel commander, Rebel commander," Owensford said.

He looked down at the screen, split to offer him views from any of the vehicles. Not much to be seen. The Helots were well dug in among their boulders. *No artillery left. No perimeter guards left. Not likely to have much communications, they may not hear me.* Peter touched his console to change communication channels. "Move in fast."

"*Sergeant Cheung, Spartan People's Liberation Army,*" a voice replied. "You got something to say, Cit?"

Sergeant. "Let me speak to your commanding officer."

"That's me, Cit." A laugh, that might or might not have been cut off short. "What you want?"

Officer dead, or escaped? No time for that— "You're surrounded, your heavy weapons are destroyed, and we have you located. Surrender now and you'll be treated as prisoners of war."

"Well, well, Baby Prince—"

"This is Colonel Ford," Peter said.

"Where's the Prince?"

"Not here." *Jesus Alana says keep them talking. About anything.* "Do you want to talk to the Prince? He's coming, he'll be here shortly."

A nasty laugh. "No need to wait for him. We got the rancher's boy," the rebel said. "Give us twenty hours headstart, and we'll let him go."

"Twenty hours? That's too much," Owensford said.

"How long?"

"Well, not twenty hours—"

"Hell, you don't mean to give us nothing," the rebel said.

"Not true," Owensford said. "Give up and you'll be well treated. Killing hostages gets you hanged."

"Yeah, well, worth just one try," the guerrilla said. "OK, we're sending him out."

Like Hell you are. Owensford switched to his command channel. "All units, stand by. Section One. Section Two. Make ready. SAS One, stand ready." Back to the enemy leader. "Don't do anything rash."

"Me? Rash? Nah, never." A figure was pushed out from behind one of the jagged boulders. Owensford upped the gain to maximum, and the face sprang out at him. Lydia's face, in a square-jawed male version. The hair was darker blond, plastered to the side of his head with blood, and one eye was swollen almost shut. The young man limped; his hands were bound behind him . . . with barbed wire.

"You see him, Cit?"

"Execute, all units execute," Peter said. Then to the rebel, "No, see what?"

Demetrios Halleck was walking upright, with care, watching where he put his feet but moving as quickly as he could.

"You see him?"

"This is Crown Prince Lysander Collins. Stand by, Sergeant Cheung, I'm coming up to talk to you."

"What the hell?" the rebel said. "Where? Show yourself—"

"I'm right over here, Sergeant."

"I don't see you—"

Mortar shells fell around the rebel position. The blast of a concussion grenade knocked the Halleck boy flat. Something moved in the shadows near where he fell.

"Pour it on," Peter ordered. "Go for it, all units, go for it, go, go, go!"

"Go," Lysander said. The sweat under his armor turned suddenly cold and gelid; like those nightmares where you waded through thick dank air, unable to turn and see what chased you.

Breaching charges flew through the air like blurring snakes; the soft *whumps* of their explosions across the minefield were lost in the hammer of the 76s and the thumping crash from the rocket howitzers. The Cataphract was tossing as they drove forward; out of the corner of one eye he saw the 6x6 truck pacing them. *That wasn't supposed to happen.* They reached the rocks, and armored men leaped out among the rebels. Another flurry of shots. Then silence.

So quickly, Lysander thought. Silence fell, broken only by the crackling of small grass fires and shouts, and moans from the wounded. Lysander halted the Cataphract and climbed down slowly. Bodies everywhere.

"Hey Sarge, maps!" someone shouted.

"Don't touch nothing! It'll keep till morning."

Shots and a grenade off to the left. Someone was running, and half a dozen Royals led by a sergeant gave chase.

Lysander carefully made his way back down the hill, out to where medics hovered over two figures. *Two.* "Status?" Lysander asked.

"This one's stable," the medic said. He indicated the Halleck boy. "Broken ribs, but I think nothing internal. The other one will make it if we get him in the tanks in time, but it's going to be close."

"Who is he?" Lysander asked.

"Corporal Owassee," a voice said from behind him. Lysander turned to see Sergeant Miscowsky. "Mine. He put his flak jacket over the kid, and they shot the shit out of him. Sir."

Lysander touched his helmet. "Dustoff. Get in here *now.*"

"Already on the way," the aerial dispatcher said.

"Sergeant, whatever that man wants, we'll get it for him," Lysander said. *Rewards and risks. Statecraft.* "We owe him. *I* owe him, big."

"Yes, sir."

"Now. Where's the rebel leader?" Lysander asked.

Sergeant Miscowsky jerked his head toward the row of boulders behind him. "We got him. Up yonder. Sir."

Lysander started forward, but Miscowsky was in the way and didn't move. For a moment Lysander stared at the man. "Let me by."

"Well, sir —"

"Prince," Owensford said from behind him.

"What's going on?" Lysander demanded.

"Maybe you don't want to know," Owensford said. "You can go, Sergeant."

"Sir." Miscowsky ambled off into the dark.

"All right," Lysander said quietly. "Just what is this? Mutiny?"

"Of course not, Your Highness. You're in total command here. Anything you order will be done. Any question you ask will be answered," Owensford said.

"The Laws of War—"

"A good officer knows what to see, and what not to see," Owensford said. "And the Laws of War apply to prisoners of war. A status this group lost when they refused to surrender while holding hostages."

"General —"

"Yes, your Highness?"

Lysander looked up the hill in time to see Miscowsky vanish behind one of the boulders. "I hate this war," Lysander said.

"We all do."

"Will they learn anything?"

"If there's anything to learn. The important thing now is to keep him drugged so he can't suicide before the Alanas can talk to him."

"He called himself Sergeant Cheung—"

"Yeah. We think he's a bit more than that," Owensford said. "You may not know it, but Croser has a bodyguard named Lee Cheung." Peter shrugged. "It's not an uncommon name, but Lee Cheung is known to have a brother who's a major in their equivalent of special forces. At the least we may find out how they knew you were out here, traitor or leak. You'll notice he did ask for you."

"I want to see that man," Lysander said. "I want to talk to him, find out why—"

"In due time, Highness." Owensford flashed a light on the trail. "Nothing more to do here, and the medics would rather we out of the way. The cleared path is marked, stay on it and be careful."

The sounds of battle had faded, and now came the

inevitable aftermath, the smells of blood and death, screams and groans of wounded and dying. "They've done this to us," Lysander said. "We can't even walk in the forest without worrying about mines. The mines will be here for fifty years, a danger to foresters, children, animals — they don't care. General, what do civilized people owe to barbarians?"

"Sir?"

"We owe them nothing, General Owensford. We owe them nothing."

✧ CHAPTER SIX

New York Times, May 17, 2094:

Luna Base. In a speech before the Grand Senate today, Grand Senator Adrian Bronson denounced anti-CoDominium partisans in both the United States and the Soviet Union.

"No man," Grand Senator Bronson said, "has done more than I to curb the CoDominium's excesses. No longer does the CoDominium pretend to be an omnicompetent government, a veritable interstellar empire. Therefore extreme measures such as this [referring to the proposed 50% cut in Fleet appropriations] are not appropriate at this time."

In other matters, Grand Senator Bronson's motion to instruct the CoDominium commander in the Sparta system to investigate terrorist activities against Fleet personnel and agents of the Bureau of Relocation was passed by acclamation. "We cannot tolerate such activities," Bronson said. "They must be uncompromisingly suppressed."

✧   ✧   ✧

I love to see a lord when he is the first to advance on horseback, armed and fearless, thus encouraging his men to valiant service; then, when the fray has begun, each must be ready to follow him willingly, because no one is held in esteem until he has given and received blows. We shall see clubs and swords, gaily coloured helmets and shields shattered and spoiled, at the beginning of the battle, and many vassals all together receiving great blows, by reason of which many horses will wander riderless, belonging to the killed and wounded. Once he has started fighting, no noble knight thinks of anything but breaking heads and arms — better a dead man than a live one who is useless. I tell you, neither in eating, drinking, nor sleeping do I find what I feel when I hear the shout "At Them" from both sides, and the neighing of riderless horses in the confusion, or the call "Help! Help!," or when I see great and small fall on the

grass of the ditches, or when I espy dead men who still have
pennoned lances in their ribs.

      —Bertran de Born, *A Poem of Chivalry*, 11th Century

❖   ❖   ❖

" . . . and we're not happy at all with the way things
are going, Major Owensford," Beatrice Frazer said.

There were nods down the table of the Battalion
Council Meeting; the Legion commander sighed
slightly and kneaded the bridge of his nose with
thumb and forefinger. This was not a staff session. It
was a meeting of the ruling body of the Fifth as an
autonomous community, just as the Regimental
Council governed Falkenberg's Legion as a whole; still
nothing resembling a democracy, but considerably
more political than a strictly military meeting of the
unit's officers alone. Beatrice Frazer and Laura Bryant
represented the civilian women and children; Sergio
Guiterrez sat at the far end with the senior NCO's.

"We were looking forward to Sparta as a permanent
base; the wives and children came here to set up real
homes while the Legion was dropping into a combat
zone on New Washington. Now we can barely go into
Sparta City."

Everyone nodded; there had been no terrorist
attacks on Legion civilians yet, but that was as much
because of caution and careful planning as anything
else.

"And the worst of it is," she went on, "that otherwise
it's close to ideal here. Not just the weather and the
food —" That brought some chuckles; Tanith's perpet-
ual steambath had been driving everyone berserk, the
Legion's civilians worst of all "— but things in general.
The Education Ministry's people have been a great
help with the children; they have *good* schools here,
and on Tanith we had to do everything ourselves. No
borloi, either."

Nods; Tanith lived by the drug trade. Drugs grown

by slaves, at that, and the general social atmosphere was about what you would expect. Nobody had been at ease with the prospect of their children growing up in a place like that, and you could only isolate from the surrounding environment so much.

"In fact," she went on, "we've made more friends here than on planets we've stayed on for years. If it wasn't for the war . . ."

"We wouldn't be here," Owensford answered dryly. "We'll coordinate with the RSMP and try to see the civilians can visit town safely, Mrs. Frazer. I'd also appreciate it if the defense drills for the women and children were stepped up. In fact, I'd like to appoint a standing committee of you, Mrs. Savage, and, hmm, Mrs. Fuller, together with Veterans Smith, Puzdocki and Shaoping, to review the procedures and suggest alternatives. Any objections?"

"We'll need access to the planning computers," Beatrice Frazer said.

"Coordinate with the Captains Alana," Owensford said. "Objections? In favor?" A unanimous show of hands. "Battalion Sergeant Guiterrez?"

The stocky chicano smiled. "Sir," he said, "with the men, we've got almost the opposite problem. They like this place too much."

Owensford frowned; like the CoDominium Marines from whom the Legion had grown, and the French Foreign Legion before *them*, desertion had always been one of Falkenberg's Legions' problems. Soldiers like soft duty, but you have to let warriors kill something once in a while. You can use men who like to polish equipment in barracks, but you'd better have some warriors, too. . . .

"Not going over the hill, exactly, sir," Guiterrez said. "Plenty of fighting. Gets downright personal. But most of our long-service people could get permanent ranks in the Spartan army a couple of jumps up from where they are, commissions even. The pay's good, they could get Citizenship, and hell, the people here *like* soldiers, sir. These are good men we're training, too, not people you'd be ashamed to serve with. And since the Legion'll be retaining a base here, it wouldn't be like cutting themselves off. You can expect a drop in reenlistments as contracts come due. This is a place we can belong."

Owensford nodded. "The CoDominium Fleet likes this place for retirement, for that matter. But we have to *win*, first, Top," he said. "Otherwise this won't be a place anyone can live."

"Win. Yes, sir. Major, dammit, they won't let us win! Major, we know who's behind most of this—"

"We've been over this already, Top. Comments noted. Now, we've received a communiqué from the Colonel —" A rustle around the table. "None of you need worry. I've given the casualty list to the chaplains.

"Came in an hour ago with the CD courier ship. The message is just short of ten Earth months old. The Regiment landed safely, took its initial objective, and has moved on Allansport; they expect some fighting there. Colonel Falkenberg approves our measures to date —" just after he landed and found out how rapidly the situation had deteriorated. *God, we thought* that *was bad.* "— but warns that mobilization on a larger scale may be needed and authorizes the necessary reassignments."

A chuckle, especially from the officers. Exactly what you'd expect from Christian Johnny.

"And a message for all of us." Owensford touched the console in front of him.

Falkenberg appeared on the screen at the far wall. The colonel was seated at his field desk and wore field uniform. "We're moving ahead of schedule here," Falkenberg said. "Light casualties. Good local support. Details attached.

"Your reports say things are rough there," Falkenberg said. "I'm sorry to hear it, but I have to say I'm not greatly surprised. I did hope you'd have some time before our enemies built up strength, but Sparta is important to Bronson and his people. It's even more important to us, the way things are developing. It's vital that you keep Sparta independent. I know you'll do that, whatever it takes.

"Administrative matters. Major Owensford is herewith promoted to Lieutenant Colonel, and authorized to accept whatever Spartan rank he feels is justified.

"Colonel Slater will now assure himself that this room is secure and all present are authorized and cleared for discussion of regimental business."

The screen went blank. Owensford looked at each person in the room, then typed in a phrase on his console. Falkenberg reappeared.

"As all of you know, there's more happening than we can usually discuss in Council meetings. I regret that, because you're being asked to endure hardships without knowing why. I can only say, what you're doing is important to us all. To the Regiment, and to whatever future civilization has out here. That future is uncertain. The CoDominium is breaking up, but it's not dead yet. It still has great power. That power is divided. Our group, the faction loosely headed by the Grants, the Blaines, Admiral Lermontov —"

"— Bloody blunt about it," George Slater said.

"— controls part of the Fleet. A smaller group is loyal to the Bronson faction in the person of Vice Admiral Townsend. Most of the Fleet is trying to stay neutral: 'No politics in the Fleet, the Fleet is our fatherland.' We can all sympathize with that view. We've all held it. It's now an obsolete notion. There is no Fleet, and we'll have to build a fatherland, a fatherland for ourselves and a home for the Fleet.

"What you're doing is significant to that effort. If things go well here, we'll have influence in New Washington, enough influence that we should be able to base naval and marine units here. That won't be enough. We'll also need bases on Sparta.

"The question inevitably arises, who do I mean when I say 'we'? I don't know. Clearly some entity larger than the Legion, and for that matter larger than whatever part of the Fleet joins our faction. I confess I don't yet know what that entity will be. I have my hopes. I think you may be in a position to know better than I do.

"We face a very uncertain future. I'll do what I can to take some of the pressure off you, but frankly, I can't do much just now. The situation here will require all our political resources until we have New Washington stabilized. Don't feel ignored, though, because what you're doing is vital. You're distracting our enemies, the enemies of the Legion, and, for that matter, the enemies of civilization. What they throw at you there they can't throw at us here. You're helping grind them down. It won't be easy, that kind of campaign never is, but I know you can do it.

"We're going to win. Never forget that. Godspeed and God bless you." The image faded.

"Bloody hell," someone said.

"A war of attrition," George Slater said. "Major — Colonel, I have a request. I won't put it as a motion until I see what you think."

"Very well," Owensford said.

"I propose that we ask my father to sit on this Council. With all due respect, none of us here is very experienced in Fleet politics —"

"And General Slater has been with Falkenberg

longer than anyone else," Owensford finished. "As you all know, Colonel Falkenberg is very sensitive to the principle of unity of command. He was therefore careful not to imply that General Slater was in any way associated with command of Legion units here. I much appreciated that. However, I agree with Captain Slater. The situation here is not what we expected. Events have moved much faster than we expected. I think we can use the experience of retired Lt. Colonel Hal Slater on this Council, and I will entertain a motion to that effect."

"So moved."

"Second."

"Moved by Regimental Sergeant Gutierrez and seconded by Mrs. Frazer. All those in favor say aye. Nays? I hear none. Let the record show the vote was unan—"

There was a brisk knock at the door. Owensford frowned. "Come."

The door opened. Owensford looked up, felt his face freeze into blankness at the junior lieutenant's expression.

"Sir," the young man said. "Sorry to interrupt. Priority message from Sparta City. The transportee shuttle has been sabotaged. There are over a thousand dead, and the . . . Sir, the CoDominium enclave Commandant has summoned all heads of government and armed forces to a meeting. Immediately, sir."

Owensford started to rise. "Wait a minute," he said. "*Heads* of armed forces? Plural?"

"Yes, sir. The summons includes the Helots . . . and they're under CoDominium safe conduct. Any action against them for the duration of the conference period or twenty-four hours thereafter will be treated as an attack on the CoDominium."

Peter looked down the table at the shocked faces as

he tried to control his own. "Gentlemen, ladies," he said formally. "I'm afraid we'll have to adjourn."

❖　　❖　　❖

"Skilly will be back in a minute."

Geoffrey Niles raised himself on one elbow to watch her go. There was a relaxed pleasure in the way the muscle clenched and relaxed in her buttocks as her hips swayed, shadowed in the dim light. *Not at all what you'd expect in some ways*, he thought. She was fastidious as a cat, when there was opportunity. One of the most frequent punishment drills for Helot recruits was for not washing; the offender was scrubbed down by their entire squad, using floor-brushes. . . .

The cave air was still chill, but he ignored that now, not pulling up the coverlet despite his nakedness; he had learned the trick of that, these last few months, of being indifferent to how you felt physically. *Learning a good deal from Skilly*, he thought with a sour grin, running over the last hour in his mind. Even exhausted, it stirred him. *God, what a lay!*

"Lot of fun, all around," he murmured to himself. Which was odd again, considering that he was still working like a slave; no harder than she, of course. Less if anything . . . "But it's rarely boring."

The thought of England and the eternal petty round, traveling in to Amalgamated's offices in the City, vacationing in the Alps or the family's private island in the Caymans. . . . *Brainless debs and endless bloody boredom.* Now *there* was something chilling. Not that there was anything wrong with inherited wealth, except that it tempted you to *waste* yourself. You couldn't really enjoy nothing but enjoyment, and once there were a certain number of credits in the account adding more was just numbers. Not many of the people he had known on Earth had anything approaching Skilly's diamond-hard concentration and single-mindedness; they scattered themselves instead, a little bit of this and that. No way to accomplish anything.

Adventure isn't the thing, he mused. He'd learned that, floating down the river holding onto the corpse of one of his men, after the Dales battle last year. Adventure was like happiness, not something you could set out to find; that way lay safaris and pointless risks that were simply bigger amusement-park rides. What really mattered was *accomplishing* something. Something big and worthwhile, and putting everything you had into it, that was what people like Grand-Uncle Bronson or Murasaki or Skilly did. Starting off with nothing and aiming to win a war and rule and reshape a planet; *that* was something worth spending your time on.

He yawned again. *Well, Grand Uncle, maybe I'll surprise you and find my own career on this little junket*, he thought. He stirred uneasily at the thought of going home now; his Sandhurst classmates wouldn't understand. . . . *I had no choice! Not really, and then it was too late —*

There was a notebook on Skilly's side of the bed, one of hundreds she kept neatly shelved, a 20cm x 10cm black-bound volume. That was another surprising thing, the way she hated to waste time. If there was nothing else to do she'd whip out one of these and start writing, thoughts and observations and plans. . . . Idly, he flipped open the front cover.

Postwar # 7, he read. There were plastic markers on the side, dividing it into sections: *pers., polit., miltry., econo.*

Personal first, he thought.

Freehand pencil sketches. Of himself, nude or in fanciful uniforms, or with Skilly. *Are we really that acrobatic?* Notes for insignia, flags. Floor-plans and elevations of houses and gardens. One picture of a ragged, big-eyed urchin, and it was several moments before he recognized a younger Skilly. A last series, showing him and Skilly and a baby; in a cradle, at her breast, playing with Niles. . . . Touched, he closed the notebook and set it down again. *Maybe she fancies the dynastic connection. Marriage into the Bronson clan. Cadet branch, but still quite a step up from Belize. And what would Grand Uncle think? But it's something to think about.*

"Definitely," he murmured, closing his eyes for a moment. In fact, it was an exciting thought. *A dynasty*, he mused. Not that Skilly had ever said anything directly against Croser, but . . . *Most dynasties start with ruthless pirates*, he reminded himself. *Or lucky soldiers, or barbarian invaders. No reason they can't become enlightened in time. Civilizations have been founded by enlightened barbarians . . . Could Skilly think that way? With a Bronson connection, could she be a satrap in a real social order? Would she accept that?*

"Up again? Jeffi really *be* a mon of iron," Skilly laughed, sliding back into the bed. Her feet were cold when she entangled them with his — they were nearly the same height — and so were her fingers as she trailed them down his chest and stomach.

"God, woman, you must be slipping something into my drinks," he said in mock-horror.

"Lots of red meat and fresh air," she said, kissing him and kneading. "But we spare you poor knees and elbows this time," she went on, rising and straddling his hips. "Skilly good to her Jeffi, hey?" she said, looking down at him heavy-lidded as she lowered onto him with taunting slowness. "Enjoy while you can, we in the field soon."

"Soon? *Ah!*" He ran his hands up to her breasts.

"Hmmm. Mmmm, nice. We been spending de

winter make life miserable for the kings, now they getting good and mad. We gots to make them spread out —" she grinned "— so they not get it together for a concentrated thrust." Her hips gave a quick downward jerk. "Too many of us to stay pure guerrilla anymore, so."

Niles laughed a little breathlessly. "You're thinking strategy at a time like *this*?"

She leaned forward against his hands, locking her own on his shoulders. The mane of curled black hair fell over his face as they began to rock together, but he could see her teeth and eyes glint through.

"Skilly is always thinking, Jeffi," she gasped. "Always."

.   .   .

Skida Thibodeau slid herself a little to one side and picked up the notebook, sparing a fond glance for the man sleeping beside her and hooking up the coverlet to warm his feet. She pulled a pencil from the spine and licked the point as she flipped the book open.

Polit. The first section was a list of books on internal-security technique; she ran down them and added another note: *secr. pol. — own budget — labr. cmps. profit — see R.Conquest, details.* Important to be thrifty. Also — *Rival grps. — balance.* But it would be easy to go too far. *see Anat. der SS-Staat.*

On to *miltry.* The first page of that carried an abbreviated star map centered on Sparta's sun, with transit-times radiating out like the spokes of a wheel. Underneath it was a note: *conscr. army — 10/15 div.*, and a list of planets. She put a checkmark beside Thurstone, then stopped for a moment.

Them first, but who next? Haven? she asked herself; it was not nearly as close, but the shimmerstone trade was valuable. On the other hand, it was still CD, and pretty worthless otherwise. Not enough people to serve as a recruiting ground for further expansion. It *did* have a refueling point . . . The pencil moved: *Haven poss. nxt.; CD goes; expl. beyond?* Time enough to think about that when the Democratic Republic started building up its navy. *Build or take. So much easier to take than build.*

She slipped the pencil back into its holder and sank down on the bed, pulling up the blankets. Niles shifted closer in his sleep, and she smiled to herself as she yawned and prepared to drop off.

Life is good, she thought contentedly. A light began to flash beside the bedside communications unit; she frowned at it, then swung out of bed and belted on a robe. *This better be important,* she thought.

❖   ❖   ❖

"Well, we know how it was done," General Desjardins said. "Those *fools* in the SCA thought they could terrorize the CoDominium into stopping involuntary transportation. They smuggled a suicide bomber on the shuttle; through the Aegis station." Most spaceships with cargo or passengers docked at the orbital transit-station, and boarded the surface shuttles there.

"Mingled with the transportees, and managed to get close enough to a coolant pump during reentry. They didn't *notice* that there were CD officers on board the shuttle as well as eleven hundred convicts!"

Owensford nodded tautly. The Royalist party was sitting in one corner of what had once been the Officer's Mess of the CoDominium Marine garrison; the dry, slightly musty air of the big dimly-lit room carried a faint ghost of banners, of raucous celebrations with bagpipers and Cossack dancers, a lingering sadness. The remaining staff of the enclave rattled around like peas in a very empty pod, and the junior officers who had brought the two parties here had

been men in their forties . . . *There, but for luck, go I,*
the mercenary thought with a shudder. Stranded here
in a lost outpost of a dying empire. He glanced up at
the group across the room, around a hastily-dusted
table of their own; Dion Croser and his NCLF gang.
Croser was talking with one of them, laughing and
slapping the man on the shoulder.

Bastard.

There was a stir at the entrance; the honor guard
there was not giving the same carefully neutral salute
they had accorded the Spartan kings and their Legion
officers.

The Helots, Owensford thought sardonically. *Meet the
enemy.*

They had come under CoDominium safe-conduct,
in a heavily armed Marine shuttle.

Pity, he thought savagely. *Otherwise they'd never
get out of here alive. They may not anyway, once I
drop my little surprise into the meeting.* Then:
Observe. Know the enemy.

The CD Commandant had insisted on seeing all
parties to the civil war, including those that did not
recognize each other as belligerents and those claim-
ing neutrality. The Royal government had spent three
days protesting the safe-conduct for the Helots; the
Marine commandant had been sympathetic — no
doubt where the CoDo garrison's sympathies lay, particularly after the violations of the Laws of War — but
standing orders left no latitude, not with a Grand
Senator breathing down their neck.

The CoDominium might be tottering towards its
grave, but the walking corpse of it still possessed a
power no planet without space-navy capacity could
ignore. Even now, a blatant violation like the shuttle
bombing could not be ignored. Not even when Sparta's
friends included influential Senators and Grand

Admiral Lermontov. Especially then, when those friends fought for their lives and any excuse might serve their enemies to bring them down. There were so many enemies, Kaslov's murderous neoStalinists in the USSR, Harmon's demented Patriot Party in the US, both openly courting nuclear war with nihilistic relish. Bronson and his opportunists playing both sides against the middle for private gain. . . .

Take a good look, he reminded himself, studying the half-dozen rebel leaders. They were in camouflage jackets and leather trousers and boots, but neatly pressed, brasswork and the badges on their berets polished. A touch of *bandido*-flamboyance here and there, a brass earring or long braided hair, a bit of swagger. Skida Thibodeau was in the midst of them and her eyes flicked over him with a steady considering look as she passed, like a predator in hot jungle thoughtfully eyeing a wild boar.

Owensford straightened slightly, feeling an instinctive bristling. *The dog and the wolf*, he thought ironically. He had studied the records and the pictures carefully, but they had not prepared him for this sleek exotic handsomeness, the graceful deadliness of a fer-de-lance.

It must have taken considerable courage to come here, anyway; there were more than a few Spartans and some Legionnaires who would have risked the CoDominium's anger to kill the enemy leaders. This was a bitter war, and the reason for it was right here. Owensford studied them carefully; one or two might not be aware of the danger they were in, several of the others were slightly stiff with the knowledge of it, under their bravado. Skilly was completely relaxed, even slightly amused. The mercenary officer felt his teeth show slightly. Most soldiers endured danger by an act of will. He had known some who enjoyed it . . .

and a few who were simply not much affected one way or another, icemen. He had never liked them; there was something missing inside in someone like that, and the Helot leader looked to be a prime example. There was a mind behind the big dark eyes. . . . *But no soul*, he decided. *None at all.*

Ace Barton leaned close and whispered: "Notice Niles," he said.

That must be the tall blond man; he felt their eyes and turned to give them a false and toothy grin as the Helots seated themselves. Skilly leaned back in her chair with arms and legs negligently crossed, and went instantly to sleep.

"Doesn't look much like the pictures." They had extensive video files on the Honorable Geoffrey Niles, and despite the unmistakable Nordic cheekbones and male-model looks, this was a different man. "Our little sprig on the Bronson family tree isn't nearly so much the silly-ass Englishman, these days," Barton replied thoughtfully.

"Can't say that it's altogether an improvement," Owensford said. Nearly two Earth years in the wilderness had thinned him down, and given him something of the feral look the others at the Helot table had. "Keeping bad company and all."

"Gentlemen, ladies." The CoDominium lieutenant called from the inner door; he had a flat Russian face, ash-blond hair turning gray and body stringy under the blue-and-scarlet dress uniform. "The Commandant will see you now."

.   .   .

"Ten-'*hut*," the garrison Sergeant-Major said. "This meeting will come to order."

There was a rustle, the military men standing to and the civilians a little straighter; the kings had already been seated, of course, being heads of state. David I looked no more worried than usual; the improvement in Alexander I was as night and day.

Colonel Boris Karantov returned the polite nods of the Spartan and Legion soldiers and ignored the Helots. He sat carefully, lowering himself down by his hands; he was in his seventies and looked older, regeneration treatments or no.

"Be seated, gentlemen, ladies." His Anglic was still slightly Russian.

"We are here to discuss violations of the Treaty of Independence governing relations between this planet and the CoDominium. And of the Laws of War. Let me first establish that the CoDominium is strictly neutral in the current conflict; I am uninterested in the rights or wrongs of that struggle as you perceive them. I remind you that this meeting is being recorded, and the records will be made available to the appropriate offices of the CoDominium Authority as well as to the Grand Senate."

There was a flat weariness to the tone, the voice of a man who has excluded everything but the performance of a job in which he no longer really believes.

"Now, a shuttle — a civilian vessel —" he pronounced it *wessle* "— under charter to the Bureau of Relocation, carrying both involuntary colonists not yet transferred to Spartan jurisdiction, and off-duty officers of the CoDominium Fleet, has been destroyed by an act of criminal terrorism. I have called all possible parties here to account for this crime. Your Majesties?"

"We, the Dual Monarchy's government denounce this abhorrent act." Alexander looked sternly toward Skida Thibodeau. "It is quite possible that this was an operation organized by this person as a provocation to discredit us. However, we are fairly sure that a dissident group called the SCA is responsible, and if — when — we catch the individuals responsible, they will be subject to trial and execution. Or turned over to you for punishment, Commandant. Sparta values its relations with the CoDominium." A subtle reminder that they had powerful friends in the Grand Senate.

Karantov nodded non-committally, his fingers rolling a light-pencil. "Still," he said judiciously, "this SCA is believed to have links to your own security *apparat*. You say this is entirely a matter of disaffected individuals, but this would be claimed in any case."

His eyes rose to Croser. "Mr. Croser, your organization has also been linked to terrorist activities. You have to say?"

Croser's nod was politely deferential. "Sir, firstly, the NCLF is purely a peaceful political party. It's true we hope to form the government after the illegal Royalist regime is rejected by the people in the upcoming referendum" — David I snorted, and Alexander almost rose in his fury, with General Desjardins laying a hand on his arm — "but we seek to use only legitimate means."

Karantov made a slight bored gesture, as if waving the Spartan through the necessary pieties.

"More to the point," Croser continued, his face and voice taking on a flatter, harsher tone. "The NCLF draws its strength from the oppressed classes — that is, from the transportees oppressed by the Royalist regime. Every transport which lands increases our just strength. It would be suicidal for us to interrupt the flow, even if we would stoop to such an atrocity as this.

"No," he went on, the mellow voice taking on a ringing quality, "the only logical candidate is the Royalists themselves — lashing out in their desperation, now that the whirlwind they created by their own actions is out of control. Through this false-front SCA, which they use to disguise actions too repulsive even for them to openly admit to. Certainly the SCA has claimed responsibility."

Bastard, Owensford thought. *But a* smart *bastard.* No way to prove that wasn't true.

Karantov's head turned toward the Helots. Their commander was sitting with one fist supporting her chin, watching the byplay between the others with lazy enjoyment.

"These NCLF *rabbiblancos* be getting some thing right every now and then, even if they be wuss weaklings," she said lightly. "The Spartan People's Liberation Army *be* a transportee army. Why we kill our own recruits?"

The CoDo officer nodded grimly; obviously loathing the speaker to the point of physical distaste at listening, equally obviously accepting the argument.

Alexander shook off the police commander's hand. "I repeat, as a provocation, of course. You would very much like to ruin our relations with the CD."

Skilly grinned insolently and leaned back with one arm hooked around the back of her chair. She examined the nails of the other hand.

"Tsk, tsk," she said, with mock-kindness. "Old man be having de fantasies. He need the doctor, bad."

"Silence!" Karantov rasped. After a moment: "Under the Treaty, I have the right to resume command of the Aegis station if the Spartan government fails to perform its duties. This will be done. Lunabase informs me that heavy shipments of involuntary colonists will be received shortly, and I will *not* allow anyone entrusted to my care to be endangered!"

"Colonel?" Skilly's voice was chocolate-smooth this time; Owensford glanced aside at her, narrow-eyed. She was keeping her own on her nails, the long black lashes drooping. "Maybe be better you land the convicts somewhere else. Safer than this dangerous city, which be too big to secure, hey? Also city is full of legitimate military target place, maybe we attack it soon."

A brilliant smile. "We Spartan People's Liberation Army promise solemn not to attack any place the shuttles land, if no Royal troops be there."

The Royal government delegation tensed; this was the real rebel ploy. Karantov pursed his lips thoughtfully, calling up the map-function of the table. It blinked from steel-gray to transparent, showing an overhead view of the Serpentine continent.

"Where would you suggest?" he said.

"Well, anywhere on the river do OK," she said blandly. "Howsomeever, all the towns have the same objection as Sparta City."

She reached over and tapped a spot on the south shore of Lake Alexander, where the railway from Olynthos circled around the Vulcan Rapids.

"This be the best spot, I think. Plenty open water, already docks for the mineral barges, and not much town. We agree not to attack there or anywhere within five kilometer."

"Commandant, that would cause considerable administrative difficulties," David I broke in.

"Three of my officers and a thousand people whose only offense was to be there when the Bureau of Relocation came through *died* just now, Your Majesty," Karantov said frostily. "This is considerably more than an administrative matter."

He glanced at the map again, then at the guerrilla leader with unconcealed suspicion.

"I and my staff will consider this matter. Provisionally, we will seal off all portions of the Aegis station dealing with BuReloc. The shuttles will take transportees to the surface —" he tapped the Lake Alexander location "— and nothing more, no other traffic."

The Spartans winced slightly; that would cost them heavily, especially in the CD credits BuReloc would no longer pay for services on Aegis, and in the fore-gone lift-capacity of the shuttle's surface-to-orbit runs.

"Furthermore, I am referring this matter to my superiors. I warn you that there will at the least be heavy fines, particularly if the culprits in the murder of my officers are not found; I am asking for reinforcements." Presently there were only about a company of Garrison Marines on Sparta. "Possibly a CoDominium blockade of this planet for violations of the Laws of War will be ordered."

This time faces paled. Bronson's aid to the Helots was already clandestine, and would not be affected. The Royal government would face riots and collapse, particularly in the cities. Sparta was only semi-industrialized, it simply could not function without off-planet supplies; was more vulnerable than a truly primitive world.

Time, Owensford thought, and cleared his throat.

"Colonel Karantov, if you please. I have a further complaint with regard to violations of the Laws of War."

Karantov raised his eyebrows, and the Helots' eyes turned to the Legion officer like turrets tracking.

"As to offenses committed against civilians, or among indigenous armed forces, that is beyond my jurisdiction." Karantov looked wistful; he was old enough to remember times when a CoDominium officer's word was law in such matters, and had been a grown man when the Fleet was still arbiter of all conflicts.

"The offense concerns a member of Falkenberg's Legion," Owensford said.

He felt a chill satisfaction as Skilly leaned over and spoke rapidly to a subordinate, who began to tap frantically at an opened laptop. A buzz broke out from Croser's party, until he cut it off with a knife-hand gesture; the Spartans leaned forward like hounds on a leash. Owensford slipped a message cube into the receptor.

"Lieutenant Deborah Lefkowitz, Falkenberg's Mercenary Legion 11A7732-ze-1," he said. A picture of her flashed up, together with her service history. Another shot of her with her husband and their two children, ages four and six. Then a full-length of her mostly-naked body, lying spread-eagled and open-eyed with its throat cut from ear to ear.

"Gene typing, finger and retina prints give positive ID," Owensford said, keeping his voice even with an effort. The Legion was very much a family. . . . *And I have to explain this to Jerry.* "She went MIA from an aircraft downed near this site during the battle of the Illyrian Dales last year. The cave was being used as a C3 post; our counter battery fire hit an ammunition dump, and the survivors evacuated quickly. Evidence that it was being used by the rebels follows."

Karantov's gray pug-dog face was emotionless as he turned it from the screen to the Helots. Owensford saw Skilly's own go equally blank, like a mask from an Egyptian grave, but the fingers of her right hand moved slightly, flexing. Everything took on a diamond clarity as he realized with an icy shock that she was calculating. On whether Karantov would order her arrest, and on how many she could kill before the guards shot her down. Geoffrey Niles was pale, looking at the photo on the screen.

The woman spoke, softly. "Skilly did not order that. If she had, Skilly would have seen that the body was disposed of with a thermite charge. And if you get she the genotypes —" sperm samples from the rapists would have yielded that "— Skilly will give you the bodies. With confessions. *Because Skilly does not like to be left holding the bag.*"

For a moment something with teeth looked out from behind the smooth features.

"Our investigation into this matter will require the perpetrators alive," the CoDominium commander said. His face and voice were near expressionless; Skilly's were as well, but her eyes flicked sideways to Owensford, and her head inclined slightly.

Good move, he translated mentally. There was nothing he could do now, after launching this torpedo.

"Field Prime has read your Laws of War, the old version and the new," Skilly said; left unstated was the shrinking field of application, as the CoDominium's power faded. "And the Mercenary Code." The influence of the free companies had grown with every passing year, particularly if you counted the armies of planets like Covenant who made their living from hiring out their fighting men. "Conducting internal trial and punishment fulfills the letter of both," she went on. "And we has no intention of doing more."

One of Karantov's fingers tapped at the table. "I did not know you were a . . . practitioner of the Code," he said with heavy irony.

Beneath the expressionless mask there was the hint of a cold snarl when Skilly spoke, an ancient anger and contempt.

"Field Prime doesn't give a pitcher of warm spit for you Code, or some dead bitch," she said, in the same soft voice. "Never no laws or codes to protect Skilly where *she* came from . . . but she doan pick fights she can no win, either. No point in paying no atteention to Spartan laws; them or us go to the wall, anyways. But only a fool get into a new battle when this one not won yet. Skilly Thibodeau be no fool. SPLA complying with your Code this time, and that all you going to get. Colonel."

"Punishment of individuals is not sufficient if the violation was policy set by leaders," Karantov said.

"My investigators should be involved." The threat of detention was unspoken.

"Skilly regrets that not possible," she said; then she grinned like a wolf. "Skilly also give standing orders anything she say when under a gun be disregarded. Can no play dis game without you willing to lay down the stakes, mon. You safe-conduct is unconditional . . . and Skilly have certain friends on Luna."

Karantov made a small wave of dismissal. "I expect the transcripts and the executions promptly," he said.

The Helots stood. "Oh, very prompt," Skilly said; the fingers of her gun-hand made that small unconscious gesture again. "You get all you ask for, Colonel, and more."

"I request that my evidence be presented to the Military Affairs Committee of the Grand Senate, and that copies be sent to the commanding officer of every registered military organization within the CoDominium," Owensford said formally. Someone involuntarily drew in a breath. It was impossible to determine who, but Peter thought it might have been Geoffrey Niles.

"Skilly don't see any need to do that. She will find your criminals. If this be record, then make the record clear, Skilly have nothing to do with that, and neither do any of her allies." The heavy-lidded eyes swept the others at the table, before she turned on her heel and left.

"Your comments are noted," Karantov said. "Colonel Owensford, your request is reasonable and will be granted. Copies of the relevant portions of this hearing will be furnished to all registered military organizations.

"We now adjourn meeting until I and my officers can consider this matter. That will be all, gentlemen, ladies, Your Majesties. Stay for a moment if you would,

Lieutenant Colonel Owensford." The CD commander emphasized his role by using Owensford's rank within Falkenberg's Legion, a registered military organization. . . .

.   .   .

"Please be seated, Piotr Stefanovich." Karantov touched a button to summon the steward. "Vodka and tonic, please. And you, Colonel?"

"Whiskey and water, thank you." They raised their glasses.

"*Spacebo*, Colonel. And congratulations on your promotion."

"Cheers, Colonel Karantov. May you not regret yours." Owensford sighed. "You played that pretty hard-nosed, Boris," he said. "On the Spartans, I mean."

The older man shrugged. "No more than I must." He looked to be certain that the recording cameras were turned off. "Of course, Piotr Stefanovich, it is clear that this is Armstrong's Black Hand *apparat*, no connection to the Spartan government. But this I cannot say in public. No more can I say Grand Admiral wishes most earnestly that you put down this revolt quickly." He paused, looking into his vodka and then snapping it back with a flick of his wrist. "No politics in the Fleet. Bah. Now is all politics."

"Maybe it's time for you to choose sides."

"Sergei and I wish you victory; Grant too, but we Russians most of all," the Russian CD officer continued softly. "This Croser, we Russians know his kind all too well; and the Thibodeau woman, yes. The True Believer, mad and brilliant, and the bandit killer follower . . . too many times has our suffering country seen the like of them." He crossed himself in Orthodox fashion, right to left. "We must hope that sin does not lie so heavy on Sparta as it does on the poor *rodina*."

"So why are you —"

"My friend, this is not the time. Some power remains, to the CoDominium, to the Senate. Enough to have me removed here if I give cause. Another time—"

"Another time may be too late."

"I think not. Your war goes badly? Surely you do not lose."

"Let's say we're not winning. Boris, the Fleet holds all the power out here."

"Power? Power to destroy, perhaps. Not to build. Not yet."

"Dammit, certainly enough power to intercept off-planet supplies to the rebels!"

"Yes, probably."

"So why—"

"Commodore Guildford has Navy command here. He is typical of new Fleet officers," Karantov said. "He chooses sides, not by principle, not by which is right side, but which side wins, which is how he is Commodore when sector like this would not rate more than Captain of Fleet."

"And he thinks Bronson will win?"

"He thinks he does not know. He thinks that by doing nothing he will anger neither side, be able to deal with winner." Boris Karantov shrugged. "Sometimes that tactic works."

"It also ensures that whoever does win will have no use for you," Peter said carefully.

"Agreed. Is this warning, Piotr Stefanovich? I tell you again, I do all I can. More and they will remove me."

"More a warning to Guildford, I think. Dammit, Boris, a surveillance satellite would make a lot of difference!"

"I will speak with Captain of Fleet Newell. You will understand, Piotr Stefanovich, there is much sympathy for you in Fleet units here. Many have families here, many have retired here, many more think to retire here. Is not popular to watch this planet destroy itself."

"We are *not* destroying ourselves. We are being destroyed. There is a difference."

"*We*, Piotr?" the CD man asked ironically.

"Yes. It's as much my fight as the Spartans. I've found something worth fighting for — dammit, it can be your fight too."

"Da. I know."

"Then for God's sake help us."

"I tell you again, it is not yet time." Karantov reached into his attaché case, and pulled out a message cube. "The latest from our observers at New Washington; somewhat more recent than official channels." A CD Fleet courier could take a direct route, through unsettled systems with no refueling stations, if there was need.

"In brief, Astoria has fallen to the Legion, and your Colonel is tearing up the Columbia Valley to meet the Friedlanders." He smiled wanly. "A swift campaign, glory or defeat, and an honorable enemy. It seems like a vision of paradise, no?"

"So Falkenberg has won?"

"When this message was made, he was winning his war," Karantov said. "He will hold the important parts of the planet. After that—" He shrugged. "Is politics, again."

"Thank you for the message."

"And is this. From Grand Admiral Sergei Mikaelovitch, news so secret that it cannot be sent except by word of mouth. The Grants have done all they can to make Bronson relinquish this feud. He will not."

"What does he want?"

Karantov shook his head. "Some say he is mad. Me, I

believe not. But whatever his plans, he is spending fortunes, and we dare not come to an open break with him. Not yet."

"We can tie him to the murder. That was his Grand Nephew there with Thibodeau! I can't think Adrian Bronson wants to be associated with atrocities."

"Nor I. Your pictures will go to Sergei Mikaelovitch, and to Grand Senate. I can do no more than that."

"It may be enough."

"And it may not. My friend, Earth's life hangs in this balance. Sergei Lermontov is no longer sure that we have *one* year, much less the ten we have all planned. Certainly we do not if things come to open fight with Bronson faction. My friend, we have done what we could!"

"It's nice to know you tried," Owensford said dryly.

Karantov snorted laughter. "Still *ami*, thinking the problem will yield to 'can do,' eh, my friend?"

"Boris, I'm beginning to doubt I can do bloody *anything*. This war . . . "

The other man nodded. "Some help I can be, perhaps. The Admiral sends you Fleet Intelligence report on Kenjiro Murasaki; we are certain now that he is mercenary Bronson has hired for Croser."

"Bronson hired him directly?" Owensford said, balancing the message cube in his fingers and then slipping it into a pouch on his belt.

Karantov nodded. "Which may yet be cause of great regret to Croser. Be careful, Piotr Stefanovich, be very careful. The Meijians have some of best computer personnel in all settled worlds, and Special Tasks, Inc. hires only best of those. Murasaki is like ghost; rumored to be here, to be there, never proven. He commands highest fees, and his chosen field is the undermining of an opponent's own weapons and personnel. I read from report. 'Subtle to a fault.

Treacherous as a snake, and bound by no soldier's honor, not even as Meijians understand it. His only scruple is loyalty to his employer for the term of the contract.' " Karantov shrugged. "From this I suspect primary motivation is aesthetic — he is artist, artist of assassination and subversion and death."

"That about describes the way things have been going," Owensford said feelingly. "All right. It's a war of attrition. The great thing is not to lose your nerve. But bloody Hell, I could still use an observation satellite."

Karantov nodded, tapping his fingers against the table. "Request has been noted. Now. Grand Admiral also sends you help, twenty computer specialists recently retired from BuInt. Experts in counter viral work. This is, you understand, of most extreme secrecy."

Owensford smiled. "Boris," he said, "it's also extremely welcome. We need them, our own people have enough to do with the Legion systems and a few here in the capital; it's getting pretty bad out there."

❖   ❖   ❖

"Interesting," the dark figure in the corner said. "Very interesting information. Not vital, of course." Keys clicked as he scanned forward through the data. "Interesting. They have discovered our origins from Fleet Intelligence. Ah, they are sending technical specialists to help the Legion. Fascinating, and incriminating if my principal could use this before the Grand Senate, which of course he cannot. No access codes, I see."

"Murasaki," the Helot commander said. "Skilly did not appreciate that little surprise back with the CoDo."

Geoffrey Niles took another drink from his canteen; water, unfortunately. *I could use a drink right now*, he thought. *God, those pictures . . .*

"Bloody right," he rasped. "Our plausible deniability is

running too sodding thin for comfort, Mr. Murasaki. If the Grand Senator has this pinned on him — and I'm pretty conspicuous — he'd lose half his influence in the Fleet, and every second merc on all the hundred planets would be taking potshots at his people and interests —"

"Jeffi," Skilly said, without taking her eyes from the Meijian.

The meeting was taking place in a farmhouse northwest of Colchis; the Movement had financed the owner, decades ago. Land on the Eurotas was cheap, and mostly free once you were a day's ride away from the river, but equipment was expensive. A few thousand Crowns had made the difference between peasant misery and modest comfort for the owner and his family, enough for ploughs, harrows, a satellite dish for the children's education. In return couriers had a safe place to stop. . . . The sound and smell of cooking came up through the floorboards of the attic. It added an unreality to the meeting, Niles thought: death and conspiracy to the scent of fresh bread and a roast.

"Jeffi," Skilly went on, "in case you not notice, mon, you working for Skilly now, not Earth Prime." She turned back to the Meijian. "Well?"

He shrugged. "Operational security in the combat zone is your responsibility," he said.

Skilly shifted slightly; the Meijian did not tense, but the chilly air of the attic was fully of a coiled alertness.

"Yoshida was in command of that post," the woman said. "He responsible, Murasaki; should have his head, too."

"No," Murasaki said flatly. "I do not abandon my people."

"Neither does Skilly," the woman said. "Ones who offed the merc fucked up by not hiding de evidence, and they pay." She smiled at the ghastly pun. "But Yoshida commander on site — he should have checked."

"Field Prime," Niles said. "If we just tightened the behavior of the troops up—"

"*Jeffi, shut up*," Skilly said. She turned her head toward him; a slight trace of fear crept down the Englishman's spine. "This the Revolution, Jeffi; we try fighting by your *rabbiblanco* rules, they kill us all in a month. That the reason their stinkin' Code there at all."

Niles fell silent; usually it was a teasing joke when Skilly referred to him as a *rabbiblanco*, white-ass. Not this time.

Murasaki chuckled softly. "Not the way our enemies would put it, but moral considerations aside, quite accurate. The Law of War certainly has a conservative effect, making it difficult to fight wars with large or radical aims. It favors established, regular forces."

He turned his attention to Skilly once more. "I would remind you that Earth Prime's main goal is to humiliate the Legion. Not merely to defeat it, but to make Falkenberg and its individual members *suffer*, to cause them pain and anguish. So I was ordered."

"Good, OK, *absolutemente*, once we win you can have them all fucked to death by donkeys — but not while it can backfire on we. Mon, Falkenberg got influence! He winning his war, too. We get him mad enough before Helots holding the planet, we gets the Legion an' twenty thousand mercs from Kali knows where, them riding down in CD assault boats pretty likely. Nobody off-planet except maybe Lermontov much care what we do to Spartans, not enough to do much, but the mercs be a different story."

"Is it certain that won't happen now?" Niles asked. "Those pictures. Properly used, they might get quite a few volunteers."

"Why?" Skilly asked. "Not they fight."

"Not everyone would agree," Niles said.

"Jeffi, you crazy. Falkenberg, maybe he get mad

enough, he talk them mercs around, but it not they fight unless they get paid."

"Yoshida shall be reprimanded," Murasaki said.

Skilly snorted. "And all you people, they out of the chain of command in my area," she said flatly. "No operations without regular Helot clearance."

"As you wish, Field Prime," Murasaki said, inclining his head. The two leaders stared at each other with mutual respect and equally absolute lack of trust. The Meijian rose and left without further word.

Niles looked from the technoninja's back to Skilly's face. *Alike*, he thought with an inward shudder. *How could I have missed it? What did that old book say about Kritias, the pupil of Socrates who had become one of the Thirty Tyrants?*

"When a man is freed from the bonds of dogma and custom, where will he run? He has gotten loose, of the soul if you like the word, or from whatever keeps a man on two feet instead of four. And now Kritias too is running on the mountains, with no more between him and his will than a wolf has."

When Niles was a child he had loved Turkish Delight; on a visit, Adrian Bronson had grown tired of his whining and bought him a whole box while they were at a county fair on the estate. Niles could remember the exact moment when pleasure turned to disgust, just before the nausea struck; he had never been able to eat the stuff again. No lessons like those you teach yourself, his grand uncle had said to his mother. . . .

"Sometimes Skilly think that one, he a sick puppy," she said meditatively, looking after the Meijian. "Likes to hurt people. But terror only effective if it be used selective . . . Or maybe he not care so much who wins? Maybe he bossman doan care?" Then her gaze sharpened, fixing on the Englishman's face.

"Ah, Jeffi, Skilly think you maybe getting second thoughts, maybe think Skilly not been telling you everything," she said, grinning at him. "Too late, me mon." She stepped closer, over the piled trunks and boxes, putting a hand under his chin. "River of fire and a river of blood between you and de old life now. You be Skilly's now, Jeffi. Skilly's and the Dreadful Bride's. Come on, we got a long ride ahead and a battle to fight."

❖ ❖ ❖

"You know, George, I'm breaking the Code," Barton said to the other officer beside him in the lounge of the blimp. "The unwritten sections, at least."

"Oh?" The other man looked up from his laptop.

The sunlight was fading outside, even from two thousand meters altitude; below the oblong shadow of the lighter-than-air craft had faded as darkness fell. They were two hundred kilometers west of Mandalay now, angling north across the bend of the Eurotas to reach the lands north of Olynthos. Below them were the vast marshes around Lake Lynkestis, not a light showing in all the area from horizon to horizon. The lounge was walled in clear plastic, a warm bubble of light in the vast black stillness; somehow the throbbing of the diesels was a lonely sound as they leaned back in their chairs with tobacco and coffee and brandy. Behind them, the riding beacons of the other five aircraft were drifting amber spots.

"Yeah. Gettin' emotionally involved with the clients."

"I know how you feel," Slater said. "Homelike here, isn't it?"

Barton pulled on his cigarette and nodded; they had a lot in common, despite Slater being half a generation younger. Both from the American southwest, he by birth and Slater by heritage. Their families were from country areas that had changed little since the coming of the CoDominium; where as recently as their teen-age years it had still been possible to pretend they lived as free men in a free country. Barton had been born in Arizona, and George Slater had visited kin there often enough. Slater's mother was a colonial from a largely American-settled planet as well.

"Better than home, if it weren't for the war," Barton said. "After we — there I go again, after the *clients* win — I'm giving serious thought about buying back my contract from the Legion and making a go of it in the Royal Army."

"Can't resist being a brigadier, eh?" Slater said, laughing silently. His face creased, leathery with long exposure to strange suns; he was a tall whipcord-lean man, brown hair sun-faded.

"It doesn't hurt," Barton said frankly. *The pay isn't spectacular*, he reminded himself. No better than what he'd been getting as a Captain in the Legion, considerably less than he'd usually made as an independent merc commander with Barton's Bulldogs, if you factored in the foreign-exchange difficulties. The opportunity to use his skills on a larger canvas was more important: it had not been easy, going back down the scale after having his own outfit. Before Falkenberg smashed it back on Tanith; that had been just business, of course. *Business, and I was on the wrong side. Didn't used to be so clear cut, right side, wrong side. Now—*

Now it's important.

"I'll be hanging up my guns in another few years no matter what," he went on, discarding a frayed toothpick and fishing another out of a pocket. He had picked that habit up on Thurstone, when tobacco was unavailable. "I'm damn near sixty, George. Long past time to think of settling down." Even with regenn, it was half a lifetime.

"Me too," Slater replied. Barton glanced over at him in surprise. "Cindy doesn't think dragging the kids from one base to another is all that good an idea," he explained. "Wants them to have a home before they leave the nest. I always wanted land of my own; anyway, it's what I was raised to. Dad doesn't talk about it much, but he still remembers losing the ranch."

And you'd waited long enough, Barton thought, with a certain wistful envy. Slater's father had been with Falkenberg since before he took over the 42nd CoDominium Marines, the unit that had followed him to become the Legion. His wife was a colonial, country-born. They had four children, from three to ten.

"For that matter," Barton said, "I think Pete Owensford wouldn't mind having a home. He may have found someone to share it with—"

"That Halleck girl?"

"Well, I notice he found reasons to visit the Halleck ranch, and now Lydia Halleck's in Sparta City for a year at University—"

"Well, well," Slater said. "Hadn't heard that last part. Hell, Ace, we're none of us getting any younger. And this is a good world, good in lots of ways."

"Can't fault the Spartans for their terms," Barton said meditatively. Lateral transfer at their brevet ranks was the least of it; automatic Citizenship, landgrants . . . with their Royal Army pay and partial Legion pensions thrown in, they would be well-to-do men by local standards.

"Mmmm-*hm*. And," Slater went on, "this place is one of the few I've seen whose government doesn't make me want to pinch my nose and 'holdeth aside the skirt of the garment.' "

Barton's face went bleak. "Yeah. I like the people, too. Which is why I've started wanting to win even more than usual." You always did; a matter of self-respect, the Code, and of course you lost fewer men that way.

"Agreed." A shrug. "Of course, we're getting a lesson in what Christian Johnny always said, remember? 'Soldiers are the cleanup crew.'"

One of Falkenberg's history lessons was on how seldom military men had much say in how their efforts were applied. Armed force was a blunt instrument in politics, liable to do more harm than good unless aimed with extreme precision. At best, it bought time and space for the political leaders to repair the political mistakes that had left no choice but violence in the first place.

The other man nodded and sipped at his brandy. *Damned good*, he thought.

"Well," he said, "at least this time we aren't hired by the ones who screwed up." *To bury the evidence under the bodies*.

"Dad's looking into another matter," George Slater said. "Loyalties. It's easy to see what holds the Spartans to their cause. The Helots are another matter. Whitlock's working on political persuasion. We should too."

"Sure," Barton said. "How?"

"Oh, maybe remind them just what their leaders do. Left their troops and ran like hell at the Dales, saved their skins by sacrificing everyone else. Get that story across, and the first time they get a setback it's every man for himself." Slater tamped tobacco into a pipe. "It's not as if the people they're following are admirable. In any way."

"Maybe their troops don't know that—"

"I'm sure they don't," Slater said. "If they did, would they stick?"

"Maybe some would. Revolutionaries. I learned all about fanatics on Thurstone, hell, before you were born. But it's something to think about." He looked at his watch. "Another day's work in Olynthos," he said. Slater would be taking over there; it was the second-largest city on Sparta, center of the Middle and Upper Valleys of the Eurotas. "And then on to the wilds of the north for me. Should be interesting."

❖   ❖   ❖

"Are you all *right*, Margreta?" Melissa asked. She had to lean close and put her ear to the young soldier's, given the noise level. "You're pale as a sheet."

"I'm fine," Margreta shouted back. Her fingers were shaking slightly as she put on her helmet; the noise level dropped immediately, as the sonic sensors automatically filtered out the background. "It's just . . . the news about Lieutenant Lefkowitz, you know? Everyone in the Legion is —" *Mostly mad enough to rip out veins with their teeth*, she thought. *With me, it's more personal. I've got to* work *with the animals who did that.*

Melissa nodded and gave the younger woman's shoulder a squeeze. Margreta smiled back. *Be here. Be ready for possible extraction*, were all the orders that had come from her clandestine Helot contact.

It had run through Fort Plataia like fire through standing grass, and the execution of the four Helots had done little to calm the anger. The CoDominium authorities had little alternative but to accept that as sufficient; the Legionnaires would not. *The Brotherhoods seem to be almost as angry*, Margreta thought. There had been a delegation of condolence, and a new rush of enlistments. Frightening to have the enemy's nature driven home so thoroughly, but there was something in knowing you had a big family to protect you . . . or at least avenge you.

The new vehicle assembly bay was even louder than usual. Armored vehicles were moving down the conveyor, and the air was full of the ugly howling rasp of heavy-duty grinding machines, the ozone-smelling flash of electrowelders and the whine of pneumatic tools. Each light tank started the line as an open frame; as it passed down computer-controlled overhead cranes swung in, first with sections of hull-armor to be welded on, then with components and engines and transmissions. Lighter parts like the roadwheels and tracks ran on trolleys up to the sides of the line, and the last thing to be added was the turret with its basket, lowered onto the Cataphract. These particular models were SP guns, with 155mm gun-howitzers in big boxy turrets.

"Just shows what you can do if you have to," Melissa said again, smiling and waving about at the vast extensions which had nearly doubled the area of von Alderheim Works # 2. This time the Legion helmet delivered it in conversational tones. "After the war, we'll have twice the capacity we did going in. Of course, most of it will be for tanks."

They had become friendly, after meeting at the University's software department. Melissa von Alderheim was more than the daughter of Sparta's wealthiest industrialist and fiancee to Lysander Collins; she was the best CAD-CAM designer on the planet. That was a rare art, these days, when design changes were mostly a matter of styling and BuInt suppressed all real change. Much of the new output of war machines was her doing.

"Two fifty per month of the AFV's, and fifty of the SP howitzers?" she said.

Melissa nodded. "It's the stabilization and optics that's the bottleneck," she said. "We're getting the Friedlander stuff through now. And an inquiry about what we're using it for."

A natural worry; Daimlerwerk Friedland AG had

lucrative markets for armored fighting vehicles all through this sector, and hiring out their panzer units was even more important to them. Vehicles were parked outside, several hectares of them waiting to be driven down to the plant's docks on Constitution Bay, everything from jeeps and trucks to the self-propelled guns she had seen under construction inside. The landing platforms were busy, barges and steamboats and diesels unloading metals and forms, loading with vehicles and engines and general goods for transshipment upriver.

"This is going to cause the enemy hard trouble," Margreta said. Then shivered. *Why am I frightened?* she thought. It was just a routine consulting trip . . . and Major Owensford said a hunch was your subconcious telling you something.

The main gate of the factory was on the other side of the complex, facing the main road into town; von Alderheim Works # 2 had been built on a greenfield site, with plenty of room for expansion.

FAMP. Almost too loud to be an explosion, a pillar of flame reaching for the sky. *Truck-bomb*, she thought numbly. Lots of big articulated trucks driving up there all the time, although *how* they had got a bomb past the checkpoints and inspections . . . *Of course. Use a legitimate load of explosives. And a suicide driver.* Who would look for a bomb in a ten-kilo load of shell filler? Even this far away the blast was perceptible, and the two Royal Army troopers guarding them wheeled, their rifles coming up automatically.

God, please, God, Margreta prayed, an atheist's desperate reflex as she cleared her pistol.

"Wait a minute," she said to herself, crouching and looking around. Nothing, except the normal work of the docks grinding to a halt as everyone turned to look at the pillar of smoke. The explosion was spectacular, but not really damaging. No secondary blasts . . . *"It's a diversion!"* she shouted. "Get —"

KRAK. A Peltast rifle; the massive 15mm round smashed through one soldier's spine and out the front of his chest in a shower of bone and blood, ignoring his body armor as if it were tissue. Impact sledged him forward with his limbs flopping like a rag doll's. Margreta drew and dove for cover; her armored torso struck Melissa at the same moment, sending the slight Spartan woman four steps back on her heels toward the shelter of an APC. The Legionnaire's free hand was reaching up to drag the other woman down into safety and—

KRAK. The 15mm round, which would have punched through Melissa's center of mass if Margreta had not moved her, struck and skimmed all along her arm from shoulder to fingertips instead, shattering bone and tearing muscle. She went down with limp finality, her head thudding into the tungsten-steel cleats of the personnel carrier's treads. *KRAK.* Into the leg of the soldier she had shot, blasting it off at the shin.

"God *damn!*" Margreta shouted, pulling her communicator free and dropping the useless pistol from the other so that she could fumble a hypo from her belt and slap it against Melissa's neck. Gray skin, rapid breathing, sweat . . . shock.

"Medic, dustoff, Ms. von Alderheim is down, repeat, dustoff soonest," she said. "Wound trauma, internal bleeding, multiple fractures of the right arm." The other Spartan trooper rose from his crouch and fired.

"Talkins, Capital Seven here," a calm voice said from her hand unit. Her chest seemed to turn tight and squeeze; that was her Helot contact's codename. "Make sure of the von Alderheim woman if you can. Quickly."

Goddam, she thought to herself. It seemed to come

from some distant part of her mind, while her body and mouth did things on their own.

"Guard Graffin von Alderheim," she said sharply, drawing her pistol and moving forward into the maze of parked vehicles. The soldier shouted uselessly behind her, and there was the heavy *bwanggg* of a Peltast round ricochetting off armor, sending him back to cover.

"God *damn*." Dangerous, but she had to get out of the vicinity of Melissa. Otherwise, it would be difficult to explain her survival.

And there were some things that you couldn't do even to keep your cover.

"God damn, we Legionnaires are supposed to *stop* this sort of thing." That stopped *her*, for a moment. *We*. We had always been her and George, after Mother went away. A helicopter went by overhead, and she shook herself back to awareness.

✧ CHAPTER SEVEN

Thomas Cook & Company: Almanac of Interstellar Travel:

Transit times for standard merchant charter:
(Standard Terran month of 30 days)
Earth — Sparta (via Tanith):	**6 months**
Tanith — New Washington/Franklin system:	**4 months**
New Washington — Sparta (via Tanith):	**9 months**

— all travel times may be reduced by 50% or more for naval couriers, warships or assault transports.

✧　　✧　　✧

When bad men combine, the good must associate; otherwise they will fall, one by one, an unpitied sacrifice in a contemptible struggle.

— Edmund Burke,
Thoughts on the Cause of the Present Discontents

✧　　✧　　✧

Further, war, which is simply the subjection of all life and property to one momentary aim, is morally vastly superior to the mere violent egoism of the individual; it develops power in the service of a supreme general idea and under a discipline which nevertheless permits supreme heroic virtue to unfold. Indeed, war alone grants to mankind the magnificent spectacle of a general submission to a general aim.

— Jakob Burkhardt, *Reflections on History*

✧　　✧　　✧

"The bones in the arm and shoulder were severely damaged. Shattered would not be too strong a word," the doctor said, with the impersonal sympathy of her craft. "Massive edema and tissue damage as well, from hydrostatic shock."

Lysander listened, but most of his attention was

elsewhere. Melissa's face was barely visible through the quartz view port in the regeneration tank universally known as a mummy case. Her head was covered with a white surgical bandage but it looked more like an old fashioned night cap. There was no makeup, but she seldom wore much anyway, and enough remained of her tan to give some illusion of healthy color. She looked relaxed, even peaceful, but very helpless, and very still. *She's always been so active. And now —*

A nurse shouldered through, studied displays and touched a few of the controls around the cocoon-like capsule of the regeneration tank, and left silently. There were half a dozen Life Guards outside the door, and a sandwich-armor slab closed off the window, but otherwise the small private room in the St. Thomas Royal Hospital was nothing out of the ordinary. Every ward was overcrowded with war casualties, and the regeneration clinics more than any.

Lysander swallowed, holding his helmet awkwardly in hands that suddenly felt too big. *Freiherr* von Alderheim was there, looking somehow deflated; Lysander's father was there as well, holding himself erect now, but with an effort that showed the stoop lurking beneath it. Recovery from the enemy's virus attack was proceding, but still slowly. Queen Adriana stood by, holding her husband's arm, almost visibly willing strength into it.

God, I hate hospitals, Lysander thought. There was the smell, of course, but that wasn't as strong as in a battlefield surgical unit. Mostly there was a *feel* of sickness to them, a concentrated misery that soaked into the walls themselves.

"That's fairly straightforward regenn work, though," Dr. Ruskin continued; her fingers touched the scanner equipment tucked into the loops of her green gown slightly nervously. This *was* rather distinguished company for a sickroom. "At least seventy-five percent, possibly complete recovery. It's the neurological damage that had us worried most of the morning. Ten hours of Sir Harlan's best work. It was, well, what he was able to do was wonderful, that's all."

"She will recover?" von Alderheim asked.

"Yes, we think so."

She doesn't sound very sure, Lysander thought.

"And she can still have children?" von Alderheim insisted.

"Yes, there were no injuries of that kind," the doctor said. This time she sounded much more confidant.

"Does she know we're here?" Queen Adriana asked.

"No, Madame," Dr. Ruskin said. "We're using a neurological hookup to keep her asleep until the regeneration stimulation process takes hold."

"So there's no point in her father and my son staying here?"

"I wish they wouldn't," Ruskin said. "We're terribly crowded, and some of the staff are awfully young; they want to see His Highness close up, and that can be disruptive. It really would be better if you go back and wait at the Palace. We'll let you know in plenty of time before we wake her up."

"She shouldn't be alone," Lysander said. "We failed her. I failed. Her and the whole planet, I can't protect them and —"

"Nonsense," the Queen said. "You can't be everywhere at once."

"I know, Mother, but—"

"And the doctor is right, Lysander, We are in the way."

"How long? Until she wakes up?" Lysander demanded.

"Nine days minimum. More likely eleven."

"Hmm. You're certain there's nothing we can do here?"

"Nothing but get in the way," the doctor said. "You could go say a few words to anyone off duty in the staff lounge. They all want to see you. But otherwise—" Her voice softened. "You needn't worry that she'll be neglected, Highness. There's no one here who doesn't love the Princess. Soon to be Princess. We'll have her well in time for the wedding, Prince Lysander. I swear it."

"Thank you. And there's work to do." He started toward the door, then went back inside the room alone after the others left. Lysander, Prince of Sparta, put both hands on the tank and spoke quietly. "I'm sorry," he said. He straightened and looked at the blocked off window as if he could see through to the city outside, to the city and the countryside beyond. "I'm sorry." He stood that way a long time. When he turned to leave, his face might have been carved from stone.

❖   ❖   ❖

Dion Croser stepped to the edge of the dais and raised his hands. Silence fell across the stadium like a ripple through the ocean of forty thousand faces, all turned toward him. Behind him his image stood, fifty meters high on the great screen; he flashed his famous grim smile and leaned his hands on the lectern. It was full night, but the blazing rectangles of light all around the upper tiers made a white day of the sloping seats, shutting out the dark and the stars. Searchlights stood between them, shining vertical pillars thousands of meters up into the sky until they merged into a canopy of white haze; between them were giant Movement banners, the black circle on red with the red = sign in its midst.

"Victory!" he said.

The word rolled and boomed back from the ampitheatre, and the crowd roared. A wave of pure noise that thudded into you like a fist in the gut. Terrifying, if you were the crowd's enemy. Exhilaration beyond words when the adoration of the many-throated beast struck. The stadium was just off Government House Square; they would be hearing it in the Palace . . . hearing it in every house in Sparta City.

Power, he thought. *This* is *power.*

The sound went on and on, building until the ground shook with it; the white-noise surf of it gradually modulating as the disciplined blocks of NCLF militants chanted.

"Dion the Leader! Dion to Power!" More and more falling in with the chant. *"DION THE LEADER! DION TO POWER!"*

He listened, waiting for the peak moment; they were like some smooth sculptor's material under his command, and he could feel threads of unity stretching out from his mind to each of theirs. The sound was unaltered, but he could feel a moment's smooth pause inside himself, like the hesitation of water at the top of a fountain's arc. He raised his hands, and silence fell like a curtain into an aching void.

"My people," he said, and there was a sigh like a vast moan.

You are my people, he thought. *Foolish and brutish and short-sighted, you are what others have made you. Made you, and then despised you for it; but you will follow me, and I will give you back your pride. Make you worthy of yourselves.*

"My people — the people of Sparta! Tonight we come here together to celebrate a great victory, a victory over oppression, over arrogant elitism. For half a year, we have campaigned together in the Constitutional referendum. Peacefully —"

— except for the riots and so forth —

"— we have gone from neighborhood to neighborhood, from town to town, explaining our just cause — the cause of democracy, of universal sufferage and human equality. Not once have we forbidden those who oppose us, those who have usurped the People's power, from arguing against us. Tonight we see the results!"

It was a warm early-summer night, and the lights and crowd made it a hot one; he could feel the thin film of sweat on his face fighting with the makeup artist's powder, and trickling down his flanks. Smell it as well. That did not bother him; it was a sign of honest labor, of the labor that had earned him this prize. He made a small motion with the fingers of his left hand, and behind him numbers sprang out across the simulacrum of his own face.

"Two thirds have voted *yes* to the great question of our day: *Should all Spartans share equally in the sovereign franchise of citizenship as their inalienable right?* The People have spoken! Let those who dare deny their voice and their right!"

Another roar, harder this time, with an undertone of guttural menace that bristled the hair along his spine.

"Fellow Spartans — fellow *citizens* —" another crashing bark of cheering "— our struggle has been long and difficult. I must confess," and he lowered his eyes, "there was a time when I too, was heedless of the sufferings of the people — better than the corrupt clique around the self-appointed kings only because I was ignorant rather than callous."

Another wash of sound, denial this time.

"Yes! But I went to *the People*, learned from *the People* —" he raised his face, letting humility slide into an expression of iron determination "— and together, we built the Movement. Only a few of us at first, but more and more as the years went by. The vanguard of the People, building their power brick by brick."

He gripped the sides of the lectern, leaning forward and letting his voice go low and confidential. The sound-system here was excellent.

"The kings thought they could stop us with bribes and lies, by having the Milice and the RSMP break heads. Many of our brave comrades —" he shot one hand out towards the NCLF contingents, with their Party banners inscribed with the names of the martyrs "— have fallen. Yet not once have we answered their provocations in kind, despite the brutalities, the brutalities that have driven some poor souls into the hills. Helots in truth, ground down under the heel of militarism — and while we cannot condone their actions, we understand only too well their reasons.

"And that is how we'll build the New Order — brick by brick, with discipline and patience. First, we'll present the results of the people's will to the kings. Then, whether they agree or not — because those same results show that *ours* is the rightful authority — we'll hold elections for the Constitutional Convention, and there we, the People's choice, will make a new Sparta, one that will produce something besides the endless taxes and war and poverty the kings and their flunkies have brought us. And then we'll elect a *government of the people!*"

"DION THE LEADER! DION TO POWER! DION! DION! DION!"

This time he let it go on much longer, falling away raggedly into silence.

"But," he said, then paused while the quiet built. "*But*. If the Royalist clique refuse to heed the people's will *then* — if they try to turn the guns of the bandits and misguided youngsters they call the Royal Spartan Army on us — why, *then* —" His lean, slab-and-angle

face contorted, and a fist crashed down on the podium.
"They'll feel the people's anger!"

A chopping gesture cut short the answering howl. "I
make not threats," he continued blandly. "United,
we'll carry the people's cause to victory. You have done
a great deal, and there's a great deal more to be done.
Tonight, enjoy your well-earned victory."

He drew himself up, and gave the Movement salute,
fists clenched and wrists crossed over his head, then
wheeled and walked briskly through the door beneath
the huge overhead display screen.

"Congratulations, Leader!"

He waved to the crowd of NCLF functionaries; his
bodyguards closed in around him, protecting from all
but a few of the hands thrust forward. Croser walked
slowly, grabbing the proffered hands and calling people by name, he made a point of knowing as many as
he could. Fragments reached him: *best speech ever*
and, *inspiring*. It was that, he thought critically; a first-
rate professional job of work, if he did say so himself.
Oratory and organization were the basic skills of the
revolutionist, and he had both.

There were only a few of the inner circle in the room
where he sat to let the specialists sponge off the makeup.
One of them was Murasaki, he thought — it was difficult
to tell, with the Meijian — but most were section-heads
and the analytical staff, going over the effect of the
referendum campaign and the meeting tonight on
public opinion.

"That should throw about one percent of the Citizen body to us," the senior statistician was saying.
"About two percent to the SCA. Unfortunately, it'll
also firm up most of the rest with this new Crown Loy-
alist Party."

Croser scowled slightly, holding out his fingers for a
cigarette before he stripped off the tunic and began to

towel down his torso; his neck and shoulders were beginning to ache slightly with the leftover tension of his performance. The Loyalist-Pragmatist merger was not unforseen, but it was still a negative development. So was the tightening loyalty of many non-Citizens to the Royalist cause; loyalty to their Citizen employers, in many cases. Particularly out in the long-settled parts of the countryside, where it was becoming a serious embarassment to the Helots. Bad enough that most of the Lower Valley had either given the referendum a "no" answer, or boycotted the whole operation. *Too many boycotted the election, and the Royals know that, know we faked it, but they aren't saying anything. Why?* But it didn't matter. Numbers didn't count. What counted was strength. *And we're gaining, and they're losing, because we know we're going to win.*

❖   ❖   ❖

Croser's image faded from the television screen. Dr. Caldwell Whitlock stared at the set for a moment. "Man could charm the scales off a snake," he said. He turned off the set and looked up at his visitor. "Drink? You look like you could use one."

"I suppose," Lysander said absently. "But it doesn't do any good."

"No, reckon not, and good thing you know that," Whitlock said. "But this time I think no harm done. Bourbon all right?"

"Sure. Dr. Whitlock, we've got to do something about that man."

"Well, yeah, you surely do," Whitlock said. One section of the book case behind his desk was hinged. It swung out, books and all, to reveal a small cabinet. Whitlock poured two drinks, added water, and handed one across his desk. "Cheers. Yes, sir, your Highness, you surely do. So why don't you?"

"What should we do?" Lysander asked.

"Turn him over to Jesus and Catherine Alana," Whitlock said. "I doubt he knows everything, but he'll sure know enough you could put a big dent in their operations."

"Just arrest him? Question him with drugs, or worse? We can't do that."

"Well, you *can* do that," Whitlock said. "Least for now you can. Give him more time and maybe you won't be able to. But right now you can, and you'd save lives by doin' it." Whitlock sipped at his drink and looked over the top of the glass at Lysander. "For instance, I expect he approved that attack on your lady."

Lysander looked as if Whitlock had struck him. "You believe that."

"Surely do. Can't believe that wasn't approved at their highest levels. Tell you another thing. I hope you got real good people watchin' that hospital. Real good, and a lot of 'em, 'cause they're likely to try again."

"Why? What did Melissa do to them?"

"She did plenty," Whitlock said. He ran his stubby fingers through his mane of white hair. "Plenty. Designed those tanks for one. Snubbed Mr. Croser and that Skilly woman at a night club for another."

"I didn't know they'd met."

"Happened when you were off-planet," Whitlock said. "People tell me things maybe they don't tell you. Story got back here you were on Tanith all set up with that hotel girl, Lady Melissa took to being squired around by the youngest Harriman boy. I guess I'm not surprised no one told you."

"No, no one did —"

"Don't reckon it mattered a lot either," Whitlock said. "Far as I can see she was pretty careful 'bout where they went, public places, avoid scandal. Sensible lady, even when she's madder'n hell at you. With good reason, too. 'Course her whole point was that you'd find out, bit of irony there you never did. Anyway, one night they went to a charity thing, and Croser was there with that Skilly. He got drunk, started talking to her about you and what you'd be doing on Tanith. I don't know what all was said, but it ended up she slapped Croser hard across the face and walked out. Looked for a minute like Croser was going to do something about that, but nothing came of it. But he sure didn't like it, and neither did that Skilly."

"I never knew — But that's not reason to have her killed!"

"Might be to him," Whitlock said. "Just might be, and if she said the wrong things about that Skilly person, there'd be another. But the real reason to kill her is to get at you. If they thought she didn't like you, thought she was goin' through with this marriage for politics, she'd be safe enough, they'd purely love to have you in a bad marriage where you're likely to do something stupid. But the way you two been carryin' on, like love birds, it's pretty clear you made up whatever problems you had, and that's not so good, the way they see it."

"What the hell is it to them?"

"Come off it, Highness," Whitlock said. "You got to know, for all practical purposes right now you *are* the nation. Oh, sure, people love your father, but they think of him as the old king, nice old man, symbol of the nation and all that, but still, he's the old king. And they trust David to do what's best if there's peace, but there ain't no peace, and they don't see there'll be any peace without you make it happen. Now most times maybe it's best you don't act like you know all this, but this is a time for some plain talk. Whatever future this experiment in the good society has got, right now it pretty much rests on you."

Lysander didn't say anything. Whitlock nodded. "So, we got that straight. Now, about Croser."

"But — Dr. Whitlock, he's been careful, there's no evidence to connect him or his political movement with any of this. No criminal acts."

"Well, that's right, and if that's what you're waiting for, you'll never get it," Whitlock said. "Son, a long time ago a man named Burke said that for evil to win all that's got to happen is that good men do nothin'. That's happening here. You're in a war, and you got to fight it like a war."

"And if we get like the enemy what's the point of winning?"

"That's what King David's always sayin'," Whitlock said. "Your father, too, sometimes, not so much now. Lysander, let me tell you something, you couldn't in a million years be like them even if you was to work at it." Whitlock studied papers on his desk for a moment. "You better think about it. I'll go on plannin' the politics for you, and Pete Owensford will go on fightin' the enemy for you, good men will go on dyin' for you, and hell, it may be enough, Prince Lysander, it just may be enough, and maybe you got a point. You've got a decent government, and Lord knows I'd hate to see it turn mean, but you better think, Your Highness. Just how many of your people are you willing to see killed just so Citizen Dion Croser can have his legal rights?"

❖ CHAPTER EIGHT

To be a general it is sufficient to pay well, command well, and hang well.

— Sir Ralph Hopton *circa* 1689

❖   ❖   ❖

The discipline enforced by firing squad or pistol is inferior to that accepted, self-imposed discipline which characterizes good soldiers. Regulations designed to keep dull-witted conscripts together on the shoulder-to-shoulder battlefields of the blackpowder era are inappropriate in an age when weapons and tactics demand dispersion on the battlefield, and when the initiative may be more important than blind obedience. In the last analysis fighting spirit centres on the morale of the individual soldier and the small group of comrades with whom he fights.

— John Keegan and Richard Holmes; *Soldiers*

❖   ❖   ❖

If I learned nothing else from war, it taught me the falseness of the belief that wealth, material resources, and industrial genius are the real sources of a nation's military power. These things are but the stage setting: those who manage them but the stage crew.

The play's the thing. Finally, every action large or small is decided by what happens there on the line where men take the final chance of life or death. And so in the final and greatest reality, that national strength lies only in the hearts and spirits of men.

— S. L. A. Marshall

❖   ❖   ❖

Crofton's Encyclopedia of the Inhabited Planets (2nd Edition):

Stora Mine: Mining settlement in the southern foothills of the *Kupros Mountains* (q.v.), north of *Lake Alexander* in the Upper

Valley section of the Eurotas river, on the planet *Sparta* (q.v.).
The initial CoDominium University survey of Sparta indicated
that the eroded volcano later christened *Storaberg* contained
unusual concentrations of metallic ores. Researchers
hypothesized that during the original uplift process which
produced the Kupros Mountains, a "plug" of freakishly
mineral-rich magma was extruded through a fissure. Over time,
the rapid erosive forces produced by Sparta's 1.22 G stripped
away the covering of softer rock, exposing the core and
depositing alluvial metal deposits extensively in the area. The
rock of northern slopes of the mountain contains up to 8%
copper, 6% lead, 2% silver and significant quantities of platinum,
palladium and thorium group metals; locally higher
concentrations are studded through the mass of the mountain
and nearby deposits of "ruddle" hematite have iron contents of
up to 83%. Exploratory mining began during the period of
CoDominium administration and full-scale exploitation
commenced with the chartering of Stora Mines Inc. in 2041.
Both open-pit and shaft mining is carried on; facilities include a
geothermal power plant, smelters and concentration plants, the
215-kilometer electrified railway to Lake Alexander, and
miscellaneous support, maintenance and repair industries.

Description: The settlement of Stora Mine lies on an eroded
peneplane at the northeastern edge of Storaberg Mt. Built-up
areas are largely confined to "ribbon" developments along the
valleys of the northeast-southwest tending ridges. The central
town is laid out on a grid basis, forming an H surrounding two
public squares, and includes a business district, public buildings
and the railroad station. Total population (2090) is 27,253,
including many temporary workers housed in company barracks.
Climate is severe, roughly analogous to northeastern Minnesota
or southern Siberia; the longer seasons make this a loose
comparison, however. The silt-filled basins and rocky hills of the
piedmont zone running down to the lakeshore have been
extensively developed to supply the mining labor force and enjoy
more moderate temperatures . . .

       ❖   ❖   ❖

There is a semi-facetious classification of officers long familiar
to many of the military fraternity. It does credit to the
understanding of its unknown originator as well as to his sense of
humor. Its lightly sketched implications when further explored
and a little amplified approached conclusions that are not so
humorous. Using the terms "brilliant," "energetic," "stupid," and
"lazy" and applying them to a selected group of people of whom

the stupidest and laziest may still be well above the average of brilliance and energy in the general community, a scale for measurement of certain aspects of individual military potential may be constructed. . . .

The Class Four officer we must study diligently, to devise the means of identifying him in, and eliminating him from, the military services. The combination of stupidity and energy is the formula of ambition other than a laudable kind. The ambition generated is too often entirely personal and totally unconcerned with any elements contributing to the general welfare that are not also an occasion of individual preferment . . . Morally courageous he is not, since this quality is all too often incompatible with personal ambition. Given experience, he may be to a degree learned. He may be cautious, crafty, cunning, and is seldom lacking in decisiveness, but he can never be wise, just, loyal, or completely honest. All too often he achieves a personally successful military career. Energetic stupidity, once invested with authority and allowed to accumulate experience, can do a convincing imitation of a hard driving professional soldier . . .

    — Joseph Maxwell Cameron, *The Anatomy of Military Merit*

      ❖   ❖   ❖

Winter still lay heavy on the southern slopes of the Kupros Mountains. The dawn was bright but hard, and the cold wind sighed mournfully through the branches of the dark pines and leafless birch-trees. These mountains were not as high as the Drakons; the quick erosion of a heavy-gravity world had scoured them down, although the peaks were still glacier-crowned fangs four thousand meters high. The lower slopes were a wilderness of canyon and gully badland, tumbled boulders larger than houses, rushing torrents and new forests just gaining a foothold amid the shattered granite and volcanic scree.

Skida Thibodeau sat looking thoughtfully down the long slope toward the foothills; Lake Alexander was invisible beyond. Cloud-shadow moved across the huge chaotic landscape, and the young sun tinged the snowdrifts with pink. An orderly handed her a cup of coffee, and she chewed on a ration bar, a leather of fruits and nuts. It was cold enough to make the hairs in her nostrils stick together when she inhaled, but snow might begin to melt by midafternoon; weather turned quickly this time of year in the Upper Valley.

"OK," she said after a moment. "Von Reuther, how are the troops?"

"Those in the latest wave from the Dales are now fully rested. The first arrifals are restless." The German-born ex-CD officer had been in charge of keeping the inflow inconspicuous until she arrived. "Some attempted to desert."

"We doan allow no deserters."

"Ja, we know how to deal with those." The German shrugged. "We have done so. But these are not regular soldiers, and we are short of non-commissioned officers. Too many were lost covering our retreat in the Dales."

"Hard fight, but we win in the Dales," Skilly said. "Victory there. Show we can stand up to the Cits."

"I agree. And so we tell the recruits," von Reuther said evenly. "But they were also told they will win soon. They believe this, but one does not learn patience in Welfare Island. The war goes on, for many longer than anything they have ever done in their miserable lives."

"You knew what kind of recruits you were getting," Skilly said. Her voice hardened. "You tell me you know how to make soldiers out of them. You say CoDo's been doing that for fifty years, taking gang-banger homeboys and making them Marines."

"And so we have, Field Prime. But we do not also hide from police while we train CoDominium Marines, ja? When they graduate they parade, people cheer, pretty girls admire uniforms. Not here." He straightened formally. "Field Prime, if you are not satisfied with my performance—"

"You not thinking of quitting on Skilly?" Everyone in the room stiffened, and tension mounted. Then, suddenly, she grinned wolfishly. "You doin' fine. Doan worry so much. Everything goin' just like we want."

The Helots had been moving men and supplies from the Dales to the Kupros in dribs and drabs since the midwinter battles. It was a long way from the Dales, north and east along the foothills. Longer when you had to move in small bodies and take extreme care not to be observed. The Kupros held few people away from the mining settlements, but there were ranches in the hill-and-basin country of the piedmont, and the odd trapper elsewhere.

"You want fighting, we do that, all right. Now listen up, everyone." The dozen or so commanders leaned closer. "Operational plans you all got, so Field Prime will tell you the general stuff again. We not trying to hold what we take, but this be no hit-and-run, either. Two overall objectives: temporary economic damage, maybe some loot, but mainly we demoralize the militia. Then it easier next time."

She dusted her hands, set the cup down on the pine needles and wrapped her arms around her knees. The hard wolfish faces about her were intent. Everything seemed very clear: von Reuther's methodical clock-mind making notes, Two-knife's rock solidness, Niles still with a little of the detached air — *not as much, maybe he getting over it; this fight show it one way or the other* — the others frowning a little. One of them raised a hand.

"Field Prime, the original planning called for maximum attack on off-world mining equipment. May I ask why that's been changed?" They were all aware of the importance of denying the Royalists foreign exchange to buy weapons systems.

"Because, Hernandez, due to our, ah, consultants, and other things which you got no need to know, the overall schedule been moved up. We be needing CD credits and Friedlander marks someday too. And maybe von Reuter getting them parades he wants sooner than we think."

Predatory grins at that. None of these men intended to live in caves for the rest of their lives.

"OK," Skilly continued. "So you got the schedule of targets, stuff they can replace but not quick. Now, basic, this is a terror raid. Remember, though, it *selective* terror. We has to show the workers they should be more afraid of us than the Royalists, and the Cits that fighting us is no way to protect their households — just the opposite, that the fact. *Useless if they think we kill everyone no matter what they do.* Understand me? We want to demoralize, not make cornered rats. Collateral damage in the course of operation be fine; any unauthorized murder, rape, looting or arson, I want punished quick and public and hard. Skilly will hang anyone not understand that.

"So," she went on, after meeting the eyes of each. "Next, we gots to have real careful timing. Troops, they full of beans and think they can lick the world, we convinced them we won the Dales fight. They believe that, doan matter what really happen." *And they do fight good. All of them.* For a moment she remembered the provisional companies left behind to protect the retreating leadership. *No omelets without eggs. Too many eggs that time, but Skilly learn.* "Good they got confidence, bad if they be getting the stuffing knocked out. Better we not believe our own propaganda; we still no able to fight the enemy on their own terms. We make them fight on *our* terms. First —"

❖   ❖   ❖

"It's a good computer system," the milita staff chief of Stora Mine said; the commander was out with the troops. "Only as good as the input, of course, but it does help us coordinate things on the security side."

"I see." Ace Barton was deliberately noncommittal.

They were a very long way indeed from Sparta City — seven thousand kilometers or more by river, about half that as the crow flew — in an area crucial to the war effort. The windows on one side of this room showed the reason why. The great openpit mine had been operating for fifty years, but it had only just begun to make a mark on the jagged side of the mountain, itself a lone outlier of the Kupros range that stretched across the northern horizon. A semicircular bite had been taken out of its side, stepping up the striated rock in smooth terraces; there were huge diesel-electric trucks at work there now, hauling down the ore blasted free from the face. Another charge went off, and hundreds of tonnes slid slowly down to lie in a rubbled pile. As the dust clouds settled, hundreds of overalled figures swarmed forward with pneumatic hammers, while others waited with scoop-loaders.

The manager — her name was Olafson — nodded when she noticed the direction of his eyes.

"Bit archaeological, the technique, but it's actually cheaper than sonic crushers and robots," she said cheerfully. "Cheaper than asteroid mining, even, *if* we watch the costs carefully. This is an unusual formation: copper, silver, thorium and platinum, iron, nickel. Mechanical crushing, then powdering, chemical separation, magnetic; we ship the easier stuff in ingot form down the railway to the lake, south to the Vulcan rapids by barge and then down to Olynthos over the railway around *those*. Powdered slurry along the same route for the more refractory materials. We run some shaft mines underground as well, and this is the collection point for a lot of independent outfits up in the hills." A scowl. "Or was, before the bandits got so bad."

She indicated the jagged line of the mountains.

"We've got a geothermal power station here as well, about 400 MW, so what with one thing and another we've become the second center of the Upper Valley, after Olynthos."

Anselm Barton had been examining the retrieval system; it was like much else on Sparta, a cobbled-together compromise. Bulky locally-made display monitors, rather than the thin-film liquid crystal units made elsewhere, and multiple terminals routed through ordinary laptops into the mainframe unit. That was a featureless cube about three times the size of a briefcase, hooked in turn to a databank about the same size.

"Earth-made?" he asked.

"Earth's systems are overpriced junk," Olafson replied with a snort; her civilian hat was deputy vice-president for operations of Storaberg Mines Inc. "No, from Xanadu. Thirty years old, and still works like a charm." She nodded again at his unspoken question. "Yes, we check for viral infiltration regularly, and we've had your people up on the link too, once a week. That what brings you here?"

"Part of it. We've brought some technicians along with us," Barton said. He was nervous about that. However careful these people were, they were working with old equipment and they were provincials. The Legion's own computers had Read Only Memory programming; efficient for military use, but not flexible enough for a civilian operation. *And Murasaki's technoninjas are just too damn good with computers.*

"Part of it. What's the rest of it?" she demanded. "You're here with your headquarters groups, Legionnaires at the landing field, and two battalions more on the way. Something's up?"

"Well, not really. Bit of paranoia. Here, show off your system."

"No problem," Olafson said. "Here's how we've

managed it. This system's got lots of capacity; we got it cheap, that's why we've got a central unit rather than a dispersed network."

She called up a map of the mine and area. "There are about six thousand people working for the Company, a thousand or so Citizens and long-term employees, the rest casuals. As many again in dependents, service industries and so forth. We've always had a Company police" — Storaberg Mines Inc. was owned by the managers and skilled employees, mostly — "which we've expanded to about five hundred men, with Citizen officers and light infantry weapons. Your Captain Alana's people checked them; we spotted half a dozen Helot plants among the recruits, and hanged them to discourage others."

"This perimeter?" Barton asked, drawing a finger along a dotted line.

The whole installation was spread out over kilometers of rough country, patches of housing or machinery sheds in pockets of flat ground separated by forest and rocky hills.

"Well, that's the problem. It's hard enough to get people to live up here anyway, you couldn't at all if you tried to cram them in cheek-to-jowl. We've got first-rate all-weather roads, though." A true rarity on Sparta, outside the capital and some of the larger towns.

"The perimeter guard is sensors and detectors, with blockhouses here" — points sprang out — "manned by the security force and by militia on rotation. If there's an alarm, all the Citizens and the reliable non-Citizens and their families concentrate here, in the Armory, or at assembly-points throughout the settlement, and move to where they're needed. All the real non-combatants, kids and so forth, head for the Armory; it's massive, mostly underground, with a cleared field of fire all around. Not that we expect an attack *here*, of course, the Helots haven't been within fifty kilometers of us, but we're also the coordinating point for the other mining settlements, and the farmlands and ranches all around the north shore of Lake Alexander. There are more of them than you'd expect, with the mines to feed. There's good land up here, it just doesn't come in big blocks like it does down in the Valley.

"And then," she continued, "we've got the woods all around the mine sown thickly with disguised sonic and visual sensors; anything suspicious is routed directly through here and to the relevant perimeter posts. Minefields all around; multiple-use, they can be set for command detonation or sonic, thermal or vibrational triggers — cost a fortune."

Barton nodded. "Okay. Now let's look at that perimeter."

"Now?"

"No time like the present." He led the way outside the room and down the corridor toward the coffee room. When they got there he ushered her inside despite her surprise, and closed the door behind him. A Legion sergeant had set up equipment on the lunch table.

"Secure, Andy?"

"Yes, sir. There was a bug, but I sort of stepped on it."

"Bug? In here?" Karen Olafson stared at the red-haired headquarters sergeant. "Are you sure?"

"Damn sure. You put it there, right?" The sergeant stared menacingly at her.

"What? General Barton—"

"She's okay, sir," Sergeant Andrew Bielskis said, continuing to study the console he had set up on the table. "That's genuine shock reaction."

"Right. Was there a bug in here, Andy?"

"Not in here, sir. But there's a couple in the corridor, and I'll bet my arse the computer system's been penetrated. Ma'am, if you'd just put your hand on this plate for me. Now the other hand here. Excellent. How's the weather outside? Know any Helots?"

Fury and curiosity were fighting it out on Karen Olafson's face. Curiosity won. "All right, General, what *is* this?"

Barton got another nod from Sergeant Bielskis. "They're planning something," Ace said. "Something big, from the number of troops they've been infiltrating into this area. Damned near a regiment."

"I — how do you know that?"

"Luck. Good and bad luck. The good luck was one of their deserters got to sleeping with a local girl, one night tried to warn her to get away before this week. Bad luck was local intelligence decided not to risk sending it on the wire—"

"Or telling me," Karen said indignantly.

"Yes, ma'am. But it took a week for the report to reach Captain Alana. Since then we've seeded some of Mace's scouts into the area. Something's up, all right. Something big and ugly."

"Oh, God— You said 'this week.' "

"Yep. So. First thing I want you to do is shut things down," Barton said. "Close off all mine operations while we do some security checks. Do it slow, make it look like routine maintenance, but start buttoning up and getting your irreplaceables secured, and I mean start right now. I'm particularly worried about that computer system. You rely on it too much."

"We can't operate without it—"

"Exactly. Andy, I want Jenny and her techs to go over this place and put in manual backups for the security stuff, especially all the control systems. That bloody computer is a point failure threat, and I don't like it. It goes down, we have a hell of a job controlling things."

"Yes, sir. We'll start in the morning—"

"No, Sergeant, you'll start tonight," Ace Barton said. "And we'll just damned well pray it's not too late."

❖   ❖   ❖

Warrant Officer Jennifer Schramm poured coffee and sprawled in a plastic chair that couldn't have been very comfortable. It was well after midnight.

"You look like you can use a break," Ace Barton said.

"General, that's a fact."

"How much have you got done?"

"About half of it," she said. "I've got manual activation lines for the mine fields. Some bypass communications, but we're running out of optical fiber."

"More coming in tomorrow," Barton said. "What does the computer know you've done?"

"Nothing, sir. Well, it knows we shut down its access to some controls for a while, but as far as it's concerned everything's normal again. What we did, we've jury rigged a manual control console. Throw a couple of big switches and the computer's bypassed, you've got manual control." She sipped coffee. "Frankly, General, I'm amazed at how much they trusted to that damn computer."

"Think it's been penetrated?"

"I *know* it has been."

Ace frowned. "How do you know?"

"Well, I don't really, but I feel it. Fault logs. They're squeaky clean, General Barton, and I don't like that. It's like something was erased, maybe. Same for access records. Some of them are missing."

"Missing?"

"Yes, sir. Again, it just looked too damn clean so I

got Andy to have a talk with a couple of the techs, and of course they were playing war games on the damn computer — and there's no record of it. Like someone wiped the access record files."

"The techs—"

"No, sir. Look, playing games might get them docked an hour's pay at worst, if anyone really gave a damn, but erasing logs, that's a firing offense, and they bloody know it."

Barton touched his communication card. "Wally."

"Honistu here."

"Wally, take a break. Come drink some coffee and put your feet up."

"Well, a little busy, but that sounds right, sir."

Jennifer looked a question.

Barton smiled. "Right. Wally's been with me a long time. My adjutant in Barton's Bulldogs. Way I asked him made it an order."

"You really think they're listening to everything?" Jennifer asked.

Ace shrugged. "This room's secure, don't know about the rest. Tell you this, if the computer's bugged, the control room is. And Andy found a bug in the corridor. It shouldn't have been there, not smart to put one there."

"Too easy to find?"

"Something like that. Not obvious, but not that hard to find either. Almost like maybe it's an early warning? Maybe so when we disable it they know we've found it? I don't know. I can't think the way the rebels do."

Major Honistu came in and closed the door. "I'm damn busy, General. What's up?"

"Sit down, Wally, and let's talk a minute. Jenny doesn't like what she's finding in the computer. More like what she's not finding."

Honistu nodded judicially. "I got the same ugly

feeling, General. Add in the intelligence reports, and we got problems."

"Right. What you're doing out there is important, but so is doing a bit of thinking while we have the chance. Let's talk."

❖   ❖   ❖

Alarms rang in the corridor.

"That'll be it," Ace Barton said. "OK, Wally, get moving. I'll be in central control." He led Warrant Officer Schramm up the corridor while Honistu ran off in the other direction.

Karen Olafson sat at the central console. An alarm *wheeped* softly, and one screen blinked red. She looked up as Barton came in. "Emergency Network. The Torrey estate is under attack."

The screen showed a man in combat armor thrown on over indoor clothes. Tall, with rather long brown hair and a flamboyant mustache, in his thirties.

"Alan, this is General Barton."

"Barton. Alan Torrey here," he said; he spoke with the accent of an American of the taxpayer class. "I'm definitely under attack, by a company or better. They overran the RSMP post up at the Velysen place, then hit here. We stopped them butt-cold."

A grim smile; Barton decided that he rather *liked* Citizen Alan Torrey.

"All my people are armed, I won't employ anyone I can't trust. That gives us nearly a hundred guns, and we've been preparing for this. The problem is the Militia reaction-force from Danniels Mill; they came running, and hit an ambush about four kilometers south of here. Had to fight their way off the road and onto a hill; they've taken better than fifty casualties, and they need help bad. I can't do it, we're holding in our bunkers but if we come out their mortars will slaughter us."

A man burst through the door of the operations control center. He was hastily buckling on armor. "General alert, Karen. General, we're sure glad you're here."

"My husband and partner," Karen said.

"Karl Olafson, general co-manager and Major of the 22nd Brotherhood, for my sins. Alan, can you give me a relay?"

"Here."

This time the screen split. "Captain Solarez here, Major Timmins is down." The new figure was crouched in a shallow hole behind a rock, with a wounded communications tech lying beside him and operating the pickup. Small-arms and explosions sounded from the background.

"Report, Captain," the militia Major said.

"I've got thirty dead, sixty wounded and three hundred effectives, that counts the walking wounded. We had to leave most of our heavy weapons with the transport. The enemy have us under visual observation and they're sending us heavy fire, medium mortars, 84 and 105mm recoilless rifles, heavy machine guns. Nothing fancy but they've got plenty of it. We've beaten off one attack already, in company strength."

A map of the militia position came up; squares indicated possible enemy dispositions. The Brotherhood fighters held a dome-shaped rise, as high as anything in the vicinity; the road wound past it, following the low ground up from the shores of the lake. The gap into the sedimentary basin that held the Torrey estate was still two kilometers north and west, but the picture-pickup showed columns of smoke from that direction.

"Major, I can hold here but not forever," the captain went on. "We've no water except the canteens, very little in the way of other supplies, and I'm taking steady losses. Either someone tries to pull us out, or we'll have to fight our way through to the Torrey's. This is obviously bigger than we thought."

"Hold," Karl Olafson said. "We'll come get you."

Ace Barton spoke. "What do you have on hand, Major?" he asked.

"Our security battalion, Brigadier," the miner replied. "There's another Brotherhood reaction-force battalion here, mobilizing now, I'll leave those. We've got a little surprise, a six-gun battery of 155mm gun-howitzers, just up from the von Alderheim plant in Olynthos. And plenty of trucks, we'll take the mine vehicles. Pick up more infantry at the rally-point at Danniels Mill, and mounted scouts to cover our flanks."

Barton picked his words with care; interfering in the local chain of command was not something to be done lightly. "This isn't going to be anything you can handle," he said. "They're risking too much for just a raid. They've got something much bigger in mind. The mine itself, for a guess. You go out there and they'll ambush you just like they did the original relief force."

Major Olafson nodded. "We'll be careful. And counting the second-line people and the perimeter guardposts, that still leaves the equivalent of a complete rifle-regiment here. It's a chance, sir," he said. "But one we've got to take."

Barton signed agreement; that instant concern was a weakness of these friends-and-neighbors militia outfits, as well as a strength.

"Hell," the militia officer went on, "with nearly a thousand men and artillery, I don't think we'll have much trouble chewing up anything they send at us."

Barton had been writing on a pad of engineering paper. He handed that to Olafson. DON'T REPLY TO

THIS. THIS ROOM IS BUGGED. GO FIND MAJOR
HONISTU AND PAY ATTENTION TO HIM. "I expect
you're right," Barton said aloud. He tapped the paper
again. "Not much can happen to a force that size.
Godspeed, then. Who'll hold operational command
here?"

"I was hoping you would, sir."

"Right." Barton wrote quickly. VITAL YOU SEE
HONISTU. He watched Olafson leave and turned back
to the console. *Bad luck. Not enough time to make a
real plan. I've got a bad feeling about this one.*

⋄   ⋄   ⋄

"Good," Skida murmured to herself.

Her face-shield was showing the input from a
pickup three kilometers south. An armored car led out
the gate between two pillboxes, trailed by a huge boxy
mine-clearing vehicle. Trucks followed it, 6x6 models
crowded with infantry in mottled-white winter
camouflage and Nemourlon armor; they towed heavy
mortars or two-wheel carts with ammunition and
supplies. A string of them, and then two of the big ore
trucks. Those pulled cannon, medium jobs with the
long barrels turned and clamped over the trails, riding
on four-wheeled carriages. More trucks . . .

She turned to the Meijians clustered around their
equipment. "This had better work," she grated.

One of them looked up and bowed slightly. "We are
downloading into the enemy mainframe even now,
Field Prime," he said politely. "There will be too little
time for the enemy to react."

As was explained before, went unspoken. The
Legion techs were doing random sweeps of the more
vital Royal Army machines, of which the Stora Mine
was one. No way to leave the pirate taps in for any
length of time.

She grunted assent and turned to a display table

showing an overview of the mine and town. Too much
here depended on the Meijians; too much on the
NCLF's secret apparat. Neither the technoninjas nor
Croser's people had ever failed her seriously before . . .
but this was the first time so large a Helot force had
depended on them so totally.

And we not just fighing the hicks. Barton. Barton
suspected something. *What was he doing here? How
much could he know?* She tried to remember what
she'd been told about Brigadier Barton. Older than
Owensford but subordinate, could something be
made of that? *Bad sign he here. Shouldn't be here. Not
now, not when things critical.*

Even in the Dales battle there had always been the
option of pulling back; they had never been so deeply
committed that the enemy could have destroyed them
all, although it had been necessary to sacrifice the better part of two battalions to get the leadership cadre
out. Now they had to attack, attack an immensely
strong defensive position with forces that were barely
superior to the Royalists even with the diversion drawing off some of their strength.

No way Skilly can win a straight fight here, she
thought. *She would need five times the troops and
more equipment for that.* But if they lost this time, the
Movement's edge would be blunted, perhaps forever.
The thought of losing the instrument she had worked
so long and hard to forge made her stomach feel tight
and sour; with an effort of will, she made her hand
stop its instinctive desire to rub soothingly. . . . *Armor
would stop it anyway.*

Niles gave her a grin and a thumbs-up; he looked
better now that combat was near and there was no
time to brood. That was another anxiety, she had serious doubts whether the Englishman had thought
through the implications of her orders.

He toughen up a lot, she thought. *Now we see if it enough.*

❖   ❖   ❖

"Where's Fatima, Eddie?"

The mechanic jerked at the voice and rolled his trolley out from under the truck. The sirens were still wailing across the maintenance compound parking-lot.

"Ah, she's sick," he said, looking up and wiping his hands on an oily rag. "I came down to see the vehicle park was ready."

Christ, I hope I didn't hit her too hard, he thought. She was a good boss, and no more a Citizen than he was. Had been the one to get him the assistant maintenance chief's job, too. But you didn't retire from the Movement, and when it gave you the word you obeyed. Or died, and your family with you, wherever you tried to hide.

Christ, how did I ever get into this? Shit, shit, shit. I don't want to kill anybody. Not even the Cits, hell the ones here haven't been so bad —

The man in militia uniform looked around; fifteen 4x4s, another ten 6x6s. Stora Mine was lavishly equipped with mechanical transport by Spartan standards, since you couldn't haul ore by horse-drawn wagon; even with the mobile Brotherhood force gone, there were still scores of trucks and vans in the settlement, a fair number of private cars as well. The emergency plan called for his two ready companies to billet here, able to reinforce anywhere in the sprawling complex.

"They OK?" the Citizen-soldier said, jerking his head toward the transports.

"Sure, sir. Ticking over normal, but I just wanted to check. You know what's happening?"

"Goddam rebels've attacked a ranch, the boss took some people out to put them down," the militiaman said.

More militia were coming up, and at a wave from the commander began loading prepositioned packs of weapons and equipment on the trucks.

"Nothing wrong here?" the mechanic asked; a man with a wife and a new baby had a right to sound worried.

Why did I listen to that bastard Sverdropov? First it had been little things, turning a blind eye to a crate on a run down to the lake, passing messages, just more union work Sverdropov said, and he'd been sore-headed back then after the last outfit he was with broke a strike with scabs. The Movement had gotten him his first job here . . . Then bigger things, and when he baulked they threatened to turn him in, then it was hanging offenses and he *had* to keep going.

"Nah, just playing safe," the militiaman said; he looked worried, but not very. "You'd better get to your shelter station, but thanks for checking, Eddie. Give my regards to Mary."

"No problem, sir," the mechanic said, zipping the equipment bag and walking toward the office with a friendly wave to the nearest troops. Sweat trickled down his ribs from his armpits despite the cold, as the left-over bombs clinked in the duffle.

❖ ❖ ❖

Legion Corporal (Headquarters Adjutant Staff) Perry Blackbird was in his last enlistment before retirement. He'd been too old to go with the Legion to New Washington. In fact he was plenty old enough to rate a desk job at headquarters, but Andy Bielskis had asked him to come along on this job. "Got a feeling on this one, Perry. Can use your nose," Bielskis had said.

And Andy had the best nose in the Legion. Perry had watched Andy grow up in the Legion. He and Andy's father had been sergeants together. Of course that was back in Blackbird's drinking days, when he went up to sergeant and back down to PFC with seasonal regularity. Now with his seniority he was paid as much as a sergeant, and he didn't have any command responsibilities, which was the way he liked it. What with Jeanine married to a farmer and Clara dead these five years, he lived alone and he'd been getting crustier and more set in his ways. "Do me good to get out," he'd told Andy. "Hell, somebody's got to watch out for you."

And there was something wrong here. Perry Blackbird wasn't sure what, but things didn't feel right. *Maybe it's I know Major Barton is worried sick, and Andy ain't too happy.* His instructions were to nose around, see how these militia carried out procedure, watch for anything suspicious, see what he could improve.

Now he watched as the mechanic went into the office. Then he turned to the militia sergeant. "Is that standard, a civilian mechanic workin' your motor pool?"

"Well, sure, this is a mine, not everyone is militia. Eddie's a sorehead sometimes, but he's all right." The Citizen sergeant's voice had an edge to it. Plainly he didn't think they needed any outsiders to tell them how to operate.

"Standard procedure during an alert is nobody's alone with a truck he ain't going to ride in," Blackbird said. "Don't you do that here?"

"Well, sure, but who the hell follows procedure all the time? Never get anything done that way."

"You like this Eddie?"

"He's all right."

"Trust him, do you? With the lives of your troops?"

"Sure — what are you getting at?"

"Why isn't he militia?"

"I don't know, never asked. What the hell do you think you're getting at?"

"Nothing, Sarge, nothing at all. But I sure am glad it

ain't me getting into one of them trucks. Have fun, Sarge." He touched his comm card. "Andy, I'm going into the maintenance office, I may need help. Send me a couple MPs, and maybe you better come a-running."

He left the militiaman staring at his back.

❖   ❖   ❖

"Captain Mace," Barton said.

The Scout commander looked up from the plotting board. The Legion techs had set up their own battle tech system in the computer center that doubled as militia HQ. "Sir."

Barton typed at his own console. "HAVE THEY FOUND THE BUGS IN HERE?"

"TWO."

"THINK THAT'S ALL?"

"NEGATIVE."

Aloud he said, "How long would it take to string landlines of our own between the perimeter bunkers, HQ, and the main interior points?"

"About a day, using all the men, sir," Mace said.

"I think we should get on that as soon as this fracas is over," Barton said.

"Sir."

Christ I'm no goddam actor. "FIND THOSE DAMN BUGS!!!" he typed. "Meantime, collect our spare communicators, and send one to the commander's bunkers. And the power and communications buildings."

"Aye, aye, sir."

Barton turned to the screens. The local militia had mobilized with smooth efficiency, fanning out to their duty posts. Second-line Brotherhood personnel were seeing the families and children to the Armory; an immensely strong position, dug into solid rock and surrounded by pillboxes. *And I don't like this one damned bit.*

"Get me the relief column."

Karl Olafson's face showed, looking up from the tail of a truck set up as a command post. From somewhere outside the field of vision came an unmistakable *booooom*, heavy artillery in action.

"Report, Major."

"Light resistance on the way here, sir. Mines, and snipers, a lot of them with Peltast rifles" — which had considerable antivehicle capacity — "we lost the armored car, and the mine-clearing vehicle is damaged. We had to stop and deploy several times, but we've pushed through to within firing range of the trapped reaction force, and with them to observe we're shooting the rebels out of their positions."

"Are you in ground contact?"

"I think so, at least, my forward patrols are running into them. Infantry screens."

"Resistance?"

"They're giving a stiff fight and then pulling back. Laying mines as they go." The militia officer grimaced, and the mercenary nodded. That was something of a Helot trademark. "But they don't have time to set complete nets, or equipment for air-delivered stuff."

Odd, Barton thought. The enemy had repeatedly shown they *did* have some capacity in that field. Not an unlimited one, but this was a fairly important action. Certainly the largest battle in the Upper Valley so far. One of the few where the Helots had operated in battalion strength.

"And they're keeping their mortars on the reaction force position, mostly."

More understandable. Causing maximum Citizen casualties seemed to be a strategic aim of the enemy high command, and the pinned-down force was a concentrated, sitting target. *And I still don't like it*. "All right, Major, carry on, but keep me in the loop."

"Yes, sir. I expect to break up the enemy concentration within the next few hours, and pursue their elements as they split up and withdraw."

Barton leaned back in the chair. *That ought to be that*, he thought. The screens showed orderly activity, the last of the children going down the elevators at the armory . . .

His Legion console screen lit. "SERGEANT BIELSKIS REPORTS REACTION FORCE VEHICLES MAY BE SABOTAGED. POSSIBLY BOMBS ABOARD. IT IS CONFIRMED THAT BOMBS WERE PLACED IN MOBILE RESERVE VEHICLES."

"Jesus Christ," Barton said.

"Sir?" Olafson said.

"Major, this computer's showing something odd. I've got a terrain plot. You see that secondary road off to your left there?"

"Yes, sir?"

"Dismount your men and go investigate it."

"Sir?"

"Now, Major. Go take a look yourself."

"General, that will delay us—"

"Major, indulge me. It won't take five minutes. I don't quite know what this thing is trying to tell me, and I'd rather have you go in strength. Now get moving, please. And stay on line with me."

Olafson reacted to the tone of command. "Yes, sir. Captain, dismount the unit, please—"

Dear God, let them get out of those trucks and I'll buy the biggest damned Easter candle—Bloody Hell. That perimeter monitor's repeating, I saw those rabbits move exactly the same way last *time I looked.* His hand reached for a button. It was 1045, exactly.

❖   ❖   ❖

"OK, shut it down, just leave the pumps working," the foreman said. "We'll pop that rockface when the alert's off."

He had half-turned when the prybar struck him behind the ear. Then he was staring at the wet stone of the tunnel floor; there was time for a moment of surprise before something hit the back of his head. The last sound he heard was crumpling bone.

"Come on, we gotta get everything in place before 1050!" the man who had struck him hissed. The six men in hard hats and overalls began taking bricks of *plastique* from their carryalls. Two of them began shoving extra loads of dynamite down the holes bored into the glistening black stone of the stope-face.

"Pumps, transformers and the conveyor," the man continued, looking nervously back over his shoulder at the long tunnel that lead towards the cage of the mine's shaft-elevator.

"Won't nobody notice the body?" one of the workers asked.

"No way, when we pop her they'll be boiling mud all through here." He glanced at his watch. "Come *on*, we've only got five minutes!"

❖   ❖   ❖

"Here, you, what're you doing there?" the power-plant supervisor asked. "This isn't your workstation."

The turbine room was quiet, except for the ever-present humming of the rotors, but that was more felt than heard. He was the only one of the supervisory staff here, most of the rest were in the militia . . .

The overalled figure at the steam inlet rose and turned. Consciously the supervisor felt only surprise; drilled reflex made him draw his sidearm as he saw the man pull a machine-pistol from his carryall. Brotherhood training brought it up two-handed, *crack-crack-crack* and the worker was spinning away with red blotches on his clothing. Hands came around the turbine housing behind the muzzle of another submachinegun, and the supervisor dropped flat as 10mm bullets slapped through the air where his chest had been, whined off metal.

Jesus God, that'll blow the steam pipe! he thought, returning fire, looking at the brick of plastic explosive. The whole floor would be flooded with superheated water from the boreholes that slanted down into the magma.

More bullets, and feet were moving off on the floor somewhere.

Two of them, he thought, snapping a new magazine into the pistol and scuttling backward. The pulse hammered in his ear, but there was no time to be dazed. *Got to report.*

There was five meters of open space between the turbine he was using as cover and the control room. The supervisor took a deep breath and leapt, rolling the last two meters. Lead flicked pits from the concrete at his back, and shattered through the windows as he sprawled through the door of the control room and slammed the metal portal behind him. Glass starred and shifted above him as he crawled to the communicator console and reached up from below; fragments cascaded over him when he reached it, as one of the attackers put another clip through the windows. He shielded his face with his gun arm and keyed the unit.

"Mine Central, Powerhouse One, rebel attack, rebel attack!"

"I am sorry, your call cannot be completed as sent. Please indicate your call direction and try again."

"God damn you!" Panic button. The Legion guys had put in a panic button. It was just over there. His legs didn't want to work, but he could still drag himself across the floor to the desk, reach up and slap the button.

Alarms hooted. Somewhere off in the distance he heard shouts.

"Move, damn you!"

"God damn it, there wasn't 'sposed to be any

mother fucking alarms," someone shouted. "Let's get the fuck out of here!"

"Hey you, shithead, get your ass back here—"

"Fuck off."

"Who's there? Sergeant, what the hell, get the Old Man! There's rebels in here. Officer of the Guard! Power house!"

There were shots, and more people shouting, and it all faded away.

◇　　◇　　◇

It was a thousand meters of rocky open field from the bunker's lip to the beginning of the woods. Brotherhood Lieutenant Hargroves squinted through the IR scanner and frowned in puzzlement.

"Brother Private Diego, you *sure* the audio sensors don't pick up anything? I got stuff moving around out there. What's on the visuals?"

"Nothing, sir. Birds, deer . . . big herd of deer. Sound and sight."

"Yeah, that might be it, but I'm not counting on it. Anything from the patrol?"

"Regular check-in blips, sir."

"Get me Central."

He picked up the microphone. "Central, this is Lieutenant Hargroves. I've got some funny readings on my direct view sensors but they don't match with the stuff through you. Could you check it? And I'd like to send out another patrol."

"Report acknowledged," a voice said. *Captain Olafson, right enough,* the militiaman thought.

"Yes, ma'am, but can I send out the patrol?"

"I'm sure you can handle it, Lieutenant?"

He frowned, uncertain. "But the *patrol,* ma'am?"

"I have full confidence in you, Lieutenant. Remember to maintain radio communications silence under all circumstances." A click.

Bullshit. There's something damned wrong here. "Hell — get me the Captain."

"No answer, sir. It's ringing through but nobody's picking it up."

"The *hell* you say!" Nobody answering in the company command bunker? "Fire up the radar! Get the damned lights on!"

"Sir, standing orders —"

"*Do* it, Diego! Everybody, stand to your guns. Markham, get on the minefield circuit."

"Shit! Sir, multiple metal contacts within three thousand meters. Multiple!"

He keyed the helmet radio. "Captain, are you there?"

"Hargroves, what the hell are you doing calling me on the hailing frequency *again*?"

"Captain, I didn't — Sir, the landlink's down and I've got radar traces —"

"Down? You reported in on it not five minutes ago!"

The desperate voice of the communications tech broke in. "Sir, we're being targeted, designator lasers and —"

Something blinked out of the sky at them behind a trail of fire. There was an explosion on the roof of the bunker that threw them all to the floor, loud enough to jar the senses.

"Radar's gone, radar's gone!"

Hargroves leapt up and to the observation slit. Men were coming out of the woods. Rocket trails slammed down out of the sky to his left and right, and more from positions among the trees. The bunker shook under repeated impacts, and he could hear screaming in the background.

"Open —"

Another streak of fire. He had time to drop down and wrap his arms around his head, before there was a slamming impact and a violet light loud enough to show through his clenched eyelids. Powdered concrete made him choke and gag, while savage heat washed across the backs of his hands. Blast bounced him back and forth in the right-angle of wall and floor. When he opened his eyes a single tear-blurred glance showed that there was nobody else alive in this chamber. He staggered erect, head and shoulders out of the gaping semicircle that *something* had bitten through the observation slit of the bunker, and keyed the helmet radio again.

"Perimeter six, under rocket attack! Answer me, somebody, *please*, they're through the wire —"

A high-pitched jamming squeal drove into his eardrums. Armed men were swarming out of the woods; a long blade of flame showed as a recoiless rifle fired, and the bunker shook again. None of the gatlings was firing. Bangalore torpedoes erupted beneath the coils of razor wire, and the enemy poured through as the earth was still falling back. They came running, screaming.

Hargroves slapped the audio intake of his helmet to zero, leaving the mike open as he wiped at the blood running down from his nose. "Minefields inoperative," he shouted, bringing up his rifle. *Aim low. Fire. One down.* "Perimeter five and four not supporting." A saw-edged *brrrrrt. brrrrrt.* came from his left, then ceased. "Correction, five still maintaining fire. Enemy is in at least battalion strength. The mine fields are inoperative. I have no reaction for—"

◆ CHAPTER NINE

If one has never personally experienced war, one cannot understand why a commander should need any brilliance and exceptional ability. Everything looks simple. Everything in war is very simple, but the simplest thing is difficult. The difficulties accumulate and end by producing a kind of friction that is inconceivable. Countless minor incidents — the kind you can never really foresee — combine to lower the general level of performance, so that one always falls far short of the intended goal.

— Clausewitz, *On Strategy*

◆　◆　◆

"Field Prime, Attack Force one here. Bunker secured," Niles said.

And I'm glad, he thought fervently. Running forward across a minefield that might be activated any moment had not been one of the more pleasant experiences of his life, with only a piece of intrusive software between him and being shredded into a dozen pieces.

The bunker listed as six on his map was more of a tangled depression of earth and crumbled ferroconcrete now, the sappers had made sure with a cratering charge centered right on the twisted wreckage of the radar pickups. There were more thumping crashes behind him, as they laid strip charges to clear real as well as virtual paths through the mines.

"This Field Prime. Proceed with Phase Two."

Niles stood, waved his hand in a circle around his head and chopped it south; the jamming that bolixed the enemy's small-unit push was unfortunately affecting their own, as well. The off-world helmetcom systems could filter it, but there were only enough of those for senior commanders. Squads rose and dashed by him, heading into the open parkland that separated the perimeter bunkers from the interior villages of the Stora Mine. The men were bowed under their burdens, bundles of Friedlander target-seeker missiles, satchel charges, flamethrowers. Others were swinging right and left, lugging machine-guns and portable gatlings, setting up blocking positions to prevent the intact bunkers from sortieing and closing the quarter-arc wedge the Helots had driven into the north face of the mine's defenses.

"Am advancing. Phase Two in progress," he said. The headquarters company had formed about him. "Follow me!"

❖   ❖   ❖

"Broadband jamming, sir," Legion Signal Corps Corporal Hiram Klingstauffer said cooly, hands dancing across his controls. "I can filter it."

"Right," Barton said. *Breath in. Breath out. Surprise is an event that takes place in the mind of a commander.* No antiradiation missiles available to him up *here*, though. The replacement shipments for the ones lost in the Dales were still on their way. The enemy's logistics seemed to operate much faster . . .

He strode over to the window and used a chair to smash out the thick double panes; cold air flooded in, and the sound of explosions and small-arms fire. Most loudly from the north, but there were flashes and crumping sounds from all around the perimeter, and that was the most accurate information he was likely to get for a while. Lights flashed and died over the mine-works south of the town as the 24-hour arclamps went off. Barton wheeled and looked at the computer displays.

Power Central. A peaceful, unmarked control booth, distance shots of humming machinery and workers attending it.

Perimeter. A light blinked on, and a militia major's voice shouted: "Long live the Revolution!"

Karen Olafson recoiled as if it had bitten her.

"Turn it off," Barton said. She looked at him blankly. "It's in enemy hands, nothing but disinformation. Forget the damned thing." He went to the Legion console and threw the big switch at the top. Lights winked. "I'm taking manual control of the defenses." *Of what Jenny's crew managed to rig, anyway. God damn it, we needed another week.* He pushed that thought aside. What he needed didn't matter any more. It was what he had that counted.

First things first. Puzzle out just what did which. There was a crude map above the manual console. Right. Infiltrators attacking the power house. Activate the minefields, detonate on contact. North side first, that's where the noise is. He threw the switch.

The response was instant. A dozen blasts, lights flared near the power house, along the whole north periphery. More explosions. Blasts all along the inner perimeter swath. Then more, in the park areas.

"What's happening?" Karen Olafson demanded.

"Somebody was where he shouldn't have been," Ace said absently. "Some of those were secondary explosions. Think you can get that thing working again?"

"I can try. I'll dump it and reboot from WORM."

WORM. Write Once, Read Many, Barton remembered. Computers weren't his specialty, but this was supposed to be a way to make sure nobody tampered with data because once it was burned into a glass disk it didn't get written over.

"Security systems only. *Now!*" Her hands moved, with gathering speed. Blood trickled down her chin from a bitten lip. The screens went blank, flickered, came back up with nothing but a red = sign in a black circle, the Helot banner. Then they flickered again and stayed blank.

"Sir," Klingstauffer said calmly. "I'm getting radio from all the militia units. They're questioning withdrawal orders they've received, demanding confirmations. The Captain in charge of Perimeter 10 through 14 registers that he is withdrawing as ordered but under protest."

"Give me a broadband over ride. In clear."

"Sir."

"Karen, turn that damn computer off. Never mind trying to restart it. Shut it down so it doesn't send out any more orders."

"Right," Karen said.

"Here's your general channel, General. No problem with the direct wires, but they're jamming hell out of radio."

"Right. No harm trying." Ace keyed the mike. "ALL UNITS, ALL UNITS, THIS IS GENERAL BARTON." *Calm, Ace, they won't hear any better if you shout. Or will they* — "Klingstauffer, send for some bull horns." He keyed the mike again. "All units, you are on your own, I say again, all commanders, ignore any other instructions, take command of your units. Act as you think best under the circumstances. The central computer system is compromised, I say again the central computer is compromised. Look around you, react to what you see, and kill the sons of bitches. Relay these orders to any other units you can find."

"Klingstauffer, get that message going on a continuous loop, general broadcast."

"Sir."

"And get runners going with bull horns to repeat it anywhere and anyhow they can."

"Right."

Barton went to the Legion direct line console. It was difficult to tell what he had there. Direct lines, but to where— He keyed one. Nothing. A second. "This is Barton, Command Central. What do I have?"

"Captain Trent, vehicle reserve. God damn, General, I'm glad to hear from you!"

"What's your status?"

"We're on foot, sir. Vehicles sabotaged, your man found out just in time, lost a truck and some troopers, it was real bad, real bad, but—"

"TRENT!"

"Yes, sir."

"Get hold of yourself. What's your status?"

"Sir. Sir, I have two companies of dismounted infantry. Five percent casualties."

"Right. Like it or not, Captain Trent, you have the only effective force I can communicate with. Captain, the mine's under attack. The perimeter's been penetrated at the north sector, possibly elsewhere. We have unreliable communications, and many of the militia have been given false orders by the central computer. Do you understand?"

"No, sir."

"Good man. I'll explain it. The central computer was briefly taken over by the enemy, Captain. God knows what it told your people to do. We have shut it down."

"Oh —"

"Right. So the one thing we do know is, they're inside the perimeter in the north sector, possibly stations 10 through 14 as well."

"Yes, sir?"

"So you've got to do something about it. First thing, get the word to all unit commanders. Two items. Item one, the mine fields are active again. Chase the bastards into the mines. Item two, all unit commanders are on their own. Act as they think best. You got that?"

Captain Trent sounded scared, but he said, "Sir. Instruct all units, disregard previous orders, act on their own judgment. And the mine fields are active again."

"That's it, son. Now take a deep breath, think about what you're going to do, and do it. You'll be fine."

"Yes, sir."

"Are any Legion people there?"

"There's a sergeant—"

"Get moving on your instructions, then put him on. And leave a communications squad to man this line at all times."

"Sir." Trent left the mike activated when he put it down. Ace Barton could hear him shouting orders in the background.

Scared as hell, but he's making sense.

"Major Olafson, weak signal," Klingstauffer said.

"Barton here. Olafson, the mine is under attack, the perimeter's penetrated, north side for certain, possibly other areas. Your vehicles may have been sabotaged. Check for bombs. Then cancel your present mission and defend the mine. I say again, the mine's under attack, your vehicles may have been sabotaged. Your instructions are to abandon your present position and return to defend the mine. Did you get all that?"

Hissing and buzzing. "— penetrated. — under attack —"

Nothing about checking vehicles. Damn. Ace repeated his instructions.

"Nothing," Klingstauffer said.

"Did we get through?"

"God knows."

"Repeat those orders, and pray." *Jesus, I could go broke buying candles and altar flowers.*

The direct line squawked. "Sergeant Bielskis, sir."

"What happened down there, Andy?"

"Turncoat, sabotaged the trucks. Blackbird smelled a rat. We've got him. Captain Trent's scared but he's steadying down."

"What I needed to hear. Andy, about that traitor. Keep him. I want him alive, Andy. That's really important."

"Yes, sir. He's scared, keeps talking about how they'll kill his family, wife and little girl—"

"Name?"

"Edward L. Bishop. Wife is Mary Margaret Ryan Bishop. Son Patrick James Bishop, age 2 months."

"Can you get his family into protective custody?"

"No, sir, they're with the other noncombatants in the main bunker."

"Best place for them. OK, Andy, you're on your own. I got other problems."

"Record this, sir. Bishop was recruited by one Leontin Sverdropov, a shop steward. I'd guess Sverdropov has biofeedback conditioning."

"Got it. Have your MP's pick him up if he can be found. Anything else, Andy?"

"No, sir. Blackbird and I'll help get The Word out to the other units."

"Do that. Command Central out." Barton took a deep breath. "Olafson, any progress?"

"There's some sort of viral bit floating around in the system RAM, every time I power down it drags in a trickle current and reboots from the infected config when we come back on line, instead of from the ROM backup."

"Right. Turn it off. Just shut it down, then go through and fix it right. For now we'll rely on manual and what the Legion installed."

"Yes, sir."

"Klingstauffer, can you get Mace?"

"Stand by one. Here, sir."

"Jamey, what's your status?"

"I've just got to my command, sir. From what I can see, they didn't expect the mine field to activate." Mace's words were punctuated by distant explosions. "They've got troops still out there in the mines, both rings."

"Serve them bloody right," Barton said. "Okay, Jamey, make me the best esitmate of the situation you can and report back."

"Roger."

"Sir," Klingstauffer said from the plotting table. "Incoming, multiples, bombardment rockets, heavy mortars too from the trajectories. Target zones follow."

Lines swam over the plotting table, and red circles marked the impacts. *Lot of those are empty space*, he thought. Then: *Of course. Air-sown mines. They're trying to immobilize us.* The sky howled outside, but the *bop* sounds of the bursting charges were not followed by the surf-roar of bomblets or the crunching detonations of HE warheads. Instead there was a multiple fluttering whirr, as the rockets split and scattered hundreds, thousands of butterfly mines. Over the blimp haven where the men of the Fifth were moving out, over the wrecked vehicles of the reaction force, around the perimeter garrisons, down the main streets.

"Incoming, bombardment rockets and mortars, multiple," the sergeant said tonelessly.

"Rather a lot, isn't it?" Barton said. He whistled softly. "Rather a lot indeed. Where'd they get it all? Like they're going for broke. Klingstauffer, can you get me General Owensford?"

"Ms. Schramm's working on the antenna now, sir. Five minutes."

"Right." *Stop. Breathe deep. Now go to the window and look out—* Secondary explosions in the mine-fields. Someone was taking some real punishment. *So are our people, with all that artillery pouring in, but the Helots have to be losing more, they're in the open.*

"Legion Headquarters, Fort Plataia sir."

"Owensford here."

"Barton. Uploading situation report." There was a warble of data. "Feed complete."

"Received." A long pause. "Jesus, Ace, what's going on up there?"

"This one's it, sir. I'd say they've committed damned near everything they have. Not just troops, look at how much ordnance they're expending."

"So why are you talking to me?"

"If you'll look close at the situation report, General Owensford, you will discover that you are God damned near the only person I *can* talk to."

"Oh. Lahr! Andy, get Jesus and Catherine in here on the double, then start looking into what direct communications we have with any unit in General Barton's Command. Move! OK, Ace, what you got from where you sit?"

"One hell of a mess, Boss. I got a bad feeling on this one. No command, no control, no communications, and no bloody intelligence."

"They any better off?"

"Some," Ace said. He took another deep breath.

"Actually, things can't be going so good for them, either. They penetrated the computer system here, good move, everything was tied to it. Used the computer to disable the mines and security systems. Had some inside help, too, saboteurs, God knows what else. But we turned the mine fields on with manual. I don't know how many of their troops are out there, but a lot of mines are going off and there's a lot of secondary explosions."

"Ace, are you telling me you have most of the Helot army trapped inside your perimeter?"

"Skipper, we just may, but it's not clear just who has who trapped. I doubt their command elements are in here. They don't much go in for Rommel style. More like Hitler."

"Well. Clarifies your objective, doesn't it?"

Barton laughed. "General, just at the frigging moment the objective is to live through all this! But yeah, I see what you mean. We got them in a killing zone. Only problem is, we don't have a lot handy to kill them with, and they seem to have plenty to do unto us."

"You have two battalions coming."

"Up river and up those roads. This'll be long over by then."

"Royal Cavalry in Olynthos. Prince Lysander went up there yesterday. I could send that. The Air Cav units could be there in a couple of hours."

"Maybe not," Ace said. "They've got bugger all equipment up here. They must have known that Air Cav was down there. This is typical Skilly. Devious. Started with a small attack on an outpost to lure out the reaction force, an ambush for the relief column to make Stora Mine commit *their* mobile force, an ambush for *that*, then the main attack — sure as God made a mule ornery, they've got something that can take out the airborne troops, and it's *already in place*."

"Good thinking, Ace. Still, I will have to report to the Prince."

"Yes, sir, but make sure he understands. Christ. He's there with the Air Cav? I didn't know that, but bugger all, it doesn't mean *they* didn't."

"It doesn't mean they did, either, Ace. Thanks to Major Cheung we plugged that Palace leak."

"They could have another. Dammit, Peter, they get me thinking they're ten feet tall—"

"The great thing —"

"Is not to lose my nerve. Yes, sir. Wilco."

"Right. You're in charge, Ace. I'll see what I can organize from here."

"Thanks. It's heating up, I better get back to it. Don't let them suck the Prince into anything stupid."

"Godspeed. Out."

Something was happening outside. A line of massive explosions slammed their way across the open space outside the control building. One struck a parked ore-hauler, throwing the hundred-tonne machine onto its side; a moment later it pinwheeled across the gravel again, as a fuel dump went up in a soft *whomp* of orange flame and black smoke. The *crump . . . crump* sounds echoed off the mountainside, were joined by others throughout the settlement as more explosive fell out of the sky.

Ace Barton took a deep breath. "Sergeant, feed counterbattery data to the perimeter posts and the armory." The armory at least had light artillery in revetments, and heavy mortars of its own. "Do what you can to get communications so we have a decent situation report. And anybody you can get to, tell them we win if we hold on. They haven't accomplished dick yet, and their surprise is over. Now all we have to do is live through this."

❖   ❖   ❖

"We got to get out of here!" someone was screaming.

"Keep moving, keep moving," Niles barked into the speaker.

They were supposed to be destroying the town, planting explosives everywhere, making the Citizens' homes uninhabitable. *If I take time to do that, we won't get out of here at all,* Niles thought. *And the mine fields are active again.* He shuddered. A few minutes earlier and he'd have been in the middle of that field when it activated. As it was he'd lost a fifth of his command to the mines. *Dead or run away and there'll be more of those. Just vanished. Where do they think they can run?* There was no safe place. If the Royals didn't find you, Skilly would. *But Skilly won't hold this area after tonight, so all they'll have to worry about is the Royals.*

Groups of infantry were moving, but it wasn't a very orderly maneuver. They were supposed to fan out and make contact with the other Helot formations that would be pouring in through the breached defenses, but not all the defense system was breached, and it wasn't at all clear just what part was. Somewhere out there he should find reinforcements, but he didn't know where. *This is becoming one monumental cock-up.*

His force was divided. He had led some across the greensward while the mines were off, but not all had made it before the field was suddenly activated. Not only had he lost men, he'd lost contact with a third of his force, who were back there in the perimeter, trapped between two mine fields. Paths would have to be cleared before they could advance or retreat, but there was no one to clear them.

"Incoming!"

Niles hit the dirt. There was a nightmare of explosions, some close, some distant. He scrabbled with his radio. "Cease that artillery on north sector, I say again, cease, you're dropping into areas we hold."

There was no acknowledgment, but eventually it stopped. Niles got up to look at the situation. Men were cursing. They knew where that barrage had come from and they didn't like it at all. "Who's fucking side are they on?" someone shouted. There were answering curses.

Niles put that out of his mind, and tried for a calm assessment of the situation. He was near a residential community. The houses were shuttered, but they weren't all empty. Fire spat from a house half a kilometer away. Helot fighters dove for cover like reeds rippling in the wind. Some returned the enemy fire, shooting wildly, while others hugged the ground and waited. The black stone blocks of the shuttered house eroded under the return fire as if they were being sandblasted, in a shower of sparks and ricochets, but it didn't stop the Spartan sniper. Finally two Helot rocketeers came up. They snapped open the collapsable fiberglas tubes, came up to kneeling position and took careful aim; these were the light unguided bunkerbusters. *Whooot*-crash. A house half a block from the target showed a spurt of flame. There were more rifle blasts and the Helot went down. His partner cursed and got the rocket launcher.

Niles tried to shout to the man to move to a different location, but he wasn't listening. He got the launcher loaded, raised up, aimed. Another *whoosh*, and this time the windows of the house blew out in a spectacular shower of fire and shards. A burning figure staggered out the door to lie and twitch for a second. One more obstacle out of the way, but it had cost them time.

Ask me to give you anything but time. Who said that? Doesn't matter. "Keep moving! Up, up, move, move," Niles urged. "You can't stay here!"

"Sir, jamming's off."

Niles cursed silently; that meant the Royalists had communications again. Continued Helot jamming would hinder their own side now more than the enemy. *And I'm in a pocket, and I don't know what I have in here.* The timetable was shot all to shit. Niles had never believed much in that timetable. Too damned complicated, too many units to get to different places, too many things had to happen at the same time. Skilly kept insisting it was a simple plan, just a simple wedge attack, breach the defenses, seek out and destroy, but it hadn't looked simple to Niles. It was hard enough just to get one unit to move on a schedule, under fire or not, and this had dozens. Niles had tried to get von Reuter to discuss it, but the German wasn't about to criticize Skilly's plan. *No one would. Afraid to sound like defeatists. So we went with this, and now —*

"Over to standard radio com," he said. "Codes. Who have we got contact with?" He punched the first channel button.

"Group Leader ben Bella here."

"Situation?"

"Codes CORNUCOPIA an' HEPHAESTUS." The warehouse and smelter areas. Forces advancing but objectives not secured. "We can't find the underground Movement liaison."

"Keep looking, have to evacuate our people."

"Sure, sure, I'll keep looking. Bloody god damn hell!"

"Problems?"

"Half my troops are dead in the fucking mines! The mines were supposed to be off!"

"Yes, I know, we took losses too," Niles said. "What else?"

"They were supposed to be off, damn it!"

"Get hold of yourself. Report."

"We've got sniper fire and infiltrators from the residential districts, and somebody's spotting for that goddam artillery of theirs, it's too damned effective, they must have their computers up again!"

Likely, actually. "Follow standing orders." Those called for blasting down any building from which hostile fire was received. He winced; a little severe . . . but what else could they do?

"Standing orders —" His subordinate broke off with laughter.

"Ben Bella? What the hell?"

"Standing orders, sir? HALF MY FUCKING MORTARS AND ROCKET LAUNCHERS ARE OUT IN THE FUCKING MINEFIELDS! I don't know where the rest are. I don't know where the ammunition is. Sir."

"Sir, sir," his communications sergeant said. "Group Leader Martins."

"A moment. All right, ben Bella, link up with the Movement people and do what you can to get back on schedule—"

He heard more laughter from ben Bella. "Schedule! That's great! Schedule." More laughter, then silence.

Can't say I like that much. "Go ahead, Martins, Niles here."

"Sir, Code WHITE GUARD." *Heavy resistance, cannot advance.* Martins was supposed to be securing the main smelter complex. Niles looked down at his map; about half a kilometer west of the blimp haven, in a tangle of workers' bunkhouses and maintenance sheds. "I've identified Legion troops, and Brotherhood first-liners, I think they're from the reserve force."

Damn, Niles thought. The truck-sabotage was supposed to have knocked them out of the fight entirely. *Well, everything couldn't work. But had anything worked since the mine fields came back on? How many survived, and how much are they worth?* His head pounded, and it was hard to think. *No way to know the situation. And back up there in central control, they had the computers back on, they knew where everything was. Barton — Barton, what the hell was Barton doing out here anyway, Barton wasn't supposed to be here, this was supposed to be provincials, amateurs, and now*

*we're fighting Barton and the Legion and those damned
SAS units will be out there waiting for us.* He shook off
the feeling of hysteria. "Martins, can you get through?
Answer in clear."

"No, sir. Everytime we punch a hole, they fire the
buildings and fall back, or pinch us off behind the
neck of the penetration. I don't have enough edge in
numbers, and these are good troops. Too many civilians running around getting in the way, too."

Another amateur, has to explain everything. *But I'm
not much more than an amateur myself, and these
Legion types, this is their business, they do this all their
lives.* "Code STALINGRAD." *Dig in and hold.*

"Bullshit."

"What?"

"I'll do what I can, but everything's fucked up,"
Martins said. "You better figure something fast, or it's
going to be bugout boogie and there won't be fuck all I
can do about it. Sir."

"Field Prime," the communications sergeant said.

This ought to be secure. Ought to be. "Marlborough
here." *Stupid code name.*

"Report."

He worked to keep his voice calm, and not to give
irrelevant complaints. Like ammunition in one place,
and guns in another, troops separated from their
commanders— "Heavy losses averaging thirty percent
due to unexpected activation of the mine field. Ben
Bella's still advancing but hasn't secured objectives.
Martins is pinned down, unable to advance at all. Part of
my troops are with me at Sugar Mike Two, but the rest
are still out at the bunkers with the minefield between
us, and I don't have a good estimate of what's with me
and what's behind. Troops are complaining that the
mines weren't supposed to detonate, and some of them
are unhappy about taking friendly fire."

"Field Prime know that. Our friends don't have any explanations, they still looking. You ought to be finishing Phase Three, mon!"

"Field Prime, that timetable cannot be kept. It doesn't even make sense any more. The surprise is over, they're organizing, their computers are up, their artillery counterfire programs are starting up, and our whole force is exposed!"

There was a pause. "You sayin' you want to run now?"

"Field Prime, I am suggesting that it is impossible to complete the mission."

"Field Prime will consider that, but not time to give up. Perimeter Ten to Fourteen pulled out when we jimmied the comm, and we overran they bunkers, now we using them." The outer defense positions had all-round fields of fire. "Swing a couple of companies up they ass, see if we can nutcracker them. We rendevous at Objective A-7, eh?"

"I will comply, but my advice is to get out before we take more losses. We've hurt them, and so far we still have an effective force, but —"

"Field Prime will consider recommendation. Now do nutcracker."

"Roger wilco."

Niles looked up. "Sutchukil, you will take A and C companies and swing east against those garrison johnnies," he said. *What's left of them. Between them there's not a full strength company, and I have no idea of what they're facing.* "Da Silva, you're in charge here. Remainder of the reserve, follow me."

He lead the way, at a steady wolf-trot rather than a sprint; they had better than a klick and a half to go. The troops followed by platoon columns, spaced out along the verges of the road on alternate sides. The composition soles of their boots rutched steadily on the light snow-covering of the roads and sidewalks. Noise was increasing from either side, small arms fire and explosions. Mortar shells went overhead, making everyone hunch their shoulders involuntarily. They landed to the east, fire support against Royalist militia probing at the Helots. Return fire went *shoomp-whirrrr* overhead in the opposite direction. The garrison was getting its heavy weapons into use.

They ran through a section of park, where pine-trees were blazing like torches, with an overwhelming stink of tar.

"Mines!" someone screamed. A butterfly mine popped up, and half a squad flopped. A leg lay improbably in the center of the path they'd been running on.

"Keep moving," Niles ordered. "Come on, we're going home!"

The men moved ahead, but cautiously now. Niles tried to hurry them.

"Fuck off," someone shouted. "You want to run through mines, you come up here in front and do it." There were shouts of agreement. "Damn right." "This de revo*lu*tion! Officers to the front!"

"Incoming!"

A box pattern of high explosive fell around them, and several mines detonated. One man screamed, but no one else seemed to be hit. "They clearing the mine field for us!" someone shouted. Others laughed and the units began to move forward again. Another round of artillery, this time behind them.

There's luck, Niles thought. "Move out, move out." He wondered how many were following him. Not as many as started. There were gaps in the ranks. *Damn fools, don't they understand, they can't stay here.* He ran on.

Finally they were through the park and into a

business district. Artillery flashed in the distance, but nothing was falling on them at the moment. Buildings were burning on either side; larger ones now as they came closer to the center of the dispersed settlement, flames licking up from the windows to soot-stain the white stucco. Heat drove out the day's chill, turned the uniforms under the armor sodden-wet; the smoke was thick and choking, billowing just over head-high. Bodies lay crumpled; he saw one half-out of the driver's door of a scorched van, pistol still in its hand. A woman dangled from a shattered shop-window, lying on her back with spears of glass through her chest, long blond hair falling a full meter to the sidewalk to rest in a pool of blood.

A bullet went overhead with a nasty *krak*. More, and a man dropped.

"Take cover!" the platoon commanders were shouting. Two men sprinted out to retrieve the wounded man. "Crew weapons, set up weapons," Niles shouted.

A machine gun crew got into action, then another crew opened up with suppressing fire against the sniper. A noncom ran from one clump of troopers to the next, assigning target sectors. *Good man. I need to get his name.*

Niles put himself behind a bullet-riddled electrocar; the Company Leader in charge of the area came sprinting across the open street with his radiotech and a squad at his heels. They dashed into the cover of the car body and crouched beside the Englishman, panting.

Nobody spared a glance for the two dead militia fighters sprawled beneath the body of the car; a man in his fifties, and a boy who probably had never shaved, both in bits and pieces of uniform and armor. The bullets that killed them had probably been a mercy, after the burning fuel drained out and down.

"Situation?" Niles said.

"Hell of a fight for this district, sir," the Helot officer replied; Steve Derex, Niles remembered. He was a tall lanky man, heavy-featured, with the fashionable guerrilla braid down his back and a nasal Welfare accent; one arm had a stained bandage around it. "We rushed them out, but they kept comin' back through the sewers and snipin', thicker'n crabs inna hoor's cunt. Got the cure for *thet*, right enough."

As if on cue, there was a massive *thump* under their feet, a sound that shuddered up through the soles of their boots into the breastbone rather than to the ears. Manhole covers all along the broad concrete roadway sprang into the air with a belch of sooty fire.

"Took a fuelin' station and jist ran the hoses down, sir," the guerrilla said with vindictive satisfaction. "Wit' youz troops, maybe we kin clear an' hold this sector."

Niles looked across the street. Two and four story buildings, offices mostly. Perhaps a laboratory or assay office. Nothing of any great importance, certainly nothing worth losing a whole battalion for. From beyond that came a steady booming sound, rolling and echoing off the cliff-line of the open pit mine just to their south. The armory, and the gun-batteries around it.

Clear and hold for what? But that's the Plan— "Let's do it, then," he said, looking at his watch. *1130 hours*, he thought. The timetable was shot all to hell, and there wasn't anything to accomplish. *What did Skilly expect to do?*

❖   ❖   ❖

"We rendezvous at Objective A-7, eh?" Skilly said, listening to the ripping canvas sound across the sky.

"Roger wilco." Niles' voice sounded hard and flat, tightly confident.

"Incoming!"

Skida went flat along with everyone else in the headquarters unit. The shot fell a thousand meters behind them, crackling echoes through the jagged hills. Then there was a flash visible even in bright noonlight, and another explosion that shuddered the ground beneath her. Secondary explosion, as piled ammunition went up.

"Goddam, that counterbattery too good!" she said. That was the fifth heavy mortar they had lost in the last fifteen minutes. There weren't many left.

"The Legionnaires are feeding the plotting data to the Royalist gunnery computers," consultant Tetsuko said, not glancing up from his consol. "Falkenberg's troops use Xanadu milspec multiband radars, difficult to jam, and their passive sensors are also very good. And the artillery is dug-in and has armored overhead protection. Not very vulnerable even to precision-guided munitions."

"Field Prime don't need explanations, Field Prime need results," Skilly said.

Crump. Crump. That heavy-mortar battery was down to two tubes, but they were maintaining fire. Skilly felt a stab of warmth; they might have been gutter-scum once, but she had shaped something different, as proud and deadly as a King Cobra.

"Report from Olynthos?"

"The Royalist airborne is not scrambling."

Sheee-it. The little Fang missiles were in perfect position, and the Royals couldn't know about them. The air cavalry was a serious problem in her Upper and Middle Valley operations already, and the Spartans were training more. Half the purpose of this raid had been to lure the helicopters out where they could be killed. "Maybe we outsmart us, cut communications too good so they don't know we here yet," she said. "We hurt them enough here, they come." And maybe the Prince, too, there was a report that he'd been seen in Olynthos. *If he there, he will come run-*

ning, not like him to send his troops out and not go. We get him and this war is half over. If we stay here, punish the Cits, maybe they send that air cav, maybe they send the Prince, we win it all. Getting rid of the airborne would be worth taking heavy losses, getting the Prince worth even more. *We could still win, win big.*

But suppose he didn't come? If the air cav didn't come? Then she grinned. *They will come next time. Next time they send everything they have, even the old king.*

"OK, the Mjollnir ready?"

"As instructed, Field Prime. We have it set up on the bunker line in the center of our penetration through the enemy defenses.

She touched her helmet. "Von Reuter?"

"Fallback complete and standing by," he said stolidly.

Von Reuter was a comfort; the man didn't give a damn for the Movement, but cared a great deal about doing his professional best. When it came to making a pursuit as costly as possible, he had a certain sadistic imaginativeness as well; anyone who came after them — *assuming we gets away at all* — would get a very bloody nose, while the Helot forces broke up into dozens of small parties and made their way to prepositioned hiding-places and supply caches. And when it was over, the Kupros Mountains would be a second place the Royal forces would be extremely cautious about entering, would have to guard continuously. It was still a good plan.

"Right," she said. "Let's go."

This time they would ride in style; the first people back out had dropped off transport. Someone had even taken time and a spray-paint can to sketch a red = on the sides of each. Skilly led the slide down the hill to the vans and trucks. As they boarded and drove bumping and crashing down the rock-strewn streambed they passed other captured vehicles heading north into the wadi-and-gully country. They were loaded with sedated wounded, or with boxes and crates of refined silver and platinum and thorium, from the looted warehouses, or medical supplies, food, clothing. . . . Money to slip off-planet through Bronson's outlets to pay for weapons, to pay troops and bribe and buy and intimidate here on Sparta. Supplies to help sustain the expanding Helot forces. They would drive the vehicles to destruction, then transfer the loot to muleback and scatter it.

" *'Make War support War,'* " Skilly quoted to herself, as they drove onto the ringroad of the base. *That chink Sun Tzu knew he business.* The background chatter hummed in her helmetphones, and the sound of combat was a continous diffuse stutter all around, louder than the roar of engines. Behind a fragment of wall the Meijians had erected the Mjollnir, a squat two-stage rocket shaped like a huge artillery shell twice the height of a man.

"Faster," she said.

There must be at least a thousand, maybe as many as two or four thousand armed Citizens within the perimeter, besides the formed units in the bunkers and the Legion soliders. Speed and the air-sown mines and disrupted communications had kept them from concentrating, but that would not last long. The trucks and vans careered down the streets, veering between wrecked and burning vehicles. The lead car went over a body with a sodden *thump*; a howling dog dashed by, its coat ablaze. Not only houses and cars were on fire, the wooded tongues of ridgeland between the built-up areas had caught as well, and smoke was drifting in billowing clouds.

Helot soldiers with MP brassards and light-wands were directing traffic, most of it people on foot moving at a run. More vans and trucks with wounded and loot passed them; parties of Movement undergrounders clung to their sides or ran back toward the perimeter, those too compromised to stay even with this degree of confusion, and the scores of transportee recruits they had picked up.

Most of those not on pickup or guard duty were laying boobytraps, everything from grenades taped to doors to huge time-detonated mines in the sewers; a lot of them were wired into the settlement power systems, and there was going to be a *very* unpleasant surprise when they got the turbines running again.

Skilly grinned like a wolf at the thought, opening the door of the van and dropping out at a run as it slowed down beside the block of buildings she wanted. The guides waved them in through doors that had been blasted off their hinges with a recoilless-rifle shell, up steel-framed stairs that sagged and creaked, into a corridor slashed and pocked with the remains of close-quarter fighting with grenade and bayonet.

"Down," the man at the head of the stairs warned. "Under observation." The building was fibrocrete, but the tall rectangle of window at the south end looked out onto enemy-held open ground and the armory-fortress. "Peltast snipers."

They squatted and duckwalked down the transverse corridor; the floor was wet and sticky, and the blanket-wrapped form of a Helot trooper lay in one doorway, the hole blasted through his helmet showing why. The corridor turned, and they were in a long room looking out over the open space. More Helots sprawled on the floor, forming heads-in starfish circles amid maps and plotting tables and a tangle of communications lines.

"Yo, Niles," Skilly said; it was safe to come to a crouch here, and she scuttled quickly over to his side. "Crack this nut yet?"

"No, Field Prime," he said. "Here, take a look." They moved to one side beyond the last of the tall narrow windows, and he offered her the thread-thin jack of a pickup camera one of his troopers was holding over a window on an extension grip. "Careful with that, Yip."

The guerrilla commander flipped down her face shield and plugged the jack into her helmet. A view of the field outside sprang into being on the inner surface of the shield's complex materials. The Brotherhood fortress had taken advantage of the proximity of the big open-pit mine a kilometer further south; nothing showed of the main bunker but a low mound of turf set in a dozen hectares of landscaped park. The plans Intelligence had stolen — Movement Intelligence and the Meijians both — showed an underground wedding cake, fibrocrete and steel running down six stories; generators, air-filtration systems, the works. The Spartans had always known it was a dangerous universe. The bunkers radiating out from it were newer, but also knitted into the park's contours, from the little gatling-pillboxes to the round covered gunpits. As she watched a hatch slid open and the barrel of a light gun appeared, a 155mm with a double-baffle muzzle brake. It fired, a pale orange flash against the noon sun, and the hatch was closed again in smooth coordination with the recoil of the cannon.

"Slick," she said.

About a second all-told, the hatch must be keyed to the lanyard of the cannon, not a practical interval to hit it with a PGM. Somebody had gotten lucky; one of the gunpits was a crater blasted open to the sky, but they could peck at them all day and not do that again, and now the Helot army was taking losses.

A van exploded, taking with it two trucks and some motorcycles, tossing men and loot in all directions. Something else exploded.

"Stop that bunching up!" Skilly screamed.

Niles looked at her, then away.

Getting hot, here, not quite like what Skilly expected. She had hoped for better results, hoped the Brotherhood gunners weren't quite that good. If they could have knocked out the bunkers and gun emplacements, a Helot force squatting on the armory roof would have eleven hundred civilians under its boots. The Royalists talked a good line about not bargaining for hostages, and held to it fairly strongly when it came to their own men . . . but it was another thing to say "go ahead" when someone had a gun in your child's ear.

She was aware that Niles was saying something.

" . . . and a lot of our people are still in there inside the perimeter."

"Pull them out."

"As I just told you, the Royals have managed to activate a number of their mine fields, and their artillery is highly accurate. We can't pull out. Much of our force is pinned down." Niles waved behind them, at the trucks going by. "I hope that loot is good, because we paid a heavy price for it."

She was still studying the gun emplacements. She seemed distracted. Then she touched a button on the side of her helmet. "Anything from Olynthos?"

"Two choppers rode out, down river."

Down river. Away from the action, and away from her missile emplacements. *Where could they be going?*

"Nothing else? Nothing? All right. We'll make them come here. Now we use the Mjollnir."

Niles frowned. "Well, that will take out one of the gun emplacements—"

"Do the big central bunker pretty good, though."

"No military targets in the central bunker. Just noncombatants."

"You thinking like a *rabbiblanco* again, Jeffi." He

frowned, a little insulted. *I've gotten beyond the naive stage, I think*, he told himself. "What do you mean?" he said stiffly.

"*Noncombatants*. Am no such, just enemies with gun and enemies without gun. Get that Mjollnir ready."

"Sk — Field Prime, they've got close to four hundred women and — well, nearly a thousand children in there, and —"

"Get me the fort, Jeffi. They get just one chance, like everybody."

"You *can't* —"

She was standing between him and the others in the room, whose eyes were on the windows or the corridor in any case. Geoffrey Niles froze as the muzzle of her Walther jabbed like a blunt steel finger into his left side, exactly where the armor latched under his armpit. Her face leaned closer to his, and she flipped up the shield; there was tension in the green-flecked brown eyes, and her voice was pitched soft.

So that nobody else will see or hear, he knew with a distant corner of his mind. *For my sake, if it comes out right.* If he passed what he suddenly realized was a carefully contrived test.

"Jeffi, Skilly want you with her when we win. But Skilly going to *win*, Jeffi my sweet." A slight smile, tender. "Welcome to Skilly's world, my mon, where she live all her life. This the real world, *and it like this every day*." The high-cheeked brown face went utterly cold. "I doan give me order twice, mon."

He was already one over the limit.

❖   ❖   ❖

"Jesus Christ, what's going *on* back there!" Karl Olafson barked. "We've been out of com link for better than half an hour!"

"Major," Barton began, "please listen closely." He

waited for a second, until the man in the screen nodded.

"The enemy partially penetrated our security systems, used them to disorganize the defenses, and launched a major attack on Stora Mine in conjunction with internal sabotage. They've overrun substantial areas of the settlement. They have taken heavy losses, and we've stopped them, but they're still out there."

Emotion rippled across the square blond-bearded face, fear, rage, astonishment. Then nothing but business; Barton nodded in chill approval. There was no *time* for anything else.

"We've relieved the Torreys, but they've abandoned the attacks. And thanks to your warnings we found the bombs in our trucks."

"Glad you got that message," Barton said. "Wasn't sure you had."

"Just heard part of it, something about sabotage, decided to look into the trucks. Thank God. All right. We're 120 klicks from you. I can be back there in two hours, three at most."

"No you can't," Barton said. "The road's mined, and I'm sure there are ambushes set up all along it."

There was a long pause. "Our families are back there, in the armory bunker."

"I know. It won't do them a bit of good for you to get killed, though."

"All right, what do you want?"

"They're beginning to realize they can't hold here," Barton said. "They'll start to retreat — and they don't have all that much choice about the route they'll take if they want to get away with the loot they've been scooping up. They have truckloads of stuff they've stolen."

"Christ. From where? Our homes?"

"Probably," Barton said. "Keep hold of yourself. The

best thing that can happen right now is for them to load up with loot they won't want to give up. Loot will slow them down as much as all the mines they've been scattering. I don't know this area all that well, but from the map it sure looks like you can cut across the ridge line and show them that two can play this ambush game."

"Christ Almighty! Harry, give me that map. Who knows this area? Yeah, get him — General, I think you have something. Davis? What's this ridge like? How long would it take to get over to here—"

Another voice. "No road, but there's good trails. Let's see, maybe fifteen klicks. Four hours? Three for those in real good shape."

"They may be past by then, but maybe not," Barton said. "I don't think they quite appreciate how hard a retreat under fire can be. Get over there and see what you can do," Barton said. "Be careful, you're not trying to stop them, just punish them as they go out, and that's *all* you do. Don't try pursuit. Don't try anything fancy. Just get where you can see them, dig in and hurt them, no need to close with them."

"Roger. OK, we're on the way."

❖   ❖   ❖

"It's the Royalist commander," Geoffrey Niles said hoarsely.

Skilly touched her helmet. "This Field Prime, Spartan People's Liberation Army."

"Major Bitterman here." A woman's voice. The central armory would be held by administrative troops. "What do you want?"

"You getting one chance to surrender, or we crack you like the egg," Skilly said flatly.

"You haven't been doing much cracking as yet, rebel." There was confidence in her voice; the armory bunker would withstand most things, short of a nuclear weapon.

"So far, Field Prime be *nice*. Major, de kids and all in there you responsibility. You put them in military zone. Better you left them out, nobody out here get hurt who not fighting. Last chance."

"I've seen what you did to our homes," Bitterman said. "And this is not a military zone. There is no military force here. This is a hospital and bomb shelter."

"Well, too bad," Skilly said. " 'Cause it military to me."

"What do you want?"

"You surrender."

"You know what you ask is impossible. I don't have the authority. I tell you this is a hospital and shelter. There are no military units here."

"They all around you out there."

"Well, yes —"

"General Barton here. Who is this?"

"Calls herself Field Prime, General," Major Bitterman said.

"Field Prime, this is General Barton."

"Good. Surrender, and I don't smash in that Armory."

"The Armory is a hospital and shelter for noncombatants," Barton said.

"I don't believe you, but I don' care much either. You surrender or we crack it open."

"General, she's bluffing," Bitterman said. "This place would withstand anything up to nukes."

"Field Prime don't bluff, as you going to find out. I give you your chance. You don't get another."

"Suppose the hospital did surrender?" Barton demanded. "What does that do for you?"

"Oh, fuck off," Skilly said. She cut the connection. "Hey, Jeffi, that bunker be one big military target. Skilly not to blame if the Cits put people over the ammo and power supply, hey?"

He nodded. "Yes . . . I suppose that's true," he said.

His shoulders straightened. *It is. A damned sight more of a military target than Dresden was, after all.* Not that it mattered, the Royalists already had evidence enough to hang them all six times over for violations of the Laws of War. *Unless we win. Winners write the laws.*

She touched her helmet again. "Tetsuko. Do it."

❖   ❖   ❖

Barton looked down at the plotting table. The Helot attack reached through the perimeter of Stora Mine like a knobbly treetrunk, with branches reaching out to touch objectives, twisting around obstacles or strongpoints. He was starting to get an accurate picture; also starting to put serious pressure on the attackers. *Daring. Bold. But they depended on their electronic edge too much. If we'd been here another week—*

If we'd been here another week they would have found out and called off the attack. Attack? Or raid? Did they have an objective other than loot and generally smashing things up?

Information was flowing in now. Disorganized as they'd been, the Brotherhood had put up a good defense, which was what Barton had intended. Defense in place was a lot simpler and easier than a coordinated attack, and these Brotherhood troops all knew each other, had worked with each other, knew what to expect. The enemy had pummeled them in a few places, but by and large the Brotherhood forces had held, and that was all they needed to do.

There was one coherent enemy force around what had been defensive post 12, and many pockets of disorganized Helots, some in minefields, others in old bunkers, but all cut off from the enemy's main body. Put screening units out to keep those groups disorganized and make sure they didn't rally, because some were in a position to do some real damage if they broke free, but otherwise leave them alone for the moment. They'd surrender soon enough when they saw they were abandoned.

That left the rest of the Helots, an organized force of fewer troops than he had in total, but larger by far than any integrated force he could put together. The Helot main body was dug in and holding, but rear elements were already withdrawing, and they were sending back a stream of heavily laden vehicles. Concentrate artillery fire on that group, especially on their escape routes. Every possible shelter, and every crossroads, had long ago been added to the target data base, so it was a matter of picking targets for indirect fire and feeding in their coordinates. Drop rounds onto the roads, knock out vehicles that would have to be cleared away before anything else could get past. Make the enemy think he was being cut off. It took steady veterans to go on advancing when they were afraid their line of retreat was cut.

Right. The artillery fire plan could be left to the local militia officers. They could read maps as well as he could, and they'd seen the terrain.

And that would be wearing the enemy down something fierce. *Which is about all I can do just now.*

Aggressive patrols to make the enemy bunch up, and aggressive artillery to pound them when they did bunch up, and meanwhile gather enough troops to mount a real counter attack. *Time's on our side now. . . .*

"Sir," the technician said. "Launch, from one of the perimeter bunker locations under enemy control." The sergeant was frowning as he tracked. "Very odd trajectory, sir. Straight up, almost. Several — better than five clicks."

Some sort of suborbital? he thought. Then: *Oh, Christ.* The whole purpose of the attack was suddenly plain. Not just to shatter the mine, to demoralize the Citizens of Stora Mine and the northlands around it. Some wounds anger, but there are others that break the spirt. *That's what the enemy intended. Had intended all along.* His hand stabbed out toward the communicator, then froze. There was nothing he could do, nothing at all.

"Sir, it's a two-stage. Computer says antifortress penetrator, heavy job. Apogee. Coming down under thrust. Coming down *fast*. Jesus, Mach 18! 20! Jesus, it's —"

The ground shook beneath their feet.

❖   ❖   ❖

"Prepare to pull out," Skilly said, raising herself to her knees and wiping blood from the corner of her mouth. The explosion had been more like an earthquake, this close.

The bunkers around the underground fortress were intact, but there was a gaping hole near the entrance to the main bunker. Smoke rose from it. It looked bad, looked terrible.

Baffles and multiple armored doors had protected the weapons posts. The steady fire continued, then the Spartan defenders realized what had happened behind them, and then every remaining weapon opened up, firing continuously with no thought of maintaining concealment. Wire-guided missiles lashed out in return from the Helot positions, beamriders. The savage exchange of fire continued for a minute, then died away. The Helot troops couldn't take the losses and dove for cover. Someone screamed near by.

"Fuck this shit, fuck it, fuck this motherfucking shit!"

"Steady," Skilly shouted. "General comm, Phase —"

RAK. Yip had raised himself to reel in the surveillance camera; the sniper bullet punched through his shoulder, upper lungs and out the other side without slowing much. Everyone dove as it whined around the room, pinging off concrete with that ugly sound that told experienced ears the thumb-sized lump of flattened metal might hit anyone from any direction. The guerrilla NCO's heels drummed briefly on the floor, as blood flooded out from nose and mouth and the massive exit wound under his left armpit.

"— Phase Five, say again, Phase Five," Skilly repeated.

Almost on the heels of her words the first of the huge demolition charges the guerrillas had cobbled together from captured blasting explosive went off, with a jarring thump that was loud even a kilometer away. The remaining militia could be expected to press their pursuit with reckless courage, and the Helots intended to make them pay for it. With explosive and steel rather than close-quarter fighting, where possible; with ambushes where it was not.

"Now, Jeffi. Now we run, and they come after us, and we kill them."

✧ CHAPTER TEN

No battle plan survives contact with the enemy.
— Helmuth von Moltke

✧ ✧ ✧

"All day for nine hours we ran. It was the contagion of bewilderment and fear and ignorance. Rumour spread at every halt, no man had his orders. Everyone had some theory and no plan beyond the frantic desire to reach his unit. In ourselves we did not know what to do. Had there been someone in authority to say, 'Stand here, do this and that' — then half our fear would have vanished. So I began to realize, sitting in my swaying car, how important the thousand dreary things in an army are. The drill, the saluting, the uniform, the very badges on your arm all tend to identify you with a solid machine and build up a feeling of security and order. In the moment of danger the soldier turns to his mechanical habits and draws strength from them." Alan Moorehead, on the retreat from Gazala, June, 1942
— Quoted in John Keegan and Richard Holmes, *Soldiers*

✧ ✧ ✧

Crofton's Encyclopedia of the Inhabited Planets (2nd Edition):

Olynthos: town at the head of navigation on the *Eurotas River* (q.v.), *Sparta*, (q.v.). Established as Fort Tanner during CoDominium administration, 2030. Communication with Lake Alexander and its mining settlements by rail and slurry-pipeline (2060), followed by rapid growth; river-port, fitting out point for outback expeditions, and industrial center. Power supplied by hydro developments on Vulcan Rapids (potential in excess of 1000 MW.). Smelters, refineries, direct-reduction steel mill, mining machinery, building supplies, explosives, general manufacturing. Pop. (2090) 66,227 not including part-time residents.
Description: The town lies on the southwestern bank of the river immediately below the Ninth Cataract of the Vulcan

Rapids, in an area known as Hecate's Pool. Most buildings are constructed of limestone blocks from nearby quarries; notable features include . . .

❖   ❖   ❖

Melissa was down, hurt and bleeding, and shells were falling all around them, but Lysander couldn't get to her. His legs were paralyzed, and when he tried to crawl filthy hands came out of the ground, reached up with slimy fingers to drag him down. Melissa moaned softly, and Lysander shouted to her, shouted that he was coming, but he couldn't move, and —

"Prince."

"I'm coming! I swear it—"

"Prince."

Lysander sat bolt upright on the cot. "Harv. I'm awake. God, what a horrible dream. Melissa, she was — What is it, Harv?"

"Urgent signals, Prince. You're needed in the orderly room. Helots attacking the Stora Mine complex."

"Right. I'll be there in five minutes." He suddenly realized where he was. "My compliments to the colonel, and can he alert the regiment."

"Already being done," Harv said. "Choppers winding up and they're rolling the armor out."

"Right. Thanks."

Colonel Bennington and his senior officers were in the staff room clustered around a map table. "Attention, please," Captain Larry Sugarman, the adjutant, said. They fell silent as Lysander came into the room.

"Carry on, please. Jamie, what's happening?"

"Sir, it's an all-out assault on the Stora Mine complex," Bennington said. "We don't have direct communications, we're getting everything on relay through the Legion Headquarters in Sparta City. General Owensford is on line and would like to speak with you when you have a moment."

Lysander leaned over to study the displays on the map table. "There's a hell of a lot more 'maybe' and 'probable' and 'could be' and plain rumor than real information here."

"Yes, sir, the Helots seem to have disabled the main computer at Stora. Disabled or worse; there are indications they got control of it."

The circles, solid, shaded, and dotted, blinked as the table was updated. Some of the dotted circles vanished, others moved to shaded. A few shaded turned solid as sightings and identifications were confirmed, but there was still more rumor than fact reported on that map table. "Better let me speak to General Owensford," Lysander said. "I'm not learning much here. I presume you're getting the regiment ready to respond."

"Yes, sir. Sergeant, see if you can get General Owensford, please."

"On line and holding, sir," the sergeant said. He handed a headset to Lysander.

"Lysander here."

"Owensford, Highness. Urgent request. Do not send out any air cav reaction force. I'll explain, but that's an urgent advice, sir."

Lysander stared at the map. New data flowed in. The impersonal circles moved or changed sizes, with bright flashes indicating battles. Friendly units shrank as he watched. Confirmed casualties. "Our people are taking a licking," Lysander said. "And they need help. I suppose you have reasons."

"Sir. This is an all out assault, regimental to brigade strength, carried out with full intelligence. They have to know where your units are. Possibly even that you're commanding them. Therefore —"

"I see," Lysander said. "Therefore they've already factored in the First Royals and think they can deal with us."

"Exactly, sir."

"Isn't that called taking counsel from our fears, General? Paralyzing ourselves because of what might happen?"

"Yes, sir, but in this case it may be wise. We don't know nearly enough. What we do know is they were willing to commit in strength to this operation knowing your force was there and ready. The plan was complex: initial attack to draw out the reaction force, ambush that, sabotage the mobile reserve, infiltrate saboteurs—"

"Jesus, and all that worked?" Lysander demanded.

"More than ought to have."

"Skilly," Lysander said.

"Yes, sir, I believe so. I have only intermittent contact with General Barton at the mine, but it's my impression he believes so, too."

"Devious," Lysander said. "So it could be a bluff to keep us from sending reinforcements."

"Sir, she's devious all right, but I can't think the Helots would risk this much on the hope that you'd think it through and not send a reaction force."

"Point taken." Lysander grinned wryly. "And she probably thinks this was a simple plan, not much to go wrong. Advice?"

"Keep your options open. You're our reserve, don't commit yet. You're closer than I am," Owensford said. "And you won't be cut off from direct contact with Barton at the mine forever. You can decide what to do when you have a better idea of what the situation is."

Lysander considered the map again. "Barton's in command at the mine?"

"Yes, sir. Local commander asked him to take over."

"All right. We'll be his reserve until the situation develops. You'll keep me up to date, and get me contact with Barton when that's possible."

"Anything we know, you'll know," Owensford said.

Lysander studied the map table. *I'd give a lot for satellite observations. Have do something about that, there must be a way to convince the CD. And what the hell am I doing, acting like I'm in charge? But it's my job, and no one else is going to do it, whether I get it right or not. And right now—* He turned to Bennington. "Jamie, get your two best pilots. Load up two ships with scouts. Have them duck out this way, down river, then swing wide and angle back, one out to each side of the valley. Straight recon mission, with the option of committing the scouts if that looks worth doing. If they've gone to this much trouble to set up an ambush of the air cav, I can't think they'll give it away attacking one ship, but the pilots should be careful anyway."

"Yes, sir. If the Helots can infiltrate a big unit they can have a couple of small ones, too."

"Good point. And any scouts they do drop will need full rocket support. But you know that."

"I'll see to it, sir."

The First Royal scouts were not as well trained as the Legion's SAS units, but they'd been trained by the Legion, and had some combat experience. *Training's over. Time to get some use out of them. For that matter it's about time for Sparta to stand up independent of Falkenberg's Legion.* "Jamie, General Owensford estimated regiment to brigade strength committed at the mine."

"Yes, sir."

"Then they can't have much left to block the roads."

"Well —"

"How much could they infiltrate up here?" Lysander demanded. "We've had regular air sweeps. Jamie, if they're good enough to have another regiment beyond what's committed already, we're going to lose anyway. Now are they that good?"

"I see your point. No, sir."

"Get the ground units moving upriver. Usual precautions, recon units lead, watch for mines, but get them moving. Keep the aviation units grounded until we figure out what Miz Skilly has in mind. Next thing, get your Intel and aviation people together and figure out where they're planning on engaging the air cav."

"Engage with what?"

"I don't know. Assume something effective."

"Missiles," Bennington said. "Right." He turned to his adjutant. "Larry, who've we got for this?"

"McCulloch and Levy, sir?"

"Good choice. And Captain Flinderman, I think. Give them the assignment and have them report when they've thought of something."

"Yes, sir."

"And get the ground units moving."

Captain Sugarman spoke quietly into his headset. Lysander turned back to the map table. After a few moments the displays changed again. Friendly unit reports became more reliable, although there was still a lot of confusion about enemy strength and locations. Lysander studied the situation carefully. The entire Stora garrison, nearly a full regiment of well equipped and trained Brotherhood troops, reinforced by Legion units, and they were reduced to ineffective and disorganized pockets. What could do that to them? Whatever it was couldn't be small, and he became more certain the enemy had committed all they had. The Helots couldn't possibly have any large strategic reserve, and not much else either. *Anti-aircraft missile units, infiltrated and —*

Infiltrated where? "Jamie?"

"Highness?"

"Have your experts consider this: a small anti-aircraft missile unit in hiding somewhere along the route from here to the mine, probably close to this base.

Not so close they can't get away once they launch their birds, but close enough to observe what we're doing. Preferably with a good escape route through terrain that would halt armor."

"Put that way, Highness—" Bennington manipulated the map controls.

"Right. I see it." Lysander increased the gain on the Decelea Forest, a university experimental arboretum and park north of Olynthos Base. It was easily large enough to hide a company of missileers, it overlooked the Valley road north, and the broken terrain and gullies extended down to the river.

"Hit us, bug out to the river. Without air we couldn't stop them crossing, and that gives them a hell of a head start in getting away," Bennington said. "It's sure where I'd put an ambush for air cav."

"Can't do any harm to send some scouts up there. We might get lucky," Lysander said. He pointed to the map table. "It's about time some luck fell our way, because it looks like we're getting lunched up there."

"Right." Bennington studied the map. "And I think I'll send some artillery units north along the main road, on up past the Decelea turnoff, but not too far past, say to about here, where they'll have that park in range—"

Lysander grinned agreement.

Bennington called his adjutant. "Larry, please ask Lieutenant Arnold to alert his men, then report here. We have a job for him."

Such a simple thing to do. Sending men off to crawl around in a forest until they can bring in artillery shells onto other men. He looked at his hand, and remembered a line from a poem. Just a line. *"The hand that signed the paper . . . these five kings did a king to death."* Why do they obey me? They're older and more experienced. He remembered Owensford, during the Dales battle, and later in the rescue of the Halleck boy.

At least they try to tell me when I'm making a mess of things. He turned back to the map table.

    .   .   .

"Royal Leader, this is Arnold. I have located our objective. We have an enemy unit under observation. They are unaware of our presence, but I can't guarantee that for long if we attempt to close. Visual and IR observation. Data transmission follows, stand by."

Images on the map table swam, dissolved, and reformed as update data flowed in. Lysander and Bennington eagerly bent over the display.

"Missiles, all right," Bennington said. "I don't recognize the type. Let's see if we have a visual." A blurred image appeared on one of the wall screens. "Still doesn't mean anything to me. You, sir?"

Lysander shook his head. "Afraid not. Okay, let's buck this back to the Capital. Maybe the Legion has something in its data base."

"Right." Bennington made adjustments. "Whatever they are, they're anti-air. Give 'em any capability you like, they were looking right down our throats here. If we'd sent the air cav out in a body to follow the highway, or even the river—"

"Yeah. How long will it take Arnold to get into position to attack them?" Lysander asked.

"We'll have to ask him, but I'd give him at least half an hour."

"Please see that your artillery is in place and ready to fire at that time."

"Yes, sir." Bennington sounded enthusiastic.

They studied the map as they waited. The First Royals regiment was poised and ready, all they needed was assurance that they could move safely. *And the right objective. If we can find the enemy we can kill them. Definitely need to talk to the CD people. There has to be a way to get some satellite observations.*

"Urgent signal from General Owensford for Prince Lysander," Sergeant Roscius said.

"Put him on the speaker. Lysander here."

"Sir —" The word was choked off. Everyone in the command room looked up, puzzled.

Owensford was quiet for a moment. Then his voice turned cold and impersonal. "Sir, the mine garrison is engaging in a spontaneous all out counterattack. It is expected that when the attack makes contact with the enemy it will be repulsed with heavy losses. The counterattack began when the garrison learned that the Helots had used an earth penetrator rocket to attack the hospital and civilian shelter area. General Barton is attempting to halt the attack and reorganize the garrison troops, but he has had limited success. The enemy is retreating. General Barton is worried about ambuscades. He is attempting to halt the pursuit until our forces are better organized.

"Civilian casualties were heavy, amounting to sixty percent in the hospital and may be as high as fifty percent among women and children in the shelter."

The command room fell silent. Someone made a deep growling sound.

"Can you get me a direct link to Stora?" Lysander asked.

"Yes, sir, but I thought I'd better tell you this first."

"Quite correct, General Owensford. I suppose there's no chance this was an accident?"

"No, sir, they threatened to attack the central shelter unless it surrendered. The attack was an earth penetrator missile, specially designed to attack hard targets. It was launched instantly after the Helots ceased communication. There was no time for evacuation. It was deliberate, sir." Owensford's icy calm was beginning to fray.

Cold fury gnawed at Lysander's stomach, but he felt a

preternatural calm. "All right. Get me General Barton."

"Yes, sir, I'll patch him through."

"Barton here."

"General, this is Lysander. Peter told me."

"Yes, sir."

"It's not your fault. You couldn't have prevented it."

"I don't see how I could have, sir. But we have five hundred dead children here, and I was in command."

"Can you get me a general circuit? I want to speak to everyone there."

"Klingstauffer, His Highness wants a general circuit. Shall I announce you, sir?"

"Yes, please."

There was a pause, then, "All units. This is General Barton in command center. His Highness Prince Lysander Collins will speak to you now. Your Highness —"

"My people. My sisters and brothers. Please listen. I share your grief, and together we will mourn Sparta's dead. That is later. For now, I have a command. I order you to live. Wherever you are, whatever you are doing, stop, take heed, think. You are what the enemy wanted you to be, enraged citizens seeking vengeance, vulnerable to their treachery.

"And THAT IS NOT ENOUGH. You shall be avenged, but you will not be avenged through haste and madness! Vengeance demands victory, and victory demands that we act together, as a disciplined army! Brothers and Sisters! Organize. Organize and obey your officers.

"People of Sparta. I am coming, I am bringing the instruments of vengeance and destruction. Wait for me. And know that this will not end today, not today, and not tomorrow. It will not end until we are avenged. More than avenged. Together we shall pursue these creatures wherever they go, relentless pursuit, until we have killed them all, killed them not only for revenge but to cleanse this land, we shall cleanse this land of all memory of these creatures. They do not deserve to breathe the same air as free men and women, and by God Almighty I swear it, they shall not!

"We came here to this empty land, and we made a home. We built a land of honor, and we offered to share it with anyone worthy, and this is their answer. They cry for their rights. We will give them their due. We will give them justice.

"My brothers and sisters, listen. Do not throw your lives away. Halt and think. Man your assigned stations. Find your officers. Obey them. Organize, make ready, and wait for me. I am coming, my people. Never doubt it. I am coming. God may have mercy on these wolves but we shall not."

❖   ❖   ❖

"Legion headquarters has identified those missiles, sir. Something new, but the Legion data base has specs on them. Fucking bastards," Captain Tyson said.

Lysander's look silenced him. "Good. Feed the performance data to the air ops commander. What I want is a good feint. Send the choppers out as if they're headed north, but turn away before they're in danger."

Tyson straightened. "Can do."

"Lieutenant Arnold reports enemy alerted," the communications sergeant said. "They're setting up their birds, like they expect us."

"They heard the speech," Lysander said. "Or someone up north heard it and sent an alert. Doesn't matter. They expect us to come running. Arnold in position?"

"Five minutes, sir. Artillery's targeted. Rockets in place."

"Get those choppers going, then. Colonel Bennington, you'll take command of this operation. Hit them, neutralize them, take some live prisoners able to tell us how they got here, then let the constabulary finish them off. I want this regiment headed north as soon as possible."

"Yes, sir. You want me to command?"

"Yes. As soon as we've defeated the ambush, I'll take the air cav and get up to Stora."

"This may not be the only missile force they have."

"May not be, but it probably is. Jamie, they can't cover the whole countryside. We're scouting alternate routes, I'll take one of those, but by God I'm going. They need me up there."

"Aye," Jamie Bennington said. "That they do, my Prince."

❖   ❖   ❖

Twenty officers and as many civilian leaders were gathered in the command center of the Stora Mine. They greeted Lysander with grim satisfaction. "We waited, Highness," someone said. "Now lead us."

Ace Barton rose wearily to attention and saluted. "Highness. You'll be taking command now. I'd like to go back to the Legion."

"Denied," Lysander said. "General, you will continue in command here." He looked at the grim faces around him. "You'll need an expert," he said. "This is General Barton's work, and he is good at it."

"Not good enough."

"I forbid that," Lysander said. "Until now we didn't know, couldn't know, the true nature of our enemy. Blaming ourselves for not foreseeing this criminal act is pointless. General Barton, you will organize the pursuit. The objective is to harass and punish the enemy, of course, but that's not the main objective. It is far more important that you avoid their traps, avoid casualties. Preserve our people, so that we can win this war and rebuild."

"Speak for yourself," someone said. An elderly captain. "We lost a daughter and two grandchildren. I don't care what happens to me as long as I take some of them with me."

"How many others feel that way?" There were mutters, but before they could answer, Lysander shouted, "That is *treason*, Captain Caldon." He paused to let that sink in. "I said treason, and I meant it. Sparta needs you alive, not dead."

He strode into the crowd, and stood among them. "We will cleanse this planet," he said. "To do that we must win this war. Not just kill a few hundred, a few thousand, while their leaders skulk off to do this again. We have to defeat them completely, defeat their soldiers and hang those who ordered this. Anything less lets them get away to kill more women and children."

There were mutters of agreement. "How, then?" Karen Olafson asked.

"It won't be easy," Lysander said. "You can't do it alone. A retreat is always faster than the pursuit unless the retreating force is utterly routed, and these weren't. They were prepared to retreat. You've already run into ambushes."

More muttered agreement. "And so did they," Karen Olafson said.

"Yes. That was good work," Lysander said. "Major Olafson hammered them well, but still they were able to screen him out and slip past. This is what they're best at."

"But — Highness, what can we do, then?" Karen demanded.

"Harass them, yes, but carefully, avoid their traps, avoid their ambushes. Kill and capture anything they leave behind. We've already cleaned them out of the Valley behind us. Four different pockets poised to ambush us, and we have destroyed them all. You can do the same. Keep them moving, make them split up into small groups and disperse. Harass them. Many will desert their cause. The rest will be so dispersed they can't do much harm. You'll have this army neutralized, and this is their main force. Brothers, sisters, you do this, and I'll do the rest. Together we'll win this war."

"What about the others? Some of our workers joined this rebellion. We've found them dead, wearing their Helot arm band," Karen Olafson said. "And that awful little man who put the bombs in the reserve force trucks. They have spies everywhere."

"We'll take the prisoners back to Sparta City and wring them out, and we'll send technicians to screen the others here," Lysander said. "But be careful. We don't want to force anyone to join the conspiracy. In fact — General Barton, you're authorized to issue a general amnesty for anyone not directly involved in atrocities."

"But —"

"He's right, Mrs. Olafson," Barton said. "Of course the amnesty won't apply to those we caught in the act."

"No, they'll go back to the capital. The important thing is to win, win and rebuild. End this war once and for all, and leave it behind us. We can do that."

"How?" Captain Caldon asked.

"We have to deprive them of their bases. We need surveillance satellites. We must halt their off-planet supplies. None of that can be done here, and most of it I'll have to do myself. I'll have to go back to the capital. It's time to win this war, but I can't leave this Helot field army intact. It has to be made ineffective, and for that I need your help. All of you, doing the best work you can. Will you help me?"

The old captain studied the prince's look, looked to his comrades, and turned back to Lysander. "As you command."

✧ CHAPTER ELEVEN

Forms of government change. Long ago James Burnham, following Hobbes, pointed out that while it is easy to convince people that government is valuable, it is not quite so obvious that any particular form of government is best. The belief that fifty percent plus one will best look out for the interests of the whole is as much a myth as the Divine Right of Kings, and certainly no more compelling than the notion that the state may be best placed in the hands of those educated to the task. Alexander Hamilton, himself "the bastard son of a Scots peddler," argued for a strong hereditary component to the United States Constitution on the grounds that an aristocracy would look to the future and not merely to the next election. Clearly he expected an open aristocracy which could be entered on merit, but he was not shy in defending hereditary rights for those who had won admission.

By the Twentieth Century it had been repeatedly proved that the qualifications required to obtain the office of chief of state were not optimum for actually performing the job; and this regardless of whether the state was a constitutional republic like the United States, or the kind of revolutionary anarchy favored by its southern neighbors. . . .

If the ancients from Aristotle to Machiavelli were agreed on one thing, it was that when a state required strong armed forces for its survival, those armed forces had better be commanded by a single person; that the political crimes of one bad ruler were infinitely preferable to the dangers of dividing military command. Better Tiberius than a committee. The first two hundred years of the United States of America seemed to disprove that thesis, partly because prior to 1950 the United States would never have dreamed of keeping a large standing army in time of peace, and even had it done so, that army would have been conscripts, not long service volunteers.

The events of the Twenty First Century demonstrated that the ancients may have been wiser than the moderns thought . . .

— From *Utopia to Imperium:* A History of Sparta
from Alexander I to the Accession of Lysander,
by Caldwell C. Whitlock, Ph.D. (University of Sparta Press, 2220)

❖   ❖   ❖

Crofton's Encyclopedia of Contemporary History and Social Issues (3rd Edition):

Interdiction: The CoDominium Grand Senate has always reserved the right to declare an *interdiction* of space travel to or from any solar system or body therein, as punishment for actions contrary to laws which the Grand Senate regards as outside the jurisdiction of even sovereign planets. The most usual cause for such action is an attack on CoDominium citizens, particularly on Fleet personnel, or a violation of the Laws of War (q.v.). Many independent planets regard interdiction as an intolerable infringement of their sovereignty, and an attempt to reduce them to the quasi-satellite status of most Earth governments.

It is noteworthy that interdiction has never been attempted against a planet with significant naval strength . . .

❖   ❖   ❖

But perhaps naval warfare best illustrates the effect of both permanent and contingent factors in limiting the scope, intensity, and duration of operations. Specialized warships are probably quite recent in origin. The first navies may have been antipiratical in purpose, though there are grounds for thinking that the advantages conferred by the ability to move forces along rivers or coasts first prompted rules to maintain warships. But at any stage of economic development, navies have always been expensive to build and have required handling by specialized crews. Their construction and operation therefore demanded considerable disposable wealth, probably the surplus of a ruler's revenue; and if the earliest form of fighting at sea was piratical rather than political in motive, we must remember that even the pirate needs capital to start in business.

— John Keegan "The Parameters of Warfare"; *MHQ: The Quarterly Journal of Military History*, Vol 5:2, Winter 1993

❖   ❖   ❖

The house stood on large open grounds. The entry drive led past a gatehouse manned by Royal Regiment soldiers, and through a small grove of elm trees. Beyond that was half an acre of well tended grass leading up to the Georgian style house. The porch was as large as many military houses.

Hal Slater answered the door himself, and waved his visitors inside. "Come in, please, Colonel Karantov. Welcome to my home. I think you met my wife some years ago?"

"Welcome, Boris," Kathryn Slater said. She wore a simple black dress of elegant design, with a firestone pin. Her earrings flashed with a shade of green that could only have been greenfire; it was clear that Kathryn Malcolm Slater was not worried about money.

"Mrs. Kathryn Slater, General Slater," Karantov acknowledged. "I present Captain of Fleet Clayton Newell."

Newell, like Karantov, wore civilian clothing, and there was nothing to indicate that they were two of the highest ranking CoDominium officers in the Sparta system. Karantov kissed Kathryn's hand, and after a moment Newell did likewise.

Hal Slater leaned on his cane to bow stiffly, and ushered them across the entry hall toward the rear of the house. "We're meeting in my study," Slater said. "It's as secure as the Legion can make it."

"I would say trustworthy, then," Karantov said.

Captain Newell stopped in the entry hall and looked around the room, at the parquet floors, columns and mirrors, original paintings on the walls. Twin curved staircases led up to a musician's balcony above the entry. "Very nice," he said.

"Mostly Kathryn's design," Slater said.

"Impressive," Newell said. "And very lovely."

"Thank you," Kathryn Slater said. "Hal was offered an official residence as Commandant of the War College, but we decided we'd rather build our own. We've lived so many places, and this will probably be our last."

"You are pleased to live on Sparta, then," Boris Karantov said.

"Very. I don't think anyone has ever appreciated us quite so much. Now, if you'll excuse me, I'll leave you to your work," Kathryn said. "You won't be disturbed. Pleased to meet you, Captain Newell."

Hal Slater led the visitors into his study. Karantov and Newell went into the room and stopped short at the sight of several others already there. Karantov bowed stiffly. "Your Highness. I expected to meet you, of course. But — Anatoly, Samuel, you I do not expect."

"I'll explain," Hal Slater said. *Russians never consider a meeting friendly if it doesn't open with a drink.* "But first, may I get you anything? I've let the servants go for the day, but we have just about anything you would like."

"Cognac, perhaps," Karantov said.

Hal opened a paneled cabinet and poured brandy from a crystal decanter into small glasses which he handed around to everyone. They all lifted them formally. "To Sparta," Slater said.

Boris Karantov looked quizzically at Slater, but raised his glass and drained it. "Sparta, then." After a moment Captain Newell did the same.

"Excellent cognac," Karantov said. "Terran?"

"Yes, from the Crimea," Hal said. *To Russians, all brandy is cognac no matter where it comes from.* "Do you care for more?"

"Not just at moment."

"Please, be seated," Slater said. "I believe everyone has met? We will have one more visitor — ah, I believe that's him now." Hal left, and came back a few moments later with Dr. Whitlock.

"Dr. Caldwell Whitlock. You'll remember him as a political consultant to Colonel John Christian Falkenberg. Dr. Whitlock is now also in the employ of the Dual Monarchy. Dr. Whitlock, Colonel Boris

Karantov, CoDominium Fleet Marines. Fleet Captain Clayton Newell, CoDominium Navy. Captain Anatoly Nosov, formerly of the CoDominium Navy, retired, now a Captain of the Royal Spartan Naval Reserve. Captain Samuel Forrest, also retired as a Captain of the CoDominium Navy, now Rear Admiral, Royal Spartan Naval Reserve. And of course you know Crown Prince Lysander. Caldwell, we just toasted Sparta's health."

"We'll say I join you in the sentiment," Whitlock said. "Highness." Whitlock bowed slightly, and turned to the others. "Gentlemen, I'm proud to meet y'all."

"Also in the employ of Sparta," Karantov said. "May I ask, Doctor, to whom do you give primary loyalty?"

"There's no cause to choose," Whitlock said. "No conflicts."

"None at all?" Karantov frowned. "Interesting."

The study was large and comfortable, lined with book cases. The furniture was leather, massive couches and chairs. Everyone found a seat. "Pleased you could all come," Hal Slater said. "I hope no one will think I am rude if we plunge right in."

"Please do," Fleet Captain Newell said. "I confess I am intrigued to learn that two of my former shipmates are now officers of the Royal Spartan Navy. Matter of fact, I didn't know Sparta *had* a navy." If you listened closely you could still hear a bit of American New Englander accent in Newell's careful speech. "Doubtless all will be explained."

"I could have introduced them as Citizen Nosov and Citizen Sir Samuel Forrest," Slater said carefully. "Citizenship was bestowed with their naval commissions, and His Majesty was pleased to confer the Order of the Golden Fleece on his new Admiral."

"Ah," Newell said. "And this offer — it is an offer, isn't it?"

Lysander smiled slightly. "It is indeed, Fleet

Captain. The Kings in Council have authorized extending Citizenship to CoDominium personnel willing to serve the Dual Monarchy. And honors, as deserved, of course."

"I see," Newell said.

"To be brief," Dr. Whitlock said, "we can offer commissions, and generous pay to our Navy Reserve, leastwise to those who join up early, being as how we don't have much Navy. Citizenship. Land. Damn good pensions, and a chance of honors, on retirement from the Spartan Navy." He looked at Karantov. "We can use experienced Fleet Marines, too."

"You have naval personnel but not ships," Newell said carefully.

"Well, that's right just at the moment," Whitlock said. "But you know how things are back around Earth. That could change pretty fast. You never know what happens to ships when a fleet starts coming apart."

"Or where Sergei Lermontov orders ships to go," Karantov said. "I take it I am included in offer?"

"Well, yes," Hal Slater said. "You'll need a place to retire in a few years anyway, Boris. Your family is already here. You can retire from the CD any time you like, and take service with the Royal Spartan Navy. And if the CD stops your pension, we'll pay it. In addition to your Spartan pay, of course."

"Is this the deal you have, Samuel?" Newell asked.

"Yes." Samuel Forrest was a big man, large enough that he must have had difficulty getting around in CD warships without bashing his head. "They guaranteed our CoDominium pensions. Did quite a bit better than that, actually. Certainly better than I expected."

"What do you want from us, Samuel?"

"We like it here," Forrest said. "The only thing wrong with Sparta is the war. Dr. Whitlock—"

"Well, everybody knows the war would end like

that—" Dr. Whitlock snapped his fingers "— if the CoDominium fleet did its proper job of intercepting arms smuggling into Sparta. That and protecting our observation satellites. Give us our satellites and stop the enemy bringing in weapons, and we'll finish the war right enough."

"I see," Newell said. He looked significantly to Karantov, then back to Lysander. "You do understand, Your Highness, that we are not in command here? Commodore Guilford does not want to be committed, to either side. He turns a blind eye to the smugglers. To his credit, he has not given Bronson's people direct assistance."

"Merely stops the rest of y'all from doing your jobs," Whitlock said. "Well, thank the Deity for small favors even so. But gentlemen, not to rush you, but where the hell did you think of running to when the CoDominium breaks up?"

Karantov inhaled sharply. "You use strong words."

"Situation calls fo' strong words," Whitlock said. "You got to be hearing the same things I am. So many factions in the Grand Senate nobody can get a coalition together. Budget crisis in the United States. Political crisis in Russia. Already had one mutiny in the fleet, ship's crew didn't want to be transferred." Whitlock shrugged. "That's what we know about. Now, here we got a good planet, stable government that *wants* y'all, wants y'all enough they're willing to give you some land, pay good money, and guarantee your CoDominium pension to boot — I don't need to tell you, if there ain't no CoDominium there ain't likely to be no CoDominium pensions. So you got all this you can look forward to."

"And all you want is —"

"All we want," Prince Lysander said softly, "is for you to do your duty. You have the reputation of men of honor, and you have done your duty to the

CoDominium. Now — now you have a duty to civilization. Make no mistake, gentlemen. We're going to win this war, and once we have won it, we will take measures to see we are never again dependent on anyone else for our protection. We will have a Navy."

"And y'all can be part of building it," Whitlock said. "You could start in any time. And of course if you retire here, it makes sense to keep this place as healthy as possible. It's goin' to be your home, so the sooner this war is over, the better for everybody — including you."

"Da," Karantov said. "But Highness will excuse me if I say we do not see you wish to *win* this war." He shrugged.

"That can be remedied," Lysander said. He stood, and the others scrambled to their feet although there was no need to. "If that is your objection, I think it will be met soon enough. Dr. Whitlock, you have full authority to negotiate for me," Lysander said. He bowed slightly. "I'll leave the specifics to Dr. Whitlock. But rest assured, rest assured, gentlemen, we do intend to win this war, and we will do whatever we must do. *Whatever* we must do. Good afternoon."

"Our Prince has grown a very great deal," Dr. Whitlock said softly after Lysander left the room. Everyone nodded.

"Negotiate," Boris Karantov said.

Caldwell Whitlock smiled broadly. "Negotiate indeed." He nodded to Slater, and Hal went to the bar and poured their glasses full of cognac again. Whitlock passed them out. "Now, what y'all want is homes, good land, good positions for your families. Education for your children and grandchildren. Let me point out, gentlemen, that one, two, maybe five percent of the developed land on Sparta belongs to rebels. Worth a whole lot. All that will come to the government when we win. We have land, honors, titles, a decent place to live. We need a navy." He raised his glass. "Here's to you."

Karantov looked to Newell, then back to Whitlock. "Falkenberg makes no mistake in choosing you as his representative," he said. "I have always thought to retire to raise horses, perhaps sail small boats on a suitable lake. What say you, Captain Newell? Lord Admiral Newell has a pleasant sound. As does Baron Karantov. To Sparta."

Clayton Newell looked at the others, then around the room. He hesitated for a long moment before he spoke. "You speak for both Falkenberg and the Dual Monarchy." Whitlock nodded. "Which means you speak for Lermontov and the Grants, even if you do not acknowledge that."

"Oh, I reckon I can say I do," Whitlock said. "Long as it's strictly among us friends. Blaines too, for that matter. But you will understand, Captain, what with the communications difficulties, sometimes we don't have orders, but we still got to act."

"And you have that authority?"

"We really are layin' all our cards on the table," Whitlock said. "Well, it's this way. Colonel Falkenberg values King Alexander and Prince Lysander a lot, and of course anything purely havin' to do with Sparta is goin' to be decided by the Spartans. Anything else is sort of up to me, and Lieutenant Colonels Slater and Owensford, acting collectively."

Newell sat in an overstuffed leather chair. "And you see no conflict of interest? Between Lermontov's interest and Sparta's?" He looked to Forrest and Nosov. "Nor do you?"

Samuel Forrest shook his head. "Not really. You have to be aware that King Alexander has been a Lermontov ally for a long time. Right now, under the CoDominium Treaty, Sparta isn't even supposed to have a foreign policy, let alone a navy, so how can there be a conflict over external matters? But the simple answer is that

King Alexander and Prince Lysander are aware of the situation, and they've left Dr. Whitlock to negotiate for them, so they must not see much conflict."

Newell stared at each one in turn for a long time, then contemplated his still full glass. Finally he said, "Clearly Boris is convinced that your Prince Lysander, and all of you, may all be trusted." He spoke slowly and carefully, measuring every word. "I will confess, what we hear from Earth is alarming, and little would surprise me. War, a coup by Admiral Lermontov, perhaps more likely a coup *against* the Grand Admiral. No one knows what to expect." He shrugged. "Look, I find your offers attractive, I'd be a fool not to. But what happens if you don't win? Suppose Boris and I help you, and you lose? We'd be gambling everything."

"We are now," Hal Slater said carefully. "We don't intend to lose."

"No one does," Newell said. "But it's not entirely in your power. You must know what you're up against. Bronson's got money, power, ambition. He has his own shipping line, and enough money to arm those ships. You could win your war, and still find this planet destroyed, with no CoDominium force to avenge you."

"Which is why we need a fleet," Samuel Forrest said. "It need not be a large fleet, just enough to take on armed merchant men. A squadron would do. I believe there is a squadron here, now." He raised his glass. "To Sparta."

Anatoly Nosov stood and held out his glass for a refill. "Let us be specific. You have four warships here. One is frigate *Volga*, Commander Vadim Dzirkals, very much a Lermontov supporter. One is cruiser *Vera Cruz*, your own, and we presume your officers will follow as you lead. One is frigate *Kirov*; I do not know Commander Chornovil, but I understand he is intelligent, and certainly he was promoted by Lermontov. More to the point, four of his bridge officers formerly served with me in *Moscva*. Fourth is destroyer *Aegir*, with American commander. I believe Captain Forrest knows him—"

"Harry Clarkson," Forrest said. "A Townsend man, but I think most of his wardroom has other sentiments."

"A fleet," Karantov said. "Perhaps sufficient no matter what Bronson sends."

"You're suggesting mutiny," Newell said. His eyes darted around the room.

"I suggest nothing," Nosov said. "But it is very much possible that soon there is no CoDominium, and it is to advantage of us all that we consider possibilities." He raised his glass. "To Sparta."

"If there is no CoDominium, those with control of naval power will have great power indeed," Newell mused. "Much could be done with a squadron of warships. Not just here."

"Well, I suppose," Dr. Whitlock said. "But then there's this. One time, Napoleon was admirin' his troops on parade. 'See the bayonets of my Guards, how they gleam,' he said. And Talleyrand said, 'You can do anything with a bayonet, Sire, except sit on it.' I'd think the same thing might apply to your warships, Captain. You can blow hell out of a planet, but where you goin' to set down? You want to face the kind of war the Spartans have been fighting? Spend your lives wondering when someone's going to kill your family? Long time ago, a man named Ortega y Gasset pointed out, rulin's not so much a matter of an iron fist as it is of a firm seat." He raised his glass. "To Sparta."

"I will drink to Sparta," Newell said. "And perhaps when Spartans have achieved that firm seat, we will continue this discussion. Until then —" He raised his glass. "To Sparta."

✧ CHAPTER TWELVE

It will be agreed that the aim of strategy is to fulfill the objectives laid down by policy, making the best use of the resources available. Now the objective may be offensive in nature (e.g., conquest or the imposition of severe terms), it may be defensive (e.g., the protection of certain areas or interests) or it may merely be the maintenance of the political *status quo*. It is therefore obvious straight away that formulae such as that attributed to Clausewitz, 'decision as a result of victory in battle,' are not applicable to all types of objective. There is only one general rule applicable to all: disregard the method by which the decision is to be reached and consider only the outcome which it is desired to achieve. The outcome desired is to force the enemy to accept the terms we wish to impose on him. In this dialectic of wills *a decision is achieved when a certain psychological effect has been produced* on the enemy: when he becomes convinced that it is useless to start or alternatively to continue the struggle.

—Général D'Armée André Beaufre,
An Introduction to Strategy, 1965

✧   ✧   ✧

From this time Cataline turned his back on politics because it involved envy and strife and was not the speediest and most effective means for attaining absolute power. He obtained quantities of money from women who hoped their husbands would be killed in a revolution, conspired with a number of senators and knights, and collected plebeians, foreigners, and slaves. Lesser leaders of the conspiracy were Cornelius Lentulus and Cethegus, then praetors. To the Sullans up and down Italy who had squandered their profits and were eager for similar doings he sent messengers, Gaius Mallius to Faesulae in Etruria and others to Picenum and Apulia, and these quietly enrolled an army for him. These facts were still secret when they were communicated to Cicero by Fulvia, a woman of position . . .

— Moses Hadas, *A History of Rome*

✧   ✧   ✧

The Senate Chamber was unusually quiet. High marble walls, a dais for the speaker, benches encircling it. The Chamber had been designed as a romanticized version of the best description they had of the place of government of ancient Sparta.

Two thrones, one to either side of the rostrum, stood empty as the Senators took their places around the room. There was an electric air, which made Senator Dion Croser nervous. What did they plan?

There was a thundering knock at the door. The Sergeant at Arms opened it, looked out, and closed the door again. "My Lord Speaker, the Kings ask admission."

The Speaker's name was Loren Scaevoli, a dry stick of a man nearing his hundredth year and looking it even with regen; he had been the youngest of the Founders. His voice had an unusual inflection to it this day, almost of glee. "Senators, the Kings ask admission to our chamber. What say you?"

"Aye and welcome!" a hundred voices shouted.

"Three cheers for His Majesty Alexander I!"

The cry ran through the chamber, and the crashing *hurrah* echoed from the high marble walls of the big semicircular room. One hundred twenty-three Senators lined the benches that encircled the dais; one hundred seventeen cheered. Dion Croser stood politely with his handful of supporters, waiting for the sound to die.

"Three cheers for King David!" If there was any less enthusiasm it was hard to notice, but when someone shouted "And for Prince Lysander!" there was no mistaking the renewed enthusiasm.

"It is the will of the Senate that the Kings be admitted," Scaevoli said formally. The Sergeant opened the door to allow them in, then closed it to exclude the Life Guards. By tradition the Kings of Sparta were guarded only by Senators when they entered the Senate chamber, and they entered only by permission, not as a matter of right.

They came down the center aisle together, walking slowly.

Something unusual, Croser thought with a prickle of interest, looking down at the Speaker's dais. He had developed a certain affection for the mock-classical atmosphere in this room, and even for the cut and thrust of Parliamentary debate. Decadent and doomed, of course, but he would miss it; even the smells of tobacco and the leather cushions.

The Kings took their places in the twin thrones on either side of the Speaker's chair. David I, solemn and grim faced, as if he dreaded what was about to happen. And Alexander, smiling, looking very healthy indeed, compared to a few months ago. *Damn him.* The waxing insanity of the Collins king had been a large part of his plans. Behind the dais the display wall was set to show the crowned mountain of the Dual Monarchy.

For now, Croser thought. *For now.*

The Privy Council, led by Crown Prince Lysander, filed in, taking their seats in the horseshoe-shaped area surrounding the thrones. That *was* unusual, except for the Budget Debates and the yearly Speech from the Thrones. Then the five Ephors, the direct representatives of the Citizens. Croser raised his eyes to the spectator's gallery that ringed the upper story of the chamber, just under the coffered ceiling. One of his supporters was arguing with the guard.

Trouble, he thought, looking down at his fingers arranging the papers on the table before him. Black folders against the creamy stone, the whole interior was lined with it . . . He tapped at the terminal built into it; the library functions were active, but not the communicator.

The senators who had escorted the Kings to their thrones filed back to the benches. The Sergeant at Arms carried in the mace of office on its crimson cushion, and the Senatorial Chaplain delivered his invocation, ending as always, "God save the State," but it seemed more than perfunctory today.

"This one hundredth seventy-eight session of the Senate of the Dual Monarchy of Sparta will now come to order. This is to be an Executive Session; I remind all members of this august body that there exists a state of apprehended insurrection."

Croser pressed a key. "Point of order, Mr. Speaker," he said, and the computers relayed his voice until it seemed to come from everywhere and nowhere. "Is this to be a closed session? Pursuant to the Senatorial Rules of Procedure and the Constitution, Article XXI, Rights of Assembly and Information Access, I protest that such action is highly irregular if not unconstitutional without prior notice."

The Speaker's eyes were almost hidden by their wrinkled pouches.

"Senator Croser, you are not recognized."

"I protest!"

"Protest is noted; please be seated, sir."

The Speaker raised the amplification. "Senators, I spy strangers. The Sergeant at Arms will clear the Senate Chamber of all who do not belong here."

Something squeezed at Croser's stomach, as the clerks and secretarial staff left their posts. Shouts came from the galleries; Guard troops were clearing them, and though their uniforms were the gray and blue and silver of ceremony, their rifles held magazines and fixed bayonets. He half-rose and chopped one hand down across his chest; above him his bodyguard

Cheung relaxed from the beginning of a move that would have ripped out a soldier's throat as he sprang to seize a weapon. The visitors were led away, out of the galleries, out of the chamber.

Croser keyed the circuit that connected him with the other NCLF representatives in the Senate. "All to be detained," he murmured. "So that nothing can get out. Although silence is a message in itself."

"*Leader, what shall we do?*" one of his supporters hissed in his ear.

"Shut up."

"But, Leader —"

"Shut up and *stay* shut up. Not one word, any of you; not under any circumstances whatsoever."

Croser forced his lips to stop curling back from his teeth, tasting sweat as he reached out calmly to take a sip of water. *What was it that old tombstone said? "I expected this, but not so soon."*

The Speaker rapped his gavel. "I recognize the President of the Council of Ephors," he said.

Citizen Selena Borah Dawson, wife of the Principal Secretary of State, and very popular in Citizen Assemblies. The Ephors functioned largely as ombudsmen, but they had certain formal duties as direct representatives of the Citizens. "Senators, I ask for a resolution which under the Constitution the Kings may not request, but which you may grant."

There was a ripple of movement. Croser hit the *record* and *playback/scan* functions. "Ah, interesting," he murmured. "See, there are the ones who knew it was coming." Excellent security on this measure, if Murasaki hadn't picked it up. A damaging blow, despite all the preparations.

"Senators, I make no speeches," Selena Dawson said. "The Speaker will show the evidence on which the request of the Citizens will be based."

The Speaker touched buttons, doing the work of his vanished clerk. The crowned mountain faded from the giant display screen above the dais, to be replaced with a close-up shot. Croser recognized it; the Velysen ranch, with the dead bodies displayed.

"Senators, bear witness," the old man said.

The image faded, to be replaced by another. This time a bleeding child, screaming by the corpse of its mother outside a burning building.

Hmmm. Croser thought. *Oh yes, the Hume Consolidated Financial Bank bombing.*

More. Burnt out ranches. A playback of Steven Armstrong's engine crew drowning before the camera as their ship sank, of his family burning in their car. Chaos and blood in a restaurant, and a young man with his ribs peeled open by the grenade he had smothered. The frozen body of Deborah Lefkowitz, as the Helots and the scavengers had left it. More still; after fifteen minutes Croser leaned back in his chair and let his eyes slide down to the panel before him, flicking through shots of the other Senator's faces. Even a few of his own NCLF appointees were looking gray; there were tears elsewhere on the benches, and not only among women. A few were looking away also, swallowing. Colleagues moved to assist one elderly representative who fainted.

"And the final horror," the Speaker said. The wall was filled with the image of the shattered bunker at the Stora Mine. The camera moved inside, to hospital beds thrown over, then came to a halt on a tangle of broken and bleeding children shielded by dying women. "A deliberate act, done with equipment imported for the purpose," Scaevoli said. "Imported from off-planet, brought all this way to be used to kill our women and children. Madame President, do the Ephors have a request of this body?"

"We do, My Lord Speaker. The State is in danger. We ask for the Ultimate Decree."

Lars Armstrong leapt to his feet. "At last!"

I might have known, Croser thought. Steven Armstrong's brother, and his successor as representative of the Maritime Products Trade Association.

Scaevoli looked to the Ephors. "Is this the request of the Ephors? Do each of you agree?" Three nods of assent. A fourth, a young man thought to be a radical fireball, stood staring in horror at the screen. He looked from that to Croser, looked defiantly to the Speaker. "Aye," he said.

The Speaker bowed, and turned to the chamber. "I recognize Senator Armstrong."

"My Lord Speaker, I move that the Senate instruct the Kings to take all measures necessary to ensure the safety of the state, effective as of this date and to run for one Spartan year before expiry or renewal."

"Mr. Speaker!" Croser said, shooting to his feet.

"I recognize Senator Croser."

"If the honorable Senator moves the Ultimate Decree —" essentially a drastic form of martial law, with the suspension of civil rights "— then surely there must be debate beyond mere assertion! Is this a deliberative body, or a rubber-stamp whose assent is secured in advance by conspiracy?"

Or a lynch mob, he thought, looking at the faces glaring at him from every corner of the chamber.

"Mr. Speaker."

"I recognize Senator Armstrong."

"Mr. Speaker." Armstrong was a tall blond man like his brother, perhaps a little heavier, with hair that was thinning on top. His smile was much like that of the carnivore piscoids his family's ships hunted. "I can best reply using words other than my own.

"*How long, O Croser, how long,*" he began, in a calm conversational tone.

"*How long will you continue your abuse of our forbearance? What bounds will you set to your display of reckless contempt? Are you not affected by the alarm of the people, by the rallying of all loyal citizens, by the convening of the senate in this safely-guarded spot, by the looks and expressions of all assembled here? Do you not perceive that your designs are exposed? The Senate is well aware of the facts, but the criminal still lives. Lives? Yes, lives; and even comes down to the Senate, takes part in the public deliberations, and marks down with ominous glances every single one of us for massacre.*

"As to why —" Armstrong pointed silently to the screen.

Croser waited out the applause. *You'll envy your brother before I'm through with you*, he thought coldly.

"Mr. Speaker," he said quietly.

"I recognize Senator Croser."

"My compliments to the Senator on his ability to paraphrase the Classics; however, he is not Marcus Tullius Cicero. Nor is this Rome. Nor am I," he went on, letting a slight sneer into his tone, "the brother of the man whose agents destroyed a shuttle with over one thousand men, women and children aboard — an atrocity I note is *not* among the disgraceful collection of demagogic propaganda to which we have been exposed! An atrocity which has imperiled the independence of Sparta."

One of Armstrong's friends gripped him by the arm as he began a lunge forward.

"If this assembly," Croser went on, "wishes to emulate the Senate of the late Roman Republic — and court the same fate at the hands of ambitious generals and mercenary armies — then at least my voice will have been heard in warning!"

He sat. *Not bad*, he thought. Not that it would make any difference, but it would be there on the record. Another Senator asked for the floor.

"I recognize Senator Hollings."

"Mr. Speaker. While I agree that a grave emergency confronts the State, I am disturbed by the reckless haste with which the Ultimate Decree has been proposed; in fact —"

Croser glanced at his wrist; a half-hour since the session began. *Longer the better*, he thought.

At last the Speaker's gavel fell. "Senators, do I hear a second for Senator Armstrong's motion?"

"I second."

"Senator Makeba seconds. Senators, a motion is before this assembly. The Ephors acting in their capacity as Protectors of the Citizens have requested the Ultimate Decree, authorizing the Kings to take all necessary actions to safeguard the State, and it has been duly moved and seconded. Duration is one year from this date, subject to renewal by vote. A two-thirds majority is necessary for the passage of this Decree. Senators, you have one minute to register your will."

A thick silence descended; despite the ventilators, Croser could smell the sweat of fear and tension. At last Scaevoli looked up from his desk and smiled at him.

"For, one hundred seven votes. Against, eight votes. Eight abstentions. The Decree is in force, as of this day, April seventeenth, 2096, and this hour."

The old man rose, moving with careful dignity. There was a slight gasp as he lifted the Mace of the Senate from its cushion; the procedure was laid down in the Constitution, but Sparta had never seen it done in all the years since the Founding. Scaevoli turned, bowing as he laid the symbol of representative power on the empty plinth equidistant between the two thrones.

"Your Majesties," he said, bowing to the left and right. "Into your hands we yield the Sword of the State. May God preserve and guide you."

"Amen," Alexander said.

He stood. After a moment David I stood as well.

"Our first act shall be to appoint Crown Prince Lysander as Master of the Forces," Alexander said. "He shall act in the name of the Kings with the authority of the Kings until such time as we shall rescind those powers." He bowed toward David.

David said, "So be it," and sat.

Alexander was still on his feet. "Senators," he said. "One man is the author of our miseries; one man is responsible for the unspeakable conspiracy which has caused so much suffering and death among Our people." He paused, as all eyes turned to Croser. "From respect for your august assembly's immunity from executive action, I now require that you place under arrest Senator Dion Croser, on charges of High Treason, and take him from this place to be delivered to duly appointed officers who shall place him in custody and hold him at our pleasure."

Croser stood; something seemed to pass from his face, as if an invisible mask had been removed.

"Very well." His voice cut through the buzz of excitement that filled the chamber, clear and carrying enough not to need amplification; half a dozen Senators were elbowing their way toward him.

"Treason?" he said coldly, then laughed. "I too have an appropriate quotation. 'Why is it that treason never prospers? Why, if it prosper, none dare *call* it treason!'"

Silence fell for a moment. "And if this is treason, rest assured I shall make the most of it. *I'll be back.*"

"Attach the leads here and here, please," Jesus Alana said.

They had selected a small staff office in the Palace for the interrogation; the chair to which Croser was strapped was already secured to the floor, and the equipment had been easy to set up.

"As you can see, gentlemen," Alana went on, "this is a completely non intrusive technique. No pain or drugs. The subject condemns himself."

Alexander and David seated themselves in one corner, determination and distaste on their faces; the Senators joined them, and Scaevoli, who watched with bright-eyed interest. Prince Lysander entered in full uniform.

"About time," he said softly, smiling at Croser. "About bloody time."

"Catherine?"

"Ready to calibrate," she replied, looking up from the desk.

"Senator Croser," Jesus Alana said politely. "You realize this system doesn't require your collaboration? Your body and nervous system cannot lie to the machines; even if you don't say a word, 'yes' and 'no' will come through as clearly as if you had shouted. Why don't you cooperate now, and save us all time and trouble, and yourself some discomfort?"

Croser could not move in the padded clamps, but he managed to spit with fair accuracy at the Legionnaire's feet. Jesus Alana sighed.

"Is your name Dion Croser?" he asked.

"Got it, positive," Catherine said.

"Are you a dolphin?"

"Negative, Jesus."

"Are you leader of the conspiracy to overthrow the Dual Monarchy?"

"Positive, ninety-seven percent. Fear reaction,

aggression. Ambivalence; he's been wondering if he's still really in charge."

This time Croser spoke: *"Om."*

"Do you know the woman known as Field Prime?"

"Om mane padme hum."

"Does she work for you?"

"No—"

"Uncertainty," said Catherine.

"With reason," Jesus answered. "You have been engaged in warfare against the Dual Monarchy. Are you in the employ of anyone off-planet? Are you in the employ of Grand Senator Bronson?"

Catherine shook her head.

Jesus Alana smiled thinly. "Have you received material and financial assistance from Grand Senator Bronson? Thank you. Do you receive much assistance from that source? Was one item of that assistance a large missile designed to penetrate and destroy fortresses? Ah, you remember that missile. Were you aware that this missile was to be employed in the attack on the Stora mines?"

"Not for that!"

"Not for what, Senator?" Jesus asked pleasantly. "You were then aware that there would be an attack on the mine. Did you approve that attack?"

"Om mane padme hum."

"To whom did you give that approval? Did you give approval to Field Prime? Thank you. Is Skida Thibodeau the person known as Field Prime?"

"Om mane padme hum."

"Where is Field Prime now? Do you want to see her? Shall we bring her to you when we have captured her? Perhaps you would care to be in the same cell?"

Croser looked as if he had swallowed a serpent. Catherine held up her thumb and forefinger joined in a circle. Her smile showed wicked glee.

"Does Senator Bronson have representatives on this planet? Ah, does he have more than one? Ah. Thank you, we will return to that point later. For now, does the term technoninja mean anything to you? Do the technoninjas work for you?"

"Doubt again, Jesus," Catherine said.

"So. Ms. Thibodeau calls herself Field Prime. Do you have a title in this movement? What is that title? Are you called President? Chairman? Something Prime? Ah. Sparta Prime? Political Prime? Movement Prime?"

"Om mane padme hum."

"City Prime? Not city but closer. Ah. Capital Prime? So. You are known as Capital Prime," Jesus said. "You see, Senator, it does you no good to evade, and I fear your bio-feedback training is not up to this task. Do you know where Field Prime is? Do you know where her primary base is located? Thank you. Do others around you know? Does the bodyguard known as Cheung know?" Jesus smiled wolfishly. "You may be pleased to know that the Cheung brothers are reunited, in the basement of the Palace. We will soon know all that they know."

"So much for your legalities," Croser said. "Lee Cheung has committed no crime. I didn't know he had a brother."

"Both lies," Catherine said.

"Ah, but under the Ultimate Decree we need not prove a crime to detain someone," Jesus said.

"It wasn't passed yet when you arrested him."

"True, but he was seen to be armed in the Senate Galleries. He was detained for proper identification, but before his release — you see, Senator, you are not the only one who can employ the law for his own purposes. We now require confirmation of information we already have. Is the primary base camp in the

Southeast? Here, on this map."

"*Om mane padme hum.*"

"Do you ever eat dogfood for breakfast?"

"*Om mane padme hum.*"

"Was your mother attractive?"

"*Om mane padme hum.*"

"In this sector then? Ah. In this river valley?"

"*Om mane padme hum.*"

"How far from the river is the entrance to that cave known as Base One? More than two hundred kilometers? More than three hundred?"

"*Om mane padme hum.*"

"Did you order the assassination of Alicia Armstrong?"

"*Om mane padme hum.*"

"Ah," Catherine said. "Reaction damping a little . . . Negative. He didn't."

"Was the bombing which killed Alicia Armstrong done on your orders."

"*Om mane padme hum.*"

"Positive, with some ambivalence, Jesus. Remarkably good control over his pulse rate," she added. "Congratulations, Senator. I've worked with few better."

"Did you intend the bombing to kill Senator Steven Armstrong?"

"*Om mane padme hum.*"

"Positive, he did."

"Is Senator Hollings a member of your conspiracy?"

"*Om mane padme hum.*"

"Negative on that, but there's some ambiguity."

"Do you consider Senator Hollings to be an unconscious supporter of your conspiracy?"

"*Om mane padme hum.*"

"Yes-no."

"A dupe?"

"Positive."

"Would you call him a useful idiot?"

"That's it," Catherine said.

"Is the moon made of dog droppings?"

"*Om mane padme hum.*"

"Is the base camp more than thirty kilometers from the bend in the river? Ah, is it more than fifteen? More than ten? More than ten but less than fifteen, then . . ."

"I'm glad that's over," Alexander said as the guards took Croser away. A look of distaste bent the Spartan king's mouth for a moment. "It's necessary, but I don't like it."

Lysander's face showed no emotion at all.

"Over for the moment, Sire," Jesus Alana said, looking up from his notes. He punched a key. "There, the RSMP and the Milice can act on the new information. There's a great deal more information yet to be got out of Croser," he added. "*Madre de Dios*, I'm happy we didn't have to beat it out of him; that one, you could pull his toenails out and get nothing."

"I can still hardly believe it," David said, shaking his head and looking at his hands. "All these years, he was . . . and this was inside him, this sewer. How could, he was meeting people and smiling at them and talking and all along . . . Is he mad?"

"No, Sire," Catherine Alana said, beginning the shutdown on her equipment as she went on:

"Thibodeau may be, technically, from the profile we've built. Human beings have a capacity to learn speech, and to develop a conscience; if they aren't taught at the right stage, conscience atrophies, and you get a feral child or a sociopath. She could be a borderline sociopath. Croser's as sane as any of us here — and as bright, IQ of about one hundred fifty-two — he's just too bloody evil to be allowed to live."

"Amen," Alexander said grimly. "And he'll hang, along with the others we catch."

"And his property goes to reward loyal Citizens," Lysander said. He leaned forward to study the form his father held in his hands. It was a proscription notice, bearing the Royal seals and signatures, describing the individuals' crimes and ending with an identical proclamation: *to be cast out from all protection of law; declared to be among the enemies-general of human kind, to be dealt with as wolves are.*

"Suitable," he said. "I just hope we catch them all."

"We won't," Jesus replied, calling up some of his notes. "They had plans; cut-outs, dispersal plans, duplicate facilities, you name it. Friend Croser was smart enough to arrange not to know a lot of details, and a lot of them will be going to ground right now. We'll sweep up a good many of the big names, and any number of the dupes who didn't know the NCLF was in the rebellion."

"We must be careful of those," Alexander said. "They have committed no crime—"

"Sire, they were at best very stupid," Lysander said. "And while we can't proscribe stupidity, we don't need to reward it. I take it, Captain, you do not consider this morning decisive."

"On the contrary, Highness, I believe it is the most decisive act since the war began. We have undoubtedly hurt them very badly, and if we can keep them on the run we may be able to end this war."

"The leadership," Alexander said. "We need Miss Thibodeau."

"And Murasaki," Jesus Alana said. "He perhaps more than the others, Sire."

"We shall proclaim rewards for both of them," Alexander said. "One million crowns, payable in CoDominium credits if so desired, for the head of

Skida Thibodeau. Two million if she is delivered alive. Half a million for Murasaki dead, one million alive. Half that for information leading to their death or capture. We'll set up ways to make it easy to tell us."

"That should prove interesting," Jesus said. "Some of those gutter scum would sell their entire families for much less. I foresee interesting times for their leadership."

"What will you do now?" Alexander asked Lysander.

"Melissa will recover," Lysander said. "I'd like to stay with her, but you've just made me Master of the Forces, and I don't suppose I'll have a free moment. I'm not protesting, it's what I asked for."

"Be careful what you wish for," Catherine Alana said softly.

"Exactly. We will need to marshal our forces against this Base One of theirs, and this time we will destroy it. It and all the equipment in it. But that isn't going to be simple."

"Indeed," Jesus Alana said. "The Legion will assist, of course, particularly with the artillery, but most of this must be primarily a Spartan effort."

"Yes. And that, I have to say, is quite satisfactory. It's not that I don't value the Legion's contributions—"

"But it's nice to have your destiny in your own hands," Catherine said. "We understand, Highness. Maybe better than you think."

✧ CHAPTER THIRTEEN

Guerrillas required a base. Although they traditionally lived partially at their enemy's expense — because of their raids against supply depots and convoys — guerrillas still needed a place that provided them an assured source of supplies, such as Mina's secluded area and powder factory. Without such a base, the need for food, fuel, equipment, and ammunition would dominate their operations, place a severe constraint both on their movements and their choice of objectives for their raids, and could drive them from one raid to another in search of supplies until they had exhausted their physical and psychological resources. In addition, a base provided a place for rest and recuperation and a point to which they could retreat. Thus, the base had to be reasonably secure from enemy attack . . .

— Archer Jones, *The Art Of War in the Western World*

✧   ✧   ✧

One of the surest means of making a retreat successfully is to familiarize the officers and soldiers with the idea that an enemy may be resisted quite as well when coming on the rear as on the front, and that the preservation of order is the only means of saving a body of troops harassed by the enemy during a retrograde movement. Rigid discipline is at all times the best preservation of good order, but it is of especial importance during a retreat. To enforce discipline, subsistence must be furnished, that the troops may not be obliged to straggle off for the purpose of getting supplies by marauding.

It is a good plan to give the command of the rear-guard to an officer of great coolness . . .

— Baron Antoine Henri de Jomini, *The Art of War*

✧   ✧   ✧

The helicopters skimmed in low over the hilltop.

The long twilight of Sparta's northern-hemisphere summer was settling over the Dales, throwing purple shadows over the forested vales between the hills. Gathering dusk made the muzzle flashes huge belches of leaf-shaped flame as the howitzers bellowed from their laager, six 155mm cannon on light-tank chassis. They and their supporting vehicles were dug in behind a two-meter berm gouged out by the engineering vehicles. A line of trucks snaked back to the south, bringing up heavy shells to feed the iron appetite of the guns. A radar vehicle stood a little to one side, its big golf-ball shaped tracking antenna rocking slightly on its gimbals; other vehicles were spotted around the enclosure, APC's for the crews, communications tanks, trucks, a field-kitchen.

Peter Owensford stood in the open doorway of the aircraft; the moment the skids touched down he tumbled out, followed by his Headquarters group. Then the lead helicopter whirled away, and the second touched down briefly to disgorge its load. The dark machines sped south, hugging the nape of the earth, the low slicing sound of their silenced blades fading quickly. The soldiers' boots swished in grass, sank into the soft fluffy purple-brown earth thrown up by spades and earthmoving machinery or simply ripped free of the sod by treads and wheels; it smelled as rich as new bread, under the overpowering sweetness of crushed grass and the diesel-explosive stink of war.

Five tubes firing, he thought, remembering to leave his mouth slightly open so the overpressure would not damage eardrums. The sixth must be deadlined for maintenance, about par for the course. The artillery barrage halted, an echoing silence broken by the squeal of bearings as the self-propelled guns shifted targets. Off on the horizon to the north light flickered, lighter weapons firing. Owensford tapped into the battalion push as he walked toward the command table set up at the rear of an APC. Shashtri had just acknowledged a request for counterbattery fire; as they walked up he could see a spyeye or RPV surveillance camera view of the target, two batteries of heavy mortars firing from within a narrow erosion-cut gully in the limestone rock. Sastri's singsong voice murmured as the little Krishnan bent over the table.

Muzzle flashes came from the enemy 160's. The table was Legion-standard equipment, either what they had brought to Sparta or one of the shipments of Friedlander battle electronics just coming in; looking down was like being suspended in an aircraft observing the Helot battery. The silence was eerie, you expected to hear the CRUMP and whistle of heavy mortars . . . giddy-making, as the viewpoint shifted. Definitely an RPV about a kilometer to one side. The muzzles of the mortars dipped as the hydraulics lowered them into loading position.

"Fire mission. HE and anti-personnel equal measures," Major Sastri said. He touched controls and a grid sprang out on the table-screen, and then a red dot centered on the enemy position. "Bearing and range, mark."

Another voice sounded, calm and flat, the battery commander. "Received and locked." Clangs and rattles from the guns as the autoloaders cycled. "Loaded basebleed HE standard. Gun one, ranging fire. Mark. Shoot."

A short massive sound, slapping dirt and grit across the firebase in a hot puff as the first gun fired and gas shot out of the twin-baffle muzzle brakes. The gun recoiled, and the vehicle rocked back on its treads slightly, digging the spades at the rear of the chassis deeper into the dirt. A sound like heavy cloth tearing faded across the sky to the north. The mortars on the screen were firing when the shell exploded eleven seconds later, on the lip of the crevasse in which they were emplaced and directly above them.

"Correction," Shashtri said. He read off numbers from the map table. "Execute fire mission, battery, fire for effect," Shashtri said.

Almost on the heels of the words the other guns of the battery opened up, cycling out the heavy shells at one every seven seconds. On the screen the narrow slit in the earth vanished; most of the 155mm rounds dropped neatly through it, to gout back out in white-light flashes. Several struck the rock lips on either side and penetrated before exploding, sending multitone cascades of chalky rubble down into the depths of the canyon. Smoke and dust billowed back, silent and dreadful; then the ammunition with the mortars detonated in a string of secondary explosions that lifted the whole hillside up in a crackle-finished dome of smoke.

The image jiggled. An operator spoke:

"Acquisition on the drone. Tracking. Evasive action." The surface rushed up and the viewpoint was jinking down a valley. Suddenly camouflage nets showed between the trees, IR-sensor enhancement. Owensford leaned forward in sharp curiosity, and then the screen went to pearly-gray blankness.

"Battery, fire mission," Sastri said thoughtfully. "Three rounds. Penetrator and impact-fuse, mark." His fingers touched a portable keyboard. "Whatever was under that net is deserving a tickle."

He looked up and saluted. "With you in a moment, sir. Captain Liu, take over. This way."

They walked downslope and south, speaking quietly; the helmet earphones filtered the huge thudding noise of the guns.

"Not having much trouble?" Owensford said.

"No indeed, sir. The preliminary artillery duel went

as expected, and now they have nothing with the range to reach us, while we can hit them as we please. The drones provide good observation, and the Spartan scouts are proving very effective as well. This is a very one-sided battle, and so long as we have ammunition it will continue to be."

"Just the kind I like," Owensford said. "Well done."

"Thank you, sir. Ah, here we are." The secondary laager was a little apart from the regimental artillery battery; one vehicle was a trailer, from which a tent had been unfolded.

They ducked inside the tent, flipping up the visors of their helmets. There were four men inside; George Slater, commander of 1st Brigade, the spearpoint force of the Royal Army columns heading north into the Dales. The Royal Army colonel commanding the 2nd Mechanized Regiment . . . *Morrientes*, Owensford remembered, he'd been a Brotherhood militia officer last year, transferred to the Field Force shortly after the first Dales campaign. A Royal Army interrogator, a sergeant; tall, wiry-slender, beak-nosed and thin-faced, with steady dark eyes. And a Helot, in the dentist-style chair, his head and limbs immobilized by clamps; his face had the glazed, wandering look of someone under questioning drugs.

Not really truth drugs, the mercenary reminded himself. All they really did was make you not give a damn, and feel very, very chatty. Individual reactions varied widely, as well, unless you had time and facilities to do up a batch adjusted to the subject's personal biochemistry. Spartan biochemists had the knowledge to do that, but the proper equipment was rare outside the University.

"Carry on," Owensford said. He caught the sergeant's eye. "Important prisoner?"

"Equivalent of colonel, sir," the interrogator said.

"I've got a transcript . . ." He bent to the captive's ear. "Is it your fault, Perrez?"

"No," the man muttered, his eyes roving the room without seeing the faces around them.

For a moment he tailed off in a mutter of Spanish. Spanglish, actually; Owensford recognized the dialect, common in the tier of states south of the Rio Grande which had once been part of Mexico. The sergeant's gentle urging brought him back to something more generally comprehensible.

"That maricon kraut von Reuter, he no pull back fast enough. If Skilly were here, no esta problema, the Cits wouldn't comprende where we were. Little shits, sneaking through the trees and spying, Skilly would get them. Two-knife would. Reuter doesn't have half the cojones Skilly does." He giggled, speculating obscenely on where she kept them.

"So where is Skilly?"

"She run off, she and Two-knife both. Gone. Bug out, baby."

"Leaving you behind with von Reuter."

"Yeah."

"Why?"

"She got a plan, that one."

"She didn't tell you the plan, did she? Ran off, leaving you behind. How do you know there was a plan, that she wasn't just saving her own skin?"

"Naw, she wouldn't do that. She wouldn't!"

"What do your troops think about the plan?"

"They don't believe no plan. They think what you say, she run off, save hide. Hey man, you got any agua?"

"Sure. Here you go. Where did you say Skilly went?"

"Didn't say. You trying to fool me! But I didn't say because I don' know where she went. Bugged out, that one, say she got a plan, and off she goes. With that Jap."

"What Jap?"

"Crazy one. Murasaki-san. Nothing working the way he expect, not any more. He go off mad, that one." The prisoner began to sing obscenely.

The sergeant got up and came over to them. "Probably not a lot more today," he said. "That stuff tires them out fast."

"Is this one guilty of atrocities?" Owensford asked.

"Not that I know of," the sergeant said. "He wasn't at Stora at all. Want me to work on atrocity stories?"

"Actually, no," Owensford said. "If he's not obviously guilty of a hanging offense I'd as soon keep it that way. Tell you what, Sergeant, you see what else you can get, then wrap him up good and turn him over to my headquarters people. I'll take him back to Sparta City. Sort of a present for His Majesty."

"Yes, sir."

Owensford led the way out of the tent. Outside he turned to Morrientes. "So we're not going to catch their leaders."

Morrientes shook his head. "This is independent corroboration," he said. "Most of the Helot high command just aren't here. Nobody's seen them in days."

"That must upset the hell out of their troops," Owensford said.

"Well, yes, sir, I'd say so, because when we advance we find abandoned equipment, weapons even, and whole platoons ready to surrender."

"Good. Keep pushing," Owensford said. "And we may even have a surprise for you. A pleasant one."

"Sir?"

"It looks like Prince Lysander has talked the CD into making sure our next satellite stays intact."

"Now that's good news."

Owensford stood for a time listening to the artillery bombardment. *What the hell plan has Skilly got this time? Whatever it is, we can see she pays like hell for it.* "Good work, Morrientes. Very good work indeed. Carry on, and Godspeed."

❖   ❖   ❖

Brigade Leader Hans von Reuter raised himself to his hands and knees, then staggered to his feet wiping at the blood at the corner of his mouth. Around him his headquarters staff were doing the same, righting pieces of equipment that had toppled when the salvo landed practically right outside the cave. His ears were ringing, and he worked his mouth carefully and spat to get the iron-and-salt taste out of his mouth.

"Location," he said. His face was impassive, a square chiseled blank. *Now I know how von Paulus felt in Stalingrad*, he thought. *Duty is duty, however.*

There were screams from outside, from men and the worse sounds of wounded horses. They grew louder as wounded were dragged inside and carried over to the improvised aid-station on the other side of the big cavern, laid down amid the glossy stalactites that sprouted from the sandy floor. Corpsmen with red M symbols on their jackets scurried among them, sorting them for triage and slapping on hyposprays of anesthetic. Outside a slow series of rifle-shots gave the horses and mules slashed by shrapnel or pulped by blast their own peace.

"Here, ah, here, sir," the plotter said, drawing a black circle on the plastic cover of the map, once the easel was back up.

"Hmmph," von Reuter grunted. *Too far.* The Royalist position was twenty kilometers back, and the only weapons he had available that might reach that far were twisted scrap under a hillside half a kilometer away.

Infiltration? he thought. *Again, no.* The enemy had gotten much better at that sort of thing; also, there were just too *many* of them, and clearly they intended to pound him to bits before advancing. They'd be inserting those SAS teams across his retreat routes, too. No dangerous subtleties or daring sweeps, just a straight hammerblow, rolling northwest and then veering northeast toward the exact location of Base One. The Royalist columns were coordinating well, with intensive patrolling between. *He* was having enough problems stopping them from infiltrating his own positions. Mostly they were bypassing or punching through any screen he put into place, the lead elements encircling the Helot blocking forces for the foot-infantry marching up behind to eliminate.

This is the set piece battle the Royals have always wanted. Now they have it.

It shouldn't have happened. When the Senate passed its Ultimate Decree the Helot army should have dispersed, disbanded if necessary. Let the Royals have the bulk of the equipment and stores, take the irreplaceable equipment and retreat to the hills and wastes with the even less replaceable trained officers and non-coms — *We did not do that in time. Field Prime was certain that we would have more time, but there was no time at all. The Legion SAS forces, then Royals, both with those damned missiles, were in place in hours. We could have fought past them if we had sent everything immediately, but Field Prime tried another plan, then another when that failed, and now I am defeated.*

Doubly defeated, because it had taken all his skill to preserve the Stora Commando as it attempted to retreat from the determined attention of the Brotherhood forces and militia. When he was ordered to return to defend Base One, the Commando was doomed as an organized force. *Except for those already extracted. Some of the best of the Commando. And many of the politicals. And it was the same here, many of the best gone before I arrived. Gone to I do not know where.*

Doubtless Field Prime has a plan, and doubtless it will be brilliant, and complex as usual. Amateurs believe simplicity means that a few things can go wrong and the plan will still work. She has no concept. Falkenberg's people well understand that no battle plan survives contact with the enemy. Field Prime has heard the words but they have no meaning to her.

Yet she has come close to success. Perhaps this time it will work.

She only has to win once.

And none of that was important. His mission now was to delay the enemy as much as possible. He could use anything left of the equipment, and delay was more important than preserving his force. *Of course they must not know that, or they will simply run away. Already they resent that Field Prime is no longer here.* Von Reuter sighed. He had taken no part in the attack on non-combatants at the Stora Mine, but he was quite certain to be tried as a war criminal for his part in the poison gas attack in the Dales; and even if he could surrender he would not. He had his professional honor to consider.

The orders are to delay. I am not told why, merely that it is important. It is not easily done. His forces simply could not move as fast as the Royals, not at foot and animal-transport speeds; it was difficult even to break contact once the Royals advanced. His heavy weapons were outranged, and could be used once and once only: then they were destroyed by the suddenly excellent enemy artillery.

They find us easily. Almost as if they have a satellite.

Surely they do not, Field Prime would have told me?

Small arms fire crackled; he looked up sharply, estimating distances.

"Evacuate," he snapped. "Company Leader Gimbowitz." The chief of the field-hospital looked up. "You have the enemy wounded here as well?"

The doctor nodded, swallowing; he knew as well as the commander what came next.

"We cannot take prisoners or wounded with us," von Reuter said regretfully. "I must ask for medical volunteers to remain with them until the enemy arrives. They will have permission to contact the Royalist commanders once their troops are in the immediate vicinity."

That made it unlikely the Helot wounded would be slaughtered. Individual soldiers of both sides were as likely as not to shoot out of hand individual soldiers of the other who tried to surrender, but the Royalist senior officers were sticklers for the Laws of War. For that matter, wounded men and medics in an organized setting were reasonably safe.

He turned. "Quickly, please," he said. "Group Leader Sandina, please see to the demolition charges on the equipment we cannot remove."

✧ CHAPTER FOURTEEN

There are two central causes of the generally poor Western military record in the field of counterinsurgency. The first is that Western armies are either not large enough or do not consider it important enough to maintain a full-time, well-qualified cadre for counterinsurgency tasks. This is perhaps a good choice, because the main task for these organizations is to ensure an adequate response in the event of higher forms of conflict. The resulting cost, of course, is to occasionally field partially qualified novices in counterinsurgency situations where professionals are required. The second cause of lackluster Western military performance is that Western peoples will not long tolerate the use of their soldiers in suppressing rebellions in a distant land, whether their soldiers are in a direct combat role or serving as advisors.

An international corporation composed of former Western officers and soldiers skilled in acceptable counterinsurgency techniques would largely solve both of these Western counterinsurgency problems . . . Considering the record of most Western governments in the field of counterinsurgency, the corporation would not have to work very hard to achieve comparatively superior results. And a commercial concern would likely attain those improvements at considerably less cost.

— Rod Paschall
LIC 2000: Special Operations and
Unconventional Warfare in the Next Century
(Institute of Land Warfare, Association of the US Army, 1990)

✧　　✧　　✧

If, in the future, war will be waged for the souls of men, then the importance of extending territorial control will go down. Long past are the days when provinces, even entire countries, were regarded simply as items of real estate to be exchanged among rulers by means of inheritance, agreement, or force. The triumph of nationalism has brought about a situation where people do not occupy a piece of land because it is valuable; on the contrary, a piece of land however remote or desolate is considered valuable because it is occupied by this people or that. To adduce but two examples out of many, since at least 1965 India and Pakistan have been at loggerheads over a glacier so remote that it can hardly even be located on a map. Between 1979 and 1988, Egypt spent nine years of diplomatic effort in order to recover Taba. Now Taba, south of Elath, is a half-mile stretch of worthless desert beach whose very existence had gone unnoticed by both Egyptians and Israelis prior to the Camp David Peace Agreements; all of a sudden it became part of each side's "sacred" patrimony and coffee-houses in Cairo were named after it....

Another effect of the postulated breakdown of conventional war will probably be a greater emphasis on the interests of men at the head of the organization, as opposed to the interest, of the organization as such ... Individual glory, profit, and booty gained directly at the expense of the civilian population will once again become important, not simply as incidental rewards but as the legitimate objectives of war. Nor is it improbable that the quest for women and sexual gratification will re-enter the picture. As the distinctions between combatants and noncombatants break down, the least we can expect is that such things will be tolerated to a greater extent than is supposed to be the case under the rules of so-called civilized warfare. In many of the low-intensity conflicts currently being waged in developing countries this is already true, and has, indeed, always been true.

— Martin van Creveld
The Transformation of War, 1991

❖   ❖   ❖

The Council Chamber was colorful, and for the moment buzzing with informal chatter. Most seats at the big conference table were taken. The conspicuous exceptions were the cabinet secretary's console at one end, and a single large arm chair at the center. The War Cabinet was already at the table. Rear Admiral Samuel Forrest, as senior Naval officer, sat between Generals Owensford and Slater, the deep midnight blue of his Navy tunic contrasting with the more colorful army garrison uniforms. Madame Elayne Rusher, the

Attorney General, was next to General Lawrence
Desjardins, Chief of the Royal Spartan Mounted Police.
Roland Dawson, Principal Secretary of State, chatted
with Lord Henry Yamaga, Secretary of State for the
Interior and Industrial Development. Eric Respari of
Finance listened to them with a sour expression.
Everyone knew that Respari had been an avid student of
the late King Jason's economics theories; now he
resembled the Freedman King in expression as well. Sir
Alfred Nathanson, called Minister of War even though
his office was administrative rather than part of the
chain of command, was hard at work on his notebook
computer. At the far end of the table Dr. Caldwell
Whitlock sat alone. He had been invited by Prince
Lysander, and if some of the regular members of the
War Cabinet resented his presence, none of them were
going to say so, especially not today.

In addition to the principal officers at the conference
table, another dozen chairs along the walls were filled
with experts: Legion Captains Jesus and Catherine
Alana, Alan Hruska, the Milice chief for Sparta City;
Spartan and Brotherhood military; Legion officers;
civilian officials, most carrying notebook computers.

The room fell silent as Horace Plummer, Secretary
to the Cabinet, came into the conference chamber
and stood just inside the door. "My lords, ladies, gentlemen, His Highness Crown Prince Lysander, Master
of the Forces by order of the Kings acting under the
Ultimate Decree of the Senate of Sparta." Everyone
stood. The military acted from habit, as perhaps did
some of the others, but some were reacting to the solemn formality of Plummer's announcement.

Lysander wore the military uniform of an officer of
the Royals but with no insignia of rank. He looked
older than his years as he took his place at the center
of the big conference table. There was only one chair

there. Previously there had always been two, and Lysander had sat across from them, where General Owensford was now. Lysander nodded pleasantly to everyone, but took his seat in silence. After a moment the others sat down as well.

"The agenda is on your screens," Plummer said.

"With his Highness's permission," Roland Dawson said, "the agenda will endure a brief wait. We understand there is good news from St. Thomas's."

Lysander frowned for a moment, then suddenly his smile returned, as if he had remembered to wear it again. "Thank you. Yes, very good news indeed. Graffin Melissa is recovering well."

"Well enough to have enjoyed a brief visit to the Palace last evening. Her father mentioned it this morning. And, Highness, I have heard that we may have better news shortly," Dawson continued relentlessly. The Principal Secretary of State was the leader of the majority party in the Senate, and by definition a politician, and not even the Ultimate Decree would change that. "I understand the Queen is consulting the Archbishop to reschedule the wedding. I understand and appreciate that Your Highness would prefer this to remain a private matter, but the Citizens will be overjoyed at the news, and I ask permission to make the announcement."

Lysander looked around the room at the eager faces. Even the dour finance minister was smiling agreement with Dawson.

"Time we had some good news to announce," Elayne Rusher said.

"The Citizens will certainly want to celebrate," Sir Alfred Nathanson said.

Lysander nodded. "I expect you're right. I'll leave the details to you, then. Now — and thank you, Roland — Mr. Plummer, if we can get back to the agenda?"

"Item One. A report from the military field commands," Horace Plummer said. "General Owensford."

"Highness. My lords and ladies. You've seen the overall figures, and the rest are in the conference room computer. I can summarize in two words. We're winning."

"Thank God," Roland Dawson said. The Principal Secretary of State mopped his brow with an already damp handkerchief. "How soon do you think this will be over?"

"Not as soon as you'd like, I'm afraid," Peter Owensford said. "We're stretched pretty thin, no reserves to speak of. Nearly everything we've got has been thrown into the two campaigns, the Stora pursuit, and the reduction of their main base. We're winning, but it isn't all that easy, there are complications. Full details are in the reports on your consoles there. Unfortunately, I must ask you not to remove electronic copies of those reports from this room. We know the computers here are clean, and they have no physical connection whatever to any other system."

"General?"

"General Desjardins?"

"Does this mean we still can't rely on our computer systems?"

"Correct," Owensford said. "We captured a fair number of Helot technicians in training at Base One, and we've learned a lot from them. Murasaki's people were deeper into our computer systems than I would have imagined. We learned that much mostly by inference and skilled questioning of Helot officers and trainees." Peter Owensford nodded acknowledgment to the Captains Alana. They smiled briefly. Both looked both overworked and triumphant.

"Unfortunately, we didn't get a single live technoninja," Owensford said. "The four we did apprehend were dead when captured, or died before they could be drugged. Interestingly there was one already dead, killed by torture, apparently by Helot experts. No one seems to know anything about that, unless Captain Alana has learned something since I last spoke with him. Yes, Jesus?"

"We have one Helot officer who said the execution was personally ordered by Field Prime, as punishment for failures during the Stora Mines operation," Jesus Alana said. "Apparently this was demanded by the senior survivors of the Stora Commando. They felt they had been betrayed, and someone should be punished."

"So," Lysander said. "The vipers are fanging each other."

"So it would appear, Highness," Owensford said. "We're beginning to see fair numbers of defecting officers. Especially in the Stora Commando group, where we got a colonel, one Hamish Beshara, code name Ben Bella. Incidentally, his *spetsnaz* brigade commander was our friend Niles." Owensford stopped. Prince Lysander's face had frozen into a mask of hate. "Ben Bella had nothing to do with the missile attack, Highness. Jesus?"

"No, my prince. To the best of my skills, no one we have captured had any notion that the missile would be used against a non-military target. Colonel Ben Bella thought its purpose was to destroy the geo-thermal generating system if, as happened, the sabotage effort failed." Jesus shrugged. "I am certain I could find evidence to convict him of wanton destruction of civilian property, but I would not care to argue the case in a CoDominium court martial. Especially since the man surrendered on promise of amnesty for all except deliberate atrocities. He has a different conception of atrocity than we, but he is convinced he committed none — and that the missile attack *was* an atrocity. He insists that he would not have allowed that had he known, and while I may doubt he would have risked his life to prevent it, it is certain he believes he would have."

"Which brings us to a decision item," Owensford said when Lysander didn't answer. "We have captured a number of Helot soldiers, and in the base camp we took prisoner other rebels. The Helots have no conception of non-combatant status. All their membership are rebels, and would be expected to fight. They are nearly all armed, and some of their women and children were killed bearing arms against our forces. Others threw away their weapons. In any case it is difficult to think of a ten year old child as an armed enemy."

"Nits make lice," someone said.

Owensford frowned. "That has been said in every revolutionary war in history," he said. "And it's no more appropriate here than it was in Palestine or Kurdistan. Your Highness, we will need policies and procedures. What shall we do with captured Helot soldiers and their non-military adherents?"

"We can't just let them go," Yamaga said. "They won't work. They wouldn't work before they became Helots, and they won't work now, and now they've got a taste for rebellion. And training with weapons. Let them loose and they'll turn criminals even if they don't rejoin the rebellion."

"They have to be taught to work," Madame Rusher said. "Work habits."

"*Arbeit macht frei*," General Desjardins said. "A much abused slogan, but I believe Madame Elayne has the essence of it. They must become convinced that work is a better alternative than banditry."

"We can use some of the soldiers in expeditionary forces," Hal Slater said. "And the Legion. But that requires transportation. I can't think we want them armed and at large on Sparta until they've been obedient for a few years." He chuckled. "Pity we can't make them involuntary colonists to somewhere else. Send them to Byer's and let them try the criminal life in Hell's-a-comin'.'"

"Now there's a thought," Yamaga said. "Pity indeed we can't do that."

"But the question is, what do we do with them *now*?" Owensford said. "We've got the island camps. The Legion training program worked all right. Last time we had transport we shipped over five hundred retrained Helots to reinforce Falkenberg on New Washington, and last I heard they were doing well enough. Of course that's the cream of the crop, the ones with enough gumption to stick it."

"You sent back a thousand more who'd volunteered and couldn't finish your course," Sir Alfred Nathanson said. "And they're something of a problem. For the moment we've been able to keep order on the Island, even have them growing their own crops. But we can't maintain concentration camps like that forever!"

"Bit of a mess for the Coast Guard," General Desjardins said. "We've been worried that the Helots would try to rescue those people. So far the only reason they haven't has been the physical isolation, but we're using resources I'd like to put to other uses. We lose a few of those wet navy craft and all those Helot soldiers are available to the rebellion again."

"We can't just shoot them," Elayne Rusher said.

"No, Madam," Finance Minister Respari agreed. "Leave aside the ethics, none of the others would ever surrender if we did that. General, Sir Alfred, I'm afraid your island camps are the only solution we have. And the camps are cheaper than the war, by a lot."

"Actually, there are two problems," Yamaga said. "There are the prisoners of war, of course. And although we can't send off all the criminals as colonists to a pleasant place like Hell's-a-comin', the CoDominium keeps dumping involuntary colonists on us. I grant you they're not quite the same situation, some of the new colonists fit in well enough, but all too many are nearly as much trouble as rebels." He shrugged. "And for a lot of them it's only a question of time before they go from being useless mouths to joining the rebellion and killing our people. Bread and circuses, that's what they want."

"Every democracy in history has wanted bread and circuses," Roland Dawson said. "Not our party, of course, but there are Citizen groups who'd rather try bread and circuses than continue the war."

"Danegeld," Hal Slater said. "Never a very wise thing to give anyone, certainly not to criminals."

"It is not what they will get," Lysander said. His voice was low, but the room became quiet when he spoke. "Build that kind of welfare state and we corrupt our own people. This government will not pay people to be poor, nor will we set up paid officials with an incentive to have poor and idle clients. General Desjardins, I take it your RSMP doesn't find Island duty pleasant."

"They hate it, Highness. So would you."

"I expect I would. Let me point out that there are advantages to this. No one wants to make a career of administering the camps, so there is no one who has a good reason to retain those camps if we find a better solution."

"No one I'd want in the RSMP," Desjardins sniffed.

"Keep it that way," Lysander said. "Too many nations have destroyed themselves by allowing potentially fatal changes to their institutions as an expedient for winning wars or settling domestic crises. Every institution you build has people who want to keep on doing what they do. It's the nature of government, to build enduring institutions, structures that stay long after their purpose is over. If you pay people to help the poor, you have people who won't be paid if there aren't any poor, so they'll be sure to find some. Sparta was created as the antithesis of that kind of welfare state, and by God it will stay that way. I'd rather lose the war than change that."

There were mutters of agreement around the table.

"Hear, hear," Whitlock said.

"That's clear, then," Lysander said. "Now let me point out that when we win this war we will have far more Helot prisoners, some of them genuine war criminals."

"Hang them," Desjardins said.

"Those we can convict of atrocities, certainly. But how many will that be?"

"Rome crucified a rebel at every milepost from Vesuvius to Rome after the Spartacus rebellion," Madame Rusher said. "That's what? No more than a thousand, surely, and it's remembered to this day. I suppose if we top that we'll get a place in the history books, but I'm not sure it's a place we want."

"Nor I," Lysander said. "I'm not sure what to do with those merely swept up in the rebellion, but there's a simple solution to what to do with the active participants in the rebel cause. They wanted to try the barbarian life. I propose to give them their wish. Turn them loose on the island. Wolf Island. They get hand tools, seeds, and a few farm animals. No weapons, and no technology. If they don't work, they starve. After a few years the survivors can try to negotiate a better deal."

"Stark," Roland Dawson said.

"It's better than they planned for us," Lysander said. "Sir Alfred, this will be your concern. Please see to it."

"Yes, Highness."

"Sir?"

"Admiral Forrest."

"This is my first cabinet meeting. I'm not certain of the procedure," Forrest said.

"We're fairly informal, Admiral," Lysander said. "If you believe you have something we should know that's relevant to the discussion, it's quite proper to speak up."

"Yes, sir. I was going to say, the news from the CoDominium is confusing and contradictory. Rumors of mutinies in the fleet. Ships beached for lack of money to repair and fuel them. Stories of rivalries, along with official documents that don't acknowledge that there's anything unusual happening at all. One thing is certain, the BuReloc transport is overdue. It may be that we won't be getting so many involuntary colonists."

"A consummation devoutly to be wished," Hal Slater said carefully. "I hear much the same as Admiral Forrest. The CD's having trouble finding enough money to operate all their ships. It's probable we won't have as much trouble with involuntary colonists as we thought we would."

"Or that it will all happen at once, with a number of ships coming simultaneously," Lysander said. "But thank you for bringing that up. I presume everyone here knows that Admiral Forrest has persuaded the local CoDominium Fleet Commander to safeguard our observation and communications satellite. We're told that they're also intercepting the clandestine arms shipments to the rebels."

"We very much owe Admiral Forrest a vote of thanks," Elayne Rusher said.

"Indeed," Lysander said. "Those Fang missiles

could have been a lot of trouble. Still can be, but at least there aren't infinite supplies of them coming in. And the other high tech gear. From all of us, and from me personally, Admiral, thank you. We won't forget."

"Thank you, Highness," Forrest said. "Of course I had considerable help from Dr. Whitlock. He can be extremely persuasive."

"Well, thank you," Whitlock said. "Most important thing is to convince the local CD people they'll be better off with us as a strong and peaceful place to call home, and the best arguments for that are Admiral Forrest and Captain Nosov."

Lysander nodded agreement. "General Owensford, please continue your report."

"Yes, Highness," Owensford said. "As I said earlier, we're winning. The renewed satellite pictures have been extremely useful, especially in the pursuit of their northern group, the force they called the Stora Commando group. I am pleased to report that the Stora Commando is no longer a threat to anyone. For a while they retreated in an organized and disciplined manner. That gave General Barton a lot of trouble, but shortly after the Ultimate Decree they became little more than disorganized stragglers.

"The change was sudden and dramatic. We have since learned that most of their leadership was evacuated, leaving the rest on their own, which was pretty demoralizing when the word spread among them. Many who hadn't taken a personal part in atrocities surrendered very soon after that. The rest are disorganized, mostly city punks in the wilderness, relentlessly pursued by outdoorsmen who enjoy their work. You could almost feel sorry for them."

"No you couldn't," Lysander said. "They demanded their rights. They'll get justice. How many criminals have we caught?"

"Not so many as I'd like, because of course the ones we could prove to be war criminals don't surrender. On the other hand, over six hundred have accepted the amnesty. Of those, nine were easily proven to be war criminals, thirty-four probably are, and four were traitors, actual Citizen supporters of the rebels."

"Probably," Roland Dawson said. "What means probable, given your — techniques?"

Jesus Alana shrugged. "It is expensive and time consuming to question every captive," he said. "And are we so certain we want the answers? If we know someone is guilty of war crimes, we must make a decision as to what to do with him."

"What happened to the Citizens?" Lysander demanded.

"The traitors are in the Capital prison, Highness, awaiting Their Majesties' pleasure. Or yours," Owensford said. "They're a different case. The Helot soldiers we let go to the Island after interrogation, but we know who they are if we really want to find them again."

"Mutilation," one of the Brotherhood intelligence officers said. "We should chop off a finger. Or toes. Make it a lot easier to find them again."

Lysander didn't answer, and there was an awkward silence. "It's much the same around their Base Camp," Owensford said at last. "Better organized, but most of their leadership has bugged out. The troops left behind were supposed to sell their lives dearly. Some did, but it's beginning to sink in that they're fighting for a lost and dreary cause, and leaders who've run away. Once again we're seeing both individuals and organized groups looking for amnesty. Others have scattered into the wastelands, but this time with not much more than they can carry." Owensford shrugged. "Frankly, I'd rather be on the Island than on the run. Better soil, and I wouldn't have to worry that Mace's Scouts were looking for me."

"But we still haven't caught their leaders."

"Other than Croser and his Capital gang, no."

"General, every one of them seems to believe Skilly has a plan," Lysander said. "Do we have any notion of what it is?"

"No, sir."

"I keep remembering the Dales," Lysander said. "Where they had a plan that couldn't possibly work, only it very nearly did, because we certainly were not expecting poison gas. Captain Alana, you saw through that one just in time. What can they be planning now?"

"I confess to thinking much on that subject," Jesus Alana said. "Alas, my prince, with little result. Nor has Catherine been more successful."

"We're winning, but they're not giving up. Not trying to make terms," Lysander said. "I take that to mean they still believe they can win."

"Clearly," Hal Slater said.

"But they're losing. Losing badly. There's no way they *can* win."

"Well," Owensford said. "Perhaps. We can hope so, but in any event there is one thing I must remind you of, Highness. It may or may not have anything to do with Skilly, but it's clear that every gain we have made could be wiped out by the CoDominium. Give the Helots enough off-planet support and we wouldn't be winning any longer."

"Admiral, is this likely?"

"No," Forrest said. "Likely, no. But of course it's possible."

"Some day," Lysander said, but he said it so softly that Peter Owensford didn't think anyone else had heard.

✦ CHAPTER FIFTEEN

Crofton's Encyclopedia of the Inhabited Planets (2nd Edition):

Corinth: Town at the head of the *Corinthian Gulf*, (q.v.), a long (700 kilometer), funnel-shaped inlet on the northeastern portion of the Serpentine Continent. Corinth, founded by settlers from New Newfoundland in 2053, is primarily a collection point for nearby ranches and a fishing-base. The Corinthian Gulf, with its deep and nutrient-rich waters, is a spawning-ground for several important species of large piscoid hunted for their leather, oil and pharmaceutical derivatives; among these are the *Mammoth Daisy*, the *Tennisnet* and the *Galleybeak*. Galleybeak caviar is noted as a delicacy on several planets, having an exotic flavor and mild stimulant and euphoric qualities. Tennisnet glands are processed for a well-known anti obesity drug. Corinth's facilities include deep water docks, small-scale ship repair facilities, warehouses and marine processing plants. Population (2091), 6,753 not including transients.

✦　　✦　　✦

Another characteristic of the year 2010, familiar to those who will have lived through the last quarter of the 20th Century, is that most of the world's low-intensity conflict will probably be insurgencies. Terrorism, in and of itself, is a weak reed when it comes to effecting political changes. On the other hand, governments have been brought down by insurgents . . .

One aspect of insurgency that promises to be a bit different in the year 2010 has to do with a shift in demography. The continued movement of Third World populations to cities makes it probable that urban underground organizations will constitute a growing percentage of insurgent movements . . .

— Rod Paschall
*LIC 2000: Special Operations and
Unconventional Warfare in the Next Century*
(Institute of Land Warfare, Association of the US Army, 1990)

❖   ❖   ❖

Geoffrey Niles woke at the sound of voices, but from long habit he lay still, eyes closed, as if still asleep. It was a habit developed at school to avoid persecution by older boys, but this time it saved him from far worse. He lay still and thought about where he was.

They were in the ranch house of a farm Skilly had bought years before. The nominal owners were a couple Skilly had found in the slums of Minetown. As usual her instinct for choosing the right people served her well: Hildy and Rose Wheeler had quietly tended the farm, increasing its value and drawing no attention to themselves, quiet non-Citizen farmers who ignored politics like many in this Corinthian district a thousand kilometers northeast of the Capital. Yet when Skilly had appeared, nearly alone and on the run, they were eager to help. Geoff had been amazed at the facilities they had quietly built up in a cave driven into the cliffs behind the ranch house. Offices, storage for weapons, residence, all waiting until Skida Thibodeau should need them.

They could relax here. Back in Sparta City they'd been in a different house every night, welcome in some, grudgingly accepted in others, flatly refused admission twice, and always afraid of betrayal even by those who seemed gladdest to see them. It had been an enormous relief to leave the capital even though that required traveling in disguise on the public rail system. Skilly had a dozen disguises, papers, business travel documents, and they'd needed them. In this time of the Ultimate Decree it wasn't enough just to buy a ticket and get on a train. You had to convince the police that you had a legitimate reason for travel, and they wrote it all down to be fed to the computer system. But they'd got here, safe for the first time in weeks. . . .

He was alone in the big bed. Skilly, dressed in a tee shirt and nothing else, sat at her communications console. She had the speaker volume low and spoke softly as if trying not to awaken him, but Niles wondered why she didn't use the headset if that was what she really wanted. For that matter there was a console in the next room.

Testing? he wondered. She had done a lot of that since the Stora incident. She still didn't trust him completely. *That was close. I could have got myself killed, and for nothing, there was nothing I could do, nothing at all.* He shuddered at the memory, Skilly's cold laugh as she launched the missile, the impersonal way she looked at the results. The worst was when she told him later that he'd been right, it hadn't been such a good idea after all. "Should have listened to my Jeffy, sometimes he got good instincts." No remorse except that it hadn't worked as she intended. *And she still thinks to found a dynasty. My God, I've got to get out of here.* He'd thought that many times since the Stora campaign, but there was no place to go. The Royals would cheerfully hang him if they could catch him, and the only places he knew to hide from the Royals were controlled by Skilly.

He lay still and listened. Skilly was talking to someone, and she wasn't happy at all. "You supposed to be working for Skilly," she said.

"My sincere apologies. I am afraid my employer neglected to tell me that." Skilly had the volume set low, and the voice was very low and quiet, so that Niles barely heard it, but he was certain that it was Murasaki. "I was told to consider your interests, as well as those of Capital Prime, but not to the neglect of my primary mission. Indeed, now that Capital Prime is regrettably detained, it is not certain that your interests and my employer's are the same."

"Why you say that?"

"Let us say that my employer had known Capital Prime for many years, and thus understood him. He has never met you. Alas, while I have great admiration for your talents as a leader, a bald narrative of events does little to justify that to someone who does not know you well. All due to bad luck and misfortune, of course, but it does not appear that you have enjoyed great success."

"Skilly told Capital Prime it was time to go underground," Skilly said. "But Capital Prime trusted you to warn him in time. Not Skilly's doing."

"Ah, no, of course not," Murasaki said. "But perhaps had you more thoroughly considered the implications of your use of our earth penetrator? Capturing the mine and its town was a boldly conceived goal, admirable in concept, possibly decisive if combined with suitable political strategy. The CoDominium will often act to aid an actual government in possession of territory. Using the earth penetrator as a means of bringing the Stora garrison to battle on favorable ground was also an admirably bold notion. Alas, it did not have the proper effect."

"That bad luck too," Skilly said. "You don' tell me that Prince Baby is up there. Everything fine until he rallies the troops, make them go back to their holes and organize. That Prince one real piece of bad luck. Best we kill that one. Him and that whole group of his. He put a price on my head, I put one on his. You kill him, now."

"Ah, I was under the impression that you were thoroughly aware that Prince Lysander had gone north. My mistake. As to his demise, this is not so easily accomplished as it would have been earlier," Murasaki said. "The Royals are, after all, very much alerted."

"They still meet sometimes," Skilly said. "Report to

the Senate. Broadcast to the people." She looked around, but Geoffrey Niles had never opened his eyes fully, and she saw him apparently still asleep. Her voice fell even lower, so that Geoff didn't hear all of what she said next. " . . . whole damn place while they in it."

"There are few reliable ways to accomplish that."

"One sure one."

"I had thought you were opposed to using that."

"Skilly not like it, because it cause trouble for the future. But right now, maybe she don't got a future unless something drastic happens."

"That is of course most unfortunate," Murasaki said. "But I have only the one device, and there is some question of where to use it. Indeed, you have been persuasive in arguing against using it at all. Certainly it will greatly upset the CoDominium elements, and it is never wise to do that without powerful reasons."

"Yeah, I understand that," Skilly said. "But think, you don' do something soon, Skilly facing the ugly, ugly jaws of defeat."

"No one understands that better than me," the soft voice said. "But we have sent you vast resources, and I fear we have very little to show for all that huge expenditure. We have embarrassed the Legion, but it seems to have survived the experience, perhaps did not even notice. The Royal Government is stronger than ever. I regret I must point this out, but you do not seem to have much to offer now. Have you established control over the politicals in Sparta City?"

"Yes."

Geoff suppressed a shudder. Regaining control of the political apparatus after the mass arrests following the Ultimate Decree had been a nightmare. There had to be secure cutouts, discontinuities in the command structure, or the entire apparatus would have fallen in

the first hours; but once the known leaders were removed, making contact with those remaining was extremely difficult, and proving that you were entitled to give them orders, and that they should continue the fight, was more difficult still. Niles's admiration for Skilly had increased enormously, but his horror at her methods had grown equally. Her energy was boundless, and she had set up a number of contingency plans just in case this happened. She was particularly skilled at blackmail, and she had enough evidence to hang most of the political leadership three times over. And one of those who had refused to take her in was found the next day with his testicles stuffed into his eye sockets.

So we have control of the politicals. It takes a lot of personal contact to do it, and we can't do that easily because Skilly insists on moving from place to place all the time. Afraid someone will try to collect the bounty, I suppose. I wonder how long she'll stay here? It's safe here, but she's not getting much done.

"You blow de Palace when the government is all there," Skilly said. "Give Skilly a week warning, hell, six hours, and it'll be all over, Skilly will own this place. No Kings, no Senate, no government. Just the organization."

"Well, it is a possibility to consider," Murasaki said. "But I think we first stay with the original plan. Let us see what that will accomplish before we attempt your way. If that fails, perhaps there is another."

"You just be sure to give Skilly notice first. Those politicals not so easy to control, not trained troops. Maybe both together? Between CD and your stuff, we knock out the government, Skilly does the rest. We take over the Capital, we win, and we only got to win once. . . ."

❖   ❖   ❖

The girl was about twenty, and she had been pretty in an unsophisticated way. Now her hair had been cut off with a bayonet, her swollen lips oozed blood, and she was missing at least one tooth. The nose was swollen as well, probably broken, one eye was black, and there were other bruises, particularly on her thighs. She was sprawled naked across a couch, and one of the Helot soldiers was fastening his trousers.

Geoffrey Niles looked at the scene with distaste. "Seems a bit of a waste," he said. *Soldiers. Warriors. My God. First the Lefkowitz girl, those pictures! Pictures sent to Luna Base and every mercenary outfit registered with the CD, and they still don't learn, they think they're going to win and then they can make the rules. Rules! And everyone knows my family is associated with this.*

"Waste, Brigade Leader? We're supposed to kill her, but there wasn't nothing said about not having some fun first."

Niles shook his head. "Odd notions of fun. In any event, I need confirmation of some information she probably has. Get her dressed. I'll bring her back when I'm through."

"They say she don't know nothing. The Legion types never told her anything much, she's no use," the Company Leader said. He finished fastening his trousers and grinned. "Course it depends on what you want to use her for, but being as what you're gettin', you sure don't need any of this."

Niles's look silenced him. "There are things we have to know. People she's seen, map locations. They weren't supposed to give her to you until we were finished. Just get her clothes. Can you dress yourself?" he asked the girl.

"Yeah." Her voice was distorted.

"Then do so."

She lay still for a moment. The Helot officer smashed his hand across her mouth. "You call him sir, and you do what he says now, bitch."

She pulled herself into a sitting position with an obvious effort. Niles watched as the girl pulled on trousers and a shirt. She had no underwear, and Niles wondered if it had been destroyed in the process of undressing her. Her only shoes were boots, and he waited for her to get those on. Although she moved slowly and carefully, nothing seemed to be broken. As she finished with her boots, Niles swiftly lifted her to her feet, pulled her hands behind her, and snapped on handcuffs. "Do you want her back?" he asked.

"Well, it might be fun to have her again before we kill her."

"We'll see. If she cooperates with us. All right — Talkins, isn't it? Come along." He pushed her out into the corridor of the cave.

"Watch her," the Helot called. "She bites. Or did. Taught her not to do that."

The passage led to cellars of the farmhouse, but halfway along it was a side passage. Niles opened that door, pushed Margreta Talkins through and followed her, carefully closing it behind him. "All right," he said. "In a minute I'm going to take those cuffs off, but I want you to be sure you understand what's happening."

"And what's that?" Margreta's speech was slurred by her swollen lips. She spat blood.

"We're getting the hell out of here," Niles said.

Her eyes widened. "We. Why?"

"Look, we don't have a lot of time," Niles said. "I want to surrender to the Royals, and I need bargaining chips. You're one of them. Now we have about an hour, maybe two, before Skilly calls in asking for me, and as long after that as it takes for her to figure out what's happened. By that time we'd better be a hell of a long way from here. Can you run?"

"A little. I'm pretty bruised. If I'd known I'd have to run, I wouldn't have fought so hard."

"Look, I'm sorry."

"Yeah. It could have been worse. All right, I'll try to keep up. Look, I don't know what's going to happen, but do me this, don't let them get me alive again, all right? OK, let's go."

"All right, we can stop for a few minutes," Niles said. "I've got some clothes and equipment stashed under the rocks here. We'll take five minutes to let you change. There are weapons here, too."

She stumbled forward and sat heavily. "I guess I'm not in as good shape as I thought."

"How'd they catch you?"

"I think they were always on to me," Margreta Talkins said. "At least since Graffin Melissa lived through that assassination attempt. They were pretty sure I could have killed her. Ever since I think they've just been using me to pass false information back to the Legion. The last thing they did was send me on a wild goose chase, so I'd give the wrong story about where they were hiding. I really thought I'd located Skilly, and getting that information out was worth anything. I guess they'd decided I wasn't any more use, because that was a setup."

Niles lifted a flat rock. "Here we are. Canteens, to begin with. Water or whiskey?"

"Water. Whiskey would be great at first, but I don't think it will help for long." She drank deeply. "Let me have the whiskey," she said suddenly. Niles handed the other canteen to her. She took a sip and gargled heavily, then spat it out. "That helps. Now if you'll hand me that bandanna and look the other way—" She laughed. "Or don't, Jesus, you'd think I'd be over any kind of modesty."

Geoff fished in the crevice under the rock, carefully not looking at her.

"Ow. That stings," she said. "I don't suppose you've got some milder form of disinfectant?"

"No. I do have some more clothes. Including underwear. Jockey shorts, a bit large for you, but better than nothing." He held them out behind him and felt her take them. "And some clean trousers and shirt. I made this cache when I heard they were bringing in a Legion prisoner, but I didn't know you'd be a girl."

"Girl," Margreta said. "Lord, man, if this hasn't made a woman of me, nothing will. But thanks, I think. You still haven't explained what this is all about."

"Actually, I did. I want out. Out of all this. Amnesty and a ticket off Sparta."

"Look, we both know I'm not worth that much, not if you were part of anything serious."

"I wasn't. Not Lefkowitz, not Stora. I was in the Dales, poison gas, technically a violation of the Laws of War, but that was against military targets."

"And the anthrax?"

"Anthrax?" Geoff said. "No, I didn't know about that."

"They used it. Ruined a whole farm valley. Look, I still don't see where I come in."

"You can talk to them. I know some things they will want to know," Geoff said. "But if they shoot me before I can tell them that, it won't do anyone any good. You they'll listen to, and I presume you have ways to make contact with the Legion. They might even provide you transportation."

"Sure, if you get me to a telephone. All right, you can turn around now. And thanks for turning your back."

She looked better, but still awful. He found a bandanna and wet it from the water canteen, then added a dash of whiskey. "Hold still, I'll clean your face. And here's a comb."

"If you have a mirror—"

"I do, but let me clean you up a bit first."

"Oh. That bad?"

She tried to laugh, but he could see tears at the

corners of her eyes. He wiped off the worst of the dried blood and semen from her face. It was hard to do without hurting her, and he winced as badly as she did when he had to touch some of her bruises.

"There were four of them," she said. "One managed twice."

"Miss Talkins —"

"I think under the circumstances, Brigade Leader Niles, you may call me Margreta," she said solemnly.

"Margreta. Jesus, I'm sorry, Margreta. Uh — and I'm Geoffrey or Geoff, of course."

"Not Jeffy?"

"My God no, never again. Speaking of which." He held up a mini-uzi. "The moment of truth. I'm going to give you this now. If you want to shoot me in retaliation for what they did to you, please make it quick. I deserve that much. Margreta, I'm very sorry they did this to you, and if I could have prevented it I would have, but there was nothing I could do. God damn it! It was like Stora, nothing I could do! I could get killed and it still wouldn't have changed anything! They'd have shot me and the rocket would have gone on schedule, and the same thing with you, until Skilly left I couldn't interfere with— Sorry. You're the one who was hurt, and I'm shouting about it."

She didn't say anything. After a moment, Geoff handed her the machine pistol. He stood and watched as she checked the loads. "They're not blanks," he said. "I'd invite you to fire a few rounds, but it might attract unwanted attention."

"I'm not going to shoot you," she said. "Back there in the cave I would have, you and them and then myself, but — Geoff, are we really going to get away?"

"I surely hope so. Now, how much of this can you carry? We still don't have a lot of time. And I hope your Legion people think enough of you to come get you."

"So do I. All right, find me that telephone."

"Oh, that's no problem. I have a communicator," Geoff said. "All we have to do is get to a place where it's safe to use it."

"Let's go, then," she said. She sounded very small and vulnerable, and Geoff Niles had never hated the war so much. He took her hand to lead her, and after a moment she let him.

✦ CHAPTER SIXTEEN

The advantage which a commander thinks he can attain through continued personal intervention is largely illusory. By engaging in it he assumes a task which really belongs to others, whose effectiveness he thus destroys. He also multiplies his own tasks to a point where he can no longer fulfill the whole of them.

— Helmuth von Moltke

✦   ✦   ✦

Crofton's Encyclopedia of Contemporary History and Social Issues (3rd Edition):

The Ban: The proudest achievement of the CoDominium era was the near absence of employment of nuclear weapons in an era of nuclear plenty. The one issue that united the Fleet, from the lowest Line Marine recruit to the Grand Admiral was insistence that the Fleet and only the Fleet had the right to possess nuclear weapons, and only the Fleet could use them: and it would not do so except under nuclear threat. Not even the Grand Senate could order nuclear bombardment.

Nuclear weapons remained a theoretical last resort to the Fleet no matter what the opposition, but the only times they were ever used was in retaliation for first use by others; on those occasions the vengeance of the CoDominium Navy could be terrible . . .

✦   ✦   ✦

The Royal Messenger had a grim expression. "General Owensford, Prince Lysander's compliments, and can you come to the war room right away."

"Certainly," Peter said. Something in the Messenger's tone made him send for his chief of staff.

He was almost finished dressing when Andy Lahr came in. "Trouble at Fort Plataia. Good morning, sir."

"Trouble?"

"There's a CoDominium squad at the gate, with an official order that no one is to enter or leave the Fort without CoDominium permission."

"Jesus Christ. What did Captain Alana do?"

"Nothing," Lahr said. "Didn't acknowledge, pending orders, but he has told everyone to stay inside, and put the Fort on alert."

"Sounds good. Tell him to hang onto that until I know what's going on."

"Already did. You got any idea of what's going on?"

"No, but I expect I'm about to find out."

Both Kings and Prince Lysander were in the war room.

"Good morning." Peter bowed. "This looks serious."

"It is," Alexander said. He held out a document. "This appears to be authentic," he said. "It's an order from the CoDominium Sector Headquarters, in the name of Vice Admiral Townsend but actually signed by General Nguyen. Sparta is directed to surrender all units of Falkenberg's Mercenary Legion to the CoDominium, for transport from Sparta to a neutral world to be agreed to after the Legion units are disarmed and embarked."

"I see. That's ridiculous," Peter said. "It's invalid on its face. Vice Admiral Townsend hasn't that authority, and certainly no Marine general acting in the admiral's name does! For that matter, the CoDominium hasn't the authority to order you to do any such thing, even if it's enacted by the Grand Senate."

"They may not have the authority," King Alexander said, "but they have the power. They brought a battlecruiser and a troop transport with a regiment of Line Marines. The Marines are to be stationed on Sparta ostensibly to protect our independence from foreign invaders — which means you. You're to be taken offplanet in the troop transport."

"What does Clay Newell have to say about this? Or Commodore Guildford for that matter? He's a trimmer. If he obeys this order he's thoroughly committed to Bronson and he knows it. I can't think he wants that."

"We don't know," Alexander said. "I've sent for Admiral Forrest. The whole War Cabinet and Privy Council. But the fact is, we've been unable to talk to anyone in CoDominium headquarters except this newcomer, a Colonel Ciotti, who is coming here shortly to present his demands. His regiment is landing now. They didn't ask permission, they sent us a courtesy information, and that after they'd landed the lead elements."

"There's more," Lysander said. "We're also directed to cease all fraternization with CoDominium personnel, and dismiss from our service any CD officers who retired less than five years ago. Some new regulation. Henceforth all communications with CoDominium personnel are to be official business through the proper channels, and no informal contacts allowed. A full interdict is laid on Sparta until we —" he found a place on the paper he was holding and read "— demonstrate good faith efforts to comply with the directives in paragraph two, to wit, to disarm and surrender to the proper CoDominium authorities all persons at present enrolled in or in the direct employ of the organization known as Falkenberg's Mercenary Legion, sometimes known as the Forty-Second, and paragraph three relative to fraternization and employment of retired CD officials. All CoDominium Marine units stationed on Sparta are directed to cooperate in enforcement of these orders."

"This can't last," Peter said. "When Lermontov hears about this, he'll rescind it."

"And by then Sparta City may be a battlefield," King

David said. "I don't even know how to send a message to Grand Admiral Lermontov. They seem to have blocked all our communications. Nothing acknowledges."

"Is our satellite still working?" Peter asked.

"Interesting question," Lysander said. He lifted the phone and spoke briefly, then set it down with a puzzled look. "Yes. Which must mean something, but I'm damned if I can figure what."

"Maybe Forrest will have a suggestion," Peter Owensford said. "Now if you'll excuse me, I'll have to inform Commandant Campbell at Fort Plataia."

"Interesting that you named it that," Lysander said.

"Yes, sir." *Plataia was the site of a major Spartan victory over Persia, the place where Thermopylae was avenged, but it was also a city: an Athenian ally, under the protection of Athens. A faithful ally. And was destroyed when the Athenians refused to come to its aid. And how much of that story does Lysander know?* "It seemed like a good idea at the time. If you'll excuse me?"

❖   ❖   ❖

"Sir, I have my orders," Marco Ciotti said.

The colonel of the 77th CoDominium Marines was a weathered man in his forties, with a blue-joweled aquiline face and eyes black enough that the pupils disappeared in them. His skin was pale from time under a faint sun, and he looked comfortable enough under Spartan gravity. But not comfortable at all with this final conference in the Palace audience chamber overlooking Government House Square. He stood at the end of the Council Chamber, facing the kings and their advisors. "I'm not supposed to even talk to you while you're employing CoDominium people in your armed services." He indicated Admiral Forrest and Captain Nosov. "I'll use my judgment on that, but I don't have any choice about the Legion. Falkenberg's

Legion will disarm and surrender, and there aren't any alternatives."

David Freedman looked withering contempt at the CoDominium colonel. "You have no alternatives," King David said. "When a stupid man is doing something he knows is wrong, he always claims it is his duty."

"It may surprise you that I read Shaw too, King David," Colonel Ciotti said. "But it doesn't change my orders."

"Highly irregular orders," Alexander said.

Outside the window Sparta City lay at midsummer peace on a clear morning, a quiet humm of traffic no louder than the sound of birds in the parks below, drifting in with the scent of roses and warm dust. *Unbelievable*, Alexander thought. *That all this can be shattered in a moment.* As if to echo his thought, the double *crack* of a hypersonic transport coming in sounded. Not a commercial flight; all such had ended when the interdict was laid on. This would be the last of the transports bringing down the CoDominium's troops. A full regiment, and the former CD people said a very good one.

Another transport snapped past, startlingly close. Two of the Brotherhood representatives, a banker and the owner of a chain of clothing stores, looked at each other with ashen faces. They stood with the other Phraetrie leaders, middle aged men, a few women. Serious people; it was a high honor on Sparta. Most of them had children up at the front, with the Royal Army or the mobilized Militia, and all of them had families and homes here in Sparta City.

"The orders are unusual. I grant you that," Colonel Ciotti said, regretful firmness in his voice. "But I have no grounds for questioning their validity."

"You don't?" Lysander asked. "Sealed orders, in the name of the Vice Admiral but signed off by a Marine

General, from a Sector Command HQ. All communications as well as commerce interdicted. Colonel, you know as well as we do that this is a political move by Grand Senator Bronson, and those orders will be rescinded the instant that Grand Admiral Lermontov hears of them."

"I don't know anything about politics," Ciotti said.

"Don't you, Marco?" Samuel Forrest asked gently. "Then you've forgotten a lot since the High Cathay campaign. You didn't used to be anyone's dupe."

"My orders forbid me even to talk to you," Ciotti said. "And I won't."

"This is a violation of the Treaty of Independence," David said. "Interference in the Dual Monarchy's internal affairs."

"That's politics too," Ciotti said. "And I won't be involved in politics. Look, Your Majesties — Major Owensford — I didn't ask to be sent here; my men and I were doing difficult work on Haven, and necessary work at that. I strongly suspect, hell, I *know*, we're being used to pursue some Grand Senator's private vendetta, and I'm pretty sure I could name the Senator. It certainly wouldn't be the first time that's happened to the Fleet. The way things are going, it may well be the last. But that's all irrelevant. The 77th has a valid order, and as of 1800 hours, the troops of Falkenberg's Legion will be in defiance of the CoDominium. If that happens, appropriate action will be taken. Please don't make it worse than it has to be by trying to get in the 77th's way, because anyone who does is going to die, and it's as simple as that. Majesties, gentlemen, ladies, good day." He rose, clicked heels and inclined his head to the monarchs, and left with his aides at his heels.

There was a moment of silence, then everyone tried to talk at once. Peter Owensford listened for a moment, then called, "Attention!" in a parade ground voice. The room fell silent for a moment.

"So. What does it mean?" Lysander demanded. He turned to Admiral Forrest. "What is happening?"

"I don't know. It doesn't make any sense at all," Forrest said. "They've cut off all communications with Karantov and Newell. I can't even get through to Commodore Guildford! Some of this is pretty obvious. Nguyen's motives are clear. He's been in bed with the Bronson faction forever, and Bronson can be pretty generous. Immunity, pardon, or hell, a new identity and a lot of money on whatever planet he likes."

"And what planet will want him after this?" King Alexander demanded.

"Majesty, there are places Bronson stands high," Anatoly Nosov said. He shrugged. "And not so many places that would welcome Nguyen in any event, but this is not important. I agree with Admiral Forrest, problem is to understand why Ciotti does this. My guess is he thinks there will be no rescinding order from Lermontov."

"But —" King Alexander's eyes widened.

"I don't think I'm going to like this, but please explain," Lysander said.

"If Grand Admiral Lermontov is alive and still holds command, he will rescind that order. Ciotti knows this. Inference is obvious."

"I agree," Admiral Forrest said.

"You're saying Lermontov is dead?" King David asked.

"Dead, or deposed, Majesty," Nosov said. "I fear so."

"Which raises other questions," Forrest said. "Just what does Ciotti know, and how does he know it?" He shrugged. "But what's important is, what will we do now?"

"What should we do?" David said simply. "Fight, or obey? Ordinarily the Kings are required to seek counsel on such matters. With the Ultimate Decree in effect I suppose we don't have to, but perhaps it's better."

There were murmurs among the councilors and observers.

"Perhaps you have a choice," Peter Owensford said. "We don't. Once we're disarmed we're helpless, and while I doubt Ciotti would be party to our slaughter, he could sure as hell deliver us to someone who would be. If they can do something this raw, God knows there's nothing they can't do—or that Bronson won't do."

"So you'll fight," Alexander said. "The Legion will fight."

"We'll try. Our fighting strength is supporting Spartan operations at Base One and Stora. Ciotti knows that, and he'll make it plenty tough for any of them to come home. What we've got left is retired troops, staff officers, some military police, the dependents, against a Line Marine regiment. Before we can get any strength transferred from the front, he'll be at the gates of Fort Plataia demanding surrender. Once he has our base and our dependents, it'll be easier to deal with the rest of us. He already has guards posted around the Fort. They're not letting anyone leave, not without a fight anyway." Owensford shrugged. "We can't even run away. Not our people at the Fort, anyway. I suppose some of the field units could disband and hide out, but they'll put a lot of pressure on you people to help them hunt us down, and nobody's going to want to abandon our dependents to Ciotti anyway."

"But what will happen?" someone asked.

For answer, Owensford pointed to the main screen. It showed Marine equipment rolling up from the shuttle docks to the CoDominium enclave; tank-transporters and personnel carriers, artillery, general cargo. The men marched behind, in battledress of synthileather over armor. The harsh male sound of their singing crashed back from the walls of the deserted streets:

> *"We've left blood in the dirt of twenty-five worlds*
> *We've built roads on a dozen more,*
> *And all that we have at the end of our hitch*
> *Buys a night with a second-rate whore.*
> *The Senate decrees, the Grand Admiral Calls*
> *The orders come down from on high.*
> *It's 'On Full Kits' and 'Sound Board Ships,'*
> *We're sending you where you can die."*

"It would have been easier to stop their landing, of course," Owensford said conversationally. "Once they're down and sorted out into their units they're a lot stronger."

"Except we don't have any way to control what lands on Sparta," Lysander said.

> *"The lands that we take, the Senate gives back*
> *Rather more often than not,*
> *But the more that are killed, the less share the loot*
> *And we won't be back to this spot."*

"And if we fight them?" Alexander asked.

> *We'll break the hearts of your women and girls*
> *We may break your arse, as well*
> *Then the Line Marines with their banners unfurled*
> *Will follow those banners to hell —"*

"What will happen? We'll probably lose," Peter Owensford said. "Ciotti's heart won't be in it — he'd never have started this if he'd thought we'd resist — but he'll fight because it's what he's done all his life and he doesn't know what else to do."

"We know the devil, his pomps, and his works,
Ah, yes! We know them well!
 When you've served out your hitch in
   the Line Marines,
You can bugger the Senate of Hell!"

"Of course the Bronson people are counting on knocking Sparta out once we don't have your help any more," Lysander said.

"I expect so," Owensford said. "Actually it's rather late for that. You've learned well. Still, you'll be hurt. Murasaki's technoninjas will have your communications in knots once they round up all the former CD technicians. You've got good universities here, but they're not prepared for what Murasaki does. Not many are. Still, we've done a pretty good job on the Helots, at Base Camp One, and the Stora Commando operation. If they'd tried this stunt a couple of months ago, who knows, they really might have knocked you out of the war. Now —" He shrugged. "You've got a better chance than we do. Preserve your strength, take it slow and careful, I think you'll be all right in the end."

"Then we'll drink with our comrades and
   throw down our packs,
We'll rest ten years on the flat of our backs,
Then it's 'On Full Kits' and out of your racks,
You must build a new road through Hell!"

"General Owensford," Lysander said. "I think you are laboring under a misconception."

"Highness?"

Lysander stared at the screen. Rank after rank of Marines swung by the pickup. The tempo of the song changed, to a flurry of drums and horns.

"The Fleet is our country, we sleep with a rifle,
No man ever begot a son on his rifle,
They pay us in gin and curse when we sin,
There's not one who can stand us unless
  we're downwind.
We're shot when we lose and turned out
  when we win,
But we bury our comrades wherever they fall,
And there's none that can face us though
  we've nothing at all!"

"You seem to think we're going to abandon you," Lysander said.

"It's the sensible thing to do," Owensford said.

"No, by God," Alexander said. "Do you think that little of us, Peter Owensford? What have we done that you think that?"

"Sire—" For some reason Peter Owensford couldn't talk.

King David raised his head from his hands. "We here in this room have no choice," he said. "But — you all know what we have here. The Life Guards, some training units, and little else. All the first line Brotherhood units are up north. There's nothing left but the second-line Militia units. Old men, and boys and women. Enough to put down riots or fight terrorists, but can we ask them to fight that?" He pointed at the screen. "General Owensford, the Freedman Life Guards are at your disposal, and me with them, but I can't order the militia to face Line Marines."

"There's no need to order them," Lysander said. He turned to the Brotherhood representatives. "Citizens and Brothers. The Kings will lead their guards in defense of the allies of Sparta. Will the Brotherhoods join us?"

"Yes, Highness." Allan Hyson, the banker, looked scared, but his voice was firm. "How could we not?"

✧ CHAPTER SEVENTEEN

There is a paradox in the study of individual military merit inasmuch as people generally believe that the fundamental strength of soldiers is derived from the mutual dependence of comradeship and its assurance of being never left to fight alone. This is superficially true, but only in the sense that the strength of mutual dependence is an end product itself. Nothing can be derived from mutual support among a group of nothings. The man in a unit who has nothing within himself of any positive value is at best a vacant file. Unit strength is built of individual strength in positive quantities, however small. The approbation of his companions in arms is the greatest reward of a soldier's life. He never wins it by relying wholly on the efforts of others to assure his survival. In battle, when a man is not acting by reflex and retains a moment for introspection, the sensation of aloneness is most vivid. It is not to right or left or backward that he looks for strength of survival, but within himself. He is lost if there is nothing there of substance.

— Joseph Maxwell Cameron,
The Anatomy of Military Merit

✧　　✧　　✧

"Urgent signal, sir," Andy Lahr said. "Captain Catherine Alana."

"Is this circuit secure?"

"Yes, sir, direct line of sight systems, the Palace to Plataia. I mean, with Murasaki I suppose we can't be sure about anything, but I'd bet on it."

"It will have to do. OK, Andy, put her on screen."

Catherine was in battle dress, armor and leather, her hair hidden under a combat helmet. "New intelligence report," she said. "Cornet Talkins has reported in.

We've arranged a pickup, but I prefer to send her to the Palace. The CoDominium might or might not let her in here, but it wouldn't be much of a favor to put her in the middle of a battle after all she's been through. They were pretty rough on her. Anyway, I told her to ask for you, code Jehosophat."

"All right, I'll arrange to have her brought in. We can send her over to St. Thomas Hospital. Any reason I should talk to her myself? Andy Bielskis is here."

"She knows where Skilly is."

"Jesus. Tell me, quick."

"Unfortunately, it's where Skilly was. A farmhouse up near Corinth. Worth raiding, but you won't get anyone important. Talkins didn't exactly escape, General, she was rescued."

"By whom?"

"Sir, you're not going to like this. By Geoffrey Niles. He's with her, and will be at the Palace shortly."

"Niles. Under some kind of amnesty?"

"Safe conduct," Catherine said. "We didn't have much time, the Helots are looking for them, and so it was kind of a package deal, I had to bring in both."

"I'll do what I can. That Stora business really got to Prince Lysander. If we can show Niles had any connection to that, Lysander will hang him and there won't be a thing I can do about it. Or want to do about it for that matter."

"Yes, sir. Anyway, I told Niles he could walk out with a reasonable head start. General, he did rescue Margreta Talkins."

"Yeah. All right, I said I'll do what I can."

"There's more. The reason Skilly isn't at the farmhouse is that she's in Sparta City, Minetown to be exact, organizing the Helot revolt to take over when the CoDominium Marines kill off the government of

Sparta. When the Marines march on us, she'll start a general uprising."

"How truly good," Owensford said. "I have to face the 77th Line Marines with all my forces up north, nothing here but secondary militia, and I get to deploy for a general uprising as well. Actually, I expected it. Nice to see that effort wasn't wasted. Any idea of just what strength she's got?"

"No, sir, and I don't think she knows either. The Ultimate Decree caught them off guard, and a lot of their politicals have deserted the cause now that it's dangerous. Of course if she looks like winning they'll be back. General, that's not the worst of it."

"Captain, just what can be worse?"

"Murasaki. He's got an atom bomb."

"Oh, boy. Do we know what he plans to do with it?"

"No, sir. Niles may know more about that. He was being cagey, holding back some information to bargain with. Of course he may be wrong, but I'd bet a lot that he believes he's not wrong, that Murasaki has a bomb and Skilly has worked out a way to use it to her advantage. Maybe you can find out more when he gets there."

"I'll try. Wish I had you here."

"Use Andy. He's better than me, almost as good as Jesus," Catherine said. "OK, sir, I'll get back to defense organization."

"Yeah. How's morale."

"Not good, but how could it be?"

"Right. Tell them to hang on. Ciotti may want to carry out his orders, but he doesn't want his bright and shiny regiment all bloodied either. I'm hoping that when he realizes he has a real fight he'll reconsider."

"Yes, sir. Well, I'd best get to work. Alana out." Catherine didn't sound as if she believed that Ciotti would reconsider, which was all right, because Owensford didn't really believe it either.

❖   ❖   ❖

The gates of the CoDominium compound swung open. Almost silently, two Suslov tanks flowed out, sensors scanning as their turrets swung the 135mm autocannon back and forth. The scouts had gone over the wall earlier; infantry followed the armor, deploying into open formations.

Lysander felt his palms sweat as he watched through the pickup from the lead tank. *God I wish I was there. Like hell I do.*

The plan was to keep the CD Marines in the urban areas, prevent their full deployment. Try to keep them from winning quickly. Every hour's delay was another chance Lermontov would send countermanding orders. *Or something. Hell, the horse may learn to sing.*

The tanks moved forward. *God, I'm glad I'm not there.* Those were better machines than his men had, and crewed by soldiers everyone called the best in the human universe.

He had put the Spartan-made armor in the forward positions, holding the Legion's handful of modern tanks and AFV's back to contain penetrations. The first of the Marine tanks was nosing down the avenue leading south, with a screening force of infantry fanned out ahead, shadowy figures darting from one piece of cover to the next.

"Now," he said.

The pickup monitor shuddered, and buried blast charges dropped the fronts of the buildings on either side into the street. A barrier of rubble slid down across the pavement in a cloud of dust and brick that billowed out to obscure the nightvision scope's view. Overhead the freight-train rumble of artillery passed, and seconds later the lead element of the 77th Marines fell under the hammer of airburst shells. Automatic weapons opened up, streams of tracer from well-covered positions further down the street killing or pinning the Marine foot soldiers. The first Suslov accelerated, rising up over the rubble that blocked the street.

The monitor shuddered again, this time as the 76mm gun of the Cataphract opened up, hammering five shells into the thinner belly armor of the medium tank. The flashes were bright; the heavier vehicle slewed around and halted. An instant later it exploded, a muffled *whump* sound and belches of yellow-orange flame through slits and hatches.

"Got him, got him!" the Cataphract's commander was saying. "We got —" The pickup went blank.

"Switch to secondary," Lysander said.

"Captain Porter here."

"Collins here."

"Highness, the rebels are making their move concurrently with the Marine attack. Power's down except for buildings with auxiliaries." That meant the whole city was dark, no streetlights, probably no water. "City com lines are completely garbled. Heavy jamming on the air. Firing in the streets, and fires, from what sensors I have left. Seems to be centered in Minetown."

Lysander nodded grimly. Every Field Force soldier and militiaman was needed to contain the Marines; so were the Milice. The unorganized reserve of the Brotherhoods would have to contain the Minetowners. That might be difficult; there were sixty thousand new chums in there, many of them hungry, and there had been no time to root out all the rebels.

"The third line will have to handle it," he said. *That's all there is,* he thought. *Ordinary people.*

Another light flashed. "Sir! Major Donald here. The Marines are —"

❖   ❖   ❖

"Where do you think you're going?"

Thomas McTiernan sucked in his gut and managed to fasten the armor; a decade as a tavern and restaurant keeper had left him a good deal heftier than he had been when he last wore the Brotherhood militia equipment. Behind him an open window looked out over a street dark except for the light of a three-quarter Cytheria and the ruddy glow of burning buildings a little further north; the low-rent district was ablaze from end to end. No fire sirens sounded, not since the rebel snipers slaughtered the first response of the amateur fire companies. He could see the flashes from shells exploding near the CoDo enclave, as well, and the staccato echoes of small-arms fire. Both were increasing, and even as he watched Marine artillery opened up from inside the enclave, firing south against the Royal guns dug in near Government House Square.

"Didn't you hear the King?" he said, turning on her. Their bedroom was plain enough; there was a hologram of a serious-looking young man in Royal Army uniform. Another of a younger man; that one had the simple starburst of the Order of Thermopylae laid across it. "I'm going to help stop the rebels, the Marines, get the bastards who hurt Julio —"

Then he took in the hunting clothes on her stout body, the shotgun firmly clutched in her hands.

"Not without me, you aren't, Thomas McTiernan," she said. "And don't say it. All the young, strong, fit ones are off with the Army, like Mike —" they both glanced toward the picture of their son in uniform "— and we're what's left."

He stared at her in silence for a moment, then snorted. "Startin' to remember why I married you, Maria," he said.

The arms case was in the back of the bedroom closet. A Peltast rifle lay there, massive and ugly-handsome and shining with careful maintenance. He threw the bandoleer over his shoulder, then ducked his head through the carrying strap, grunting as he came erect. *These mothers are* heavy, he thought. One of his knees gave a warning twinge, legacy of an ancient soccer game. *Hope I don't have to sprint much.*

His daughter was waiting at the head of the stairs, a gangling buck-toothed girl with a mop of carrot-colored hair, just turned thirteen and adding pimples to her mass of freckles. She was wearing the brown cotton-drill uniform of the Royal Spartan Scouts, complete with neckerchief, and carrying the scope-sighted .22 rifle they trained with. Her father opened his mouth, hesitated.

"Just keep your head down and don't do anything damn-fool, understand?" he growled.

"Yes, Papa," she said.

Damn sight more respectful than she usually is, he thought, working his mouth to moisten it. *Christ, I wish I was twenty again.* A young man didn't think he could die. A young man didn't have responsibilities . . . *A young man didn't see his son after he'd thrown himself on a grenade in his own home.*

They came out into the courtyard that was the patio of the family business, and a shadowy figure leaped back with a cry.

"Jesus, Thom!"

"Ah, Eddie," McTiernan said, recognizing the neighbor who had the appliance-repair shop down at the corner. "Sorry."

They walked out into the street. A crowd was gathering; he recognized most of them, but it was odd to see the same faces you passed the time of day with milling around with guns in their hands.

"Thom, we're putting up a barricade at the end of the street. Mind if we use your van?"

He winced — that was three years scrimping and saving — then nodded and threw the man the keys.

"Hey, sprout, get your bike," a younger voice said. "Mr. Kennedy says we gotta be couriers to the other parts of the neighborhood."

His daughter gave him a brief kiss on the cheek and dashed away; Maria McTiernan came back out of the door, her shotgun slung muzzle-down along her back and two large hampers in her hand.

"Sandwiches," she said, to his unspoken question. "They'll need sandwiches at the barricade."

"Eddie," he said, struck with a thought. He hoisted the Peltast rifle up with the butt resting on one hip.

"Yeah?"

"Get me a couple of people, will you?" He pointed to the library at the end of the street with his free hand; it was a neo-Californian period piece, with a square four-story tower at one corner. "With someone to watch my back, I could do a lot of good from up there with this jackhammer."

"Yeah! Hey, Forchsen, Mrs. Brust, c'mon over here!"

Somebody pedaled up, breathless, shouted in a voice just beginning to break.

"Hey, I'm from Jefferson street! My Dad sent me to tell you the Minetowners are coming right up Paine Avenue, must be thousands of them, molotovs and guns and all, they've got some trucks covered with boilerplate, too. Coming through where the Marines blew down the buildings."

A growl ran through the householders, mechanics, storekeepers, clerks. The crowd flowed toward the barricade, into firing positions in upper floors; McTiernan heard window-glass being hammered out with rifle butts as he lumbered wheezing toward the library, gasping thanks as Mrs. Brust the schoolteacher came up to take some of the weight off his shoulder.

Her machinepistol clanked against him with every stride, to a mutter of "*sorry, sorry.*"

On Burke Avenue, on scores of others like it, the Battle of Sparta City had begun.

⬥   ⬥   ⬥

"Report, Group Leader Derex?" Kenjiro Murasaki said, indicating the map table. The commander of the Helot regulars infiltrated into Sparta City looked exhausted, his armor dark with grime and smoke.

"Not so good, sir," he said. "Here." The map showed Minetown as a solid splotch of Movement red, with long tangled pseudopods reaching out across the city; there was another, smaller block on the other side of the Sacred way, and a scattering like measles almost to Government House Square. From the Co-Dominium enclave a single broad straight arrow drove south, overlapping the Movement forces.

"Trouble is, them Minetowners ain't gettin' out as much as we'd like," the Helot said regretfully. "Well, not surprisin'. Handing 'em guns don't make them fuckers soldiers, sir. Too many barricades and Cits with guns. Not milishy — the milishy fightin' the Marines — just Cits, but they kin shoot. Nearly got me, b'God; snipers thicker'n dogshit out there. Peltast rifles, too, them armored cars ain't worth jack shit against them fuckers." A look of grudging respect made the Helot's face longer than ever.

"Well, anyways, when the Minetowners *do* git out, 'n overrun places with Cits in 'em, they just stops to loot, rape and burn and drink anythin' they kin find, transmission fluid included. Then the Milice flyin' squads hits and drives 'em back. Our own fires is getting so outa hand they're blockin' us too. Too many of 'em round the edges of Minetown."

"Flying squads?" Murasaki said thoughtfully. "How do they coordinate, without communications?" Much of the Royal Army equipment was still functioning, but the ordinary city facilities were frozen.

The Helot officer brayed laughter. Murasaki frowned, and it sobered the tall man down to a grin.

"They ain't using the com, sir. They's usin' Evil Scuts."

"Eagle Scouts?" the Meijian said, baffled.

"Little motherfuckers're on rooftops and in attic winders all over town, anywhere Cits live, blinkin' at each other with flashlights. Morse code." This time the admiration was ungrudged. "Runnin' messages by bicycle, too."

"Dispose of them."

"How, sir? I ain't got but the one Group, seven hundred countin' every booger and ass-wipe. Y' Movement gunmen will have to do it."

Murasaki nodded thoughtfully. *Surprising*, he thought. Analysis had indicated the blockade and CoDominium intervention would frighten the populace into sitting this out.

"Recommendations?"

"Sure, sir. Them Minetowners don't have the discipline to overrun even weak forces, but they got more'n enough numbers and firepower, with what we handed out. Your cell-leaders —" he jerked a thumb at the men and women behind him, in civilian clothes but armed and wearing = sign armbands "— keep tryin' to lead from the front. Like tryin' to stiffen up a pitcher of spit with a handful of buckshot, just wastin' men who're willing to fight. Put automatic weapons teams *behind* the crowds. Fire on anyone who retreats. Set the fires in the *center* of Minetown, big ones. They'll charge the barricades if you get them too crazy-scared of what's behind them to stop."

The technoninja nodded.

"Do it. Now. Also, detach two companies for the *Endlosung* attack on Fort Plataia."

The Helot hesitated. "Sir —"

"It is essential."

Orders crackled out.

❖   ❖   ❖

"Glad to see you, Cornet Talkins," Owensford said. "Highness, I present Cornet Margreta Talkins. She holds commissions in both the Legion and the Royal Intelligence Corps. Talkins, Crown Prince Lysander."

"I'm proud to meet you, Highness," Margreta said. She looked down at her ill fitting clothing with embarrassment. "They didn't tell me I was to meet you—"

Lysander took her hand and kissed her fingers. "I'm very pleased to meet you. We'll repeat the introduction at a more pleasant event," Lysander said. He turned to her companion. "I can't say I'm pleased to see you, Niles. Frankly, I'd rather talk to a snake."

"I wish I could resent that," Geoffrey Niles said. "But unfortunately I understand all too well."

"Were you at Stora?" Lysander demanded.

"At Stora, yes, Highness. But I had nothing to do with the attack on the Armory. I would have prevented it if I could."

"You knew it was to take place?"

"I knew we had an earth penetrator missile. I did not know its target until less than five minutes before the launch. I protested the targeting, and was told that if I continued to protest I would be shot. I did not order that target, nor did I pass along any orders concerning that missile."

"Sergeant Bielskis?" Owensford asked.

"No hesitations, and no doubts," Andy Bielskis said. "If he's faking that, he's the best I ever saw. I'd say genuine, sir."

"If you like I'll submit to any questioning technique you want to employ," Niles said. "The only violation of the Laws of War that I have been involved in or condoned was the gas attack in the Dales, and that was against military targets only. There weren't even any civilians in the area."

"All right, we'll hold that one in abeyance," Owensford said. "Cornet, what was promised to Mr. Niles?"

"Free passage out if he didn't talk us into a better deal, and a reasonable head start before pursuit."

"Talkins, you sound exhausted. I suppose it's best you're here as long as we're talking to Grand Senator Bronson's nephew, but as soon as we're done I want you to go check into St. Thomas's," Owensford said.

"Thanks, sir, but I reckon I can still fight."

"There's no need," Lysander said.

"Every need," Margreta said. "Highness, I intend to accept Citizenship just as soon as I'm discharged. This is my home, and I'll sure feel better when we've got these scum cleaned out of it." She touched her bruised cheeks and black eye. "And I reckon I have some personal reasons, too."

"Well, I can't argue that," Owensford said. "All right, Niles, you hinted that you want a better deal than a safe conduct out of here. What do you want and what will you trade?"

"What I want is a free pardon," Niles said.

"Not a ticket off-planet?"

"If I have to take that I'll do it, but I'd rather earn the right to stay here," Geoff said. "Stay here, help rebuild. Help undo some of the damage I've caused." He looked significantly at Margreta. "Marry, work for Citizenship."

"Why this change of heart?"

"It would take a long time to explain, and we don't have a long time," Geoff said. "You learn a lot about a society from fighting it. And about its leaders. And what I learned was to admire you people."

"And what do you have to bargain with?" Owensford demanded.

"Information. I'll give it all to you, and you determine what it's worth. I'll accept your valuation."

Lysander look coldly at him for a while. "All right. Spill it."

Geoff told them of the conversation he had heard between Skilly and Murasaki. "I didn't actually hear the word 'nuke,' " he said, "but I can't think what else it could be. Murasaki has one, but only one, nuclear weapon, and he intends to deploy it either to destroy the Palace, or Legion Headquarters at Fort Plataia. If it was left to Skilly it would be the Palace, but my guess is that Murasaki prefers Plataia."

"But you don't know it's a nuke," Lysander said, "and in any event you don't know where it is. Where it is now, or where it is going to be. Who would know?"

"Skilly, and Murasaki," Geoff said. "And maybe not Skilly. Murasaki is crazy. Apparently Grand Uncle gave him the assignment of undermining Sparta, and the secondary but almost equally important goal of punishing Falkenberg's Legion."

"Sounds a bit odd," Owensford said. "The Legion's on New Washington. We're just some odd bits and pieces."

"Including the families," Niles said. "Murasaki would delight in the anguish it would cause Falkenberg and his people on New Washington if they heard their families were killed. Or captured by Bronson people."

"That must take real hate," Owensford said. "Is Bronson that crazy?"

Niles shook his head slowly. "General, I don't know. I used to think he was crazy like a fox. That's still the way to bet it."

"All right," Lysander said. "General, your evaluation? Is his information worth what he asks?"

"It's close. Talkins, have you a recommendation regarding this man?" Owensford said.

"He saved my life," she said. "And he — was very much a gentleman."

"Well, you have a large favor coming from the Crown," Lysander said.

"Oh. Well, if it's large enough to cover his pardon, I'll ask for it," Margreta said.

Lysander nodded. "So be it. Geoffrey Niles, you have a free pardon for all acts committed since you arrived on Sparta to this moment. Cornet Talkins, you've still got a favor coming, you didn't use more than half your credit on this."

"So," Owensford said. "Sergeant, take Mr. Niles to a conference room and see if he remembers anything else worth knowing. Particularly clues about where this Gotterdammerung is going to go off."

Lysander stood. "I don't suppose I can be much help with that. Cornet Talkins, please go to St. Thomas's. It won't be any picnic. I'm afraid the hospital is going to end up as part of the defense system."

❖   ❖   ❖

"The next push with their armor may get through," Lysander said bluntly, to the officers grouped around them. "We're sopping up their infantry, us and the Citizens, but we've got to get more antitank teams out there —"

It had been only five hours since the attack began. *Five hours. God.* He could hear his own words as he briefed his men, but somewhere beneath it was running a stream of memory, smashed buildings and men gaping in death around burning iron. *Only five hours and we're already back to Government House Square.* The St. Thomas Hospital had been the only building suitable for a redoubt.

"Sir, rebels, they're in the main ventilation shafts on level four!"

Lysander jerked his head up from the map. "Bloody

hell! Come on — not you, just the riflemen."

The machine-gunner at the window nodded, tapping off another expert short burst at the shadowy figures darting between the burning cars in the lot below. *God Damn.* The CoDo Marines were not cooperating with the Helots deliberately, but the *effect* could be the same.

Lysander lead the way out of the orderly room they had taken over as tactical HQ at a pounding run. Wounded men and the sick evacuated from the lower levels looked up at him as he passed, slalomed off the wall at the axial corridor with the rifle squad at his heels. This *was* level four; his redoubt. And Melissa's room was quite close to where the main airshaft branched off from the service core.

"There!" he shouted.

There was movement behind the grillwork screen, across from her door. He fired from the hip as he ran, walking the bullets up the wall and into the meter-square grille. More movement, a jerk. A flash of white light, and suddenly he was lying against the door and the door was open, and Melissa was looking at him. Smiling. Then horrified, and beginning to struggle out of bed. She had a pistol in one hand, and a book in the other. Some distant part of him recognized it; the Church of Sparta *Book of Hours*.

"No, stay there, darling, *please.*"

"Bastards," he wheezed, levering himself over so that he faced the corridor. The door swung shut behind him. Thin, no protection.

Pain stabbed into his ribs, making him cough. That was a mistake, because white light ran behind his eyelids and the world rocked, and vomiting would *really* be a mistake if his ribs were in the state he thought they where. *Already* in *hospital, nothing I can do.*

"Bastards," he gritted again, and used the rifle to

climb to his knees. *"Bastards!"* The men who had followed him here were down, moving or still but down. An arm dangled out of the black hole up near the roof where the screen had been, shredded and dripping, a head and shoulders and too many teeth showing where blast had ripped the skin and muscle off a skull like a glove off a hand. The body jerked and trembled. *Not alive. Moving. More of them in the shaft.*

Lysander slumped against the wall, ignoring the gratings under his chest. The armor would hold it for a while. He clamped the rifle between his side and his arm, brought up the wavering muzzle.

"Bastards!"

Bang and *ptank* as a bullet slammed through the thin lath and thinner metal behind it, the aluminum airshaft itself. Hollow booming as something big thrashed around in that strait space, and the hole began to leak red down the gray-white plaster of the hospital wall.

"Bastards!"

Another shot, another, recoil hammering into his side, spacing them down the length of the corridor, the length of the hidden shaft. Someone came up behind him, another rifleman, firing with him, slow and deliberate. Then a thunderclap; fire shot out around the body stuck in the hole like a cork in a bottle, and plaster showered down as the metal ballooned. Harv came trotting down the corridor reloading his grenade launcher, calling over his shoulder for stretcher-bearers.

Lysander looked to see who his companion was. "Well, Cornet Talkins. I think you've earned another favor. Now do me one. Stay with Melissa."

"Aye aye, sir."

Harv brought the medics up. "Lady, I sure thank you," he said. "It was supposed to be me with the Prince, and—" He gestured to the medics.

"I can stand," Lysander gritted. "I can't sprint but I can command. Get me up. Back to the war room. *Now*."

❖   ❖   ❖

Centrifugal force kept the outer rim of the space station at .9 gee, which was comfortable compared to Sparta. Everyone knew that high gravity was much better for your health, people in high gravity planets lived longer due to the increased exercise, but .9 gee was still a relief. Sergeant Wallace and the 77th Captain whose name Boris Karantov couldn't remember had remarked on it. They'd talked about many things in an attempt to be pleasant, and to take Karantov's mind off the fact that he was a prisoner in his own office.

After a while they turned on the television screens. They showed the battles in Sparta City from the view of the Marines of the 77th. The battle wasn't going smoothly. In five hours they'd made a wreck of part of the city, but they hadn't stopped the city resistance at all. And now there were other scenes, of rebels attacking the citizens although they carefully avoided fighting any units of the 77th.

Boris Karantov watched the battle with horror. He maintained a chilly silence until the Marine lieutenant had left the room. Then he spoke to the polite Line Marine sergeant. "Sergeant Wallace, good men are being killed down there. Your comrades, Legionnaires, Spartans. And you are illegally detaining legitimate CoDominium authorities who could end this madness."

The Line Marine sergeant didn't like his situation at all. "Sir, the Captain told me—"

"Sergeant, do you deny that I am senior CoDominium Marine officer in this system?"

"No, sir."

"Then forget your captain. I am giving you orders: assist me in regaining control of this station."

"Colonel, I can't do that—"

"Sergeant, you will do that. Or shoot me now. If you disobey this order and I am alive when this is over, Sergeant Wallace, I will have you hanged in low gravity, and the last thing you will see will be recordings of that." He pointed at the screens. "Or do you tell me you join military services to accomplish that?"

"Jesus, Colonel, all I know is they tell me —" He lowered his voice. "Colonel, the story is you're all Lermontov people, and Lermontov is out. Arrested. Admiral Townsend is in charge now."

"And you believe Fleet will go over to Townsend, which is to say, Bronson?"

"God damn, Colonel, we don't know jack shit about politics, I know I got my orders."

"Which are rescinded," a voice said from behind him. "Sergeant, if you reach for that weapon I will cheerfully cut your throat. Colonel, if you'll relieve him of that sidearm — there. Thank you."

"Thank you. Now who are you?" Karantov demanded.

"Master Sergeant Hiram Laramie, SAS, Falkenberg's Legion, at your service, Colonel. When we couldn't raise communications, Colonel Owensford sent us up to have a look."

"How the fuck did you get here?" Sergeant Wallace demanded,

"I confess curiosity myself," Karantov said.

"Navy helped," Laramie said. "They was getting worried they couldn't reach Captain Newell or any of their own officers, sir, so they was glad to help us come take a look. Lieutenant Deighton's looking to help Captain Newell, sir."

"What have you done with the others of the 77th?"

"Got 'em handcuffed outside," Laramie said. "Sergeant Wallace, if you'll put your hands behind you — careful, now, and nobody gets hurt. Thank you. Colonel, General Owensford would like mightily to speak with you. Shall I get him for you?"

"Yes, please, Sergeant. And please to find out status of Fleet Captain Newell, if you will . . ."

◆   ◆   ◆

Marine Captain Saunders Laubenthal slid up behind the windowsill and looked out onto the street outside. The dead from the last Spartan counterattack littered it; many were down below, where his men had had to clear them out with grenades.

We took the street, he thought bitterly. *And now there's another bloody street to take.*

"Irony," he muttered to himself.

"Sir?" Sandeli said.

The black was the senior sergeant now, and second-in-command of the company since Lieutenant Cernkov had been carried back to the enclave and the regeneration stimulators. The unit had taken twenty percent casualties in the night's fighting.

"I was planning to retire here," Laubenthal said absently. "Gods, if these are militia we're fighting, I'd hate to see their best. They just don't give up."

From another window fire stabbed out across the street toward the Spartan positions. A body pitched forward to tumble off a balcony and forward to the pavement two stories below, a rifle rattling beside it.

"Got them pretty well suppressed, sir," Sandeli said.

Hint. "All right; tell first platoon to —"

A sound interrupted him, a high-pitched shrieking from further down the street to the north, back along their path. Then a scatter of running figures; they were pushing a handcart before them, with a uniformed Spartan wired to the front of it and a thicker mob behind. The uniform was on fire, and the mob behind fell on the Spartan wounded in the street below the Marine position with clubs and tools and bayoneted rifles. More screams rose, and the flood of ragged humanity spilled over to the building the Royalists still held; the Marines had done their work of suppressing fire all too well.

"Kaak," Sandeli muttered in his native tongue: *shit*.

Captain Laubenthal stood and touched the side of his helmet. *"The last bloody straw,"* he muttered. *"Damned* if I'll see good soldiers murdered."

"Sir?"

"It appears that we're out of touch with HQ, sergeant," he said. "I do not seem to hear a thing. A Company! Open fire, selective. Drive off those jackals and rescue the Spartans."

"Sir?"

"You heard me, soldier!"

"Fucking A, sir! Carruthers. New targets! Clean house!" He turned back to his captain. "Sir, I hope you never get that mother fucking radio working again."

❖   ❖   ❖

"Owensford here."

"Deighton here, sir. I have Fleet Captain Newell and Colonel Karantov with me."

"Thank God. Boris, what's happening up there?"

"Ciotti's people had us under house arrest," Karantov said.

"Thought it was something like that. Guildford too?"

"Sir, they've taken him somewhere else, possibly aboard that battlecruiser *Patton*, sir," Lieutenant Deighton said.

"Thank you. But you have returned control of the CD space station to Fleet Captain Newell and Colonel Karantov?"

"I can do that now, sir. Fleet Captain, Colonel, any time you'd like you can relieve my troops with those you've selected."

"I will see to this," Boris Karantov said. "I also wish to see that my landing craft is made ready. Piotr Stefanovich, my thanks. We will speak again."

"General Slater, let me add my thanks as well," Newell said. "I can't say I enjoyed being under arrest."

"No, sir. If you'll pardon me, Captain, what the hell is going on? Has Ciotti lost his mind?"

"Not quite," Newell said. "According to the sergeant who was holding Colonel Karantov prisoner, Ciotti got, along with his orders to come here and arrest you, a message to the effect that Lermontov has been deposed. It doesn't seem to have been an official order signed by the Grand Senate, but a message from someone at Fleet Headquarters. There was another from the Grand Senate, or maybe from a Senate Committee."

"Or an individual Grand Senator?"

"Possibly. Since Ciotti's the only one we know who read it, I don't have the details. All I know is, we got word Ciotti was coming with special orders, and as soon as he got here he used his troops to take control of this station. We didn't suspect a thing. I couldn't figure out what was his hurry, but then not long after Ciotti's takeover here, Signals got a long coded message from Fleet Headquarters. Ciotti's people can't decode it, and my people said they couldn't, but that may have been a story for Ciotti. I'm checking on that now."

"From Fleet Headquarters, but can't be decoded by Fleet signal officers," Owensford said. "Captain, if all else fails, perhaps Colonel Karantov can decode it. Or King Alexander."

"Hmm. I see," Newell said. "All right, I'll have a copy sent down to you. If you can read it, I expect you ought to."

"Meanwhile, what do you intend to do?" Owensford asked. "With Guildford out of communications, you're the senior Fleet official in this system."

"Until Guildford shows up again," Newell said. "Or we get authenticated orders from Fleet Headquarters."

"And if Lermontov has been thrown out in a Bronson coup?" Owensford asked.

"I'll think about that. Now, if you'll excuse me, General, I thank you for the rescue, but there are serious matters demanding my attention. I want to get to my ship!"

"Certainly. When you get the urgent parts done, Admiral Forrest and Captain Nosov would like to speak with you."

Newell grinned. "I just expect they — I have an intercom light, Colonel Karantov wants to be patched in. Just a moment. Boris?"

"Da. Piotr Stefanovich?"

"I'm here, Boris."

"Do not surrender. I am departing for planetary surface," he said. "Godspeed my friend."

❖   ❖   ❖

"Are we going to die, Mrs. Fuller?" the girl said.

Juanita Fuller looked around the bombproof shelter at the sea of faces; there were fifty children here, and hers was the ultimate responsibility. A dozen shelters like this . . . The one who had asked the question was just too young to be up above helping with the last-ditch defense, around eleven. Her face was grave behind the CBW suit's transparent visor, but some of the others were sniffling back tears.

Mark! something wailed inside her. But Cornet Mark Fuller was with Aviation Company of the Legion on New Washington. *Lieutenant by now. If he's still alive. We didn't have enough time!* A few months, just

enough to begin healing from her horrible captivity in
the escaped-convict settlement on Tanith. Now she
was supposed to face danger like an officer's lady . . .
I'm just a girl, I'm only nineteen.

"Of course we aren't going to die, Roberta," she
said, putting a teasing note into her voice. "*You* just
want a chance to get up there and fire a gun." The
miniuzi hung heavy on her hip. *I did all right on the
firing range. Could I use it on a man?*

"Let's have a song, everybody," she said. "Because
there's no school today . . .

> *Little bunny froo-froo*
> *Hoppin' through the forest —* "

Roberta began to sing, and then the others took it up:

> "Pickin' up the field mice
> *Whackin' 'em on the head!*"

"Jodie! Do *not* whack Angie on the head!"

❖   ❖   ❖

"Something funny that I didn't notice, Kinnie?"
Captain Jesus Alana asked. The motion sensors said a
company level attack was coming out of them through
the fire and smoke of the night; the Legion had pulled
back to its original encampment, setting incendiaries in
the huge Royal Army logistics buildings that made up
much of the base.

Base commander, he thought. *Base commander of a
rifle platoon.* Adult hands were far too few in Fort
Plataia to spare anyone from the firing line.

Hassan al'Jinnah chuckled again. "Just reminds me
of old times, sor," he said, stroking the stock of his
machine-gun. "Ah, here they come." The Berber had
been a long-service man when the Legion was still the

42nd CoDominium Marines and John Christian Falkenberg III had been a shavetail second lieutenant; for the last twenty-five years his job had been chief mess steward. "Reminds me of Kennicott, sor."

A very good steward, since he was devoutly Muslim and never touched alcohol. The cocking lever of his rifle made a *tch-clack* sound as he eased it backward and chambered a round.

Jesus Alana pressed his eyes to the vision block. The dark outside slipped away, replaced by a silvery day like none waking eyes had ever seen. The vast stores area in the western extension of the base was a pillar of flame behind the advancing Helots; two light tanks in the lead, and an infantry screen following. They came at a cautious trot, the AFV's taking advantage of each building, and the foot soldiers moving forward by squads and sections.

"Pretty drill," he said, and pressed the stud. The ground erupted in a line of orange fire. He blinked; when he opened his eyes again his wife was beside him, whistling through her teeth.

Cathy only does that when she's really *nervous*, he thought, unslinging his rifle. Her grenade launcher spat out its five rounds, *choonk-choonk-choonk-choonk*.

There were no living targets when he brought up his weapon. "Doubt they'll try that again," he said thoughtfully. "And it can't have been their whole effort."

The posts reported in, except for one. "Three?" he said. "Post three?"

Mortar shells whistled overhead. *Landline cut?* Possibly, and he had no one to spare to look.

"They'll be back. At least once," he said.

"Twice," al' Jinneh said. "Care for a bet, sor? Bottle of Cavaret Zinfandel?"

"Against what?"

"Blue Mountain coffee, sor. Half a pound."

"Done. Though you win either way, Mess Steward."

◇   ◇   ◇

Lieutenant Colonel Scott Farley studied the map table, then looked up to Colonel Marco Ciotti. "Six companies fail to report, Colonel."

"The communications environment is very bad," Ciotti said. "But this is strange. Send messengers with new equipment and orders to report instantly."

"Yes, sir." *Is it that he doesn't know, or he doesn't want to know? Six companies don't report. We know two went over to the enemy! Could it be all six? Six companies of Line Marines gone over to the enemy! Nothing like that has happened in thirty years. Of course they haven't exactly gone over, but they're helping the Spartans put down the Minetown rebellion, and a damned good thing, too. Surely Ciotti knows?*

"The assault on Fort Plataia has been repulsed," Ciotti said.

"Yes sir."

"Have them regroup and wait for assistance. Sergeant Kramer, get me Captain Donovic on the *Patton*."

"Yes, sir. Have to relay through the space station, sir."

"That's all right."

"Yes, sir. It'll be a minute."

Scott Farley watched the map display, but his attention was on the colonel. He had a very good idea what Ciotti had in mind, and he didn't like it.

"Here's Captain Donovic, sir.

"Ciotti here. Captain, I'm losing far too many men in this operation. I need your help. Please set up to bombard designated targets in the Government House and Fort Plataia areas."

"You really think that's necessary?" Donovic asked. "Guildford isn't going to like it."

"I see no point in telling Commodore Guildford until the battle is over," Ciotti said. "I also see no point in continuing to take casualties from these people. They were given every opportunity for honorable surrender, but it is clear they intend to fight long after the result is inevitable. Why should I let our Marines be slaughtered in this senseless action?"

Senseless. It's senseless, all right, Lt. Col. Farley thought. *But not the way you think! God damn, God damn, damn—*

"Colonel, I'm not sure this is wise," Captain Donovic said.

"What is unwise is holding off any longer," Ciotti said. "You know what is at stake here, and time is not on our side. Now please make ready for kinetic energy weapon bombardments. I will designate targets. It will not take long, and we will finish the resistance, at Fort Plataia and in the city itself. We can then proceed with our plans."

"All right," Donovic said. "I don't like it, but I like failure even less, and as you say, time isn't exactly our friend here. Sound general quarters. Battle stations. Prepare for planetary bombardment." Alarm klaxons hooted in the background.

"Captain Donovic."

The voice was strange. Everyone in the map table room looked up, startled.

"Who the hell is that?" Donovic demanded.

"This is Fleet Captain Samuel Newell. I am apparently the senior CoDominium officer present. Captain Donovic, I forbid you to use your ship to take part in this battle. You will please secure from general quarters and report to me in person. You will find me aboard *Vera Cruz*."

"How the hell —" Ciotti said.

"You're not the system commander," Donovic said.

"No, I understand that Commodore Guildford is a guest aboard your ship, Captain Donovic," Newell said. "I trust he is better pleased with that status than I was in my own offices on the space station. I have not heard you order your ship secured from general quarters, Captain, and I am waiting."

"Be damned if I'll take orders from you."

"Very well," Newell said. "Commander Taylor, sound general quarters. Battle stations. Divisions report when cleared for action."

"*Vera Cruz*. A cruiser," Donovic said. "This is a battle cruiser. You're bluffing."

"Am I? Taylor, general signal to the squadron. Continue previous deployment. Battle stations, prepare for fleet action against the battlecruiser *Patton*. All units to report when ready for action."

"*Volga* on station and ready for action, sir!"

"*Kirov* cleared for action, will be on station in five minutes, sir!"

"Newell, you've lost your mind! Are you going to fire on me? We need unity in the Fleet, not this!"

"Exactly, Captain Donovic," Newell said. "And you're going to achieve unity by bombarding an independent planet against the direct orders of the system commanders? Ever think that our families are down there on Sparta where you've helped start a God damned war?"

"*Aegir* sounding general quarters now. On station in twenty minutes."

"You're not Commander Clarkson!" Donovic shouted.

"No, sir, this is Lieutenant Commander Nielsen."

"Where's Clarkson?"

"He's not available, sir," Nielsen said. "Proceeding with general quarters, Captain Newell."

"Thank you. Captain Donovic, I am still waiting."

There was a long pause. Then: "You know, there's never been a fleet action like this, four smaller ships against a battle cruiser. I think we can take you, Newell."

"Plus the space station. All units, prepare for general engagement."

"But we'd be hurt pretty bad. And what the hell, we might not win. Robbie, secure from general quarters. Captain Newell, you'll understand if I decline your invitation to join you aboard your ship, but I agree we'll need to continue this conversation without so many eavesdroppers.

"Colonel Ciotti, I regret that your request for fire support has been overruled by the acting system commander. I fear you're on your own. Good luck."

The speakers went silent. Ciotti cursed quietly. "All right. We'll have to do it on our own." He looked at the map table. "Maybe we won't have to take the Palace. It looks like the rebels are about to do that."

❖   ❖   ❖

"GO!" Group Leader Derex was screaming like a madman. *"Go! Go! Go!"*

The Helots streamed toward the palace steps. One unit dashed to the flagstaff to haul down the crowned mountain of the Dual Monarchy. Their leader had begun to unfasten the halyards when a group burst out of the palace.

An old man, and ten of the ceremonial Life Guards. They didn't look ceremonial at all though, as they deployed on the huge steps, hiding behind the Doric columns and the great lion statues.

Someone fired four times. The elderly leader of the Guards took another step forward, stumbled, and fell. For a moment there was a lull in the fighting. A woman burst out of the palace and ran to bend over him. She was still for a moment, then she stood.

"Spartans! They have killed the King! The Helots have killed the King!"

A moment of hushed silence; then a roar. From the palace, from the buildings around the square, from tunnels, seemingly from the sky itself, the cry was repeated. "Spartans! The Helots have killed the King!"

And another cry, wordless, an animal sound of rage. The Life Guards charged forward, firing coldly and efficiently and rapidly. They reached the party around the flagstaff, and the only Helots still standing were battered to the ground. One of the guards fell on the Helot soldier and beat him with his rifle butt.

And from the square came militia, wounded soldiers, old men and women, children barely old enough to seize weapons from the fallen. They came out and they came out to kill.

Derex watched his command dissolve, vanish, not so much beaten as destroyed. Men threw down their weapons to run, and that was no good either. The enemy was out now, out in the open, out where they could be killed, but they weren't dying, it was his men who were being slaughtered, shot, stabbed, strangled, beaten to death with baseball bats. A woman sat on a Helot's chest and pounded at his head with an iron frying pan.

Derex stood to rally the men, and a grenade landed nearby. He threw himself away from it, to the ground, but the world had turned to slow motion, he couldn't fall fast enough, and the sound of the grenade was louder than anything he had ever heard in his life.

❖   ❖   ❖

The screens panned down a street where outnumbered Spartan militia battled a Helot mob. The pickup was back far enough that it didn't show all the details, but there were enough.

Farley looked at the others in the room. Colonel Ciotti, looking unhappier by the minute, like a man out

on a limb with no way off it. Major Bannister, staring at
the map table with tears in his eyes, unable to look at
his colonel. Sergeant Major Immanual Kramer, who
didn't look much better. Lieutenant Beeson, who kept
looking at the monitor screens as if he hoped they'd go
away.

We're on the wrong side, Farley thought. *And I'm
senior man except for the Colonel. I should do something. But—*

The cry came through the speaker system. "Spartans! They have killed the King!"

Ciotti looked up from the map. "Sorry to hear that."

"Sorry to hear that," Lt. Colonel Farley said. Something burst inside his head. "Sorry to hear that! Sorry
to hear that!"

"Control yourself, Scott," Ciotti said.

Scott Farley stood stiffly for a moment. He looked
to the others in the room. They didn't move. He put
his hand to his pistol. Ciotti stared in disbelief, and still
no one moved.

"Colonel," Farley said. "We're on the wrong side here."

"How dare you—"

"I dare because I'm right," Farley said. "And you know
it, Colonel. I don't know what was in those goddam coded
messages, I don't know what Bronson promised you, but
Colonel, it couldn't possibly be worth this!"

"Spartans! They have killed the King! The Helots
have killed the King!"

"Thank God!" Lieutenant Beeson said.

"Beeson?" Ciotti said.

"It wasn't us, it was the Helots," Beeson said. "Colonel Farley's right, sir, we're on the wrong side."

"Farley, I will overlook—"

"No, sir, no you won't, because I won't back off,"
Farley said. "Colonel, I can't take this. I'm relieving
you of command. Bannister, general orders, all units.

Cease operations against the Spartans, and assist the Spartans against those barbarians."

Bannister stood frozen.

"Do it and I'll have you in a cell with this mutineer," Ciotti said. "Sergeant Major."

"Sir?"

"Please conduct Colonel Farley to the Provost Marshal for confinement. Bannister, order the renewed assault on Fort Plataia."

Bannister didn't move.

Neither did Sergeant Major Kramer.

"Spartans! They have killed the King!"

Ciotti looked around wildly. His pistol was hung neatly with his uniform tunic in the cloak room. "Sergeant Major —"

Kramer shook himself, as if to wake up. "No, sir."

"Sergeant, you've been with me twenty years!"

"I'm with you now, Colonel. I'll always be with you. But — we're on the wrong side, Colonel, it's the wrong fucking side, and you know it, sir, you have to know it."

Farley nodded slowly. "Sergeant Major, I think Colonel Ciotti has had a mild stroke. He needs rest. Please take him to his quarters and look after him. Major Bannister, please send that order."

Bannister nodded slowly. He raised the microphone. "All units," he said. "Attention to orders."

When Colonel Karantov and his Fleet Marine guards arrived ten minutes later, he found the 77th in full cooperation with the Spartan forces. The battle of Sparta City was over.

✧ CHAPTER EIGHTEEN

A well-hidden secret of the principate had been revealed: it was possible, it seemed, for an emperor to be chosen outside Rome.

— Tacitus, *HISTORIES*, I, 4:

✧   ✧   ✧

Surveying this watershed year of 1941, from which mankind has descended into its present predicament, the historian cannot but be astounded by the decisive role of individual will. Hitler and Stalin played chess with humanity. In all essentials, it was Stalin's personal insecurity, his obsessive fear of Germany, that led him to sign the fatal pact, and it was his greed and illusion — no one else's — which kept it operative, a screen of false security behind which Hitler prepared his murderous spring. It was Hitler, no one else, who determined on a war of annihilation against Russia, canceled then postponed it, and reinstated it as the centerpiece of his strategy, as, how, and when he chose. Neither man represented irresistible or even potent historical forces. Neither at any stage conducted any process of consultation with their peoples, or even spoke for self-appointed collegiate bodies. Both were solitary and unadvised in the manner in which they took these fateful steps, being guided by personal prejudices of the crudest kind and by their own arbitrary visions. Their lieutenants obeyed blindly or in apathetic terror and the vast nations over which they ruled seem to have had no choice but to stumble in their wake toward mutual destruction. We have here the very opposite of historical determinism — the apotheosis of the single autocrat. Thus it is, when the moral restraints of religion and tradition, hierarchy and precedent, are removed, the power to suspend or unleash catastrophic events does not devolve on the impersonal benevolence of the masses but falls into the hands of men who are isolated by the very totality of their evil natures.

— Paul Johnson, *Modern Times:*
The World from the Twenties to the Nineties (rev. ed. 1991)

❖   ❖   ❖

There is danger that, if the Court does not temper its doc-
trinaire logic with a little practical wisdom, it will convert the
Bill of Rights into a suicide pact.
— Justice Robert Houghwout Jackson,
Terminiello v. *Chicago* 337 US 1, 37 (1949)

❖   ❖   ❖

As with any complex event, many factors were important in
the transformation of Sparta from a nation founded by university
professors seeking to establish the good society to the nucleus of
what is formally called the Spartan Hegemony and which in all
but name is the first interstellar empire; but analysts are
universally agreed that much of the change can be traced to the
will and intent of one man, Lysander I, Collins King of Sparta. It
remains for us to examine how Lysander, originally very much in
agreement with the Spartan Founders that the best policy for
Sparta would be an armed neutrality on the Swiss model, came
to embrace the necessity of empire.

We must also understand that although Lysander did accept
the necessity of an empire uniting a number of planets, he did
not come to it willingly. Indeed, it was thrust upon him in a
surprising manner . . .

—From the preface to *From Utopia to Imperium: A History of
Sparta from Alexander I to the Accession of Lysander*, by Caldwell
C. Whitlock, Ph.D. (University of Sparta Press, 2220)

❖   ❖   ❖

The war room was nearly deserted. Harv sat
motionless at one end, and Lysander was in the center,
his head bowed over the displays, although it was
doubtful that they gave him much information. Two
orderlies and a communications technician were still
on duty. The lights flickered off, then back on, as Peter
entered.

"Sire."

Lysander stared at him.

"Victory, your Majesty. The CoDominium forces
have changed sides, and the Helots are defeated.
More than defeated. Annihilated for the most part."

"Thank you." Lysander tried to stand, but his legs

wouldn't hold him. He cursed. "Another hour— If the battle's over I should go to Mother."

"She's under sedation at St. Thomas's, sire," Peter said. "And while the battle is over, there are a great many things to be done. Beginning with evacuation of the Palace. I've come to escort you."

"You really believe in that atom bomb?" Lysander demanded.

"I don't disbelieve in it," Peter said. "I'm also ordering Fort Plataia evacuated. Just in case."

"Good idea. A bomb here would get Government Square. St. Thomas's —"

"Yes, sire, I'm working on that, too. We don't have much transportation, though, and it's not going to be easy. The Queen Mother and Graffin Melissa will be out of there in five minutes. A couple of hours to get everyone."

"I suppose it's best. All right, General, where shall we go?"

"With your permission, Sire, I won't tell you until we're on the way. We've checked this room many times, but still—"

Lysander shuddered. "Won't we *ever* be free of those vermin? General, you have no idea how weary I am of living this way, scared of the very walls — anyway, let's go. I trust you'll have good communications and status displays where you're taking me."

Owensford led him out through the Palace. The corridors were mostly deserted. Peter tried to steer Lysander toward the back gates, but that wasn't possible. Lysander broke free and went to the front gates. "Where?" he demanded.

Peter Owensford sighed and led him to the place where King Alexander had died. A blanket still lay on the marble steps. "It was there, sire. The Helots were going to raise their flag, but the King brought out his guards and prevented that."

Lysander knelt and lifted the blanket to reveal the blood stained marble. He stared across the public square, to the flagstaff where the Crowned Mountain proudly flew. "Get lights on that flag," he said. "I want it to stay there until we can put up a statue. All right, General, let's go."

.   .   .

The command caravan was parked ten kilometers from the Palace. Most of both the Legion and Spartan military staff officers were there. Admiral Forrest waited impatiently as Lysander limped in, leaning heavily on a cane, and was seated with the assistance of two orderlies.

"Highness — uh, excuse me. Sire. General Owensford," he began eagerly.

"I gather Ciotti is talking," Owensford said.

"Oh, yeah. It was this way. Ciotti got the order to arrest the Legion and pronounce an interdict on Sparta. It looked legitimate enough, even though it was signed by Nguyen in Townsend's name. What made it suspicious was the other messages he got.

"First, there was a long report on the breakup of the CoDominium. The Grand Senate is dissolved, but there's not enough stability on Earth to have another election, and a lot of places aren't even stable enough to appoint new Senators."

"Jesus," Owensford said.

"There's more. The Senate dissolved, but apparently a small group of Senators got together again in the Senate Chamber, and declared the adjournment invalid on some technical grounds. That meant this Rump was in theory a legitimate Senate, or at least could call itself that. It proceeded to pass a number of resolutions, one of them the order to imprison all mercenaries on Sparta, another deposing Grand Admiral Lermontov and ordering his arrest.

"Then there was another message, apparently from Bronson himself as the new Chairman of the Naval Affairs Committee. It promises Ciotti promotion to Lieutenant General in command of this system, provided that he gains control here."

"So the swine wasn't just following orders," Lysander said.

"Well, Sire, he can plead that he was," Forrest said. "He did have orders. I'd have questioned them, myself, but he can plead that he considered them valid."

"So what's his status?"

"Karantov has sent him up to the space station under guard. Lieutenant Colonel Farley is confirmed as commander of the 77th. My guess is that Ciotti will be sent off on *Patton*."

Lysander turned to Owensford. "General, I want you to request that Karantov turn him over to us for trial."

Peter shook his head. "Sire, I don't think that would be a good idea. I don't think Karantov will do it. He's not going to put a CoDominium regimental commander up before a mercenary court martial, and if he turns Ciotti over to you, what's to prevent Sparta from demanding the heads of every CD officer who ever did you harm? As Admiral Forrest says, Ciotti can plead that he had valid orders. Sire, if you do make that request it'll come better through your government than through me. My advice is that you don't ask at all."

"I'll consider that advice," Lysander said.

"He's lost his regiment because of what he did," Peter Owensford said.

"I suppose. He's getting off easy. General, what's the status of that atom bomb?"

"We're searching," Owensford said. "Of course we don't know there is one."

"But you think there is."

"I think we can't take any chances, Majesty. Now we have another problem. Do you have the passwords to your late father's computer system? In particular, where he kept his codes?"

"Possibly," Lysander said. "When the fighting started he gave me a disk."

"We have a long message from Fleet Headquarters that no one seems able to decode," Owensford said. "We suspect it's from Grand Admiral Lermontov, in which case your father might be the only one in this system with a key."

"You don't?"

"No, sir, nor does Karantov. Whitlock may have one. Or Slater. We're trying to find them now."

"Are they missing?"

"Unfortunately," Owensford said. "When last seen, General Slater and his cadets and instructors were driving a Minetown mob off their campus, and we think Whitlock was with him."

"You think they're all right?"

"Yes, Sire," Peter said. "Hal Slater has been through more battles than anyone on this planet, and they weren't facing what you call first class opposition."

"And he'd have code keys you don't have?"

"It's possible," Owensford said. "Lermontov has known Hal nearly as long as he's known Falkenberg. But our best bet is to see if you can find your father's codes."

"All right. I suppose the simplest thing is to start with this disk. Where do you have your code equipment?" Lysander got to his feet and leaned heavily on his cane. "Harv, I can use some help. Let's go, General."

⋅　　　⋅　　　⋅

"General, I have someone calling for you. It may be the rebel commander."

Lysander looked up from the code machine. "Perhaps you should talk to her. On the speaker, please."

"Yes, Sire. All right, put her on." He lifted the microphone. "Owensford here."

"Hiyo, Petie. You be remembering Skilly, I think."

"I remember you."

"You sound cold, Petie. Like you don' like me."

Owensford made frantic hand signals. The technicians nodded agreement. *Keep her talking.* "I presume you have a message for me."

"Sure, I want to know if you wan' take up that job offer I make you. Or maybe you want to hire me? That's what you done with Barton after you defeat him, no? So maybe you hire me."

"Well, we could discuss it," Owensford said.

There was a long hard laugh. "Why, Petie, you tryin' to stall me! Lyin' to me, too. But I don' be on here long enough for you to trace where I am, Petie, so maybe we ought to talk serious. I guess Jeffi told you about Murasaki's big surprise."

"What would that be?"

"Oh, come on, now," Skilly said. Her chuckle was loud in the handset. "I know you talk to him, because we see him go into that palace, him and that spy chick you send us. So he tol' you about Murasaki's bomb, which is why you frantic to get everyone out of Government Square and your Fort. Ever stop to think I know you evacuate those people? Maybe I even know where you are. If I don' know now, I find out soon enough, and you can't keep running all the time. Can't govern no country when you can't stop long enough to go to the pot.

"Now you think you goin' find that bomb, or find Skilly, and you maybe right. Maybe right. Skilly down to the triarii now, not many Skilly's people left, who knows, maybe one turn she in for all that money."

"So what do you want?" Owensford asked.

"Skilly want what Niles gets, a ticket off this planet," she said. "You give me that, I give you the bomb. Murasaki too, if you fast enough to catch him, but I don' promise Murasaki. He clever and he fast. But you get his bomb."

"You ask for too much," Owensford said. "You and Niles aren't the same case."

"Yeah, he white ass *gent*leman," she said. "But I suppose what you mean is Stora Mine. Skilly sorry about that. Bad thing, but if it end the war, kindness after all. Thought it work, thought North Valley would surrender, but your people tougher than we think. And Baby Prince up there to rally the troops, too. Anyway, that water over the spilled milk. Question now is, maybe you catch Skilly and maybe you don't, and meanwhile you going to lose a lot of Citizens and a lot of that city, cause Skilly got nothing left to bargain with."

"We don't even have a way to get you off-planet," Owensford said. "Just at the moment, space is controlled by elements of the CD Navy and it's not certain just who they're loyal to. They like us some, but they hate you a lot, and I doubt we could talk them into letting you leave Sparta even if we wanted to."

"Now, Petie, you wouldn't lie to Skilly, would you? Damn I wish I have one of those gadgets you like so much, but I bet you got your phones jiggered same way I do, filter out all that overtone stuff before it goes out, no? Anyway, I make you one last offer. You take the price off Skilly's head, and you stop looking for Skilly. Outlaw Skilly, that all right. Skilly take care of herself. Any cop on or off duty shoot Skilly on sight, that all right, it happen anyway. But you don' send police tracking me. Or Legion either. Skilly sorry about that Stora Mine business, but nothing she can do."

"We take the price off your head, and you're no

longer officially wanted, but you remain an outlaw, to be dealt with as wolves are."

"Right. Without that reward, people get tired of looking for Skilly after a while. They hate Skilly, but they get over it, get on with their lives, if they don' get rich chasing she. Skilly like a better deal, but time getting short. I take that one."

"And in return?"

"I give you that bomb and the last place I know Murasaki at, and we quits."

"I have to refer this to His Majesty."

"Yo. And Petie, you tell His Majesty, Skilly not order anyone to kill his father. That fortunes of war, Dreadful Bride claim him, maybe, but it was nothing deliberate."

"Right. I'll be back in a few minutes."

"Don' take too long," Skilly said. "And don' be delaying thinking you track this call. You track it, all right, but when you get there you find it first relay and you got more tracking to do. Skilly can talk until that bomb go off, you not find she that way, but you lose a lot of you city."

"All right. Be right back." He turned to Lysander. "Sire, you heard."

"Yes. I presume she means it."

"I certainly wouldn't bet most of the Capital on it being a bluff," Owensford said. "And that's exactly what you would be doing."

"I hate letting her get away," Lysander said.

"Maybe she won't."

"Whatever. All right. I hate this, but I don't see what else we can do. Tell her I'll issue the proclamation rescinding the reward, and we'll both issue orders to our forces not to expend official effort in hunting for her. That's as soon as we find the bomb, of course."

"Right." Owensford activated the communications

set. "You got it," he said. "Reward called off, no official efforts to find you."

"Legion too," Skilly said. "Your word on that."

"Legion too. Our word, mine and His Majesty's. That's as soon as we find the bomb."

"Yah, I figure you do it that way. All right. At the southeast corner of Government Square, keep going southeast you come to the King Jason Hotel. It probably surprise you a lot, but I own that hotel. Well, someone else name on the papers, but I pay for it. The Royal Arms restaurant there, in the basement, there's a big meat locker. The far wall of that meat locker opens up, there's another room behind it. You'll find the bomb in there, and I think you better hurry, I don't think Murasaki leave much time. That was last place I know him to be, too, but I don't think he there now."

Owensford thumbed off the microphone. "Deighton! Get bomb disposal and a tac unit moving to the King Jason Hotel, southeast corner of Government Square. There's a nuke there, details after they're on the way. Murasaki was last seen there, but I don't expect you to catch him."

"Nuke. King Jason Hotel. On the way, skipper."

"Why won't we catch Murasaki?" Lysander asked.

"He'll have a way off planet. Bronson has agents here, they'll be on their way. The interesting part is they didn't take Skilly. I don't think they like her." He thumbed the microphone back on. "All right, bomb disposal is on the way."

"Aww, Petie, I thought you go yourself. That way, if the city go up, I know you with it. Anyway, Petie, Skilly wish she never start this. Too bad I can't stay around and watch you hang Croser, but I probably see it on TV."

"Miss Thibodeau."

"Who's that? That you, King Lysander?"

"Yes."

"Well, Majesty, excuse me, but I don' have long to talk. You take that reward off like you promise, you hear?"

"I will keep my promise," Lysander said.

"An' you don' know why you want to talk with me. It okay, Majesty, it okay to be curious about such like me. You want to stare into that empty empty abyss, and you doin' it, and the abyss stares right back, your Majesty. I tell you this, Skilly means it when she say she sorry she start this, and sorry she not listen to Jeffi about that business with the rocket. Now Skilly gone."

"Signal lost," a technician said. "Carrier lost."

"All right, General," Lysander said. "I've stared into the abyss, and I'm not about to become like that. We gave her a promise. Presuming your people find and disarm that bomb, we'll keep our word."

"Of course, sir. No reward, no official pursuit."

"So why are you looking so smug?" Lysander demanded.

"Well, sir, you may remember Sergeant Taras Miscowsky from the incident at the Halleck ranch?"

"Indeed. I remember more than him. I'm reliably informed that you've been seeing quite a lot of the Senator's grand-daughter."

"Yes, sire. But back to a less pleasant subject. Sergeant Miscowsky has been on campaign for a long time now. Accumulated considerable leave. He served with Jerry Lefkowitz, Sire, and he doesn't need any promise of reward to keep him on her track until he can send her head to Lefkowitz. I've sent for him. He'll be on leave status from the time he lands. That's not an official act. Nor is it official if the Officers Mess wants to take up a collection to help Miscowsky enjoy his vacation."

"Sir, I've got some leave coming too," Sergeant Andy Bielskis said from the doorway. "Excuse me,

Colonel, didn't mean to eavesdrop, but if it's all the same to you, Taras and I get along just fine, and I think we'd enjoy taking a vacation together."

"You were at Stora, weren't you?" Owensford asked.

"Yes, sir, that I was."

"We might need you—"

"I don't suppose it will take Taras and me very long," Andy Bielskis said. "Not long at all."

❖   ❖   ❖

"Where the devil have you been?" Owensford demanded.

Hal Slater grinned sheepishly. "Well —"

"He was chasin' rebels," Caldwell Whitlock said. "Doin' pretty good at it, too. General Slater's got a pretty good shootin' eye for a busted up old geezer who can't walk without a cane."

"Why, Professor," Hal said. He eyed Whitlock's ample stomach. "Apparently Dr. Whitlock chose to swallow his enemy. Anyway, Peter, have you decoded Lermontov's message yet?"

"No, we don't seem to be able to."

"You wouldn't. King Alexander had the code."

"We thought of that, and we think we have his codes, but I'm afraid Lysander hasn't been able to figure out how to use it."

"I'll show him," Slater said. "We need to go tell him about this, but it might be better if we talk about the situation first."

"All right. Coffee?"

"Yes, please, I could use some."

"I'll make it myself." Owensford closed the door and latched it. "Coffee, Caldwell?"

"Yeah, sure. Peter, we have got ourselves a first class mess, and it doesn't help at all that King Alexander's dead."

"Have a seat and tell me about it." Owensford

spooned coffee beans into the grinder. "No Sumatra Lintong. No Jamaica. Just local, I'm afraid."

"Right now I'll be grateful for anything," Hal said. "Peter, it's hard to know where to start."

"Start at the—"

"Beginning, go through to the end, and then stop. Yeah," Whitlock said. "Beginning. Lermontov's truly deposed. In gaol if not dead, and my guess is dead. This message was recorded and coded and set up to be sent in the event anything happened to him. It's updated with some other last minute stuff. Oh. Falkenberg won, by the way. New Washington campaign is over, Franklin gave up, and whatever passes for a government on New Washington has proclaimed John Christian Falkenberg as Protector."

Owensford whistled. "Won and won big, then. Wait a minute. Protector. Anything about that political girl, Glenda Ruth Horton, I guess her name was?"

"Yeah, I think so, but we're still decoding the Falkenberg reports. They were included in this message from Lermontov, so they didn't break in clear."

"You think the Colonel married her?" Hal Slater asked.

"You know him better than I do."

"It's certainly a possibility," Slater said. "Which makes things interesting, since we're all pretty well settled *here*. Kathryn isn't going to move again."

"Miriam Ann likes it here," Whitlock said. "Took her a while to get used to the gravity and the short day, but she likes the company. Take a powerful lot to move her now. Me too, of course."

"I never did ask where you finally settled in," Owensford said. "Sorry, been so busy."

"That's all right. I bought a spread near Hal's new place, off that park area the War College uses sometimes. Interesting neighbors. After we had that meetin' at Hal and Kathryn's, Captain Newell started looking around there. He hasn't bought in yet, but we've got, what, Hal? Maybe a dozen CoDominium navy families settled around the area. Makes for good company. I hear you're gettin' pretty serious, you staying on Sparta?"

"Yes. Lydia likes the outback. So do I. We'll keep a ranch out in the Valley, but there's too much work here. We've been looking for something near the Capital."

"Bring her out to meet Miriam Ann," Whitlock said. "I expect Miriam Ann and Kathryn can help her find a place she'll like. Better do it quick, though, I hear there's more CD people looking at land around there, you'll want to get 40 or 50 acres before the prices get too high."

"I'll do that. Thanks." Peter poured more coffee. "All right. Back to work. So Lermontov is definitely out."

"And these are his final orders," Hal Slater said.

"Call it his will," Whitlock said. "Grand Admiral Sergei Mikaelovich Lermontov's legacy to the Fleet."

"I hate to think that," Owensford said. "One damned good man. All right. What are the Grand Admiral's last orders?"

"Lots of stuff addressed to the Fleet, about loyalty, and what the CoDominium Fleet was for," Whitlock said. "Pretty damn good, too. Political scientists will be mining that for a century. But it boils down to this. The CoDominium existed to keep the peace. Now it's broken up, gone, and those who tore it up don't want peace. They're going to come around demanding loyalty from the Fleet, and they don't deserve it. Factions are going to try to use the Fleet, but it'll be to start wars for their own purposes."

"Jesus, that's prophetic enough," Owensford said.

"Right. By the way, there's another message encoded inside this one, encoded in the authentication code Lermontov used to send messages to the Fleet, and of course it's addressed to the Fleet. I sent that up to Boris," Hal said.

"Think his nose will be out of joint that you had the key and he didn't?" Owensford asked.

"Don't know," Hal said.

"I expect yes, but not too bad," Whitlock said. "We put a lot of stress on Hal being one of Lermontov's oldest friends —"

"So was Boris," Hal said.

"And one of Falkenberg's oldest friends, and that's going to be real relevant," Whitlock said. "You see, once he got through warning the Fleet what evil people would do to get control of them and their ships, he gave his last orders. He ordered them to obey his successor as they would him. But he didn't know who his successor would be. Let me read some of that.

"Brothers and sisters in arms, we cannot name my true successor now. We can be certain that the Rump of the Grand Senate will attempt to name a successor. We can be certain that successors will name themselves. How shall we choose among them? I do not believe that we can, yet we — you, for if you read this, I will not be with you — you must stay together. You must have unity. To that end, you can form a council of captains to advise your new commander, and I urge you to do that, but I do not believe that a council of captains can long govern, or even name a commander for you.

"I cannot name a commander for you.

"I will name a group that you can obey with honor. It consists of people you know. Two are young, but you will understand why they are named. The third is older and you will understand that choice also. The fourth some of you will know and some of you will not. My brothers and sisters in arms, I command you: until they themselves shall name a successor to me, you will accept your orders from John Grant; Carleton Blaine;

John Christian Falkenberg; and King Alexander of Sparta. They do not always agree, and that is well, for they can work together and they will, and when they are together they have great wisdom. When they speak together you must obey them as you would me.

"Farewell. We have done our best, for civilization, for the human race. We have not failed in our duties. Those to whom we owed obedience failed us. We have not rebelled against legitimate authority. The authority vanished. Now there is no legitimate authority.

"John Grant. Carleton Blaine. John Christian Falkenberg. Alexander of Sparta. They are my heirs, and they will find you an honorable path to follow. Stay together. Act in honor.

"Good-bye, and Godspeed.

"Sergei Mikaelovich Lermontov, Grand Admiral."

"Holy Christ," Owensford said. "That's Lermontov all right." He wiped at something in his eye. "I guess the Old Man's really gone. But Alexander is dead. What do we do?"

"Don't leave much room for maneuver," Whitlock said. "Four was an unwieldy number anyway. Now it's three. A Grant, a Blaine, and Christian Johnny. I think the Fleet will like that."

"Then you think the Fleet will obey that order?" Hal Slater asked.

"Some will," Whitlock said. "Let's look here at this system. Karantov will. Newell will think about it for a while. He's got all that Navy power, and he can see the potential, but he's pretty smart. He understands you can bash a planet, but you can't take it over, not with any four ships. Life by blackmail isn't much of a life. Besides, down deep he's a good man. He'll come around, and he'll bring those others who stood with him.

"Donovic, now, he's not going to accept this. He'll head off toward Earth. He's that kind, he'll go to see if there's anything worth picking left on the bones of his mother. So figure, that's one out of five here won't accept Lermontov's heirs. Say two out of five on average, but they won't all defect in the same direction. Some'll sell their services to the highest bidder. Hell, that's about what's happened here, it's just we got the bids in early."

"Only now this comes," Hal Slater said thoughtfully.

"So maybe one in five goes over to Bronson?" Owensford asked.

"Sounds as good a guess as any," Whitlock said. "And two in five stick with us. I presume it's us? We all together in this?"

"One for all," Hal Slater said.

"And all for one," Owensford added. "Except where does he come in?" He jerked his thumb toward the door.

Whitlock looked at each of his companions.

❖   ❖   ❖

The flags of Sparta stood at half mast. All but one. Outside the steps of the Palace the Crowned Mountain stood out proudly at the peak of the flagstaff. At night a dozen spotlights illuminated it.

Most of the wreckage had been cleaned up in Government Square. Many walls would be pockmarked for decades, but the debris was gone. Traffic was thin, but commerce had begun again in the two weeks since the battle ended. Sparta had buried a king, and had yet to crown his son, but Lysander was still Master of the Forces, and had more work to do than ever.

"Prince."

Lysander looked up from his desk. There were a million details to attend to. During the battles he had given orders to the soldiers, and things happened. Now he hardly saw the soldiers. He gave orders to civilians, and something might happen or might not.

"Aw hell, excuse me. King," Harv said. "You'd think I'd get used to it."

"Maybe I should issue a special edict," Lysander said, smiling. "Permitting you to use any title you feel like. You've earned it."

"Don't know about that. Sorry to disturb you, but there's a bunch of military people to see you. Officers, and they brought some enlisted people too, sergeants and like that. About fifty. Say they'd like to see you in the audience chamber whenever it's convenient, and they'll wait."

Lysander frowned. "Well, all right —"

"I think maybe I want some of the Life Guards with us when we meet that crew," Harv said.

"Whatever for?"

"Prince — Majesty, I plain don't like it. All these military and navy people, most of 'em in CoDominium uniforms, General Owensford dressed down as a light colonel of the Legion, General Slater in Royal Sparta uniform like Admiral Forrest, and they come with petty officers and sergeants and every one of them wearing sidearms. I been watching them, the last week they been thick as thieves, Majesty. Talking to each other, but not to you."

"Well, Harv, if that group has come to demand my resignation, a dozen Life Guards won't change anything. Among them they've got enough power to slag this planet. Tell them I'll be pleased to receive them in the audience chamber in ten minutes, and don't bother with the Life Guards."

"Well, if you say so, Prince —"

"I just did, Harv."

"Yes, sir."

Lysander found Melissa and Queen Adriana in the family quarters. "I seem to be scheduled to hold an audience," he said. "Actually it's not scheduled, it's more that it's demanded. Right now. By all the military officers in the system. Mine, the old CoDominium, the Legion —"

"Surely the Legion is ours," Melissa said.

"I thought so," Lysander said.

"You look worried," Queen Adriana said.

"Mother, I don't know. Harv's worried, and I guess that's got me thinking."

"That they're here to depose you?"

"Mother, I don't know. I have no reason to believe that, but I never had the military demand to see me in a body before, either. Anyway, I don't think I ought to keep them waiting. Melissa, take Mother to the country lodge. Harv has a driver waiting—"

"I'll do no such thing," Melissa said. "I'm coming with you."

Queen Adriana laughed. "I think you've got the wind up for nothing, boy. They probably want something, titles and honors and promotions. Soldiers like that sort of thing. But I'll tell you this, whatever they want, those Helots couldn't chase me out of this palace, and I'm certainly not going to run from our own soldiers. Now let's go see what they want. But first, you change to your best tunic, and put your orders on. If we're going to be deposed, we may as well be dressed for it!"

. . . .

The delegation filed in. There were nearly fifty of them, and as Harv had said, they wore many different uniforms. Hal Slater in Legion dress, but still wearing a Royalist shoulder badge, seemed to be their leader, followed closely by Fleet Captain Newell and Colonel Karantov in CoDominium. Just behind them was his own Rear Admiral Forrest. Then Colonel Farley of the 77th. The Captains Alana. Legion Senior Sergeant

Guiterrez, and other Legion Officers. And last of all, behind the enlisted men, in clothing more colorful than the military uniforms, Dr. Whitlock came in carrying a brief case.

Lysander received them sitting, with the Dowager Queen and Melissa seated next to him. When they had all filed in, Lysander stood and acknowledged their bows. "I regret that King David is not in the city," Lysander said.

"Sire, it was you we came to see," Hal Slater said. He bowed, then bowed again to Queen Adriana. "Madam. Graffina Melissa."

"General, we are pleased to see you, but this is unexpected."

"Yes, sire, we know it is," Slater said. "We'll be as brief as possible, but the matter is a bit complex.

"Sire, everyone here is familiar with the long messages that constitute Admiral Lermontov's last will, and of course you have read the copy addressed to your late father."

"Yes, General."

"That document named a council of four to succeed Grand Admiral Lermontov. With King Alexander deceased that left three. The purpose of the council is to hold the Fleet together until some new governing structure can be formed to keep the peace." Hal Slater spoke carefully, as if lecturing at the War College rather than speaking to his sovereign.

"That left us all with a problem," Slater said. "Two problems, actually. The first is that a council that's physically dispersed across lightyears of space can't command. Decisions are going to be needed. Right here in this system we have a divided command. I hold a commission as an officer of the Royal Army and as such I am responsible to the Dual Monarchy; under the Ultimate Decree, to your majesty personally.

However, I also have another office. With General Owensford and Dr. Whitlock I am a spokesman for Colonel Falkenberg, and meanwhile he has become Protector of New Washington, as well as a member of the Grand Admiral's succession council.

"Fleet Captain Newell finds himself under orders to obey a council that has never met. One of its members is dead, and no other member of that council is present in this system, yet it is in this system that his interests lie. Owensford, Whitlock, and I know that this system was important to Lermontov, and to Falkenberg. We know that Carleton Blaine as governor of Tanith offered alliance to Sparta. We're certain that Captain Newell and his squadron should stay here and protect Sparta. But whose orders do they follow?"

Lysander shook his head in wonder. "Are you asking me, General Owensford?"

"Permit me, sire," Dr. Whitlock said. He came forward. "There's a sense in which I don't belong in here, but maybe I better explain something. King Lysander, if there's one thing history shows us, the worst kind of government anyone ever had was a council of soldiers. Maybe one soldier can govern and maybe not, but investing supreme power in a council of military officers is about the worst thing that can happen. Lermontov knew that. He made up a council of two officers and two politicians in the hopes they'd balance off, but you'll note he cautioned them to name someone as commander as soon as they could. What he didn't put in that public last will he put in private messages to me and Hal Slater. I've shown those to the other Fleet people here. What he told us to do was use our judgment on whether to offer command to King Alexander. We also know Colonel Falkenberg approved hailing King Alexander as commander if the necessity came up."

Before Lysander could react to that, Hal Slater began to speak. "The CoDominium is gone. Something has to take its place, and we have no time to build anything," Hal said. "There aren't many people we can follow. Falkenberg has always made it clear that he won't accept supreme command. So we've been discussing this, and we've all agreed, and we've come to tell you that agreement."

Hal Slater limped forward. He was joined by Peter Owensford, then Fleet Captain Newell. Boris Karantov and Colonel Farley. Admiral Forrest. They stood in a row.

"This is just a little awkward," Hal said. "We've lost the ceremony for this over the past thousand years. But we mean every word of it." He raised his arm, not outstretched as Germans once did, but high, palm forward. "Hail. Ave. Ave, Lysander, Imperator."

The greeting was said carefully, self consciously at first, then repeated, this time with more enthusiasm. "Ave Lysander, Imperator."

It was echoed by the others in the room, officers and petty officers, representatives of the Fleet, voices blending together into a mighty shout that rang through the palace, and was echoed back to the audience chamber. The words washed over him, and Lysander stood, his expression unreadable.

"AVE, LYSANDER. AVE,
LYSANDER, IMPERATOR."

"Bring us together," Caldwell Whitlock said, his voice low and almost unheard, and then the cry rang through the palace again.

"AVE. AVE LYSANDER, IMPERATOR!"

The End